There were no flowers at Byron Morrow's grave. It was a small plot near the woods that ran along the churchyard's boundary. He'd been buried next to his wife, Elaine. Her headstone was weathered, the corners worn smooth by many rains and winters. But Mr. Morrow's was new, its edges clean and sharp as Max knelt to brush the snow away.

He had just finished when he noticed that someone was watching him.

The figure was standing in the woods, just beyond the lantern's light. It did not move, but there was something unsettling and sinister about its quiet surveillance. Drawing the *gae bolga*, Max hoisted up the lantern.

"Who is that?" he hissed. "Show yourself!"

The figure glided smoothly forward, emerging from the dark wood so that the lantern shone full upon his white and smiling face.

THE TAPESTRY · BOOK 4

THE MAELSTROM

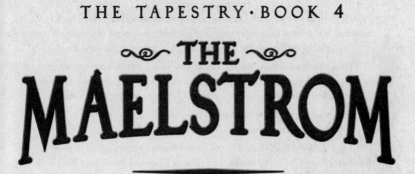

ROWAN ACADEMY

WRITTEN AND ILLUSTRATED BY

HENRY H. NEFF

A YEARLING BOOK

This is a work of fiction. Names, characters, places, and incidents either are the product of the author's imagination or are used fictitiously. Any resemblance to actual persons, living or dead, events, or locales is entirely coincidental.

Text, map, and interior illustrations copyright © 2012 by Henry H. Neff
Cover art copyright © 2012 by Cory Godbey

All rights reserved. Published in the United States by Yearling, an imprint of Random House Children's Books, a division of Random House, Inc., New York. Originally published in hardcover in the United States by Random House Children's Books, New York, in 2012.

Yearling and the jumping horse design are registered trademarks of Random House, Inc.

Visit us on the Web! randomhouse.com/kids

RowanAcademy.com

Educators and librarians, for a variety of teaching tools, visit us at RHTeachersLibrarians.com

The Library of Congress has cataloged the hardcover edition of this work as follows:
Neff, Henry H.
The maelstrom / Henry H. Neff. — 1st ed.
p. cm. — (Tapestry ; bk. 4)
Summary: "With the return of the sorcerer Bram, and the disappearance of Astaroth, Rowan Academy must prepare to battle the demon Prusias."
— Provided by publisher.
ISBN 978-0-375-85707-2 (trade) — ISBN 978-0-375-95707-9 (lib. bdg.) —
ISBN 978-0-375-89329-2 (ebook)
[1. Magic—Fiction. 2. Demonology—Fiction. 3. Witches—Fiction.
4. Schools—Fiction.] I. Title.
PZ7.N388Fie 2010   [Fic]—dc23   2012006610

ISBN 978-0-375-87148-1 (pbk.)

Printed in the United States of America

10 9 8 7 6 5 4 3 2 1

First Yearling Edition 2013

For Charlie,
as he begins his own great adventure

CONTENTS

THE MAELSTROM

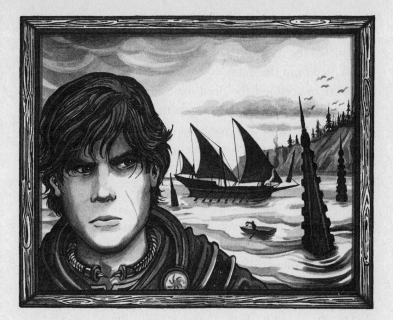

~ 1 ~

THE XEBEC

The harbormaster's bell rang clear and cold as the xebec slipped past the tall breakers and entered Rowan Harbor. Witch-fire burned at its prow, an oily plume of green flames that sputtered in the breeze and cast a spectral gleam on the dark swells. A dozen fishermen and smugglers scattered out of its path, coaxing their smaller vessels beyond reach of the ship's oars as it skimmed toward the main dock like a huge black dragonfly.

On the cliffs above, Max McDaniels slung off his heavy pack and stopped to watch the ship's progress. Despite the predawn gloom, he could make out a weather worker on the xebec's deck. The witch was crouching near the fire like an old spider as she piloted the craft through a minefield of broken stone towers that jutted from the water.

Max understood the need for caution. He was curious to see how such a ship would navigate the towers, but he was even more curious as to who was aboard and why they were here. Rowan's shores had become treacherous to visitors. The jagged pillars represented more than just a danger to the ship's hull; they symbolized all that had changed since May Day.

Just six months earlier, those broken and barnacled spires had belonged to Gràvenmuir. The demons had called it an embassy but it had really been an occupation, a base from which they could influence Rowan's affairs and keep a close eye on the only humans who might challenge their rule. It had been a darkly beautiful structure, a Gothic sculpture of black towers and battlements encasing gilded halls where demons held court, oversaw trade, and ensured that Rowan honored the terms of her surrender.

All of that was history.

On May Day, Elias Bram had obliterated the embassy and fired a shot heard around the world. Max had witnessed the event, but even now it seemed a dream. It was difficult to believe that a single person was capable of such an astonishing act, much less a man who was supposed to have died centuries ago.

Max replayed the sequence in his mind. Once Bram had halted at Gràvenmuir's gates, the sorcerer had spread his arms wide. With a roar, the surrounding cliffs had broken, shearing clean away as though struck by a chisel. And as they plummeted, so did Gràvenmuir—cast down into the sea along with everyone inside.

Gràvenmuir's plunge to the sea had been eerily silent. And during that surreal interlude, Max had realized—with awful, numbing clarity—that the world was about to change. The moment's scale and implications had been exhilarating and terrifying. There would be no more deliberations or debate. In that instant, Elias Bram had dictated Rowan's path, and mankind's fate would hang in the balance. Shocked by this realization, a part of Max had clung to the absurd hope that the silence would continue indefinitely. For as long as it held, they might pause to consider this momentous course.

Seconds later those hopes vanished. Gràvenmuir struck the water with an astounding crash. The impact jolted people from sleep for miles around and shattered the windows in Old Tom and Maggie.

The awful din soon subsided, fading like a summer storm as the sea rushed in to swallow up the dead and dying. All that remained of Gràvenmuir were those jagged spires, lurking at the water's surface to bare their teeth at low tide.

A shout and the sound of many footsteps snapped Max from his thoughts. Turning, he saw a motley troop of youths hurrying toward him along the cliff's edge from the north. They clanked along, carrying spears and lanterns as they threaded through the pines and sought to keep up with their leader, who skidded to a stop before him and promptly drew her sword.

"Who are you?" she panted. "Identify yourself and explain why you're breaking curfew."

Max merely stared, confused, as the others arrived, surrounding him and leveling their long spears, their breath fogging in the November chill.

"What is this?" Max finally asked, giving a bewildered turn. He failed to recognize a single one of the frightened, eager faces. They couldn't be Rowan students. For one, they'd obviously had little training, as evidenced by their sloppy perimeter and the fact that most were out of breath. For another, their clothes were mostly homespun and heavily patched—a ragtag array of leather jerkins, woolen leggings, and mismatched boots. Refugees, Max guessed, and recently arrived by their appearance.

"We'll ask the questions," snapped the leader. She had coarse black hair and a sallow, ferretlike face. Max waited for the punch line, some clue that she was joking. There was none. "Answer up," she pressed. "Who are you and why are you breaking curfew?"

"I'm Max McDaniels," he replied. "And I didn't know about any curfew. I've been away."

"Then you're an intruder and our captive," she declared. "Get his blade, Jack."

This order was directed at a skinny youth with a tumble of red tangles peeking from beneath a worn leather cap. Glancing at the short sword and its owner, the boy licked his lips like a scolded dog.

"Let's call an Agent, Tam," he whined. "He looks dangerous."

"Follow orders," she seethed, "or I'll have you thrown down in the Hollows!"

"Look," said Max calmly, "you must be new to Rowan. We're on the same side. If you let me—"

"Old or new don't matter," interrupted the girl, jabbing her sword mere inches from Max's face. "You ain't from Rowan. You look like you been livin' in a ditch. You're the most pathetic demon I've ever seen, and I've seen my share. Now get his blade, Jack, and be quick about it!"

Before Jack could obey, another girl spoke up.

"Max McDaniels," she mused, repeating it to herself. "I think I heard that name, Tam. I'm sure I have. Maybe he's telling the truth."

"You don't see demons like I do, Kat," said Tam, her voice taut and hateful. "That's why they put me in charge. Don't believe anything this demon says."

At Tam's third, furious order to confiscate Max's weapon, Jack inched forward and reached for it.

"Tam," said Max pointedly, "I don't know what this little patrol is supposed to be or anything about a curfew. But I can assure you that I belong here and that none of you even wants to see this sword, much less touch it."

These words exerted a powerful effect. Jack promptly backed away and stared at the weapon with superstitious awe. But Tam remained undaunted.

"Well, *this* sword is iron, demon," she threatened, inching closer. "These spears are iron and thrice blessed. Surrender or we'll call one of the Red Branch!"

"They're already here."

Pulling back his sleeve, Max revealed a tattoo upon his inner wrist. Inked in red, it depicted an upraised hand wrapped with a slender cord. A casual observer might not have looked twice, but for those who knew better, the tattoo was a warning as clear as the mark on a black widow's belly. It was the sign of the Red Branch, the elite among Rowan's warriors. Only twelve people bore such marks, and they were the most dangerous Agents in the world.

"I *told* you I'd heard that name!" exclaimed Kat.

"Well, I haven't," Tam snapped, her sword arm trembling. "And demons are false, Kat. He might fool you, but he can't fool me. I see his shine."

Max was genuinely surprised to hear such a claim.

"Is that so?" he wondered, cocking his head to appraise her. "That's a rare gift you have, but not all who shine are demons, Tam. I applaud your courage, but use your head. Would an intruder hang about in the open to watch the harbor? Wouldn't an intruder have fled or attacked when you came running?"

"Answer some questions, then," she snapped. "Who is the Great Matriarch?"

"YaYa."

"And who played fiddle at the Samhain Feast?"

"I wasn't here," replied Max, "but I'd guess it was Nolan."

"Well, what's the name of the sad old brute who lives on Crofter's Hill?"

"No idea." Max shrugged. "No one was living there four months ago."

Tam snorted dubiously, and Max grew weary of the game.

"Oh, run me through if you want," he sighed, stepping between her and a twitchy boy with an unfortunate mustache. Desiring a better view of the xebec, Max walked down to the very edge of the cliff and retrieved a weathered spyglass. His would-be captors trailed uncertainly after him, dragging their spears and muttering to one another.

By now, the xebec was moored alongside the customhouse, and several remote figures could be seen hurrying about the pier. Despite her flurry of orders, Tam's companions had apparently tired of playing soldier and seemed more intrigued by what Max was studying through his spyglass.

"Have you seen other ships like these?" Max asked, gesturing at the xebec.

"No," said Jack, dropping his spear in the rough gorse and peering down. "I ain't seen anything that big, but I haven't been here very long. Why doesn't she burn up from all that fire?"

"That's witch-fire," Max explained. "A witch is on that ship. You can see her there—that dark shape by the mainmast. The fire strengthens their weather magic."

At the mention of a witch, several children hissed.

"I care less about the witch than who she's working for," said Max. "Demons hire witches as weather workers. If you're hunting demons, Tam, I think you'll find one on that ship."

"But I've got one right here," she insisted. "And you don't

know there's a demon on that ship. It could just be a trader from Jakarün or Zenuvia."

"Do you see any cargo on the deck?" inquired Max, handing her the telescope.

She scanned from stem to stern. "No"—she frowned—"but that doesn't mean there aren't goods stowed below. Maybe it's a smuggler."

"Possibly," Max allowed. "But that would be a big ship for a smuggler. At any rate, most smugglers don't fly royal banners from their masts." He pointed to a plum-colored pennant and its pyramid of three gold coins. "Do you know whose standard that is?"

Tam barely glanced at it.

"No," she muttered, passing the glass along. "I was taught only the mark of my brayma."

The statement told Max a great deal about her. *Brayma* was a demon word, a title used for the lord of a fief. Some controlled vast territories and others small, but all enjoyed absolute authority over those who lived on their lands. While some braymas were indifferent to their subjects, Max knew most were tyrants whose appetites and cruelty far exceeded human norms. Tam's brayma must have fit this description.

From the girl's accent, Max guessed she'd lived in Dùn. That was Aamon's realm and comprised much of what had once been Russia and northern Asia. Tam was undoubtedly a runaway slave. Max had to respect anyone who had survived such a life, much less escaped and journeyed all the way to Rowan.

"You live here now," he said gently. "You have no brayma anymore."

"So where is that ship from?" she asked, still wary.

"It's from Blys," Max replied. "And it's no merchant—that

standard belongs to the king himself. The white pennon beneath is a sign of truce. Apparently, Prusias wants to talk."

"D-do you think the king is aboard?" stuttered a boy with terrible burn scars.

"I doubt it," said Max. "It's not his style to slip quietly into port. If Prusias visits us again, he'll be leading an army."

"So war *is* coming here," moaned Jack with gloomy resignation. "I thought I'd finally found someplace safe, but everyone keeps talking of war. They say Rowan broke the peace and it's only a matter of time before the demons come for us."

Max gazed down at Gràvenmuir's ruins, its spires littering the harbor like barrow markers.

"They may be right," he admitted soberly. "War may come here. But keep your chin up. I've been traveling far and wide these past few months. Rowan's not the only one who kicked the hornet's nest. At the moment, the demons fear Astaroth and each other far more than they do us. So do your duty, learn to handle that spear, and pray you never need to use it."

Stretching his tired limbs, Max gestured for the spyglass.

"And now I have to go," he announced. "The Director probably had warning of that ship, but I need to make certain."

"But you can't just leave," said Jack, grinning up at him. "You're our prisoner. You gotta pay a ransom or something."

With an amused grunt, Max dug into his pack and retrieved a leather pouch. "A Zenuvian kraken for each and a piece of maridian heartglass for your fearless captain." He handed the smooth disk of pearly, translucent stone to Tam. "I won that off a smuggler in Khoreshi. He said if you hold it up to the hunter's moon, the stone will reveal your true love."

"Does it work?" she wondered, turning it over.

"Didn't dare peek. But you give it a try someday and let us know."

Flushing pink, she studied the heartglass until Jack hooted and she threatened to brain him. His captivity ended, Max turned for the Manse. The others followed along, peppering him with questions as his long strides took him past the academic buildings. He was glad to see Maggie, stout and solid, her pale gray stone peeking modestly from beneath her ivy. Beyond her was Old Tom, stately and elegant with his tall clock tower and broad sweep of marble steps. They had almost reached the Manse when Max noticed someone sitting on the edge of the fountain at its steps, watching their approach with a bemused expression. When their eyes met, the man tipped his cap.

"Back where you belong and in one piece besides," he drawled. "Who'd have thought?"

Grinning, Max strode over to greet Rowan's chief game warden. It was unusual to find Nolan outside the Sanctuary, but Max was glad he had. The man's wry, weather-beaten face was as warm and welcome as a winter fire. With a laugh, Nolan popped up and embraced him.

"You know, I think you're taller than Cooper," he observed, sizing Max up. "Shoot, you'll be catching Bob next."

"He might be big, but we still took him prisoner," Jack announced.

"I can see that, son," quipped Nolan. "Hope you weren't too rough. You have any idea who you've captured?"

"He *says* he's Max McDaniels," muttered Tam. "Whatever that means."

Nolan scratched his graying side whiskers and cocked an eyebrow. "Well, I'll give you a hint what that means. Take a good look around this place, young lady. Without our Max, I don't think it'd be here. Heck, I don't think *I'd* be here. So let's show a little respect. Why, you're just lucky Hannah didn't hear you."

"Who's she?" said Tam, scuffing her boots. "His girlfriend?"

"I hope not," Nolan chuckled. "She's a goose. Anyway, y'all head off now and leave Max be. I need a private word with him. And curfew's about over, so try not to assault anyone till breakfast."

Once they'd finally shuffled out of earshot, Nolan shook his head. "Breaks my heart," he sighed. "We've got hundreds of those kids showing up every day now, scared and starving. They all want to help, but mostly they just get underfoot. Anyway, we got word you'd returned when you passed by Wyndle Farm. Director asked me to keep a lookout for you."

"Why'd she bother you?" asked Max. "Why not send an Agent?"

"They're all busy. Been scrambling since the watchtowers caught sight of that ship. Half the Red Branch is already here. Cooper was up north, but he's on his way. In the meantime, Richter wants you to clean up and report to Founder's Hall. Military uniform."

"No rest for the weary."

"Not today," said Nolan, his blue eyes tracking the gulls beyond the cliffs. "Anyway, I've done my duty and you'd better get going. I don't know who's on that ship or what they want, but I feel better knowing we've got our Hound."

Within the hour, Max climbed the shallow flight of stairs that led to Founder's Hall. Situated in a new wing of the Manse, Founder's Hall served as an audience chamber when the Director's offices would not suffice. It was the largest of many additions made to the Manse as Rowan Academy evolved from a secret school of magic into an independent nation.

Despite all of these changes, Rowan's seal remained the same. It was engraved upon the doors: a sun, star, and moon set above a flowering rowan tree. Stopping to gaze at it, he glimpsed his reflection in the sun's polished silver. Hot water might have removed the dirt, but it could not wash away months of hard travel. Max's wavy black hair now fell almost to his shoulders and framed a face that could no longer be called boyish. He still resembled his mother; they shared the same dark eyes and high cheekbones that had won him many an admirer. But as Max grew to manhood, the blood of his father told.

And that father was not a mortal man; he was Lugh the Long-Handed, an Irish sun deity who had been king of the Tuatha Dé Danaan. Like other heroes before him, Max straddled the boundary between mortal and immortal. Old Magic coursed in his veins—vast primal energies from ancient days when the world was shaped. Among his kin, Max could name gods, giants, and heroes—not only Lugh, but also Balor of the Evil Eye, and Cúchulain, whom Max resembled.

To a mortal, the Old Magic's gifts were great, but they were also dangerous. In battle, the same monstrous forces that destroyed Max's enemies also threatened to consume him. Like Cúchulain, Max became something else entirely . . . wild, indomitable, and terrifying.

Rowan's recruiters had known right away that Max was exceptional, but none foresaw how rapidly his abilities would develop. During his first year at Rowan, Max shattered records that had stood for centuries. At thirteen, his skills were such that only William Cooper, Rowan's top Agent, would train with him. That very year, the Red Branch had inducted Max into their elite ranks while his peers were still studying basic combat. But no others in the Red Branch had traveled to the Sidh or mastered Scathach's feats as Max had done. They had not been blooded in Prusias's Arena or crowned Champion of Blys. And no mortal—Red Branch or otherwise—possessed a weapon like the *gae bolga*.

The awful blade hung at his hip, lurking in a dark scabbard gilded with wolves and ravens. The *gae bolga* had not always been a sword. It had been a spear when Cúchulain wielded it, a barbed and grisly weapon that claimed the lives of friends and foes alike. With Cúchulain's death, the broken spear's pieces were salvaged and kept in a vault by his comrades in the Red Branch. Many kings and warriors had tried to possess the legendary weapon, but the *gae bolga* screamed at their touch and would not suffer them to hold it. Centuries passed until one arrived whom the spear deemed worthy.

While Max had successfully claimed the broken artifact, he did not have the skill to mend it. With his friends, he sought the aid of his distant kinsman, the last of the ancient Fomorians. The giant confirmed what Max had feared ever since the weapon had called to him. The *gae bolga* was a sentient thing, the living relic of a dark and terrible goddess. The Morrígan herself had made the weapon and it was infused with her essence and lust for blood and battle.

With great reluctance and difficulty, the Fomorian reforged the weapon. The *gae bolga* was now unbreakable, and its gruesome blade could shear through flesh, bone, steel, and spirit with terrifying ease. The demons dreaded it. While most mortal weapons could only cause them pain, the *gae bolga* could slay even the greatest among them. In battle, the blade keened like a banshee and the wounds it made would never heal. The Fomorian had warned that a warrior could never truly wield such a weapon; it would always wield him. Even Max was frightened of it and kept it sheathed unless in dire need. He had not drawn it since May Day.

Will we need you today, I wonder?

A student came in answer to his knock, a Third Year apprentice, judging from her sky-blue robes. Admitting him inside, she ushered Max past several tapestries and into a large oval hall whose rosewood walls swept toward a high-domed ceiling of wrought iron and colored glass. Seven living rowan trees were spaced evenly about the perimeter, each pair flanking an illuminated case. At the room's center was a great stone table. Many others had already arrived and stood conversing in quiet clusters. The tension was palpable.

"The Director says you're to have the Steward's Chair," said the apprentice, gesturing toward a high-backed seat at the table's far end.

"That's Cooper's place."

"No, sir," she said, consulting her sheet. "He is to take the Fool's Perch."

Max raised an eyebrow. As commander of the Red Branch, William Cooper should have had the Steward's Chair and sat at the Director's right hand. It was a place of honor, signifying that its occupant was the leader's most trusted and capable servant—one who might rule in his or her stead. Conversely, the Fool's Perch was the seat positioned nearest visitors, and its title stemmed from a time when negotiations might well turn bloody. Depending on its occupant, the Fool's Perch was viewed with dread or black humor, but rarely indifference.

Such names were once echoes from a distant past, but Rowan's traditions were no longer consigned to deep vaults or special ceremonies; they had been dusted off and woven into everyday life. Student apprentices now dressed in the ancient manner, donning hooded robes whose colors ranged from First-Year brown to Sixth-Year scarlet. In addition to their robes, all students wore magechains, silver necklaces whose weight and value increased as they attained various proficiencies. Max glanced at the apprentice's chain.

"Is Herb Lore to be your specialty?" he asked, noting the prevalence of green stones threaded among an assortment of iron keys and silver runes.

"I want it to be," the girl whispered, her hand straying to a bright tourmaline. "Miss Boon thinks my talents lie in Firecraft, but can I help it if I like plants?"

Max sympathized but knew red garnets and fire opals were destined to join the girl's beloved malachite, jade, and tourmaline. No student could long defy Hazel Benson Boon; she was too smart, too patient, and far too stubborn.

He saw the young teacher ahead, standing by an illuminated case and addressing a trio of Promethean Scholars with folded arms and a forward lean. That the nearby case held Macon's Quill struck Max as no mere coincidence. It was the very prize Miss Boon had won not once but twice during her student days. For all her aloof reserve, he knew she was sinfully proud of the achievement. Catching sight of Max, she ended her conversation with the scholars with a final emphatic point.

"That will do, Siddanhi," said Miss Boon, coming over. Once the girl departed, the teacher turned and appraised Max with her mismatched eyes. One was brown and the other blue, leading many students to theorize that the unusual feature was related somehow to her gifts in mystics. Miss Boon dismissed this as nonsense, but her eyes did underscore the many contrasts in her personality and appearance. Her hair was stylishly short, but her glasses were old-fashioned. Despite her bookish nature, she'd shared some of Max's most dangerous adventures. And apparently—in spite of the fact that she was not yet thirty—Hazel Benson Boon had recently joined Rowan's most venerable faction of Mystics, the Promethean Scholars.

"Congratulations," said Max, nodding at the telltale robes—inky black with amber trim.

"I suppose I should be pleased," she mused, considering a sleeve. "In truth, it's just because Ms. Kraken didn't want them. As you know, we lost many of the scholars during The Siege, but now they're rebuilding their ranks and want to include someone on the faculty. When Annika declined, I was the natural choice." Her brow furrowed and she pursed her lips. "However, I can hardly see the point if they won't even listen to my counsel."

"Counsel on what?"

"Bram!" she hissed. "They practically worship him—utterly refuse to acknowledge the dangers."

"Will he be here?"

"Hopefully not," she muttered, smoothing her robes. "The Director has asked him to stay away, but who has any idea what he'll do? He knows we can't prevent him from attending."

"I'm sure David will speak to him," Max reassured her. "He'll listen to David."

"Let's hope," she sighed. "It's a dark and disturbing day, but at least you're home and William is on his way. He's been gone nearly as long as you have." Standing on tiptoe, she craned her neck hopefully at the door. "I take it your presence means your mission was a success?"

Max coughed into his fist. "You know that DarkMatter operations are classified, Miss Boon."

"Yes, indeed," she replied. "But if you're going to cite regulations and clam up, I'll advise you to lose that unfortunate smirk. Small wonder William likes to play cards with you. May I at least ask if you plan to resume your studies? Does such an apparent stickler for the rules need me to remind him that the Manse dormitories are for actively enrolled students?"

"You expelled David and he still lives there."

"A fair point," she conceded. "But as we both know, David

Menlo has no further need of formal education, while you persevere in a state of appalling ignorance. It's a wonder you can still read. If your duties prevent you from joining scheduled classes, we'll just have to find you some tutors. . . ."

Only Miss Boon could delve right into academic schedules and curricula while everyone else was fretting about demonic ships and resurrected sorcerers. Max knew she did it to distract herself; he even found her unwavering commitment to his studies oddly comforting. But there were larger matters at hand, and when Old Tom chimed seven o'clock, it was time for all to take their places.

Miss Boon joined the Promethean Scholars as they occupied stone benches set within alcoves along the walls. Max settled into the Steward's Chair and discovered that he did not care for its rigidity or the rough iron rivets that pressed into his back. It was a heavy, thronelike chair and came with heavy expectations—expectations concerning statecraft, diplomacy, and governance. Max far preferred the Fool's Perch.

Four other members of the Red Branch were present at the table. Like Max, each wore a hauberk of black mail beneath a dark gray tunic along with black boots and breeches. While the Mystics and scholars fairly bent beneath their glittering magechains, the Red Branch never displayed any insignia other than the small tattoo at their wrists. Their scars told their stories.

Max knew them by name and reputation, but he did not know them well. Members of the Red Branch often worked alone and lived abroad. They might disappear for months or even years as they traveled the globe, looking after Rowan's darkest, most dangerous business. Max's predecessor, Antonio de Lorca, had been gregarious and charming, but he seemed to be an exception. As a rule, the order's members were quiet and reinforced Max's belief that those who'd seen the most often said the least.

He nodded hello to Ben Polk, a balding, slope-shouldered Agent with the disquieting habit of looking one not in the eye but just beyond their shoulder. There was nothing overtly impressive about the man; he was of average height with a plain and utterly forgettable face. But Max knew that this seemingly unremarkable person was over two hundred years old, was shockingly quick with a knife, and had single-handedly exterminated a secret society of necromancers. Max could not say he *liked* Ben Polk, but he certainly respected his abilities. The same held true for the others around the table: Natasha Kiraly; Matheus; and wrinkled Xiùměi, whose ancient sword looked shaving-sharp. They were knights and assassins and everything in between, but they were not friends. Max had only one friend in the Red Branch, but the Fool's Perch remained empty.

When the bronze doors opened, all heads turned to see Gabrielle Richter stride into the hall accompanied by her chief advisers. The Director wore a teacher's simple navy robes, a choice that struck Max as a message: *We are first and foremost a school.* Her silver hair was pulled back, emphasizing the hard lines of her face. Her expression was calm but strong and purposeful as she made directly for the central table, while Miss Awolowo, Ms. Kraken, and others found places in the alcoves.

"The Blyssian ambassador will be here shortly," she announced. "I've been assured that the ambassador comes in good faith, but we will be vigilant. We may call on some of you to speak, but otherwise I ask that you remain quiet. If the ambassador or any of his entourage should threaten violence in this hall, you are to destroy them outright. Rowan desires peace, but only peace with honor."

There was apprehension on some faces but approval on most.

The Director slid into the seat next to Max and patted his arm as she looked toward the doors. The sounds of heavy booted feet were coming down the corridor. A moment later, the captain of the Harbor Guard stepped beyond the hall's threshold and rapped the flagstones with his halberd. His voice filled the chamber.

"An ambassador from Blys desires admittance to the Founder's Hall. He has sailed under banner of truce and sworn a pledge of peace. Shall he enter?"

"He shall," replied Ms. Richter.

"Then I give you Lord Naberius, Keeper of the Opal Road and High Ambassador of Blys."

"They do like their titles," the Director sighed.

As the Harbor Guard stepped aside, thirty malakhim marched silently into the room bearing a colossal gold palanquin on their shoulders. The malakhim were dressed in hooded black robes, their faces hidden behind obsidian masks whose cracks and gouges marred their serene, angelic features. Their movements were so smooth, so graceful that it seemed their burden was no burden at all. But when they lowered the palanquin upon the floor, Founder's Hall trembled and several flagstones cracked.

Even when resting upon the floor, the palanquin loomed over the table and the malakhim that flanked it. It stood twenty feet tall, an enormous cube whose golden frame was fashioned in the shape of twining dragons and scepters. Its sides were made of thick glass plates whose warding runes glowed faintly against the deep purple curtains that hid the litter's interior. The curtains remained closed, but a voice issued out—a seductive tenor that flicked and probed at one's ears like a serpent's tongue.

"Greetings from Blys, Madam Director," said the voice. "I am honored so many should attend this audience, but I had hoped for a more private discussion."

"They would hear Prusias's words and I would hear their counsel," said Ms. Richter.

The litter's drapes stirred as though something huge had turned or shifted within.

"There is one here who has waged open war against my king and violated every term of the peace," the ambassador observed coldly. "It grieves me to see the Hound present, much less in a place of honor. Is this an insult? Or an oversight?"

"Neither," replied Ms. Richter. "Max McDaniels knows the King of Blys well. He has been a guest in Prusias's palace and his dungeons. Who better to hear your lord's words and judge them? And if we speak of insults, what are we to make of an ambassador who addresses this court from behind glass and curtains?"

"The runeglass is a necessary precaution," sniffed the demon. "These shores have grown inhospitable to my kind." This was most certainly true. Since the events of Walpurgisnacht, many more rowan trees had been planted along the cliffs, as had whole gardens of the otherworldly flowers called blood petals. The former were merely an irritation to evil spirits, but the latter were dangerous. "These drapes are merely meant as a courtesy," Naberius continued. "My form is not fair to mortals."

"We will not be swayed by a pretty face," remarked Ms. Richter.

"That is just what Prusias said when I urged him to send a fairer emissary," laughed the demon. "My king has every faith in your sound judgment, Madam Director. He knows that Rowan and Blys shall enjoy a long and prosperous friendship once we address the unpleasant matter of your rebellion."

"Against whom has Rowan rebelled?" inquired Ms. Richter frankly.

"Are you speaking in earnest?"

"Always."

The demon began to chuckle. Those from Rowan watched uneasily as strange forms pressed and flopped repulsively against the runeglass, obscured by the purple silks. It looked as though some giant octopus sought to escape an undersized aquarium. The curtains were thrust aside and several of the scholars gasped.

There was no visible connection between the thing behind the glass and its honeyed voice. How such an alien form produced the necessary sounds was a mystery. The ambassador's head resembled an ancient and sickly vulture that had been skinned and endowed with the large and multifaceted eyes of an insect. Perched atop a long, glutinous neck, the head swayed like a serpent's behind the runeglass. While Naberius surveyed the hall, his pale, larval body slowly slid about the glassed interior, oozing pus upon his nest of scarlet cushions and blankets of golden samite.

"Let us review history," he said, his throat pulsing with each syllable. "Two years ago, you signed a treaty, Gabrielle Richter. In exchange for Rowan's peaceful independence, you agreed to abide by Astaroth's edicts and look to your own affairs and people. Do I misspeak?"

"No," replied Ms. Richter. "As you say, I was there."

"Very good," said Naberius. "But despite these generous terms, Rowan has violated almost every provision of the accord. We know that you have been consorting with humans beyond your borders, teaching them to read, recruiting the *mèhrun* among them, and permitting them to settle your lands. Each of these activities is strictly forbidden by the treaty *you* signed, Madam Director. . . ." The demon cocked his head at the

Director, allowing the charges to resonate. "But King Prusias appreciates that humans are more sentimental than daemona. My lord admires this trait, as he admires so much about your kind. Had the transgressions stopped there, he might have been moved to overlook them in his desire to keep the peace. But as we know, the transgressions did not stop. . . ."

"Please continue," said Ms. Richter, folding her hands beneath her chin. Her expression was open and thoughtful, as though she were listening to charges levied against someone else.

"You have attacked my king, murdered his vassals, and destroyed our embassy," the ambassador seethed, heaving his body forward so that its bulk flattened against the runeglass in a white, corpulent smear. His hideous head loomed and swayed above them. "Rowan's provocations have been so brazen that news of my impending visit nearly triggered an uprising in Blys. The braymas are howling for war, not diplomacy. They want your head, Madam Director, along with those of every man, woman, and child within this realm."

"What is stopping them?" inquired Ms. Richter calmly, meeting the ambassador's gaze.

"Prusias," replied Naberius, his voice softening. He eased away from the glass, settling back down onto his cushions. "It is my king—wronged and wounded Prusias—who stands between you and annihilation. Despite Rowan's recent madness, he would still extend an olive branch. Provided she makes amends . . ."

"That is very generous of him," said Ms. Richter. "What terms would he require?"

"There are but three," replied the demon. "Rowan shall swear everlasting fealty to Prusias. Rowan shall rebuild Gràven-muir. And Rowan shall deliver both Elias Bram and the Hound's sword to my king's keeping."

"Just the sword?" wondered Ms. Richter. "Not its owner?"

"The Hound himself is of no consequence," said the ambassador, coldly eyeing Max. "The Atropos have already cut his thread and entered his name in the Grey Book. He is already dead. King Prusias requires only his blasphemous sword as the final proof of your allegiance."

Throughout this chilling interlude, Max betrayed no emotion. He had never heard of any Atropos or an ominous Grey Book, but it was clear that Ms. Richter had. Her self-control was excellent, but Max was sitting right beside her. At mention of the Atropos, her face lost some of its color.

"What have you to say?" inquired Lord Naberius. "Will Rowan join with Prusias and help him bring peace to the realms?"

"You have spoken plainly," replied the Director, "so I will do the same. If Rowan had committed the treasons of which you speak, I might be more amenable to your terms. But these attacks you mention and Gràvenmuir's destruction were committed without Rowan's blessing or knowledge."

A long silence ensued while the ambassador circled slowly about the palanquin. His glittering amethyst eyes never left Ms. Richter's. When at last he spoke, his throat flushed an angry crimson.

"The Hound sits at your right hand and you have the impudence to deny Rowan's treason!"

"It is truth," the Director replied, spreading her hands. "Almost two years ago, Max McDaniels left these shores, sailed to your lands, and lived quietly in the countryside. He might still be doing so had your king not found him and pressed him into service. Did Prusias not proclaim Max the Champion of Blys in his very own arena? If Blys's own champion has attacked its ruler, it would seem an internal matter for your kingdom. It is hardly Rowan's treason."

"What of David Menlo, then?" demanded the ambassador. "Do you deny that he orchestrated the events on Walpurgisnacht? Do you deny that he poisoned Astaroth?"

"Another curious charge," Ms. Richter observed. "David Menlo was expelled from this school for insubordination long before Walpurgisnacht. We reported this to Gràvenmuir and subsequently declared the Little Sorcerer an outlaw. Furthermore, David Menlo did not poison anyone. Astaroth willingly consumed the boy's potions before his entire court after demonstrating their considerable danger. Tell me, ambassador, if I seize your blade, praise its edge, and cut my throat, should Rowan hold you responsible?"

"You are cutting it now."

Ms. Richter looked up at the swaying head and laughed, brushing away the threat like a cobweb. "Come, sir," she chided. "You're taking this too personally! Emissaries must have thicker skins. You have made accusations and I am answering them. Let us turn to the issue of Gràvenmuir and its unexpected destruction by Elias Bram. Does Prusias intend to hold us answerable for the actions of a man we believed had died centuries ago, before Rowan was even founded?"

The ambassador regained his composure, easing back onto his cushions and regarding Ms. Richter and the Red Branch with brooding malevolence.

"You maintain Rowan's innocence and disavow these criminals, and yet here they reside. We know they shelter and sup beneath this very roof. If Rowan were truly innocent in these affairs, Madam Director, you would have delivered these outlaws and outsiders as a token of good faith and allegiance. Why have you not done so?"

"For the simple reason that the task is well beyond my power." Ms. Richter shrugged. "Why doesn't Prusias bring Yuga to heel?

I hear she has devoured all of Holbrymn and is now drifting into Raikos. . . ."

Max had heard tales of Patient Yuga. She had been a humble imp until her cleverness enabled her to escape her long servitude and become a being so dreadful that even the greatest demons now feared her. Yuga took the form of a massive storm that moved slowly over the lands, mindlessly devouring all in her path. While Prusias had sought to placate her with the vast duchy of Holbrymn, it sounded as though Yuga had already consumed all of her subjects and now desired more.

"Yuga is not your concern," hissed Naberius. "And you misunderstand your position. Prusias does not answer to Rowan; it is Rowan that answers to him."

"Would King Aamon agree?" inquired Ms. Richter. "Would Rashaverak or Queen Lilith? The other rulers might find it rather presumptuous for Prusias to claim Rowan as his vassal state. Our treaty was with Astaroth, not his servants or their kingdoms."

Naberius uncoiled once again. His heavy head reared up to gaze at them. "Prusias is Astaroth's servant no longer. Astaroth was a fool. He allowed a mortal to deceive and weaken him before his nobles. None will follow him again. It is Prusias whom you should seek to please, Madam Director. Only Prusias is strong enough to impose harmony across the four kingdoms and ensure the peace we all desire."

"I hear the other kingdoms intend to resist this 'imposition of harmony,'" remarked Ms. Richter. "Is it true that Dùn and Jakarün have formed an alliance, or am I misinformed?"

"It makes no difference," the demon sneered. "Prusias is strongest. The others will surrender or be crushed and their lands awarded to those who aided my king. Rowan could benefit if she is wise enough to reconcile with Blys and swear fealty.

Despite your deflections, Madam Director, Prusias will hold Rowan accountable for whatever Prusias chooses. My king is giving you an opportunity to make amends before war is declared. I urge you to seize this chance, for he will suffer no cravens or neutrals once battle is joined. Rowan is either with him or against him. . . ."

Ms. Richter nodded. "The choice is plain, but difficult. I must have time to consider Prusias's offer and see if we can even procure the coin that he requires. Gràvenmuir we can rebuild, a sword we can surrender, but to deliver Elias Bram . . . I simply do not know."

Sinking back to the litter's cushions, the ambassador slid beneath his samite covers like a glutted snake returning to its burrow.

"You have my sympathies," he observed. "You are unlucky in your subjects. If Bram or your Hound had any honor, they would relieve you of this burden and make the necessary sacrifices. Rowan has until the winter solstice to swear fealty and fulfill my lord's demands. I will await your answer upon my ship. Until then, I leave you to your council and your Hound to the Atropos. . . ."

The curtains closed as the malakhim raised the massive palanquin upon their shoulders. In their long black robes, they seemed to glide from Founder's Hall. Max watched them go, his mind racing with Rowan's dilemma and this unexpected threat from the mysterious Atropos. It was only when the great doors boomed shut that he remembered William Cooper and the Fool's Perch. The chair was still empty.

~ 2 ~

ARCHMAGE

Following Lord Naberius's departure, Founder's Hall became a hive of hushed and anxious conversations. Ms. Richter cut these short, thanking all for their attendance and reminding them that the winter solstice was still six weeks away. Theirs was a pressing deadline, she acknowledged, but sufficient to gather additional intelligence and make an informed decision. Once she dismissed the attendees, many offered their support and assured the Director that she had done well. She thanked them and promised to follow up with each for their advice and counsel. When Miss Boon filed past, Ms. Richter asked her to remain behind.

The teacher nodded and glanced anxiously at the empty seat where Cooper should have been.

"It's okay, Miss Boon," Max assured her. "Cooper will be back soon."

"Oh, it's not that," she muttered irritably, dabbing at her face with a sleeve. "Of course William's fine. I know he's fine. He probably got stuck with some incompetent of the Harbor Guard. It's *you* I'm worried about."

Max waved off the ambassador's dark pronouncements. "If I had a shiny lune for every time I've been threatened . . . ," he quipped. When this failed to elicit even the hint of a smile, Max merely shrugged. "Just because Prusias says I'm a dead man doesn't make it so."

Miss Boon nodded appreciatively, but her apparent worry remained.

The hall had almost emptied when Ms. Richter called Ben Polk over.

"I know you're busy," she said, "but I would appreciate it if you would track down Agent Cooper. It's not like him to miss something like this. He has been helping the coastal settlements see to their defenses and was at Sphinx Point just yesterday."

Ben Polk touched two fingers to his forehead and spoke in a voice so eerily flat and distant that he might have been daydreaming. "I'll have him home by evenfall, Director. And then I'm off for Dùn, 'less you need me for anything else round here. . . ."

Max felt a chill as those unblinking glassy eyes wandered over him and settled on his sword. He knew that if the Director ordered Ben Polk to acquire the *gae bolga*, the Agent would instantly do his utmost. The prospect that such a task might require him to take Max's life or surrender his own would be of no consequence. A killer like Ben Polk had no time for hesitation, doubts, or morality. If he'd ever possessed such things, they'd been cast aside a long time ago. Ms. Richter caught the man's suggestion at once.

"No," she replied firmly. "Once you've accounted for Agent Cooper, we need you in Dùn. The goblin carrack *Mungröl* sails on Sunday. The goblins might be slower, but that ship's made for rough seas."

As Agent Polk departed, a flock of apprentices and gnomish domovoi arrived to straighten up Founder's Hall. Ms. Richter took one of the domovoi aside, pointing out the flagstones the palanquin had cracked. "I'd like these replaced as soon as possible," she said. "And let's channel some fresh air in here. I want all evidence of that visitor scoured from this place. What a foul messenger. What a foul message!" She added this last reflection in an undertone before her attention snapped back to Max and Miss Boon. Stopping a passing apprentice, she drained a cup of coffee from the boy's tray and then beckoned the others to follow as she strode from the hall.

She chose one of the Manse's less trafficked staircases, leading them up the marble steps while the sprawling mansion hummed and echoed with the din of a new school day. Footsteps drummed and doors opened and slammed shut, accompanied by shouts and laughter from the dormitory wings. A disheveled Second Year came racing down the staircase, carrying far too many books and chomping maniacally upon a slice of ham. Upon glimpsing the Director, the boy gave a prepubescent yelp and spun awkwardly to avoid hitting her. Books and breakfast went flying as the boy crashed into Miss Boon, flinging his arms about her waist to break his fall. Both parties were mortified. Stammering incoherent apologies, the student stooped to gather up his things and braced for the inevitable tirade. He was saved by the stampede that soon followed.

More students came dashing down the narrow staircase, a blur of scrubbed faces, books, and wet hair that clung to cowls of gray, blue, and brown wool. Bidding the Director a startled good day, they swarmed past their unfortunate classmate and continued to chatter about the latest gossip, homework, and exams. Max watched them go, more than a little envious as they dashed off to study composition, divination, or whatever else occupied their busy schedules. His former classmates would be diving into their second hour of Advanced Conjuration, each resplendent in their silver magechains and a Fifth Year's fine viridian robes.

By the time they'd reached the third floor, the flood of students had thinned to a handful of stragglers, woefully late and destined for mucking out the Sanctuary stables or patrolling the raw and windy coast. Winding their way through a maze of corridors, the three finally passed the Bacon Library and veered down a disused hallway to a suite of old classrooms. Those classrooms had been converted into an apartment that was now occupied by a living, breathing dead man.

Was Elias Bram dead? In truth, Max did not know. To label the man *undead* seemed wrong. *Undead* evoked ghouls and wights and revenants—creatures with rotting flesh and spectral eyes and a ravenous hatred of the living.

But while Elias Bram did not fit this description, he neither fit conventional definitions for the living. For one, Bram's sacred apple had turned to gold, which was only supposed to occur upon one's death. For another, it was common knowledge that Astaroth had devoured the man centuries ago. But what if the Demon had kept some vital spark of Bram intact? Astaroth had spoken of past victims "contributing to his essence," but Max assumed he'd been speaking metaphorically. If Elias Bram's living spirit had persevered all this time, Max was not certain how to classify him.

Regardless of whether Bram was living or dead, Max still regarded him with a mixture of superstitious awe and fear. The man's legend loomed over everything at Rowan. Even the lowliest apprentice could recite basic facts about his life. He was revered as something of a saint and a demigod—a being whose name, likeness, and history were woven into the surroundings and daily life. For Rowan students, Elias Bram was Sir Isaac Newton, Hercules, and Merlin rolled into one.

For Mystics, however, Bram was Stradivari—a virtuoso of magic whose results could not be duplicated by later generations despite every effort to divine his methods. Even Bram's most mundane ledgers and notes were treasured documents, meticulously preserved and jealously guarded by scholars who spent lifetimes scrutinizing them in the hope of some veiled cipher or insight. It was not just his magic that was a mystery, but also the man himself. How had a shipwrecked orphan come to claim Solas's Gwydion Chair of Mystics by the age of twenty? It defied explanation.

If a book held the answers, many might have followed in Bram's footsteps. But to Max's knowledge, there had only been one. And that remarkable being was Max's very own roommate and closest companion, the mysterious David Menlo. Like Elias Bram, David was a true sorcerer, a prodigy whose genius with magic often allowed him to bypass the ancient formulae and incantations that were a Mystic's tools in trade. Once, Miss Boon had remarked—with a tinge of professional envy—that David's talents were like a composer simply improvising an entire symphony. Ever since David's power became apparent, the scholars sought to analyze him with the same fervor with which they studied Bram's papers. As it happened, the connection between the two was closer than any had imagined: David Menlo was Elias Bram's grandson.

David's initial claim that Bram was his grandfather was met with skepticism. After all, David Menlo was only a teenager while Elias Bram had died during the seventeenth century. The only possible link between David and Bram was through the Archmage's wife and daughter, who had fled Astaroth's forces and sailed west with the refugees who would found Rowan.

The pair had arrived safely in America, but Elias Bram's wife, Brigit, had died shortly thereafter. According to the histories, Elias had promised his wife that he would rejoin her in the new land. Day after day, Brigit Bram stood on Rowan's rocky beach and gazed into the east, awaiting a husband who was not coming. Legend had it that one evening she took up her lantern and simply waded into the sea until the waves closed over her. Her body had never been found, but some insisted that her passing coincided with the appearance of a large rock off Rowan's shore. Romantics claimed that its silhouette resembled a woman staring out to sea and named it Brigit's Vigil.

Little was known of Bram's daughter. Her name was Emer and the historians rarely mentioned her. From the few accounts, it seemed that Emer was a sickly, simpleminded child who had been shunned by the community even before she'd been orphaned. There was no indication that Emer had ever studied at Solas or Rowan, and all mention of her ceased after her mother's passing. As there was no gravestone bearing her name or any documentation of her death, the scholars concluded that the unfortunate girl had been driven away or left to fend for herself in the wild.

Where Emer went or how she managed to survive, Max did not know. But by now it was clear that the Old Magic was in her. For one, she was now centuries old and yet looked no more than forty. For another, she had given birth to David, whose own ties to the Old Magic were plainly evident. Miss Boon theorized that Bram's unfortunate daughter had inherited all of the Archmage's power and none of his constitution. As most mortals were far too fragile a vessel for the Old Magic, the teacher surmised that its energies had overwhelmed Emer's mind just as they had overtaxed David's body. For Max, this seemed as logical an explanation as any.

When they finally reached the ironbound door, Miss Boon cleared her throat. "Are you certain anyone's here?" she hissed. "He's often away, you know."

The sound of a child's laughter answered the question. Drawing herself up, Ms. Richter knocked. A moment later the door was opened by a wizened domovoi with blue-tinted spectacles pulling an empty cart. He peered up at them, his lumpish face grinning amiably.

"Jacob!" exclaimed Ms. Richter, sounding surprised and somewhat relieved. "Here I was expecting Elias Bram and instead I find the estimable Jacob Quills. What brings you up from the Archives?"

The creature bowed and touched a bristly knuckle to his forehead. "I've been seeing to the Archmage's books, Director," he replied. "Our lord's been catching up on what he's missed, and three centuries makes for a crowded nightstand." With a chuckle, the domovoi stood aside to let them enter before slipping out the door, pulling his wobbly cart.

Bram's quarters comprised several old classrooms that had been modified into an apartment with a large common area, two small bedrooms, a snug study, and an old-fashioned privy. The walls were cream-colored plaster whose only adornment were the latest maps of Rowan's territory and the Four Kingdoms. Turkish rugs had been strewn upon the floor, although they were barely visible beneath stacks of books, unrolled scrolls, and loose-leaf parchments. Bay windows faced south and west, but they offered little light on such a damp and gloomy morning. To compensate, several lanterns had been lit in the common room and a small fire flickered in the fieldstone hearth.

Of the four people gathered around that fire, David Menlo was closest. He sat with his back resting comfortably against an ottoman while little Mina flicked marbles toward him across the floor. David glanced up at the group as they filed in. He was a blond boy of about sixteen, very small for his age, whose youthful face was offset by an expression of frank intelligence that made him seem much older. When his eyes met Max's, they brightened with pleasure.

While David could convey volumes with a nod, Mina was more demonstrative. Shouting Max's name, the seven-year-old barreled into him with an energy and exuberance he'd not have imagined possible when he'd stumbled upon her in Blys nearly two years ago. Then she'd been a mere wisp of a girl, an unwashed and half-starved creature gathering firewood for the farmhouse where she lived with fellow orphans and several adults. The adults had not been welcoming and soon sent Max on his way. It was only by chance that he returned and found that Mina had been left as an offering to placate a monster that lived in a nearby well. Max had slain the monster, but it was weeks before the traumatized child would even speak, much less smile. And it was months before Max realized that the quiet girl who shadowed his every step was a Mystic of uncommon ability.

In many ways, Mina owed her life to both of the boys. Max had rescued her from the well; David had rescued her from Prusias, smuggling the entire household to Rowan before the demon could harm them. While Mina's former housemates now attended school with other refugees, her emerging magical talents required a different sort of education.

Apparently this education had already begun. Squirming out of Max's arms, Mina showed him not only a missing tooth but also her magechain.

"Look at that," said Max, cooing over the chain along with the departed incisor that had been set to dangle alongside minor feats in Firecraft, Herb Lore, and Illusion. "You'll be Archmage in no time!"

"That's what Uncle 'Lias says," she crowed, her dark eyes flashing with delight. Spinning about on her stocking feet, she laughed and raced back to her seat, anxious to resume her game of marbles.

Until the mention of his name, the gray-robed figure by the fire had resembled one of his own statues, huge and unmoving. But now Elias Bram leaned forward in his wooden chair. His voice was deep, its accent tinged with a faint Irish lilt. "That won't do, Mina," he chided softly. "We have company and you must make your leg for the Director. There's a good girl."

As Mina stood and made a proper curtsy, Max regarded Bram. Even when sitting quietly in his chair, Elias Bram exuded a gargantuan presence. Max suspected that Bram could sit unannounced among a host of kings and queens and dominate the gathering without ever saying a word.

He was rangy and rawboned with a high forehead, darkly chiseled features, and a beard to match his mane of snarled gray hair. He was physically imposing and seemed to simmer with a quiet, almost feral intensity. Within his pale gray eyes, one sensed an unyielding sense of purpose and conviction. For Max, the combined effect of the man's legend and individual presence was more than a little frightening. He had not felt anything like it since Astaroth. People would either devote their lives to such a person or seek to tear him limb from limb.

"The ambassador has gone," said Ms. Richter, brushing a

strand of silver hair from her eyes. "He's returned to his ship to await our answer."

"An ultimatum, I gather," Bram muttered, rising to heat some water and retrieve some chairs from his study. When they had been seated, the Archmage stooped to address Mrs. Menlo, who had been sitting mute by the hearth stroking a calico cat. "Hear me, Emer," Bram murmured, smoothing her gray-blond hair. "Your pa and little David have to speak of serious matters. Take Mina to the Sanctuary to visit our YaYa. There's to be a Matching this morning and I know you'll like to see it. I'll come find you when we're finished."

David's mother blinked and nodded and reached for a nearby shawl.

"Can Lila come?" she wondered, her voice lacking all inflection. She smiled distantly at her father's response. "Let's go, Mina," she called, as though the girl were far away and not already retrieving their shoes. "Let's visit YaYa and watch the Matching. It will be fun."

The pair departed, with Mina clutching Mrs. Menlo's hand as they tottered out, each wrapped in navy cloaks. Cleaning her paws, Lila gazed out the window and seemed to reconsider the excursion. Nudged by Bram, the cat mewed and darted out the door, vanishing with a churlish swish of her tail.

As the water heated, Bram rummaged through various cupboards and retrieved an array of chipped cups, mismatched saucers, and old spoons. He arranged them on a small folding table that doubled as a chessboard. Something about the scene struck Max as odd, and it took a moment for him to realize what it was.

"You're not using any magic," he remarked, louder perhaps than he'd intended. Any Second Year apprentice would have been tempted to heat the kettle with a flick of their fingers. Had a Fifth Year been present, there would have been no searching for saucers and cups; they would have flown from the cupboard and stood at attention. And yet here was history's greatest sorcerer methodically setting out cups and plates like any ordinary host.

"The fire's hot," Bram rumbled. "The kettle's good. The water will boil soon enough. Do you shave with the Morrígan's blade?"

Max glanced down at the *gae bolga*. "Of course not."

"Wise boy," said Bram. "Simple jobs don't require dangerous tools. You and David can finish up while the Director shares her news."

David measured out the tea leaves before grinding coffee for himself. Strong black coffee was his vice of choice, and god help the librarian who tried to confiscate his beloved thermos when David ventured down into the Archives. One could almost trace his studies by the rings left on faded tomes and forbidden grimoires.

"How was Zenuvia?" he whispered, leaning a shoulder into Max.

"Hot," Max muttered, reaching for the kettle. "But worth it, I think. I'll tell you more later."

Serving the drinks, the two boys sat next to each other on the hearth bench while their elders sat facing one another in the chairs. Despite Bram's attempts to be cordial, Max could tell that Ms. Richter and Miss Boon were nervous.

"Thank you for the tea," said Ms. Richter, stirring hers pensively. "And thank you for honoring my request not to interfere with this morning's audience. . . ."

Bram nodded and sat quietly as the Director recounted the ambassador's visit, the looming threat of war among the kingdoms, and Prusias's ultimatum. When Ms. Richter indicated that Elias Bram was to be handed over as Prusias's final condition, the man remained stoic. The only reaction he offered was a surprised grunt when he learned that Lord Naberius had been the envoy. When Ms. Richter finished, Bram tapped his knee.

"You have not told me all," he remarked, his soft tone an invitation rather than accusation.

"No," Ms. Richter confessed, sipping her tea. "I thought it better if we focus on the bigger picture."

"Better to share everything now," Bram suggested.

Glancing at Hazel, Ms. Richter detailed Cooper's unexpected absence from the morning audience.

"And this is out of character?" inquired Bram.

"Very much so," the Director sighed. "It may be coincidental and it may not. We've dispatched another member of the Red Branch to search for him. With any luck, they'll both be back by nightfall."

Bram nodded but still looked expectant. "Something else remains. You have saved it for last, Director, because it frightens you."

Glancing gravely at Max, Ms. Richter cleared her throat. "Prusias has revived the Atropos. They have entered Max's name into the Grey Book. That is why they are content to seize only his sword; they say he is already dead. . . ."

Bram's chair creaked as the big man turned to gaze at Max. "The boy looks alive to me. He is strong and has no family. The Atropos will find him more difficult than most."

"What are the Atropos?" asked Max, looking to the rest. "I've never even heard of them."

"An ancient assassins' guild," answered Ms. Richter. "They take their name from one of the three Moirae—the Greek Fates. Clotho spun the threads of life, and Lachesis measured a length for each man, woman, and child. And when Atropos cut a mortal's thread, that person's life was ended. . . ."

Max laughed. "The Four Kingdoms are riddled with

assassins and 'dark brotherhoods,' each claiming to be more secretive and deadly than the next. I've faced worse, Ms. Richter. Please don't worry about me."

"No, Max," interjected Miss Boon urgently. "She's absolutely right to be concerned. It's been centuries since the Atropos were destroyed, and it's a terrible development if they've been revived. At one time, to even mention their name might lead one to the gallows."

Max's smile faded. "Why was everyone so afraid of them?"

"They were fanatics," she explained. "Fanatical in their desire to slay any whose name had been entered in their Grey Book. They believed that once a name had been recorded, that person had reached the end of his or her life. To live even a second longer was an affront to the Fates. Accordingly, the guild sent their target a message informing him that his time had come. If the person surrendered willingly, it was said his death was swift and painless."

"What if he refused?" asked Max.

Miss Boon's face darkened. "If the target refused the summons, the Atropos expanded the contract to include all of his blood relatives, born *and* unborn. In such a case, the contract might remain open for decades—even centuries—until the Atropos were satisfied that their original target had died along with all who shared his blood."

"There are many horror stories," Ms. Richter muttered, breaking the ensuing silence. "Fear of the Atropos skyrocketed when they closed several contracts centuries after the original target had been slain. By then, of course, there were hundreds of relatives and descendants who were living in distant lands and under different names. It did not matter. The Atropos did not rest until each had been hunted down. As you can imagine, many with noble blood lived in constant fear that some distant ancestor's name was in the Grey Book and that it was only a matter of time before the Atropos came for them."

"Why only those with noble blood?" Max wondered.

"To hire the guild was an exceedingly costly proposition," explained Miss Boon. "Only the oldest families, greatest orders, and wealthiest merchants had such deep coffers. One did not contact the Atropos for personal revenge; one employed them to eliminate extremely powerful enemies and subvert nations. The Atropos themselves were brutal, but as their reputation grew, they rarely had to lift a finger. The terror they inspired led others to do their work for them. There are many sad accounts in which families turned on their own. Bodies were left at crossroads in the hope that the Atropos would be appeased. The merest suspicion that one's name had been recorded in the Grey Book could trigger outright panic and murder."

Max found it all too easy to imagine the nightmares that might unfold. Old Tom began to chime the Westminster Quarters. Outside, Max heard shouts and laughter. Rising, he walked to the nearest window and gazed down at the paths and gardens below. A group of Sixth Years was hurrying down the cobbled way that led to the Smithy. Their bright scarlet robes flapped behind them, a welcome contrast to the gloomy morning. His breath misted the diamond-shaped panes.

"What sort of person would even think to hire such an organization?" he muttered hoarsely.

"Many sorts," lamented Ms. Richter, rising to refill cups and place more wood on the fire. "Early on, some viewed the Atropos as a useful tool—a check against those whose excesses had brought a just doom upon them. The Atropos were expensive, but they were effective and always honored their contracts. One did not need to worry about blackmail, betrayal, or the other hazards common to such dealings. The guild kept their patron's identity as great a secret as their own. It was said that the Atropos did not always know who hired them; they required only a name and payment of their princely fees."

Hanging the kettle back over the fire, Ms. Richter glanced at Max's gilded scabbard.

"But any weapon so tempting and perilous will have unforeseen consequences," she reflected. "It was inevitable the Atropos would eventually harm those whom their patron never intended. As noble houses intermarried and family trees intertwined, the dangers posed by the guild increased a hundredfold. Some unwittingly caused the deaths of their distant descendants. There are even tales of poor fools who paid for their *own* execution!"

"What?" Max exclaimed. "How could something like that happen?"

"Paternity is not always as described," Bram remarked, his gaze rising to meet Max's. "Trace the bloodlines of servants and stable boys and you'll find that many lead to the local manor. And royal courts are justly famous for their intrigues. I could name kings who sired less than half their 'royal brood.' The Atropos do not care about surnames or cuckold's horns; they care only about the blood in one's veins. And if one has hired them to slay an enemy who turns out to be a distant relation . . ."

Max returned to sit by his roommate, who was staring somberly at the fire. "So what happened to them?" he asked. "How were the Atropos disbanded?"

"The threat they posed became intolerable," replied Ms. Richter. "What had once been a useful tool had spiraled out of control. People stopped hiring them, but old contracts could not be canceled, nor could the guild be enticed to stop hunting the kin of those who had fled their death summons. For the Atropos, this aspect was sacred—divine retribution against those who had sought to cheat the Fates.

"Even the most powerful rulers lived in fear," she continued. "But none dared take action until Charles V. The Holy Roman Emperor had been born in the Burgundian Low Countries, and when the Atropos were suspected of several murders in the region, Charles feared that his own house was next. He reached out to the other great powers—even the Ottomans—and despite their differences, they all agreed that the Atropos must be ended for the common good. These rulers united in a quiet campaign to identify and eliminate the guild. The tables were turned and the Atropos became the hunted. The Red Branch was involved."

"I'm glad," said Max.

"So were many others," said Ms. Richter. "The Atropos were destroyed, but so was the emperor. Despite the Red Branch's assurances, Charles could not quell his fear that some small faction of the guild had survived and would seek vengeance. Abdicating his titles, he retired to a monastery where he surrounded himself with hundreds of clocks."

"Why clocks?" Max wondered. "Wouldn't guards have served better?"

"He thought he was doomed," muttered Miss Boon sadly. "The ticking of the clocks reminded him a man's life was short and ever dwindling. Whether the clocks gave him comfort or simply fed his fears, no one knows. He died within a few years."

"The Atropos?" Max wondered, a chill creeping up his arms.

"No," Bram snapped, his eyes flashing. "The man died of fear and gout. Let his folly be a lesson to you, Max McDaniels. The Atropos are formidable, but they are *not* the Fates, and fear was ever their greatest weapon. You and I will speak more of this, but other matters press. Director, you have told me of

Prusias and his ultimatum, but what of Astaroth? Did Naberius mention him?"

"He did," said Ms. Richter, glancing out the window as rain pattered on the glass. "He said that David had humiliated Astaroth before all and that none would follow him again. It would seem the demons scorn him and will no longer bend to his will."

"Then they are fools," said Bram quietly. "And *we* are fools if we share their beliefs. It is Astaroth who poses the true peril, not Prusias or any other ambitious demon among the kingdoms."

"Six months have passed," said Miss Boon quietly, "and we have heard and seen nothing of Astaroth."

Bram shook his head. "That troubles me far more than grand displays of his power. What are six months to Astaroth, Director? Whether six months or six millennia, it is all the same to him. He is weakened, yes, but he still possesses the Book of Thoth, and while he has it, he still controls the strings. Astaroth may lie hidden and forgotten for a day or a century, but when he chooses to jerk those strings, the world will jump."

"Why don't his former servants and fellow demons share your fear?" asked Ms. Boon.

"Because they don't truly understand him," replied Bram gravely. "The daemona believe that Astaroth is one of their kind—an ancient spirit, cruel and clever. I suspect they are mistaken."

The Archmage said nothing for some time. No one dared speak, but Max glanced at David, who hugged his knees and stared at his grandfather. Max guessed the two had already discussed this topic. The rain fell harder now, the drops drumming against the window while the first winds of winter swept past in sudden gales and moaned within the chimney.

Bram cleared his throat. "I believe Astaroth is something

else entirely," he muttered. "He has masqueraded as a demon for ages and fooled them, but I suspect that Astaroth is something far older and stranger than Prusias or any of his ilk."

"How do you know this?" asked Ms. Richter quietly.

"He was my prison for many years," explained Bram, studying his hands. "I have glimpsed what lies beneath that grinning mask, and it is no demon. Astaroth is no corrupted steward or wild spirit from the first days—he is not from this world or any other within our little universe. Prusias and the others are deadly enemies, but their motives and desires are clear. We can understand Prusias's greed and lust for power—we know what he covets, and this makes him far less terrifying than one so alien as Astaroth. My liberation has weakened this outsider, but he is still lurking about—unaccounted for and still possessing the Book. Prusias may menace the world's kingdoms, but Astaroth is a threat to the world itself. . . ."

As the man lapsed into silence, the logs cracked and a plume of sparks momentarily brightened the darkening room. Indeed it was dark, Max reflected—too murky for midday and far too dismal to discuss such disturbing matters. Reaching past David, he put another log upon the fire and rose to light several more candles. Watching the flames catch upon the wicks, Max reflected upon Bram's assertion that Astaroth was no demon but something else. It was a disturbing revelation, but it also echoed and reinforced Max's own hazy misgivings. Other than Bram, Max had spent more time with Astaroth than anyone at Rowan, and there were occasions when he had stared into those merry, black eyes and sensed naught but the void behind them. Prusias could be a bloodthirsty tyrant, but his sensibilities and tastes were far more human. Max was reluctant to admit it, but there had been moments when he'd actually enjoyed the demon's humor and energetic company. He had never enjoyed Astaroth's. No matter how courtly or chivalrous Astaroth's manners may have been, his grinning white face had always seemed an impenetrable mask.

"You claim that Astaroth is the greater threat and I believe you," said Ms. Richter solemnly. "But you also say that he may lurk for a thousand years and take no action. That is too abstract a problem for our present dilemma. Rowan is threatened *now*, Archmage. Due to your actions, we have six short weeks to make amends with Prusias or gird for war."

At this hint of reproach, Bram's expression hardened into a stone mask. Seconds ticked by slowly. When he finally spoke, the man's voice was quiet but unyielding.

"I have put you in a hard place," he acknowledged. "Perhaps I should have consulted you before casting that abomination into the sea. In my outrage, I may have cost Rowan a few days to prepare her defenses. For that I apologize. But let me be clear, Director . . . Gràvenmuir was doomed the moment I saw her. And despite this farce of an overture, Prusias has no intention of sparing Rowan. That was plain when he set the Morrígan blade and my person as conditions for peace. These are the only weapons he fears. If Rowan is foolish enough to weaken herself and surrender these things for a demon's promise, Prusias will merely laugh and launch his ships." The Archmage rested his elbows upon his knees and gazed gravely at the Director. "Prusias *is* coming for Rowan, Gabrielle Richter. The only questions are how soon and whether or not he succeeds."

Ms. Richter's cup clattered in its saucer as she set it down.

"I'm well aware of this," she retorted stiffly. "But we do appreciate you clarifying the key points. I suppose it's my responsibility as a leader to swallow my pride and glean whatever other insights our exalted Archmage has to offer. He has started a war and has now been kind enough to admit as much. Perhaps he might also suggest a way to *win*."

A ghost of a smile flickered in Bram's pale eyes. He inclined his head. "Well said, Director. But I think it best if I concentrate my energies on Astaroth and leave the defense of Rowan to you and your counselors. I would not wish others to think that the 'exalted Archmage' has superseded your authority. And if it's strategy you desire, my grandson can serve you better than I."

At Ms. Richter's invitation, David unfolded from his perch and began to pace back and forth like he often did while deep in thought.

"Prusias has millions; we have thousands," he mused. "Even if he engages the bulk of his forces against the other kingdoms, he could still dispatch an army to Rowan much larger than anything we can muster. We must do everything we can to delay that outcome for as long as possible—stall negotiations with Naberius, sabotage shipyards in Blys, disrupt his trade, and incite his enemies to attack him."

"Very sensible," remarked Ms. Richter smartly. "Many of these initiatives are already in place. In fact, I believe Max has news to report from Zenuvia?"

"I do," said Max, shoving aside thoughts of Astaroth and the Atropos. "Traveling along its coasts, I heard a very consistent message among the smugglers. It could be false intelligence, of course, but I don't think so. The rumor is that Lilith opposes Prusias but will not join with Aamon or Rashaverak until battle has begun. Her reasoning is clear enough—given the distance between Zenuvia and Blys, it's unlikely that Prusias would attack her with a force of any real size until he's defeated the alliance between the other kingdoms. Should that happen, the queen could claim she never opposed him and sue for better terms. If Aamon and Rashaverak are winning, however, Lilith can join the fray and tip the balance at a critical moment. In either case, she limits her risk and may even be able to seize her allies' kingdoms should the war cripple them."

Ms. Richter nodded her approval. "What of our agreements with the Khoreshi smugglers? Are they still in place?"

"For the moment," Max reported. "But they're opportunists. Since Gràvenmuir, they've charged us triple market prices plus hazard freight and compensation for any lost ships. If Rowan goes to war, we should expect those costs to multiply tenfold."

"Are those prices worth it?" she inquired, arching an eyebrow.

Max considered this. "I think so. As David says, if and when Prusias attacks, we're likely to face a force much larger than our own. In addition, our own Agents and Mystics will be spread very thin; the majority of our army will consist of refugees who have little to no training. We need that iron ore from the Zenuvian mines. For some reason it's far more effective on the demons and other spirits. I've brought a raw sample to share with dvergar. Perhaps they can replicate its properties. If we can equip the refugees with such weapons, they become much more valuable."

Ms. Richter made a note within a slim notebook. "And what of the nonhumans? Are any of the goblins and vyes open to discussions?"

"Unclear at this stage." Max shrugged. "The greedier goblin clans might be, but the language barrier is difficult and I didn't trust my contact. In any case, the bribes they demanded at every stage were enormous, and I'd already spent most of my funds on the smugglers. As for the vyes, from what I could gather, they're not content in the new order—they feel they've been cheated and supplanted by the demons. But they're too wary to discuss anything openly. They're afraid that everyone is a demon in disguise, probing for potential traitors. We'll have to keep trying."

Ms. Richter flicked her eyes to David, who had been listening intently. "What do you make of Max's report?"

"It's good information," he commented, "and we should certainly acquire as much of the iron as we can. But I can't help but focus on Prusias. Something's wrong . . . something's *off*."

Bram raised his head at this and gazed at his grandson.

"Grandfather," said David, "you have summoned Prusias before. Have you ever summoned the other monarchs?"

"Aamon," replied Bram, touching his fingertips together and searching his memory. "Aamon knows many old secrets, but I've not called the others. What troubles you?"

"Prusias's confidence," replied David. "He knows you are here. He knows Max has reforged the Morrígan's blade, and he knows the other monarchs are likely to unite against him. But despite this, he gloats like he's already won."

"Prusias always bullies," grunted Max, recalling his own unpleasant history with the demon.

"Yes," said David. "But this seems different. I think Prusias has a trick up his sleeve."

"The cane?" inquired Miss Boon. The magic that created Gràvenmuir had come from Prusias's cane, and David had long suspected that it contained a page from the Book of Thoth.

"I don't think so," replied David, rubbing the stump where his right hand had once been. "He's had that for some time. His latest tone sounds like there's been a new development, something that will ensure victory. . . ."

"The Workshop," breathed Max. "Prusias has been protecting and sponsoring them even after Astaroth banished modern technologies. I rode pod tubes up to the Arena."

"That's precisely my worry," David confessed. "We no longer have modern technologies, but the Workshop does. And Prusias has the Workshop. . . ."

Max's hopes dwindled. What use were iron-tipped arrows against guns or tanks? The others seemed to share his apprehensions.

At length, Bram spoke. "It is a long time since I had dealings with the Workshop," he reflected. "But when last I did, they broke their neutrality and helped me safeguard the Book of Thoth. Their first love was always their machines, but perhaps we can convince them to aid us again."

"The Workshop did nothing to resist Astaroth," observed Miss Boon bitterly. "As long as Prusias is the one ensuring that their technologies do not fade, I can't imagine that they'll join us. Why would they risk their machines or their lives on such a risky prospect?"

"That's probably true," said David. "But we should at least reestablish contact through all possible channels. If nothing else, we might gain insight into what they're doing. At this stage, information and intelligence is everything. Rowan has to win the war of spies before it can win a war of weapons. . . ."

As David continued to discuss spy networks, sabotage, and civil defense, Max found that Elias Bram was staring at him. The appraisal was trancelike and unblinking, reminding Max of when another had gazed at him years earlier on a train bound for Chicago. Of course, trains and Chicago no longer existed; Astaroth had used the Book of Thoth to refashion the world and strip away much that mankind had built or invented. Among the humans who survived Astaroth's rise to power, few could even recall their former way of life—their memories of such things had faded. But some who'd been gifted with magic could recall the past with varying degrees of clarity. Max remembered everything, including that fateful day when a stranger's dead white eye had locked on to him.

"Stop looking at me," he growled, stalking back over to the

window. The rain had ceased and the walkways shone slick and wet, their puddles reflecting the gray skies. The others ceased their conversation and turned to see what was the disturbance.

"I must have a word with Max," Bram announced, rising abruptly from his chair. "I'll leave you three to your discussions while the boy accompanies me to the Sanctuary. It's time Emer came home and Mina has her lessons."

"We'll go with you," offered Miss Boon, her unease and suspicion evident.

"I don't intend to spirit away your Hound, Hazel Boon," Bram chuckled. "I just need a private word with him, assuming the lad can forgive my manners."

Max nodded, his irritation giving way to curiosity.

"Whatever you have to say to Max you can say in front of us," said Ms. Richter.

"I'm afraid I can't," replied the Archmage curtly. "Good day to you both. David will see you out." Taking up a heavy mantle from a stand by the door, Bram swept it over his shoulders and held the door open for Max.

The famous pair took a shortcut across Bacon Library, ignoring the curious stares from a score of students hunched over their books and manuscripts. Exiting the Manse through a pair of French doors, they braced themselves as the November gales whipped past them. Max envied the Archmage's heavy cloak.

It was ten minutes of brisk, silent walking until they'd traversed the orchards and wound around the stables and Smithy to reach the stone wall that separated Old College (as the original campus was now known) from Rowan's Sanctuary. A stout oaken door was set into the wall, some twelve feet tall and six feet wide and traced with fine golden runes. It was propped open to reveal an arching canopy of interlacing trunks and twisting branches, a shadowy green tunnel through the dense sea of trees beyond.

Once inside the tunnel, the Archmage removed his mantle and stamped the mud and water from his boots. The air within the hedge was always distinctive—the earthy smell of foliage and an eddying of warm and cool currents akin to where a river meets the sea. Peering far ahead, Max glimpsed bright sunlight at the tunnel's end. There was not always much difference between the weather in the Old College and the Sanctuary, but today it was pronounced. Max was happy to leave the oppressive damp behind.

"So what is it that you need to tell me?" asked Max.

"When we're through," said Bram, gesturing ahead.

The path was no longer paved and their footsteps made little noise. As they walked, Max became increasingly aware of how intensely alive the surrounding forest really was. The overhanging branches and surrounding trees was a symphony of chirrups and squawks and the patter of little feet scurrying through the underbrush. As they walked, he listened to these sounds and thought of Ms. Richter and the many difficult choices before her.

"How is Mina doing?" he wondered, just as they emerged into the clearing. "I didn't know you were giving her lessons yourself. Is she really so special?"

"She is," Bram replied, shielding his eyes from the sunlight. "I had foreseen three children of the Old Magic, but I hardly suspected that you would coexist. And yet here you are."

"And it's a wonder we're here and not with the witches," Max remarked sharply. He recalled all too well the bargain Elias Bram had once struck to acquire the Book of Thoth. In return for the artifact, the Archmage had promised the witches three children of the Old Magic. Centuries later, when the witches had learned of Max and David, they had tried to collect a portion of their rightful prize. Rowan denied their claim and ultimately triggered the very curse that helped enable Astaroth's victory. In the aftermath, Rowan and the witches had reached an unsteady truce, but great hostility and mistrust remained.

"That was a hard bargain," Bram reflected solemnly. "But I'd strike it again."

"Even now?" asked Max. "Even knowing that your own grandson is one of the three?"

"Yes," he replied firmly. "Better that my family, my blood, should bear these burdens."

"And why is that?" snapped Max.

The Archmage stopped and turned to stare Max squarely in the eye. His voice was deadly quiet. "Because we can."

"David's already sacrificed plenty."

"He has more to give," remarked Bram stoically. "And so do I. And so do *you*, Max McDaniels. That is why I wished to speak with you about the Atropos."

Placing a hand on Max's shoulder, Bram guided him through the large settlement that had sprouted up just inside the Sanctuary. Even since Max had last seen it, the township had grown considerably. Hundreds of buildings now rose in shingled clusters around cobblestone lanes crowded with wagons and carts and a host of people and creatures. At last count, some four thousand residents now lived in the township proper, a sizable number but still a manageable sum and significantly less than the towns and villages that were forming throughout the wider realm. While the settlements outside the Sanctuary and the Old College were predominately human, Rowan Township boasted a more diverse population that included snobbish fauns, willowy dryads, mischievous lutins, and solemn dvergar with braided beards. Though a distinct minority, these creatures and others could be spied amid the crush of humans, carts, and livestock that milled about the streets and storefronts.

As in Bacon Library, the sight of Max McDaniels and Elias Bram walking together elicited a great many stares. As they strolled across the cobblestones and central plaza, they encountered hesitant smiles, some doffed caps, and even a toothless crone who fell to her knees and begged for a blessing from the Archmage. But there were wary looks, too, and mutterings in their wake as the pair passed by. Few had ever seen Elias Bram and never with Max McDaniels. To find the pair together and in close counsel could only bode ill.

Bram's counsel did not begin until they'd left the township behind, their fingertips nearly brushing the tall grasses and wildflowers that carpeted a broad plain fringed by forested mountains and dotted by pillars of dark rock. When they were approaching the Warming Lodge, the Archmage stopped.

"The Matching must be over," he observed, nodding toward the building and its shimmering lagoon. "Let's hope each creature found a steward and each child a charge. YaYa was hopeful."

Max reflected wistfully back to the day when a wonderfully rare and mischievous lymrill had chosen him to be his keeper. It seemed ages ago. Nick was gone now, having surrendered his life, claws, and quills to strengthen the Morrígan's blade. Max had yet to fill the void in his heart. YaYa herself had suggested that he take another charge, but Max had refused any matching. There was only one Nick and Max had lost him. He would not lose another.

"Has Mina been matched?" he inquired.

"No charge has chosen her," replied Bram. "But when the match is right, one will. So many things are moving that it is hard to keep track of little Mina as closely as we should. I had thought to ask you to look after her, but this business with the Atropos has ruined those plans. I must find the girl a new guardian."

"I can look after Mina," Max protested. "I've been doing it since I met her."

"No," said Bram. "It is better that the Enemy know nothing about her until she's older. You would only bring scrutiny. David and I will keep her under close watch, to see to her lessons and her safety. At the present moment, it is *your* safety that concerns me. I wished to speak with you privately because the others left out an important detail regarding the Atropos. Perhaps this was mere coincidence, but I cannot take the chance."

"And what was the detail?" asked Max.

"Those targeted by the Atropos were rarely slain by strangers," observed Bram sadly. "The guild was talented at infiltration, and their members could be found in the most secret and select societies. They were very successful at using others to do their work through threats, trickery, and even spiritual possession. There were skilled summoners and spiritwracks among their ranks. Many of their victims were slain by a trusted friend whose mind and body were not their own."

"So what are you saying?" asked Max. "That I can't trust Ms. Richter or Miss Boon?"

"No," said Bram, staring hard at him. "I'm saying that you cannot trust *anyone*. Trust is a luxury you can no longer afford, Max McDaniels. When they come for you, they will not come as a stranger in the shadows. The Atropos will be someone you know."

~ 3 ~
CROFTER'S HILL

Twilight was falling, the pink sky deepening to periwinkle. One by one, the stars emerged to form their marvelous patterns and shine their soft light on the path. Max's boots scuffed upon the gravel as he strode alone, scanning the hills.

He spied his destination up ahead, a large house atop a distant rise. Its windows were bright yellow squares set against the manor's black silhouette. Even from this distance, Max heard laughter and a fiddle's notes dancing on the breeze. Ten minutes of brisk walking would see him there. Reaching deep into his pocket, he retrieved an apple and flung it far ahead. Breaking into a run, he chased after to see if he could catch it before it fell. He ran faster and faster, but the apple's trajectory continued to rise. It grew ever smaller until Max feared it would never return to earth but simply drift away like a tiny red balloon. He laughed with disbelief as the object finally reached its impossible zenith and began a slow, arcing descent.

But as he raced to catch it, Max discovered that he was not alone. There were other footsteps on the road. Glancing over his shoulder, he glimpsed a dark figure racing after him. Moonlight flashed on a face as the figure emerged from a shadow. It was Cooper, the man's pale and ruined face set in grim determination as he flew down the path and closed the gap between them.

Others soon joined in, converging from the surrounding hedges to form a sprinting pack that chased after Max. Among the bobbing blur of faces, Max spied Nolan frothing like a rabid animal. Others soon became clear—Miss Boon, Ms. Richter, and even Mr. Morrow, who tore after him with a look of frenzied, wild-eyed hate. With every panicked swivel of his head, Max spied an old friend among the pack—Cynthia Gilley, Monsieur Renard, even Nigel Bristow. The most disturbing was Julie Teller. Max's former girlfriend wept as she ran, scratching her pretty face to bloody ribbons.

His pursuers were gaining. No matter how fast Max ran, the pack closed in on him. Panting, predatory grins leered at him in the moonlight as their bare feet churned up gravel and mud. Cooper was almost upon him. Reaching forward, the man slashed a kris at Max's neck. As the blade grazed the skin, Max tensed and bolted ahead, his attention riveted on the falling apple. If he could just catch it, everything would be okay. His pursuers couldn't touch him then. They would have to leave him be.

The apple was just ahead, plunging like a tiny meteor.

Max leaped to catch it, stretching forth his hand and feeling it strike his palm. His fingers snapped shut like a trap as he spilled onto the road, rolling and tumbling along the wet gravel. For several seconds, he simply lay panting with his eyes shut tight. But no pack fell upon him; no knives or teeth or fingers tore at his flesh or pried the apple loose from his grasp.

Max opened his eyes. His tumble had left him facing the direction from which he'd come. The road was empty. There were no pursuers, only the peaceful sounds and sights of nightfall. *Where had they gone? What had driven them off?*

Climbing wearily to his feet, Max opened his hand to gaze at the apple. For several heartbeats, he merely gaped. This was not the apple he'd thrown; this apple was much heavier and made entirely of gold. Within its smooth, mirrorlike surface, Max could even make out his reflection. But as he stared at his distorted, panting image, Max noticed another, darker shape behind him.

It was a wolfhound.

Of course it was. The wolfhound was *always* here, always waiting for Max on this twilight road. It would never let him inside the house. Within the apple, Max saw its dark jaws hanging open over his shoulder. A rumble sounded in its throat before a blast of hot breath fogged the apple's surface. The reflections disappeared.

Slowly, Max turned and looked up into the animal's monstrous face. It loomed above him, more massive than Astaroth's direwolves and even YaYa. The moonlight gleamed in its huge, wet eyes as it appraised Max like some ancient and terrible god. Pressing its shaggy forehead against his, the wolfhound forced him backward along the road and spoke in its gruff, rasping voice.

"What are you about?" it demanded. *"Answer quick or I'll gobble you up!"*

Dropping the apple, Max drew the *gae bolga* from its scabbard and plunged the blade into the animal's chest. The wolfhound gave a shuddering howl, a long-echoing scream that threatened to shatter the very world. . . .

"WAKE UP!"

Opening his eyes, Max saw David Menlo standing over his bed and shaking him with as much strength as the small boy could muster. His face was pale and panicked as he shook Max again.

"I'm awake," Max gasped, sucking air like a drowning man. "I'm okay . . . I'm awake."

David backed away, giving his roommate space to recover. Max's heart was pounding unbearably fast, each beat a painful, percussive jolt as sweat coursed down his body. Kicking his soaking covers aside, Max simply lay still for a moment and tried to gather his wits.

"I've never heard a scream like that," David whispered. "That must have been some nightmare."

"It was the wolfhound," Max panted. "It's always that damned wolfhound. What time is it?"

"Almost eight," David replied. "But you don't have classes. You can go back to sleep."

"No," said Max hurriedly. "No, I should get up. I have things to do."

"No, you don't," said David mildly. "You've just returned from a long journey and earned a few days of rest. There will be plenty for you to do, Max, but not today. Let me buy you breakfast."

"You don't have to buy me breakfast. Let's just go to the dining hall. I want to see Bob."

"Alas," said David, tossing Max a towel from a nearby hook, "the dining hall is for students and we no longer qualify. Besides, you won't find Bob down there. He doesn't work in the kitchens anymore."

"What do you mean?" asked Max, propping up on his elbows. "Bob *lives* off the kitchens."

"Not anymore," said David sadly. "He retired from cooking and built a cottage on Crofter's Hill. He spends most of his time up there now. I visited once, but he didn't seem to like it. I haven't bothered him since."

Max was dumbstruck. His mind flashed back to the refugee Tam and the questions she'd posed to him: *What's the name of the sad old brute who lives on Crofter's Hill?* The girl had been talking about Bob! It didn't make any sense; the ogre had been Rowan's head chef for generations and loved his job. Something was very wrong.

Swinging his legs out of bed, Max wiped away the sweat with the towel. "Thanks for waking me," he said, padding down to the lower level of their room to wash his face. Filling a basin, he closed his eyes and sank his face into the cold water. Slowly, the drumming in his temples subsided and the muscles in his neck uncoiled. Breathing deep, he gazed up at the room's domed ceiling.

The stars beyond the glass were comfortably present. As Max watched, the constellation Orion was outlined in gossamer threads of tiny golden lights. Gradually, the outline dissipated. A moment later, the threads reappeared to illuminate the Little Dipper. It was such a soothing room, always quiet and contemplative. Beds on the upstairs level, a comfortable study below, and the clearest, most spectacular view of the heavens one could wish for.

"So . . . breakfast?" inquired David from the top of the stairs. "I'm partial to the Hanged Man, but there are some new places we could try near the east end. Lucia seems to like the Pot and Kettle. It's your choice, of course, but the Hanged Man does have excellent coffee. . . ."

* * *

In truth, Max had no choice in the matter. As the pair wandered the cobbled streets of Rowan Township, they passed any number of suitable establishments, but David found fault with each. The Pot and Kettle was too crowded, the Trestle too sterile, the Black Dragon too snooty. When David recounted a recent case of food poisoning at the Cheery Turnip, Max finally gave up and suggested the Hanged Man.

"If you insist," said David happily. "I'm sure they'll be able to squeeze us in."

The cafe stood alone, some thirty yards beyond even the humblest shops on the township's northwest edge. As they approached, Max saw that the place was little more than a ramshackle bungalow of salvaged pine boards built around a withered ash tree. By way of a sign, a crude scarecrow dangled from a branch, its rickety legs blackened from smoke that billowed from a stovepipe chimney. Within an adjoining pen, a spotted sow sprawled listlessly on her side while a dozen chickens squawked and squabbled over scattered kernels.

"This is great," Max deadpanned. "Much better than all those other places."

"Oh, I know it doesn't look like much," said David, "but it's got character! You can keep your Black Dragon with its polished brass and working bathrooms—I'll choose the Hanged Man every time. Marta takes good care of me, and I daresay I'm her best customer. . . ."

Following his friend inside, Max concluded that David was not merely the Hanged Man's best customer but its sole source of revenue. The cafe was empty, most of its chairs standing atop a half-dozen small tables arranged around the tree trunk. Coughing into his sleeve, Max peered through the oily haze and spied an enormous figure half sprawled and asleep at the farthest table. Reaching past Max, David rang a little triangle hanging from a hook.

"There he is, there he is," the figure murmured, still unmoving.

"Take your time, Marta," said David. "I've brought a friend today."

"Have you?" replied the woman, her massive head rotating up from the crook of her forearm to blink at Max. "He's pretty," she muttered. "Tall. Lashes like a doe."

"Um . . . thanks?" said Max as Marta rose heavily to her feet.

"Ain't nothing," she replied, tucking a wad of tobacco under a rubbery lip and tying back her mop of stringy red hair. "If I'd known David was bringing a lordling, I'd have washed up."

"You look fine," Max assured her.

"Ax," she grunted, spitting a brown gob into a tin cup.

"Excuse me?" said Max, thoroughly confused.

The woman hooked her thumb at an appalling scar that stretched from her temple across what remained of her nose.

"Oh," said Max, now wishing he were somewhere, *anywhere* else. "I'd hate to see the other guy," he added with a weak laugh.

"That some kinda joke?"

"No, ma'am."

"Ain't no other guy," she muttered, hefting up a sack of coffee beans. "Slipped while slaughtering a hog. The usual, David?"

"If you would," David replied, arranging a pair of chairs around a nearby table.

"What about you?" rumbled Marta, pouring the beans into a long-handled roasting basket. "We got eggs, bacon, ham, chops, chicken, toast, and a bit o' cream," she added, nodding toward a stone jug. "Apples too."

"Eggs and coffee sound great," said Max. "Bacon, too, if it's no trouble."

"No trouble," Marta grunted, seizing up a dented ax and lumbering toward the sow's pen.

"Let's skip the bacon," uttered Max quickly.

Marta merely shrugged. While she set to preparing their meal, Max and David sat and talked, as they hadn't in many months. Throughout breakfast, a great weight seemed to lift slowly from Max's shoulders. There were no other customers, no one to stare at the famous pair and debate whether they were Rowan's blessing or curse. Marta didn't even seem to know who he was.

As they ate, Max shared stories from Zenuvia. He described its teeming bazaars and spice markets, the crystalline spires of maridian sealords, and the strange townships found throughout its archipelagos. When he shared an anecdote about a fox-faced kitsune in a Khoreshi opium den, David raised an eyebrow.

"What were you doing in a place like that?"

"Smuggler owned it," Max replied, attacking his eggs. "The kitsune hung around the shop. She tried to teach me a song on her belyaël. Turns out you really need six fingers to play that thing."

"Guess I'll stick to whistling," quipped David, glancing at the stump where his right hand used to be.

The pair dissolved into laughter. Marta glanced up from kneading a mound of dough. "You two are worse'n a sewing circle," she griped. "Giggle, giggle, snort, snort. Liked it better when David sat quiet with his coffee 'n' toast."

"I'm sorry, Marta," said David, wiping a tear from his eye. "We're not laughing at you. We just haven't had a chance to catch up in a long time."

"Not since I left for Zenuvia," Max observed, tearing a hunk off the warm black bread.

"No," said David thoughtfully. "Longer than that. In truth,

it's been years, Max. I couldn't really afford to have friends while I was trying to rescue my family. I accepted it as part of the job, but until now I don't think I really realized just how lonely I've been."

"Well," said Max, "thanks to you, your family's back together. No need to be lonely anymore."

"True," said David. "But my family's . . . unusual. I love them, of course, but what I've really missed is my friend."

"Me too," replied Max. "I don't even know when the last time was that I had a good laugh. Works wonders. Wish we had Connor back—he was always good for a laugh or three."

David nodded sympathetically. Their friend Connor Lynch had left Rowan and was living in Blys, having swapped a soul in exchange for a barony and the chance to fulfill a vendetta. Ever impulsive and mischievous, Connor had been the quickest wit in their class before he sailed off on Prusias's galleon. Max missed him dearly. "Anyway," he sighed. "I'm not complaining. It's nice to sit still for five minutes and not have to look over my shoulder."

"Enjoy it while it lasts," said David, declining the bread's heel. "After you and my grandfather left, Ms. Richter and I talked strategy for the rest of the afternoon. The Director agrees with me that the Workshop's activities are a priority. And given this development with the Atropos, she doesn't want your whereabouts known for very long. I think it's safe to say that a DarkMatter assignment is imminent. Probably this week."

Max's smile faded. He stared down at the Red Branch tattoo, hating it.

"Fair enough," he muttered. "Better sooner than later, I guess."

"Soon," said David. "But not immediately. We'll need a few days to prepare, and I have some things to do before we leave."

Max almost choked on his coffee. *"W-we?"* he sputtered, wiping his mouth. "You're coming along?"

"Yes," said David, smiling. "It's not official yet, but Ms. Richter seems in favor of it. I think she just wants to get rid of me. Expulsion wasn't enough."

"Please," said Max. "She probably wishes she had ten more David Menlos."

"Oh, I'm not sure about that," said his roommate. "In any case, at the moment there's only one David Menlo and he'll be accompanying you to Blys. Cloak-and-dagger stuff, Max. Very exciting. Assuming we survive, I'm confident the Red Branch will have no choice but to make me an honorary member."

"We might have vacancies," Max reflected grimly. "Any word on Cooper?"

"Sadly no," said David, gratefully accepting more coffee. "I ran into Miss Boon in the Archives last night, and she said there'd been no word from him. Or Ben Polk . . ."

Max sat up straight. "I should go after them. You said yourself that we have a week before our mission. I could be back in plenty of time."

David shook his head. "You are the absolute last person the Director would send. Others will go."

"She thinks the Atropos are trying to lure me out?"

"She thinks it's a distinct possibility," replied David, frowning. "And so do I. It is well known that you have no remaining family. Cooper's the Red Branch commander and your good friend. He's a natural target for anyone trying to hurt you."

Max frowned and considered the situation. "If anyone's dumb enough to kidnap William Cooper, I almost feel sorry for them," he muttered. "Talk about catching a tiger by the tail. First mistake they make, he'll escape and have their heads. And Ben Polk? He gives me nightmares and he's on *our* side."

"Exactly," said David. "Those two can look after themselves. And if Ms. Richter doesn't hear from them very soon, rest assured that she'll launch the biggest search-and-rescue operation since those Potentials went missing."

"But can't you find them?" Max wondered aloud. David could utilize their observatory like an enormous crystal ball and often referred to it as his little window on the world. But the sorcerer merely shrugged.

"I've tried," he said. "Scrying has become impossible. Either I'm losing my touch or they're being held in some place with special protections."

"But then that means they're in danger," exclaimed Max. "Even more reason for me—"

"To do your job and let others do theirs," interjected David. "Cooper would want you focused on the Workshop."

Max nodded. Deep down he knew David was right, but it did not sit well. It was Cooper who had come to his rescue many times. Without him, Max would still be festering and going mad in Prusias's dungeons. And now when the man might be hurt or need his help, Max was being told to look away and concentrate on the bigger picture. *But what's more important than a friend in need?*

"I know what you're thinking," said David quietly. "I can see it in your face. Your instinct is to race off and help your friends. But if the Atropos are involved, that's just what they want you to do."

Breathing deep, Max drummed his fingers and looked about. Marta had shaped the dough into a dozen loaves that had been baking in the brick oven. Given the empty cafe, it seemed a trifle optimistic. Still, they did look good, as Marta removed them and set them on racks to cool. Max fished in his pockets.

"How much for one of those?"

"Ten," grunted the woman, staring into the oven.

"Coppers or silver?" asked Max, sorting the coins in his palm.

"Where'd you find this one, David?" Marta cackled. "It's ten *coppers*, Your Highness."

Gulping down his coffee, Max plunked the coins onto the table. "If you let me borrow that basket, I'll take all of them."

Marta hurried over to sweep up the coins, laughing as she held up a silver lune. "You can keep the bloody basket."

David leaned back, bemused. "Where are you going with a dozen loaves of bread?"

"Crofter's Hill. And you're going, too."

It was a forty-minute walk to Crofter's Hill—a tall, sparsely covered knoll that rose above the Sanctuary plains. It was a peculiar place to build a house, for the hill was unusually steep and exposed, its rocky soil apparently incapable of sustaining much more than a few fenced tomato vines and a billy goat that eyed the boys suspiciously as they reached its windswept summit.

The lone house atop Crofter's Hill was a large, heavy-timbered cottage built with wattle and daub and supporting a steep roof of gray thatch. Several steps led up to a broad porch where ceramic planters flanked a twelve-foot door made of knotted pine planks. Only two windows were visible. They were set on either side of the door and hidden by rough wooden shutters that banged and creaked with every whistling gust.

Max knocked hard on the door and waited for an answer. When none came, he knocked again while David shivered and gazed far down at the Warming Lodge, where reflected clouds drifted across the surface of its placid lagoon. When Max knocked a third time, David wrapped his cloak tighter.

"Maybe he isn't home." He shivered.

Max pointed toward a pair of muddy boots sitting by a planter and knocked again.

"*Leave it!*" boomed a deep voice with a Russian accent. "Your money is by the rosemary."

Puzzled, Max turned and spied a worn envelope tucked beneath a nearby planter where the herb was growing, tall and fragrant. Pressing his ear against the door, Max knocked louder.

"Bob, open the door. It's Max and David."

Silence, and then at last a heavy shuffling. Bolts slid back and the door cracked open. From the dark interior, Bob stared down at them, an elderly ogre whose ten-foot frame had grown thin, almost spare. He had not shaved in days. Bristly white stubble covered a sunken, toothless jaw whose lips were drawn in a hard line.

"Max," he croaked, peering closer and fumbling for the monocle dangling from a chain behind his ear. His nostrils quivered, as if taking in their scent. "Is that really you? And David, too. I thought you were the deliveryman."

"Can we come in?" asked Max.

"Why?"

The question simply hung in the air. There was no suspicion or malice in the ogre's tone, but Max almost wished there was. Their absence was heartbreaking, as though Bob could not conceive why anyone would want to visit.

"Because . . . we want to see you," replied Max hesitantly. "We brought you some bread."

The ogre glanced down at the basket. "You boys should save your money. I have enough to eat."

"Okay," said Max. "But can we still come in?"

"Very well," Bob sighed, opening the door wider to admit them.

The cottage was dark and musty inside, lit only by a pair

of oil lamps. In the corner was an enormous bed heaped with blankets and furs, but there was little other furniture and only a small kitchen where coals glowed through the grate of a cast-iron stove. Setting the basket on a counter, Max peered around until he spied a pair of crates that would serve as chairs for him and David. He dragged them near the enormous kitchen stool that Bob had brought with him from the Manse.

"Can I open the shutters?" asked David.

"If you like," the ogre murmured, shambling to the kitchen sink where dirty plates and bowls were heaped three feet high. Max's heart sank as he watched Bob fumble about in search for clean mugs or cups.

"We just ate," said Max. "Down at the Hanged Man. That's where we got the bread."

"I see," Bob muttered. Pulling up his suspenders, he eased onto his stool and rested his elbows upon his knees. A tremor began in one of his gnarled hands. He glowered at it a moment, before covering it with the other and setting them on his lap.

"So," said Max, breaking the silence. "I just returned from Zenuvia."

"Welcome home," said Bob as David opened the shutters. Sun streamed into the cottage, dusty bands of daylight that made the ogre blink. "How was your trip?"

Bob listened dutifully as Max shared tales from the distant kingdom. Max focused on the fantastic things and strange foods he'd eaten rather than the grim news of Prusias's ultimatum, the Atropos, or the looming threat of war. The ogre did not seem to be in any condition to hear of such things. When Max had finished, Bob simply sat passively by and waited for more.

"It's good to be back," Max concluded. "But I was surprised to hear that you retired and moved up here. I thought you liked working in the kitchens. . . ." He hoped this would cue a response, but none was forthcoming. The ogre merely turned his attention to David.

"And what of you?"

"Oh," said David, sitting up. "Well, I've been busy tutoring Mina. Have you met her yet?"

Bob shook his craggy head.

"We'll have to bring her by for a visit," said David. "She's very talented. And I've been assisting the Director. Looking after my mother. Those kinds of things, I guess."

"That is good," said Bob distractedly.

An uncomfortable silence ensued. David craned his head about to study the cottage, but Max stared at Bob. The ogre wilted and finally rocked up from the stool to putter about the kitchen.

"You boys will want something sweet," he mumbled, rummaging through various tins.

"We don't want anything sweet," said Max. "We want to know how you're doing. We want to know what's new with you."

This last sentence seemed to irritate the ogre. Veering away from the kitchen, he paced like a caged animal and fought to control the tremor in his hand. Glancing down at his stained shirttail, he stuffed it into his gray trousers and stalked to one of the windows.

"Bob is tired," he rumbled. "You should go now."

"No," said Max firmly. "Not until you talk to us."

"BOB IS FINE!" the ogre roared, wrenching the door open. *"He has no sweets. He has no news to share. He has nothing to say!"*

The windows were still humming when David finally spoke. "We should leave," he said quietly. "I have a lesson with Mina this afternoon."

"You go ahead," said Max. "I'll see you later."

Walking to the door, David looked up at Bob, who towered above him, breathing heavily.

"I really do think you'd like to meet Mina," he said.

Bob's shame over his outburst was painfully apparent. Closing his eyes, he shook his head in self-reproach and collected himself. "Bring her by," he sighed. "Just give Bob notice. It is hard to meet new people without . . . without being ready."

The door closed and the ogre turned to face Max. "What is it you want?" he asked softly.

"I want you to talk to me," said Max plainly. "What's wrong?"

Shuffling back to his stool, the ogre sat and stared at his trembling hand. "You don't know what it is to be old, *malyenki*," he rumbled. "Bob does not see so well. His hand won't stay still. Every day things get harder. People visit. Nice people. You. Ms. Richter. Others. Everyone wants to know how Bob is doing. He does not want to disappoint them, but he has nothing to say. Bob has no news to share. He does not want to be a burden."

"You're not a burden," insisted Max. "You've been looking after people for so long. It's okay to let others look after you."

"Bob doesn't like visits," the ogre sighed. "He always feels worse after."

"I don't think retiring was such a good idea. Why did you leave the kitchens?"

"Bob said it was his hand," he explained. "But that was little fib. In truth, it was Mum. Bob worked with her for a long time. When more potatoes or roasts were needed, he would call out for his little Mum or peek in her cupboard. But she was gone. It was no good. The other cooks became frightened. They thought your Bob was getting . . . confused."

"Have you tried to write her?" Max asked.

The ogre shook his head. "If Bob had not made her confess, she would still be at Rowan. It is Bob's fault that his Mum went away."

"You can't really believe that," replied Max. "Mum's confession is what saved her at the trial. It was Bellagrog who made her leave Rowan. Not you."

Bob could only shrug. Max's mind raced for solutions.

"Hey!" he exclaimed. "If you don't want to be in the Manse's kitchens, why don't you open a restaurant in the township? You could still cook, but in a different setting. I bet you'd be a hit!"

"Twenty years ago perhaps," mused the ogre, rubbing his stubble. "But not now."

"I see," said Max, rising to pace about the melancholy room and gaze up at the roof's timbers. "So this isn't really a house. It's a coffin—a nice roomy coffin where you can sit in the dark and wait to die. Is that the plan?"

The ogre glowered at Max. A nearly subsonic rumbling emanated from deep in his chest.

"Don't tell Bob his business."

Max walked out the front door and seized up an enormous spade that was propped against the porch railing. Sinking it into the hilltop, he scooped up a shovelful of dirt and squeezed past Bob, who had followed and now stood by the door.

"What are you doing?" the ogre asked.

Max ignored him. Swinging the spade, he let the dirt fly. It landed with a cloud of dust on the hardwood, scattering dirt and pebbles. Turning, Max marched past Bob and went outside to fill the spade again. The ogre watched silently as Max heaped more dirt upon the cottage floor. But on the fourth trip, Bob blocked his way.

"Stop it," he growled. The rumble resumed in his chest.

"No," said Max, swinging the spade back. "You were good enough to bury my parents. I'm returning the favor. Shut up and get out of the way. Dead ogres don't talk."

When Bob wouldn't move, Max emptied the shovel anyway. The dirt thudded against the ogre's broad chest, spilling down his shirtfront.

Bob's face contorted. Snatching the spade, the ogre abruptly snapped it in two and seized Max by the collar. In a blink, Max's feet were dangling five feet above the porch. Tears brimmed in the ogre's bright blue eyes; his nostrils flared like those of an angry bull. Max put up no resistance but merely patted his friend's trembling hand.

"For a dead ogre, you're pretty lively."

Bob blinked. Exhaling slowly, he lowered Max down to the porch and released him.

"You're not dead, Bob, and you're not dying," said Max gently. "Dark days are coming and Rowan needs you. It needs your wisdom and strength. Don't push everyone away."

Placing his great hand on Max's shoulder, the ogre bowed his head as though in silent prayer. From far off, Old Tom's chimes sounded. The notes were barely audible above the wind, but when they'd finished, the ogre opened his eyes. His hand stopped trembling.

"Bob will not let you down."

~ 4 ~

DREGS AND DRIFTWOOD

Three days later, the cottage on Crofter's Hill was filled to capacity. Its doors were propped open, a cool breeze skimming across as dozens of children sat silent as church mice, their attention fixed upon the ogre's pale eyes and knuckled skull. Hunched upon his stool, Bob recited a poem in a voice that rumbled like old millstones:

> *"We know not the Maker*
> *But we know his works*
> *We smell the badger in his burrow and see*
>   *old troll on his mountain*

We fear the giants on their isles, wild as the storm
We envy men and their warm fires
We scorn the goblins and their low houses
Warm blood our wine; winter's heart our home
Where stones crack and rivers freeze and woods grow quiet
You will find the ogre
And when all is dust and the lands bled dry
You will find him still"

When his slow verse was finished, the ogre blinked as though waking from a dream. Tapping his chin, he frowned. "There is more, I think, but Bob remembers not."

"Tell us another, then," pleaded Claudia, a thickset twelve-year-old with shiny black braids. Among the orphans Max had met in Blys, Claudia was the natural leader—a bold and gregarious child who was always inventing new games and activities. Following his previous visit to Bob, Max had sought her out and asked if she might like to meet a real ogre. The girl had nearly fainted with excitement. Within the hour, she had recruited an entire troop of fellow refugees eager to make the trek up Crofter's Hill.

Bob smiled as Claudia clambered onto his knee across from a toddler who was busy drooling on the ogre's flannel shirt. "You can tell us a story about Max!" she proclaimed.

"It is almost suppertime," the ogre observed, his eyes tracing the hazy sunlight that streamed through the windows. "And Bob knows not the verse for him."

"But Max should have a song," she insisted. "We can sing about the time he fought Skeedle's troll on Broadbrim Mountain."

"Or when he saved Mina from the monster," suggested a skinny youth named Paolo.

"How about when he rode off with a demon in a fiery carriage?" chimed a cheerful lump nicknamed Porcellino. "We could write a verse about that!"

"Bob believes you could," replied the ogre solemnly. "But it is unwise to sing songs of the living. The Fates might think their tale is finished. And our Max's tale is not finished yet, is it, *malyenki*?"

"Not yet." Max smiled, giving Mina's hand a squeeze. Scooting her off his lap, Max stood and stretched. "In fact, I'm running late to train with Sarah. Would you mind walking them back to Wainwright Lane? It's by the dunes."

Bob nodded and turned to Isabella, a dark-haired woman knitting by the hearth.

"Would you like to stay for supper?" he inquired. "Bob can cook and after he can see you and the little ones safe to your doors. He would not mind."

At this, the children erupted in such howls of delight that Isabella had no choice but to accept. Bidding Max farewell, Bob turned his attention to the matter of supper, lumbering about the kitchen and issuing slow, patient orders to his many eager helpers. Within minutes, they were boiling water, emptying the pantry, mixing dough, and picking tomatoes off the vine. When Porcellino dropped a sack of flour, Max skirted the mess to slip outside. Mina followed.

"Don't you want to stay and cook?" he asked. Shaking her head, she stopped to pet the billy goat, which bleated amiably and lay down on the grass.

"I have lessons with David."

"Ah. Are you enjoying them?"

"Oh yes," she replied, leaving the goat to go trotting down the hill, jumping from rock to rock. Max trotted after. "David's a very good teacher," she chattered. "So patient and wicked. I should not care to cross words with him."

"Cross swords," Max clarified.

"Words," she laughed. "I should not cross *words* with patient, wicked David. He's as patient and even wickeder than Uncle 'Lias."

"Speaking of words," Max reflected. "I don't believe *wickeder* is one of them."

"It is within the circles," she remarked, "and if it's not, it should be."

"What circles?" asked Max.

"You know the ones I mean," she said knowingly. The girl chased after a butterfly at the base of the hill. It flew to Mina's finger as though obeying a silent command. She stared at its golden brilliance, her eyes shining like opals.

"Mina, are you talking about *summoning* circles?" asked Max, his smile fading as he came up beside her. Astaroth had forbidden summoning spirits and demons. Even if one was willing to risk such a transgression, it was a profoundly hazardous exercise—one that had cost David Menlo his hand. David had been thirteen when he attempted such dangerous activities; Mina was but seven. Ignoring Max's question, she merely blew the butterfly a kiss and watched it flutter away.

"Mina," pressed Max. "What have they been teaching you?"

"Rules." Mina shrugged, squatting to investigate a chipmunk hole. "How some spirits fear iron and running streams and others special words. They have to answer David when he calls, but they *want* to see me."

Max's mouth went dry.

"Who does?" he croaked. "Who wants to see you?"

"Outsiders," she replied, peering down the hole. "Scary ones with fiery crowns and faceless ones made of blue smoke and faerie queens so pretty you could stare at them for days! There are others, too—others who call out from places only I can see. Not even Uncle 'Lias can see them."

"So he's there, too," Max remarked. "The Archmage is showing you these things?"

But Mina didn't appear to have heard him.

"You have to look deep in the circle's center," she continued dreamily, taking his fingers once again. "And you can't look too hard or you won't see it. I try to picture the skinniest space between the chalk and the floor and then—oh, Max! There are so many places! Some are like a forest of shimmering towers so tall they make Old Tom look like a toadstool. Others are smaller than my thumb and close like a flower as soon as I look at them. But they're not flowers—they're little worlds made of water and mist and light. When I look deep down in the circle, everything's bending and moving and overlapping. It's like seeing all the places at once through a curvy glass that won't stay still. It makes my head ache, but they're so very pretty and thin and far, far away. And everyone in them wants to see me, Max. They all hurry out to see little Mina!"

Max pressed Mina on exactly *who* wanted to see her, but her only response was to laugh and repeat the statement with a shy but unmistakable pride. Throughout their conversation, Max kept his voice and manner calm, but inwardly he was reeling. It was unconscionable to involve a child—even one so obviously gifted—in such risky endeavors. He needed to speak with David.

"What if I asked you to stop taking these lessons?" he said quietly. "What if you went back to living with Isabella and Claudia and the rest?"

Mina's smile vanished. Letting go of his hand, she stopped to stare up at him. "We must be what we will be." There was a Rowan seal embroidered on Max's shirt, and Mina reached up to touch each of the sigil's symbols with her finger. "Wild Max must be Rowan's sun and wise David her magical moon, and Mina must be a bright little star that shines far above all."

Max gazed down at the standard. For years it had seemed little more than a charming bit of heraldry. But did the celestial symbols above the Rowan tree represent something else? Did the sun, moon, and star stand for three children of the Old Magic? There were so many strange portents of late and none stranger than this little girl he'd rescued in Blys.

"Did the spirits tell you that?" he wondered.

"Uncle 'Lias," she replied distractedly. Her attention had now shifted across the Sanctuary lagoon, where refugees and Rowan students were popping in and out of the Warming Lodge. Mina watched them with quiet, attentive curiosity. Max knew what she was thinking.

"A charge will choose you," he assured her.

"I know," she sighed. "He is searching for me. But he cannot come to me yet—he is not strong enough. I must be patient."

"You already know what your charge will be?"

"Oh yes," Mina whispered. "I saw him in the circle. He's wilder than you, Max. Even terrible Prusias will fear him! When the gulls cry out and the waters run red, he'll rise from the sea to find me. . . ."

She grinned and clapped but would say no more. As the pair walked, Max reflected upon how much Mina had changed. The shy, nearly mute child from the farmhouse was gone, consigned to a past that might have been another existence. There was something of David in her now, an abstracted quality that made Max feel as though his questions were intruding upon a mind feverishly preoccupied with weightier matters. While David bore Max's queries with weary patience, Mina was still young enough to believe that sheer enthusiasm was sufficient to explain the wildly complex concepts that she apparently mastered with instinctive ease. She might have been speaking another language; Max simply could not conceive of more than four dimensions or send his spirit on shadow walks or perceive the pervasive, Brownian buzz of ancient incantations. When she noticed that his nods were a polite appeasement rather than a meeting of minds, she ceased her breathless discourse and talked instead about her favorite bakery.

"You sound like you're hungry." Max smiled, spying the shop in question. "Let me get you something?"

"No thank you. Uncle 'Lias will have food waiting and I mustn't be late."

"Listen," said Max. "Why don't you come to the training grounds with me? I'm meeting my friend Sarah. You'll like her."

"But the Archmage is waiting."

"I don't care who's waiting," Max retorted. "I don't want you doing such dangerous things."

Mina glanced at him. "You once saved me from a monster and chased it down its well. Was that dangerous?"

"Of course," said Max. "But I'm older. You're only seven, Mina."

"I might be seven, but I can go on shadow walks and make out the secret places. Can you?"

Max shook his head and acknowledged her point with a rueful smile. "No, I can't do those things. I don't even understand them."

The little girl hugged him, her cheeks pink from their long walk and the cold. Already streetlamps were glowing with witch-fire, bathing nearby windows and awnings with a golden light. Turning her face up to his, Mina gazed at him with fierce adoration.

"I'm going down a well, too, Max. It's just a different one

than yours. But don't worry about your little Mina. She knows the way out."

Standing on her tiptoes, she kissed his cheek and ran off down the central lane, her shoes smacking on the cobbles as she cried hello and goodbye to the baker's wife. Max watched her go, resolved to speak with David and Bram and do what little he could to protect her. *What's been seen cannot be unseen. Mina is seeing too much, too soon.*

It was nearly dark by the time Max exited the hedge tunnel. His breath frosted in the night air as his boots crunched on brittle leaves. Curfew would be in several hours and the paths were crowded with students hurrying off to libraries, their mage-chains glittering by the light of lamps and lanterns. He said hello to a few but kept to the edge of the path and never passed within close reach. In the dark, it was not easy to determine if an approaching figure carried a book or a knife. Bram's words echoed in Max's mind: *When they come for you, they will not come as a stranger in the shadows. The Atropos will be someone you know.*

He skirted the orchard and the Manse, hurrying down to the sea where the xebec lay anchored in Rowan Harbor. There'd been no word of Cooper or Ben Polk, and Max itched to speak with the hunched figure sitting near the xebec's prow, silhouetted against the green witch-fire. The witch was just a weather worker, but she might have heard or seen something of value.

Turning away, he veered north along the coast and toward the training grounds that Sarah had mentioned. As he walked, the elegance of the academic quad gave way to a wilder setting. Here the trees grew thicker and the smoke of a hundred cooking fires scented the air. Up ahead, there were shouts and laughter, punctuated now and again by the ring of steel striking steel.

Through a gap in the trees, Max glimpsed a broad clearing

that resembled both a military post and a gypsy camp. Long, low buildings and colorful tents lined the perimeter, surrounding archery ranges, sparring pits, and open-air smithies. It was chaos within; thousands of refugees huddled around bonfires and waited in long lines to hone their skills at archery or hand-to-hand combat. A small army of hogs, goats, and dogs scampered atop mounds of garbage, sifting through the waste for scraps of food. A shrill ring rose above the din. A crowd by one of the sparring pits gave a throaty cheer.

"Don't go in unless you plan to burn your clothes," warned a nearby voice.

He turned to see a boyish creature with curling brown hair and the hind legs of a deer. It was a Normandy faun, stepping gingerly through the underbrush before stopping to sniff at the base of a shaggy oak. Max recognized him at once; he was the twin brother to Connor Lynch's former charge, Kyra.

"Kellen," said Max. "What are you doing out here?"

"Truffles," replied the faun, scraping at the soil with a hand shovel. "A cruel joke that they grow so near this abominable camp with its dogs and their reek, no? If the pigs should find them"—he shuddered at the thought—"I will throw myself into the sea."

"A bit dramatic," said Max.

"Monsieur has clearly never tasted truffles."

"How is Kyra doing?" inquired Max. "Has she heard anything from Connor?"

"*Non,*" replied the faun testily, probing another patch of dirt. "And do not mention his name. Two years have passed and poor Kyra is still so ashamed. A human leaving a faun? It is not done!"

"They weren't dating," Max chuckled. "He was just her steward."

"Tell that to my sister," Kellen grumbled, prizing out a beloved truffle and sniffing at it rapturously. He waved Max away. "Go swing your silly sword and thump your chest with the flea-bitten commoners. And when you itch, don't say Kellen didn't warn you."

"Always a pleasure," said Max, stepping into the clearing.

But as he strolled through the camp in search of Sarah, Max had to admit that the faun had a point. The clearing was very large, but it was packed with people dressed in filthy leggings, shirts, and jackets. Most were unwashed and some looked ill, gazing at him with rheumy eyes from within their tents. Why Sarah had chosen such a place to train was beyond him—Rowan offered pristine facilities for its students to hone their skills.

He finally found her in the midst of an exercise area, hanging by her fingertips from a crossbar.

"You're late," she chided. "I started without you."

Without the slightest tremor, she raised her chin above the bar. Her sculpted arms were bare, the firelight gleaming on each muscle as they twitched beneath her ebony skin. At thirteen, Sarah Amankwe had only been growing into her considerable looks and athleticism. At eighteen, her beauty had blossomed in spectacular fashion. She had a dancer's carriage and her close-cropped hair only seemed to accentuate her long neck and elegant features. Max was hardly surprised by her crowd of spectators.

But Sarah took no notice of them. Exhaling slowly, she completed another repetition and then another. Each was as smooth and effortless as the last. At fifty, Max stopped counting. The crowd of spectators grew. Some grinned with disbelief at the display, but others appeared sullen and almost resentful. None looked away until she had finished.

"Your turn," she said, dropping from the bar and shaking out her arms.

"Where are Cynthia and Lucia?" Max asked.

"Studying," Sarah laughed. "We have an exam tomorrow and they want to be Mystics, not Agents like yours truly. You couldn't coax Cynthia out here for anything. Now, if you're finished stalling . . ."

Max grinned and jumped up to take hold of the bar.

"What's your best?" he asked.

"One hundred forty," she replied coolly. "One hundred and forty *perfect* ones. No cheating."

"Renard must love you," Max grunted, spacing his hands.

He stopped well short of Sarah's staggering number, doing only enough repetitions to get loose. The onlookers chuffed, some disappointed and others apparently pleased. Several catcalls rose above the clatter of training swords and laughter. Max turned his head and eyed a gang of young men and women warming their hands by a fire as they waited their turn for the sparring pits. That they were a tough-looking set was no surprise; anyone who made their way to Rowan from outside was bound to have seen more than their share of fighting. What surprised Max was the unmistakable hostility stamped on each and every face. Sarah wheeled at them.

"Watch your mouths," she snapped.

"I'd rather watch yours," quipped the leader with an insolent lift of his chin. He looked to be nineteen or twenty, a wiry youth with jagged brown hair that poked from beneath a leather cap. One eye was nearly swollen shut from a recent blow and his nose had been broken several times. In his eyes, Max saw the hard, hungry look of a scavenger.

You've killed before. And more than once.

"Cretins," Sarah muttered. She took Max's arm. "Let's go to the sparring pits. I need you to help me with my footwork."

"Don't we have to wait?" asked Max, eyeing the snaking lines.

"We get priority," she explained. "If we had to wait behind

them, we'd never get anything done. A thousand arrive every day, and most are no better than criminals. You'd think they'd be grateful for a bit of food and shelter, but all I hear are complaints about them being second-class citizens. They're already pestering Ms. Richter. As if she doesn't have enough to do."

"Why don't you just train on campus?" asked Max.

"I usually do," she replied, "but Renard's overworked and has asked Rolf and me to help with the First and Second Years. A few of my prized pupils wanted to see the camp and so we brought them here tonight. There they are—by the archery range."

Max saw Rolf Luger standing behind a score of Rowan Second Years, conspicuous among the refugees. That Monsieur Renard would choose Sarah and Rolf for such a task came as no surprise. Since they arrived at Rowan, the two had been at the top of their class and captained many of the athletic teams. At Rolf's command, the students notched their arrows and drew their bowstrings taut.

"Loose!" Rolf cried.

Twenty arrows thudded into their straw targets fifty paces away. Most were admirably centered.

"Pretty good, aren't they?" said Sarah, smiling. "Weapons training has been intensified tenfold since Gràvenmuir was destroyed. Anything but a bull's-eye is considered a miss, even for the First Years. What do you think?"

"I think they'd be better off hunting," Max observed candidly. "Or shooting on the run. I don't like this kind of training. You get too used to perfect."

Sarah appeared crestfallen. "I—I thought you'd be impressed."

"I *am* impressed," Max assured her. "It's no easy thing to consistently hit a small target. But we're not training for an archery contest. We're training for war. These kids are getting accustomed to taking their time and shooting with a steady heart rate at stationary targets. What happens when they're too scared to breathe and a vye is closing at ten yards a stride? I doubt two in twenty would hit their mark."

Sarah listened carefully to the feedback. "I want my group to be tops," she said. "You've got real experience, Max. We'll make whatever changes you suggest. What would you do in my place?"

"Stress training," Max replied, watching the group loose another perfect volley. "Have them shoot while fatigued. Use blunted arrows at multiple live targets—targets that are *attacking*. Do they know how to restring a bow in the field or fletch an arrow?"

Sarah shook her head.

"I didn't think so," Max continued. "We may not have the course anymore, Sarah, but we need to mimic real combat as best we can. If Prusias attacks, his soldiers are not going to wait at fifty paces until we're good and ready to shoot them. If Agents and instructors are spread too thin, ask some of the refugees for help."

"What are they going to teach us?" wondered Sarah. "How to spit, swear, and gripe?"

Max shrugged. "Your students have technique but no experience. The refugees have experience but no technique. Maybe you have things to teach each other. These people have survived some of the worst stuff you could ever imagine."

Sarah nodded but looked doubtfully at the lines of ragtag youths and adults crowded around the sparring pits. "Come on," she said. "I've got an exam tomorrow and told Cynthia I'd meet her in Bacon by nine. Besides, I owe you a bruise or two for critiquing my perfect little archers. . . ."

For nearly an hour, Max tested Sarah's skills in the sparring pit while Rolf and the Second Years gathered around to watch.

Sarah had chosen a *naginata,* a Japanese polearm whose steel blade had been blunted and wrapped with leather strips coated in phosphoroil. The wooden gladius Max was using was considerably shorter. With Sarah's catlike quickness and balance, it was challenging to get within ten feet of her. Whenever he darted in to attack, he found Sarah's blade waiting—poised and ready in her skilled hands.

But Max was skilled, too, and experience had taught him patience.

"Are you giving your best?" Sarah panted, laboring to ward off another attack. Despite her conditioning, she was growing fatigued. At last Max saw an opening. Feinting a lunge to the left, he spun around on his heel and rapped her sharply across the knuckles with the gladius. Hissing with pain, Sarah dropped the weapon. Snatching it out of the air, Max swept her legs out from beneath her. With a thud, Sarah fell onto her back, the gladius poised at her throat.

Breathing heavily, she glowered at him. "So you've just been playing with me."

"Not at all," said Max, helping her up. "You're just tired. Your initial attack was excellent—legitimately superb—but you expended almost all of your energy. An experienced opponent will play possum and let you wear yourself out. Focus on your breathing, Sarah. Don't think of me as an adversary; think of me as a puzzle. Find the patterns and solve the puzzle. If you haven't spent all your energy, you'll be able to capitalize when opportunities arise. Your problem isn't your skill or strength; you have both in spades. Your problem is pacing. . . ."

"Go on," said Sarah, catching a towel tossed by one of the Second Years. "You were going to say something else."

"Well, it's more than pacing," Max finally conceded. "You're afraid to actually hit me."

Sarah laughed and tossed the towel at him. "Of course I am! Who wants to ruin *that* face?"

"I'm serious," Max replied. "You have all the skill in the world, but you strike *at* your target when you should be striking *through* it. You're holding back because you're afraid you'll hurt someone. That's a habit that will get you killed. In the Kingdoms, they play for keeps."

"That's what I keep telling her," Rolf called out, sounding superior.

"Hmm," said Sarah, pivoting on her heel. "Seems like someone's forgetting that I've beaten him the last five matches. And since when have you been in the Kingdoms?"

Rolf reddened but cracked a reluctant smile as the Second Years began to needle him. But another voice broke in, rough and raw. Max turned to see the tough-looking youth from before. He and his friends had gathered around one end of the pit and were looking down at them.

"I been in the Kingdoms," he said, a grim smile on his face as he leaned on a battered broadsword. "Ain't no 'tap-tap-I-scored-a-point' nonsense there. You'd be in a vye's belly, sweets. Now get outta my pit."

He spat, the gob landing inches from Sarah's boot.

Max walked across the pit.

"Careful, Ajax," warned one of the boy's companions. "He's in the Red Branch."

"Red Branch?" the spitter scoffed. "I hear two of them's gone missing. Nothing so special about them—not even this one. Shoot, I just watched 'im fight. He's good, but rumor's always better than the real thing, isn't it? Umbra'd have his teeth for a necklace. And if he don't get outta my pit, she will."

As Ajax said this, a dark figure stepped to the edge of the pit and looked down at Max. Umbra wore leather armor sewn together from mismatched pieces she'd evidently scavenged or stolen. She clutched an infantry spear whose nicked, oiled blade gleamed razor-sharp in the firelight. Thick, wild tangles of black hair hung about her head, shadowing her features until she brushed it aside to reveal the tanned skin and chiseled features of an Inuit girl. Umbra was no older than Max. Her black eyes stared at him, hard as iron.

Max met and held her gaze before flicking his attention back to Ajax.

"No one's taking my teeth," he said quietly. "And you've got ten seconds to tell me what the problem is before I take yours."

Tension saturated the air, that almost tangible, sickly calm that often preceded a fight. Rolf hurried around the pit toward Ajax and the other refugees.

"Everyone relax," he pleaded. "This is stupid—we're all on the same side!"

"Sure we are," Ajax jeered. "That's why you're wearing new boots but I can almost see my toes. Shut your mouth before you get the beating of your life. Think your little pupils will look up to you then, Blondie?"

Rolf stopped in midstride and looked imploringly at Max and Sarah.

"I'm still waiting," said Max calmly.

Ajax glared at him. "Two years ago, a brayma took the last of my sisters," he said. "Thought it was all over, but then someone told me 'bout this place. So I cut loose and clawed my way here—eight thousand miles through two kingdoms. And what's my welcome? I get to sleep in a tent and gobble down slop while you feast like lords in your marble Manse. Shoot, I can handle that. But what I can't goddamn stomach is the idea that I gotta step aside for a bunch of bookworm sissies whenever they decide to go slumming. I'll be dead and buried 'fore I let that happen. We ain't just dregs and driftwood."

Ajax's expression was defiant. By the time he'd finished, he was breathing hard, exhaling frosty gusts that scattered on the breeze. Max smiled.

"Sarah . . . meet your new training partner."

"What?" she exclaimed. "I don't need him!"

"He is exactly what you need," Max said, climbing out of the sparring pit. Walking around the pit's perimeter, he approached the refugees. When Umbra stepped in front of Ajax, Max stopped and held up his hands.

"What you say is fair," he acknowledged. "It's not right that you're living this way and have to step aside for us whenever we please. Rowan can do better and will. Its students have a lot to learn from you, Ajax. If I can get you better food and equipment, will you and your friends help train our students?"

The boy blinked. Anger gave way to confused surprise. Ajax glanced at his comrades, who offered noncommittal shrugs.

"Sure," he grunted, turning back to Max. "I guess we could do that. Once you make good."

"I'll make good—you have my word. I'm Max McDaniels."

Ajax's dour, battle-scarred face broke out in a rogue's grin.

"Hell," he laughed, "we know who you are. Looks like you're off the hook, Umbra."

With an almost imperceptible nod, Umbra stood aside. The conflict averted, Max called over Sarah, Rolf, and the Second Years while Ajax introduced him to the rest of his motley troop. However, even as Sarah and the others came up behind him, Max sensed that something was amiss with Umbra. The girl had never relaxed her grip on her spear; her dark, inscrutable eyes remained fixed on him with unsettling intensity. She reminded

Max of a viper, coiled and lethal. He casually shifted his hand to the pommel of the *gae bolga*. Behind him, Rolf laughed.

"Everyone friends now?" he inquired, clasping Max's shoulder.

In a blur, Umbra struck.

Her spear caught Rolf squarely in the throat, its impact so sudden and savage that he barely gasped. Max knew his friend was dead even before he staggered back and collapsed into his students. The Second Years didn't even seem to realize what had happened until they saw the blood. Then they screamed.

Max had already drawn his sword. The *gae bolga* hummed greedily, its blade vibrating like a tuning fork, tasting the air for the first time since Walpurgisnacht. Umbra retreated a step, but her fierce eyes never left Max.

"He meant you harm."

She spoke these words with such calm conviction that Max held his attack. The girl was either utterly insane or . . . Backing slowly beyond the lethal reach of her spear, he glanced down at Rolf. The boy's eyes were already blank; his lips were parted on the verge of a scream that had never come. His entire throat was an open wound that gleamed wet and black in the moonlight.

But it was not this gruesome spectacle that made Max's blood run cold. It was the cruel-looking knife that Rolf clutched in his right hand. Max had seen its wavy blade many times before. The knife belonged to William Cooper.

~ 5 ~

LAQUEUS DIABOLI

Bedlam followed Rolf's death, a crush of bodies as refugees rushed forward to see what had happened. Agents arrived within minutes, forcing the crowds back and questioning Max and the rest. Sarah had been inconsolable, weeping over Rolf's body as one Agent led the Second Years away. She'd screamed at Umbra, vowing revenge, but the refugee girl didn't appear to have heard her. She simply stood by, leaning on her blood-stained spear and gazing stoically at the boy she had slain.

Word arrived swiftly from the Manse; Max was to report immediately. He knew Ms. Richter's concern. The scene at the sparring pit was too frenzied and chaotic; there might be more assassins lurking in the mob. Leaving Sarah in the care of another Agent, Max hurried away through the crowd, pushing and jostling through their ranks until he was free of them.

Miss Boon was waiting in the Manse's foyer. She was composed but had clearly been crying. Rolf's death no doubt hit her hard; he had been an uncommonly talented and industrious student. But it occurred to Max that she had another reason to grieve; the appearance of Cooper's notorious dagger was a clear sign that the man was either dead or in mortal peril.

"Are you all right?" she asked.

"I'm okay," he said. "I take it you heard about the knife?"

Miss Boon nodded before gesturing weakly at his face and clothes. Wiping his cheek, Max felt that it was sticky. Glancing down, he now realized that his shirt was spattered with Rolf's blood. "Go clean yourself up," she said heavily. "We'll be waiting for you in the Archmage's chambers. Would you like a guard?"

Max shook his head. "Rolf was my friend and he meant to kill me. Why should I trust a random guard? For all I know, you're one of the Atropos, Miss Boon."

She nodded sadly. "We'll be waiting for you. David says time is important. Be quick and be vigilant."

Heading to the dormitories, Max ducked into the bathroom. It was nearly empty. The only occupants were the dozing domovoi attendant and a First Year who nearly swallowed his toothbrush when he registered Max's gruesome appearance. Max gnored him, turning on one of the silvery faucets and scrubbing roughly at his hands and face until they were clean. Peeling off his shirt and jacket, he stuffed them into a wastebasket.

Back in his room, Max dressed quickly. He pulled on a gray doublet of quilted cotton before donning a hauberk of black steel rings. Over this he slipped the simple tunic of the Red Branch and a leather baldric to which he belted the *gae bolga*. Max's enemies might be able to infiltrate Rowan, but they would not find him unarmored or unprepared.

Ten minutes later he stood before the Archmage's door. The Director herself answered his knock.

"There are only friends here," she said, sensing his wariness.

"How do I know that?"

"David has made certain."

Looking past her, Max saw his roommate sitting by the fire in Bram's chair. Their eyes met and David gave a small, reassuring smile. Stepping past Ms. Richter, Max walked inside.

There were others within, but Max hardly noticed them. His attention was fixed on Rolf's corpse, which lay upon a long table in the middle of the common room. The boy's neck had been cleaned and bandaged and someone had had the decency to place coppers on his eyelids. But whether due to rigor mortis or careless oversight, Rolf's mouth remained open—frozen on the threshold of a scream. It was several seconds before Max realized that the body was lying within a summoning circle.

In the dark room, the hexagram glowed faintly orange, as though embers simmered beneath the floorboards. Glancing about, Max realized that all of the room's rugs and clutter had been cleared away to reveal many such circles upon the floor. Some were large with complex symbols and runes about their periphery while others were small and simple. While each was etched with a jeweler's skill upon the hardwood floor, only Rolf's was glowing.

Max looked to the room's other inhabitants. Bram was absent, but Mina was on the floor near Mrs. Menlo, who was rocking in her favorite chair and stroking Lila. Miss Boon sat on a long bench beneath three frosted windows. At her feet blinked a pair of feral yellow eyes.

"What is that?" exclaimed Max.

"Don't be frightened," said Miss Boon. "Grendel is Cooper's charge."

The rest of the creature's body seemed to materialize from thin air. At first glance, Grendel looked like an ash-gray panther. As the creature rose and approached, however, Max saw that his snout and ears were more wolflike, while his coat was dappled with a tiger's camouflaging bands. With each breath, Grendel's body faded into his surroundings so that he nearly disappeared. Only the eyes remained, fierce and predatory. Growling deep in his throat, the animal circled Max, gliding once against him before padding back to settle at Miss Boon's feet.

"So that's a Cheshirewulf," Max muttered. He'd read about them but had never seen one before. The creatures were very rare and dreaded by superstitious farmers and foresters in the north. It was said that they could smell blood from miles away and that no homestead was safe if one wandered into the vicinity. Like many magical creatures, Cheshirewulfs had been hunted to near extinction. Cooper had never mentioned Grendel before, and Max imagined that the creature probably lived deep in the Sanctuary among other wild charges whose stewards had died or no longer looked after them. "What's he doing here?"

"He showed up yesterday," replied Miss Boon, stroking the animal's scruff. "We rarely see Grendel, but when William went missing . . . It's as though he knew." Her voice broke and she checked herself.

"We're hoping Grendel can help," explained Ms. Richter. "Some doing of the Enemy has rendered scrying ineffective. If we cannot find Agents Cooper and Polk using magical means, we must use more conventional methods. The bond between charge and steward is very strong, and Cheshirewulfs are legendary trackers. Perhaps Grendel can succeed where we have failed."

Max nodded before glancing back at Rolf's body. "Has any-one told his family yet?" he asked quietly. "I think they live near Wyndle Farm."

"Nigel's already on his way," replied Ms. Richter. "We must work quickly. They will naturally want to see the body and I would not keep it from them. But we must have answers."

"What are you planning to do?" asked Max uneasily. "Some sort of autopsy?"

"That's exactly what we're going to do," David declared, ris-ing from his chair. "Not a physical autopsy but a spiritual one. I doubt Rolf was any kind of traitor; in fact, I doubt he was acting of his own will at all. The Atropos often used possession as a tool for assassinations. I think Rolf was the unfortunate vessel they chose. But we need to be certain, and we need to know if there are others in our midst."

"How are you going to do that?" Max wondered.

"*Laqueus Diaboli*," replied David, directing Mina to get up and choose a beaker from among a dozen standing upon the chessboard. "That would serve," he remarked, glancing at her selection. "But I think the iron and antimony mixture might prove better." The girl retrieved a different vial filled with metallic powder and brought it to David, but he shook his head. "I trust you to do it."

With unblinking concentration, Mina set to pouring the beaker's fine grains so that they filled up the circle about the hexagram's perimeter. Once David was satisfied with her prog-ress, he returned his attention to Max.

"*Laqueus Diaboli* is a very old trick," he explained. "A sort of reverse exorcism that most scholars have forgotten. Instead of driving an evil spirit out of Rolf's body, we're going to try and snare it back in. When a spirit possesses a human, they're like a parasite attaching their own life force to their victim's. It takes time for that connection to fade entirely, and it's likely that some remnant of that spirit's essence is still bound to Rolf's soul."

"But hasn't his soul already gone?" asked Max.

"I don't think so," David replied sadly, regarding the deceased. "A soul—particularly a young one—often stays with its body for some time. Some take hours or even days to realize that their body has died. My hope is that Rolf's soul or some part of it is still inside. If a spirit did possess him, we might be able to reel it back. That will do, Mina. . . ."

Having finished her task, the girl took Mrs. Menlo's hand and quietly led her into the guest bedroom and closed the door.

Once David heard its bolt slide into place, he continued. "Even before Astaroth's edicts, most Mystics considered summoning taboo," he said. "It's often associated with necromancy and black magic of the worst sort. I know that none of you have much experience with calling spirits, much less the sort of demon that might come tonight. I need to prepare you for some things."

At David's direction, Max took a seat next to Ms. Richter and Miss Boon. Grendel was breathing heavily, growling low with each exhale.

"It may be that nothing happens," David mused, leaning over the circle to sprinkle its interior with a fine talc. "There's always the slim possibility that Rolf Luger was working with the Atropos of his own volition. There's also the chance that his soul departed swiftly. In either case, no spirit will answer our summons. But if one does . . ." Setting down the powder, he placed white candles about the circle's perimeter. At his command, they kindled into flame—seven golden lights that shone like stars about the circle's ruddy glow. "The demon will try to conceal its presence," continued the sorcerer. "Once discovered, it will lie; it will seek to deceive us until we discover its name.

The summoner normally has this information—it's the usual way of calling upon a spirit. Since we're using another means to summon it, we'll have to extract its name. Until we do, it will seek to mislead and manipulate us. The demon cannot physically leave the circle, but you must ignore whatever it says. Its words will be designed to hurt us, to turn us against one another and play upon whatever fears it can divine. Do not listen or speak to it. Let me do the talking. The demon will give six false names before it reveals the true one. . . ."

Placing incense within an ancient-looking thurible, David began slowly walking counterclockwise around the circle. A thin yellow smoke trickled from the censer, filling the air with a sulfurous fug. The boy spoke evenly in Latin, saying each phrase forward and backward until he moved on to the next. Three times he walked around the corpse, never pausing or gazing at the body. David's attention was rigidly fixed on the circle. It was growing brighter.

When he'd finished, David seated himself by the fireplace and calmly struck a silver church bell. Its pure note reverberated in the room before fading slowly, reluctantly to silence. Max watched the circle intently, but nothing happened. The minutes ticked by. Outside, Max heard Old Tom chime ten o'clock. There were calls and laughter from the paths below and the patter of footsteps as students raced to reach the Manse before curfew. When the final chime sounded, the campus grew quiet once more.

More minutes ticked by and Max began to grow restless. His gaze wandered about the room, taking in the maps and a small Rembrandt hanging above an armillary sphere. Max knew that Bram and the Dutch artist had been close friends. Astaroth's very prison had been a Rembrandt. It seemed like ages ago that Max's own blood had enabled Astaroth to escape its confines.

He would never forget the Demon's prim smile, so ancient and knowing. Shifting his position, Max's eyes wandered along the walls and nooks, skimming the books and rugs that had been moved aside to reveal the summoning circles. His gaze paused at the mirror hanging between Bram's study and the bedroom. Max's heart skipped a beat.

Rolf's reflection shone in the mirror.

The dead boy was staring at them from its depths, his face as white as alabaster. Max bolted upright.

"What is it?" hissed Miss Boon.

"The mirror!" he gasped. "Rolf—"

Sitting forward, David gestured furiously for them to be silent. Glancing at Rolf's corpse, Max saw that it was still lying on the table, its arms neatly folded. Sitting back, Max tried to calm himself. He was sweating now; the room's silence and the mounting tension were nearly unbearable. Closing his eyes, Max counted to sixty. Opening them, he peered at the mirror. It showed nothing more than the reflections of Ms. Richter, Miss Boon, and himself sitting in a row beneath the moonlit windows.

Grendel began to growl. The Cheshirewulf bared its teeth in a jagged grimace as the animal's ears pricked forward. One by one, the candles began to gutter, as though a breeze was eddying about Rolf's body. From the corner of his eye, Max saw David point a finger at the circle.

A footprint had appeared upon the talc—a hideous, four-pronged print that might have belonged to a man-sized bird of prey. A second footprint appeared, slow and cautious, as though whatever was in the circle was creeping about its perimeter. David stood.

"We know you are here. Reveal yourself."

Nothing happened.

"*Tempus volat hora fugit*—time flies, the hour flees," David said testily, seizing the talc shaker and striding over to the circle. Throwing its remaining contents into the air, he stepped back as the cloud of particles plumed and settled around the invisible demon, revealing a glimpse of its silhouette. For an instant Max could perceive a tall and horned shape, hunched and gangling with arms that nearly reached the floor. There was a hiss as it realized what David had done. A second later it vanished.

Rolf's body gave a spasm, as though receiving an electric jolt. To Max's horror, the corpse sat up, the coppers falling from its eyes as it swung its legs off the table. Grimacing, the corpse eased onto unsteady legs and examined the circle's inscriptions. It spoke in a chilling chorus of intertwining voices, young and old, male and female.

"*Coddle, hobble, gobble the codding kiddie,*" it muttered, stooping to peer at a sigil. "*We'll gorge upon his bell, book, and candlezzzz. . . .*" Three times, the demon repeated the strange verse, ending each with a gurgling, flylike buzzing. When it appeared satisfied by the circle's merits, it turned to David.

"What dost thou want, sickly spawn of moon and womb and mandrake?"

"*Mortui vivos docent.* The dead must teach the living," remarked David with a wry smile. "But first, tell me your name."

The demon laughed, its voices jingling like change from within Rolf's bandaged throat.

"Flee to your grandsire's shadow," it tittered. "'Cower all the moanday, tearsday, wailsday, thumpsday, frightday, shatterday till the fear of the Law!'"

Walking over to his table, David struck the silver bell again. Its note rang out in the dark room, clear and true. With a moan, the corpse clapped its hands over its ears and shuffled to the circle's farthest point.

"Apparently, you know who I am," said David. "So I'm going to forgo the niceties. I will have your name and you will answer my questions or I'll have you bound within a pig of iron and cast to the bottom of the sea. Salt and iron for all eternity, demon. Most unpleasant. So tell me your name and answer my questions and perhaps we'll let you make amends."

"I am Namalya," replied the corpse, speaking in a woman's voice. "And I am punished unjustly. Even now the poor boy's family is searching for the body of their son. How they wail and cry and gnash their teeth! They shall curse your name forever, David Menlo. You desecrate the dead!"

The sorcerer was unmoved.

"My friend was desecrated when you possessed him. And you lie. Namalya is not your name." Pivoting upon his heel, David made to strike the bell. With a hiss, Rolf's corpse rushed forward, stopping only at the circle's edge. Its voice became a deafening baritone.

"I AM MOLOCH!" it bellowed. "Great Moloch, swollen with the blood of innocents!"

When the corpse's eyes went white and blank, David actually laughed.

"This is not my first summoning," he said, shaking his head wearily. "Do you think to frighten us with carnival tricks? You are small in power but great in mischief. Your actions have caused my friend's death. I will have your name and the truth or I will break you."

The corpse swiveled its head toward Max and spoke in Rolf's own voice, as though the boy's vocal cords had not been severed by Umbra's spear. "It is *you* who are to blame for my death. If you had only surrendered to the Atropos, none of this would have happened. What will you tell my mother, Max? Will you tell her that I had to die so you might live?"

In his heart, Max knew there was truth in the demon's words. He had not struck the blow that killed Rolf Luger, but he might as well have. His classmate was dead because of him. His grief must have shown, for the demon smiled and turned its attention to Miss Boon.

"We have your man," he sniggered. "He cries out for a merciful death, but we shall not give it to him. Have you ever *seen* someone on the rack? Your man is strong, but no one is that strong. . . ."

Miss Boon remained silent, but her hands were shaking, worrying at the ends of her sleeves.

"You can help him," the demon hissed. "This son of the Sidh is all that stands between you and the one you desire. All your life, you feared that you'd never experience love, Hazel Benson Boon. You thought your books would make you happy, but there you sit with a hollow heart in a scholar's robes. Do not throw away your only chance at happiness. . . ."

"David," warned Ms. Richter. "I think you must silence him."

"You have nothing to fear, Gabrielle Richter," cackled the demon, flicking his eyes to her. "I know better than to think I can move one so cold as you. After Rowan recruited you away from your nothing life in that nothing town, you never went back, did you? Naturally, you were ashamed of your father's drinking and the way decent folk scorned your mother. A pity they died in that fire before you got a chance to say goodbye. I'm sure you were the last thing on their minds, beautiful and brilliant Gabrielle who went off to a something life in a something town and never looked back. I'm sure they'd be proud. I know you must be. . . ."

"Are you going to silence this thing, or must I?" Ms. Richter snapped, glaring at David. Her voice was steel, but Max saw that her eyes were bright with tears. Reaching over, he took her hand. She gripped it fiercely and took Miss Boon's in turn. David appeared unmoved by her plea. Within the circle, Rolf's corpse had climbed back atop the table where it sat idly dangling its legs and leering at them.

"Your name," David commanded, thoughtfully examining the bell. "I won't ask nicely again."

"We shall have each of you," the demon hissed, speaking with many voices. "*Koukerros* for all and for all a good night!"

"As you will," said David, marching swiftly toward the circle.

The corpse's smile faded. "H-haven't you forgotten your little bell?"

"You had your chance." David pointed at the circle. "*Sol Invictus.*"

Unconquerable sun. It had been the motto of Solas, the ancient school of magic that Astaroth had broken long ago. As soon as David said the words, the powder that Mina had sprinkled about the circle burst into purple-blue flames. With a shriek, Rolf's corpse flipped over onto the table, screeching and scrabbling madly at the wood as though the circle's flames were coursing through every bone and nerve.

"*Graeling!*" it screamed in a little girl's voice. "I am called Graeling!"

"A lie," replied David, folding his arms.

The demon moaned and writhed, its eyes going black. When next it spoke, Max realized that Graeling's voice had been stripped from the chorus. So had the voices of Moloch and Namalya. The corpse spun around, staring at David as though every vein and capillary would burst.

"I am Legion," it panted, hugging itself and rocking while

the circle's flames blazed with sparking, phosphorescent intensity. "Legion with a thousand faces, a million faces . . ."

The sorcerer shook his head and the demon sobbed pitiably. The rest of the names came quickly. When David declared them false, the corresponding voice was stripped away. Soon, only one voice remained—the wheezing rasp of an old man.

"Ghöllah is my name. What is it you wish to know?"

The flames died away, retreating into the floor so that they shimmered like violet coals within the etched designs. Max sat forward.

"Are there other assassins at Rowan?" inquired David.

"Of course."

"Who are they?"

"I do not know." The corpse grinned maliciously at Max. "I was summoned and I served. I may have failed, but the Atropos will not. The son of the Sidh will not escape them."

"Where are William Cooper and Ben Polk?" asked David.

"I do not know." The demon shrugged. "My summoner only gave me the scarred man's knife."

Miss Boon stood. "S-so you never saw William on the rack," she stammered. "It was just a lie."

"If you like," the demon chuckled. "I've seen the rack."

"Why did they arm you with William Cooper's blade?" asked David.

"It is the kris of Mpu Gandring," replied the demon. "Its blade is accursed. My masters fear no ordinary weapon can slay the Sidh prince."

David paused at this. Several seconds passed before he spoke. "Do the Atropos know Max's geis?" he asked softly.

"No," replied the demon. "But they are searching, scrying, lying, pining for it. They care not whether they slay the Hound of Rowan or he slays himself. They care only that he dies."

"What were the terms of your service to the Atropos?" asked David.

"Nothing fancy," the demon tittered. "Ghöllah was to get close to Sidh boy and murder him. If Ghöllah succeeds, he is free. If he fails, he must report back."

"Where specifically?"

"A grotto," the demon hissed. "A grotto in the sea cliffs north of Rowan's outer walls. A day's ride. Last question, vile sorcerer, before our bargain is fulfilled."

"Certainly," said David. "Can you detect if another being is possessed?"

"Of course we know our own," the demon scoffed. "Mortal flesh is a flimsy cloak."

"Excellent," said David, walking over to a bookcase and opening a carved wooden box upon its topmost shelf. Fishing inside, he selected a silver ring. Rolf's corpse watched him, its eyes dark and mistrustful. When the sorcerer returned, the demon hissed and retreated to the table's edge.

"You shall warn my friend of peril," said David, holding up the ring. "For seven years, you shall inhabit this and warm its metal to a scald whenever you detect your own kind nearby. You shall serve faithfully and true. In seven years, your service shall end and you will be free to go. I give you Solomon's Pledge. The choice is yours, Ghöllah—you can wear silver for seven years or a pig of iron for all eternity."

"But my service to the Atropos is not complete," the demon reflected. "I must report my failure."

"You may report your failure in seven years."

The corpse shook its head as though weighing all options and liking none.

"They are a dangerous enemy, Sorcerer."

"So am I."

"Very well," the demon sighed. "I agree to your terms, curse you. Seven years, not a second longer."

David tossed the ring inside the circle. Snatching it out of the air, the corpse stared at the object upon its palm with a look of unmitigated loathing. With an awful snarl, it closed its fist about the ring and toppled over, lifeless once again. The simmering flames about the circle died away so that only the seven candles remained, merry and golden.

"An ugly business," mused David wearily. "But it is finished." Stooping, he blew out the candles and knocked gently on the bedroom door. The door unbolted and Mina slipped out alone. "There is a ring in the body's hand," said David. "Give it to our Max and tell him what it is."

If the corpse frightened Mina, the girl did not let it show. Without a hint of squeamishness, she retrieved the ring from Rolf's clenched fist and turned it over in her fingers.

"There is a demon in this ring," she declared, half turning to David. The boy nodded and gestured for her to go on. "His name is . . . Ghöllah. And he promises to warn fierce Max if there are others about. Seven years he will serve and he has vowed revenge against you."

"I'd expect nothing less," said David, smiling.

"She can tell all that from merely handling it?" wondered Miss Boon.

"Of course I can," said Mina, coming over to Max. "It cannot keep secrets from me."

Max thanked her, studying the ring as she placed it on his finger.

David turned to Ms. Richter. "Are there any others from the Red Branch still at Rowan?"

"Xiùměi and Matheus are still here," she replied. "And Peter Varga returned two days ago."

"What of the Vanguard or the Minstrels?" he inquired, referring to other elite cadres of Agents. There were several such groups at Rowan. They were not as skilled or exclusive as the Red Branch, but each had their own specialties.

"Fifteen," she said. "Perhaps twenty."

"Good," said David. "I would send them along with the Cheshirewulf to the area Ghöllah described. I don't know if they'll find Cooper and Ben Polk, but it's a starting point. Even if the Atropos have moved, Grendel should be on the scent."

The Cheshirewulf twitched and growled at the mention of his name.

"I'm going, too," said Miss Boon, rising.

"Hazel," said Ms. Richter, "best to leave this—"

"*No*, Director!" flashed the young teacher. "If they could have possessed William by now, they would have sent him for Max instead of using Rolf. William's too strong-willed to give in easily, but if they're torturing him . . ."

Ms. Richter relented. "I'll give the order," she sighed. "We'll put Xiùměi in charge. She has the most experience with this sort of thing. Take Grendel and prepare yourself for a journey. I would pack for at least a week."

"My students—"

"Will be fine," Ms. Richter assured her. "We'll see to your classes; you see to William."

The two women embraced. With a parting glance at Rolf's body, Miss Boon hurried out of Bram's chambers with Grendel at her side. When the door closed, the Director turned to the two boys. Her face was grave.

"There's something else," she said softly. "War has broken out. I had word earlier this evening. Aamon has declared war on Prusias. His armies are marching on Blys from the east. Rashaverak is attacking from the south. Given this development and the events this evening, I want you to leave for Blys at once—before Prusias can blockade our shores. Make contact with the Workshop through the one we discussed, David. The Workshop would be a valuable ally in the days ahead, and perhaps the war will give them an opportunity to break free from Prusias's grasp. Even if they refuse to join us, we need intelligence. We need to know how Prusias intends to use their technologies should the war come to Rowan. Sir Alistair has already prepared a dossier for you."

"Alistair Wesley?" Max exclaimed, remembering his old etiquette instructor. He had long regarded the departed teacher as a vain and patronizing fop. The man had accepted Prusias's offer of land and titles and abandoned Rowan two years earlier. "Isn't he an earl or something, lording it up in Blys?"

"Sir Alistair is one of our finest intelligence operatives," replied Ms. Richter firmly. "And he accepted that awful mission at my request, so please show some respect."

"How have you been in contact with him?" asked David. "I thought scrying was impossible."

"Laqueus Diaboli isn't the only old trick in use tonight," observed the Director. "We've been communicating with Alistair using Florentine spypaper the domovoi discovered in the Archives."

"Ah," said David, understanding at once. "I should like to see some."

"There is some in your dossier," said Ms. Richter. "It contains all of Alistair's recommendations regarding the Workshop, along with my comments and notes. Do not write upon the sheets unless you wish the contents to be transcribed back to those in Sir Alistair's keeping. That could be very dangerous."

"Understood," said David, taking a portfolio from the Director. He gazed about his grandfather's room, absorbing each detail as though he might not see it again. "What will you do with the body?" he asked.

"The moomenhovens will prepare Rolf for burial and we will arrange a service," Ms. Richter sighed. "Sarah and the Second Years are with Miss Awolowo. As to the refugees, we shall have to see what to do with them. . . ."

"They didn't do anything wrong," said Max quickly. "Ajax and the rest . . . they're valuable. They've seen a lot more than Rowan's students and they're tougher for it. The girl who killed Rolf . . . Umbra. Her strike was faster than anything I've seen since the Arena. We shouldn't overlook these people, Ms. Richter. There's real trouble brewing unless we break down the barriers between us."

"I'll look into it," she promised. "Now you must be off. I feel better knowing that you have that ring, but be vigilant, Max. You must be wary of everyone you meet. Both of you."

"Don't worry about us," said Max.

"We'll be back well before the solstice," said David, blushing as Ms. Richter embraced them and kissed each boy on the cheek. "Please consider the additional defenses I recommended. Tell Mina or my grandfather to help if the builders or Mystics are overtaxed."

"Your grandfather doesn't often do as he's told," said Ms. Richter, tapping her chin. "I don't suppose you know where he is or what he's doing."

"I don't ask and he doesn't tell," said David. He laughed. "Secrecy's a family trait, I guess. Will you look in on Mina and my mother while we're away? Ms. Kraken can instruct her in transmutation in my absence. She's been anxious to learn, but I've had her focused on other things. Which reminds me . . ."

Producing a key from his pocket, David went over to a

writing desk. Unlocking a small box, he retrieved a polished teardrop of lapis lazuli. Mina could hardly stand still as Max unfastened her magechain so that her teacher could thread the stone upon it.

"For identifying the ring," said David. "Be a good girl while I'm gone. And stay out of my trove."

Mina stiffened.

"I know that you've been at it, you little thief," David chided, mussing her hair. "Breaking into my chest, trying on charms of every rank and putting on fashion shows for my mother. For shame, Mina."

"A thief wouldn't put them back," retorted the girl, polishing her newly won stone and peering up at him affectionately. "Be safe, wise David and fierce Max. I will miss you." Hugging them both farewell, the girl hurried off to her bedroom, stopping only to close Rolf's eyes and place the coppers back atop the lids.

"What a strange child," muttered the Director when the door had closed. "I don't know whether she's our savior or . . . something else." She turned to Max. "You still have the *Ormenheid*?"

"Not on me," replied Max. "But she's in my room."

"How fast do you think that ship can sail to Blys?" asked Ms. Richter. "We have only five weeks until Lord Naberius will expect an answer."

"When David was aboard, I think she averaged sixteen knots," he said, doing the math in his head. "Two weeks. Maybe a little longer."

David shook his head. "Don't fret, Ms. Richter," he said, stuffing the portfolio into his enchanted pack. "Unless something goes very wrong, we'll be in Blys by dawn."

Pleasantly ignoring the Director's shock and subsequent

questions, David bade her farewell and whisked Max from the room. A minute later, the boys were cutting swiftly across Bacon Library.

"And how are we going to be in Blys by dawn?" Max hissed.

But David did not reply as they wove through tables and study carrels packed with students poring over manuscripts or staring into space and mouthing the words to various incantations. There were midterms this week. Exams seemed an absurd notion with Rowan tottering at the edge of war, but Max knew that Old College would have to be nearly overrun before Ms. Richter would cancel classes. Max was about to press David further when he caught the indignant eye of a Highland hare glaring at them from the librarian's desk. Swallowing his question, he hurried after David and the two boys disappeared down a narrow stairwell beyond the stacks.

"We're going to take my tunnel," David explained, standing aside as a phalanx of anxious-looking First Years trudged past. "No seats in Bacon," he warned them. "Try Archimedes—it's usually less crowded."

As the students moaned and reversed course, David slipped by them. Max followed but eyed each warily until he realized his ring had not grown warm.

"The tunnel will get us fairly close to your old farmhouse and Broadbrim Mountain," David continued. "From there, it's a two-week journey overland to Piter's Folly."

"What the heck is Piter's Folly?" asked Max.

"It's all in the dossier," said David, patting his pack and continuing down the stairs. "Do you need anything from outside our room? Anything from the Red Branch vault?"

Max shook his head. He'd already borrowed a longsword from the Red Branch's treasury as a less dangerous alternative to the *gae bolga*. The temptations he'd experienced earlier when he'd unsheathed the Morrígan blade had confirmed his lurking fears. He simply could not trust himself with the *gae bolga* in his hand and with friends nearby. The blade was a living thing that hungered for blood; it did not care whose so long as it drank deep. It must be a weapon of last resort.

"Do you have any money on you?" asked David as they approached the dormitory levels.

"A few lunes and coppers."

"That should be enough," remarked David, descending yet another flight of stairs until they were below the ground floor.

"Is the tunnel down here?" Max wondered. "We haven't packed yet."

"The tunnel's in our room," David explained. "We need to recruit someone first, and he's usually playing cards right about now. What time is it?"

"A little past midnight."

"Good," David chuckled. "Things will be in full swing."

Leaving the staircase, David hurried down a narrow, curving hallway of rough stone. Max had not spent much time in the Manse's underground levels—he was not even sure how many there were. It was plainly evident that nonhuman creatures lived down here. The corridor had a barnlike smell, an aroma of sawdust, wet grass, and warm fur. Torchlight flickered on many doors of different shapes and sizes—oval doors with brass moldings, square panels with centered rings, and narrow porticos whose blue pillars were marked with elegant runes and inelegant graffiti. David went to the nearest and knocked.

The door cracked open, allowing cigar smoke to trickle out into the hallway. Max heard music within, the tinkling of glasses, and raucous laughter. "The games are full, gentlemen," said a brusque voice with a French accent. The door promptly shut in the sorcerer's face. Narrowing his eyes, David knocked again.

"We want the smee."

The door swung open. As smoke plumed into the hallway, Max looked down and saw a raffish red-capped lutin puffing on a miniature cigar. Flicking ash from his velvet lapel, the elfin creature gazed back into the hazy room and gave a derisive snort.

"You are welcome to him. I will even waive admission."

Ducking beneath the archway, Max followed David into a small casino in which dozens of patrons were playing games of chance or quaffing drinks at a travertine bar. Lutins were notorious gamblers, but Max saw a host of other creatures in attendance. A pair of satyrs had joined several lutins at a poker table while a jostling throng of domovoi was crowded around the craps table, shouting, stamping, and pleading with every roll of the dice. Max heard the smee's theatrical baritone well before he saw him.

"Let's paint it red, Lady Fortune!"

They found the yamlike creature sitting beneath a potted palm, where he was propped on a striped chaise and sipping rum punch through a long straw. Although he had no visible eyes, the smee was avidly following the action at a roulette wheel via a mirror angled above the table. The ball skittered across a blur of numbers, bouncing along until the wheel finally slowed and it settled into a numbered pocket. Several players cheered. The smee drooped like a soggy croissant and sipped dejectedly at his drink.

"One left, Toby," called a pretty faun at the table. She was apparently placing the limbless smee's bets on his behalf. "What you want to do?"

"That's your gratuity," he sulked before suddenly perking up. "Unless! Unlessss the lady cares to let it ride on a romantic journey of chance and excitement?"

Rolling her eyes, the faun slipped the chip within her purse and checked her makeup.

"The game is rigged!" roared the smee, knocking over his drink with an angry butt of his dusky head. The glass tottered off the table and shattered. "Scoundrels one and all, you'd cheat a hero of his . . . of his . . ." He trailed off, apparently at a loss.

"I believe the word he's searching for is *dignity*?" sniffed a lutin, sorting his pile of chips.

"Wealth," suggested another.

"Impossible," put in a third. "He's never had either."

As the table erupted in laughter, the smee slid farther down his pillow.

"Done to death by slanderous tongue was the Hero that here lies," he murmured.

"I thought that must be a hero," remarked Max, pulling up a chair.

The smee nearly rolled off the chaise with shock. "Max!" he cried, catching himself and straightening. "David! What are you two doing here?"

"Looking for you," replied David. "We've got a secret mission and could use your help. What do you say, Toby? *'Once more into the breach, dear friends'*?"

The smee flipped about to address the nonplussed faun. "Did you hear that, succubus?" he cried. "Rowan's greatest champions have come requesting my aid. They need me! Find someone else to endure your frivolous poppycock and threadbare 'epiphanies.' I have important work to do. . . ."

As Max carried him out of the speakeasy, Toby preened like a sultan, swooning with pride and an excess of rum. By the time they'd reached the observatory, however, the smee's mood had sobered.

"Are we setting out right away?" he wondered, watching as Max and David stuffed clothes, bedrolls, and cooking gear into their packs. "Perhaps we should discuss strategy. I mean . . . I don't even know what the mission is about!"

"We'll tell you when we get there," Max muttered, buckling the longsword opposite the *gae bolga*.

"And where is 'there' precisely?" inquired the smee delicately.

"Blys," answered David, deftly fastening his pack with his only hand.

"But . . . but there are rumors of war in Blys," exclaimed Toby. "Isn't that . . . *dangerous*?"

"It's not a vacation," Max quipped, throwing another pair of woolly socks into his pack; in the wilderness, one could never have enough woolly socks. He slipped a warm black cloak over his shoulders, fastening it with the ivory brooch Scathach had given him in the Sidh.

"Do you have *Ormenheid*?" asked David, plucking a small glass vial from a shelf and slipping it into his belt pouch. Max nodded and patted his pocket where the dvergars' marvelous vessel had shrunk down to the size of a matchbox. When set upon the water and given the proper command, the miniature would expand into a Viking longship that could navigate and sail itself against wind, wave, and tide.

"On second thought," reflected Toby, "perhaps I over-indulged this evening. My head isn't quite right. I'm feeling downright tipsy. Call me a scalawag, gentlemen, but I think I'd best sleep it off. . . ."

"Sorry, Toby," said Max, plucking up the smee by one end. "This will have to do." He unceremoniously dunked the creature into a nearby pitcher of water. "Better?"

"Invigorated," groused the smee. "And now I will ask you to kindly put me down and *never* to grab me by that particular part of my anatomy again."

Horrified, Max promptly dropped the smee onto its pillow.

David cleared his throat. "If you're ready, we'll be off."

"So where is the tunnel?" asked Max.

"The same place you tried two years ago," said David, smiling. "But this time, my nosy friend, you'll have the password. . . ."

Max reddened, remembering back to the time when he'd suspected David was going mad. He'd known David was leaving Rowan through some secret passage in their room and had been determined to follow. He'd discovered that David's bed served as some sort of gateway, but the password had foiled him and he never made his way through.

Carrying the indignant smee, Max followed his roommate along the ledge on the observatory's upper level toward David's bed. Drawing aside its moon-stitched curtains, David unveiled a sleigh bed, half buried beneath unwashed coffee mugs, innumerable manuscripts, half a moldy sandwich, and some sort of grimacing iguana preserved in spirits of wine.

"Here we are," he said, oblivious to the mess as he sat near the headboard and swept some papers aside to clear a place for Max. As they had before, the grains in the wood began to swirl about, dancing in and out of focus as they rearranged themselves.

"Take my hand, Max," David commanded. "Hold it tightly and keep a firm grip on Toby."

Max did so, staring at the headboard with breathless anticipation as the grains formed a familiar pattern.

Password?

Max's roommate said nothing. He merely gazed up at the

glass-domed ceiling and the stars beyond while the seconds ticked by.

"David," Max hissed. "It's asking you for the password."

"Shhh," replied the little sorcerer, still staring up at the stars.

Confused, Max followed his friend's eyes up to the heavens. A new constellation was forming in the dome, its contours illuminated by slender threads of golden light that connected its stars. A moment later, Max was gazing at an enormous sea creature, its form outlined against the infinite space beyond. At last David spoke.

"Cetus."

A painful jolt accompanied a flash, followed by a spinning blur of lights that brought bile to Max's throat. Instinctively, he shut his eyes.

When he opened them, he was in Blys.

~ 6 ~

TO THE RAVENSWOOD SPUR

When he opened his eyes, Max found that he was still clutching Toby and sitting next to David as he had at Rowan. But they were no longer in their room; they were sitting on a moldy cot in a run-down villa. A dreary dawn peeked through holes in the sagging roof. Birds were roosting in the rafters, cooing softly and rustling their feathers whenever any icy draft came sweeping through. David released Max's hand.

"How do you feel?"

Max did not reply. He was on the verge of vomiting. Every organ seemed out of place and confused, as though they were still traveling thousands of miles in an instant. Even the room's dim light caused stabs of pain in Max's head. Shutting his eyes, he lay back on the bed and waited for the nausea to pass. The smee stirred in his hand.

"Wh-where are we?" Toby stammered.

"Blys," replied David. "In Prusias's own province. The capital city is a hundred miles or so south. We're not so far from Max's old house. We'll pass it on our way to Broadbrim Mountain."

"Why are we going there?" asked Max, releasing Toby and sitting up.

"Let's have a seat," said David, gesturing toward a splintered table in the room's center. "We'll examine Sir Alistair's dossier and discuss the plan. I already have some things in mind."

"May I finally slip into something more comfortable?" asked Toby. "It's emasculating to be plucked up like a stray sock and carried about all the time."

"Of course," said David. "We're not at Rowan—you're free to take whatever shape you like."

Smees were doppelgängers extraordinaire, creatures capable of mimicking not only another being's shape, but also its mannerisms, speech, and aura. When Max had first met Toby, the smee was masquerading as a ten-ton selkie to win the affections (and servitude) of the Sanctuary's selkie sisters, Helga and Frigga. When his fraud was discovered, Toby had been forced to reveal his true shape before all assembled and was thereafter banned from changing shape while at Rowan. When put to a more noble purpose, however, the smee's talents were exceedingly useful. Not even the terrible demon Mad'raast had been able to penetrate Toby's disguise when they'd sailed *Ormenheid* through the Straits that previous spring.

But it was not a fat merchant who bounded onto the table; it was a squirrel monkey with tawny fur and black, intelligent eyes.

"I'd almost forgotten what it's like to have arms and legs!" Toby crowed, swinging his limbs about and peeking back at his prehensile tail. "How luxuriant."

Ignoring the smee's ensuing acrobatics, David set his pack upon the table and pulled out Ms. Richter's portfolio. When Max asked about light, David directed him to a cobwebbed corner where several lanterns had been stashed along with candles and a small container of oil.

"Why not glowspheres?" Max wondered, setting the lanterns on the table.

"No magic," muttered David, unfolding a map and laying out several sheets of oily-looking paper. "It leaves a trace. No magic unless it's absolutely necessary."

Using flint and tinder, Max lit the lanterns and came around so he could look at Sir Alistair's notes. David had already read the first parchment and handed it to Max. "Careful handling that," the sorcerer warned. "Florentine spypaper's very old and extremely fragile. Remember—any marks you make on its surface will be transmitted to its twin."

Holding the sheet delicately by its edges, Max leaned forward to examine it by the lantern's warm yellow light. The paper was covered in tiny writing and diagrams that had faded or sunk into the paper so that they initially appeared to be little more than abstract patterns and blemishes. But peering closely, Max could make out faint sentences of coded Italian, French, and Russian, along with a cross-section of a castle tower and a patent drawing for some sort of loom. Atop these faded secrets was Sir Alistair's writing, penned in pristine script. The message was encrypted, however, and utterly nonsensical until David handed Max an oval of rose-colored glass. Once Max peered through the lens, the message became clear.

Evil is brewing—or building—in the Workshop. I've seen its members at royal gatherings, and while never a particularly sociable set, they appear exceedingly nervous and afraid to say or do the wrong thing. My sources say that Prusias has taken a more active interest in their endeavors and has commissioned something secret, some sort of war machine to help him conquer the other kingdoms. The demon's malakhim have been sent to observe the Workshop's progress, and I hear that the children of some key engineers have been "apprenticed" to loyal braymas throughout Blys as a means of keeping their parents industrious.

The Workshop itself is a fortress, and I fear that direct communication—much less infiltration—has become impossible. We must pass along information and gather intelligence using less direct means. Our opportunity may reside with an influential smuggler—a woman who lives in a settlement called Piter's Folly. She is called Madam Petra, but you may remember her as Petra Kosa—the Olympic medalist who later became a cause célèbre in the art world. She's an interesting, exceedingly capable woman who has been very savvy at positioning herself with various factions to become a major player within the region. No one can build or buy anything near Piter's Folly without her approval. Even the goblins pay her tribute when they drive their caravans past on the Ravenswood Spur. She'd be a valuable ally and may be able to contact the Workshop on our behalf or provide intelligence on their initiatives.

We must tread carefully, however. She has spurned our previous efforts to develop a relationship for fear that Prusias will learn of it and crush both her and her enterprise. The immediate and highly public nature of these rejections suggests that she suspects informers among her staff. She will not meet directly with strangers, and her assistants screen all of her appointments and visitors. In order to speak candidly with Madam Petra,

I believe we must masquerade as someone with whom she is familiar and already does business. We must smuggle ourselves in to see the smuggler. While she trades with other human settlements and some demons, she also does a brisk business with the wealthier goblin clans, including the Blackhorns, Highboots, and Broadbrims. . . .

"Ah," said Max, glancing at David. "That's why you want to go to Broadbrim Mountain. You think Skeedle can help us get in to see the smuggler."

His roommate nodded and handed over the second sheet. Putting the first aside, Max took up the decrypting lens once again.

Piter's Folly is located in the duchy of Bryllbatha near the borders with Raikos and Holbrymn. It is named after its founder, who was ridiculed for building so remote a shelter when the troubles began. Piter is deceased (officially, he drowned; unofficially, Madam Petra had him killed), but what started as his own private haven has grown into one of the largest human settlements in Blys. There's no official census, of course, but my contacts estimate that several thousand people live there, protected by the island's vast moat of surrounding lake and an expensive arrangement with the duchy's braymas. The Ravenswood Spur is the closest road. It cuts through the old Carpathians and passes close to the settlement on its way to feed into the Iron Highway that runs east toward Aamon's kingdom. It's a notoriously dangerous stretch of country, and the Agents must be wary of criminals—particularly as war looms and food grows scarce.

In addition to bandits, there are also Prusias's spies to consider. Prusias trusts few of his vassals and fears treachery at every turn. The kingdom is riddled with informants, and it is unlikely that the conspicuous use of magic or force will go unnoticed. A low profile is best.

While Aamon's armies threaten from the east, perhaps the greatest danger and most unpredictable element is Yuga. You may have heard that the demoness has devoured most of her duchy and has been encroaching upon other territories. Piter's Folly is not far from Yuga's own borders or from Raikos, where she is reputed to be feeding. The more skittish settlers are preparing to flee the island and move west.

This is a dangerous assignment, but an essential one. We must open up a communications channel to the Workshop and learn whatever we can about Prusias's war machine. Perhaps Aamon and Rashaverak will eliminate Prusias for us, but they are just as likely to turn upon Rowan themselves. We must prepare for war in any event.

Sol Invictus,
Alistair Wesley

When Max finished, he stood and gazed over David's shoulder at the map he was studying. Piter's Folly was far away—almost a thousand miles across what had once been called the Alps and Carpathians. And winter was nearly here.

"It will take us weeks to get there," Max estimated. "And that's assuming the roads and bridges are open. Couldn't we have tunneled closer?"

"Unfortunately, no," replied David. "It's not an easy task to create a link between our room and a distant destination. I only have several such outposts in Blys. This outpost is closest to Broadbrim Mountain, but I have another that's nearer to Piter's Folly. If we're lucky, we can use it to return to Rowan."

"What do you mean, 'if we're lucky'?" asked Toby anxiously.

"Assuming it still exists." David shrugged. "The locations are out of the way, but we're entering a war zone. There's nothing to say that an army hasn't destroyed it or refugees haven't taken up residence. The outpost is in Raikos—close to the border between Blys and Dùn."

"And Yuga," Max reflected grimly. "Can we use this outpost to jump to the other?"

"They don't work that way," answered David. "Each linkage requires a lot of time and energy, and I didn't have enough of either to establish connections between the outposts. Each tunnel is like a spoke that connects back to the observatory, but they don't connect to each other."

"Well," said Toby, "I suppose you'll have to conjure up a horse and carriage like you did when we stormed old Prusias's castle, eh?"

"Sorry," replied David. "No magic. Until we reach Broadbrim Mountain and can hitch up with a goblin cart, we're either walking or . . ."

The squirrel monkey's face drooped.

"I'm to be a steed, aren't I?"

"It would be faster," Max reflected. "A nice big horse with room for two. It's just sixty miles or so, Toby, and the switchbacks to the Broadbrim guardstones aren't too steep. I know this country."

"Well, goody for you," replied Toby acidly. "I suppose when we're in territory that I know, I'll be welcome to sit on your back and cry 'giddy up!' and 'whoa, there!' for a day or two. It's humiliating. I'm a spy, not a steed!"

"Can you be both?" asked David plaintively.

They headed north. Toby had become a shaggy black horse, and as the disgruntled smee cantered up the road, Max found his sense of adventure returning. The air was cold but bracing, bending the tall grass and the wild thistle as winter settled over

the land. The sun was rising, trying to peek from behind a jigsaw canopy of crowding storm clouds. Occasionally its golden
rays streamed through to warm the gray landscape and give it a
dreamlike quality. The road was empty; the only sounds were
those of the wind and the steady clip of hoofs upon the ancient
Roman stones.

By early afternoon, the land became hillier, the grass growing in thick tussocks as the road wound through stands of
spruce, ash, and poplar. Even the smells became familiar to Max
as they neared his old farmhouse. Ahead he saw its stone chimney peeking from behind a hilltop.

"Let's have a look," Max said, glancing back at his roommate,
whose cramped expression had not changed since morning.

"It might be inhabited," chattered David, his face blue with
cold.

"I'm sure Toby could do with a rest. There might be food.
And I know there's clean water nearby. . . ."

"If you insist."

Toby was more than ready for a rest. As they slowed to a
trot, the smee was snorting and sucking at the air, trying to
catch his breath while steam rose off his flanks. Dismounting,
Max and David stretched their aching limbs and led the grum-
bling smee around a wooded hill where they could approach the
house from a less exposed position.

"I've really got to get into training," grumbled Toby. "Too
much roulette."

"Shhh . . . ," said Max, creeping forward to peer through a
gap in the fragrant pines.

There was the farmhouse, but sadly not as Max remembered
it. Its red door had been kicked in and the shutters torn away
while the wind rippled over puddles in the animal paddock. The

windows were dark, and it appeared that much of the roof had burned away in a fire. A feral cat was lounging in the doorway, yawning and cleaning its fur.

"It looks uninhabited," whispered Max, motioning the others to follow.

The three emerged from the woody fringe of the farmhouse's clearing, stepping through the small orchard where Toby turned up his nose at the fallen remains of rotted fruit. The paddock was empty, except for the scattered bones of two sheep. Max glanced at the dark stones of a nearby well, remembering the pulpy, giggling monster that had lived in its depths. Toby was ambling toward it on weary legs.

"Don't water there," said Max quickly. "There's a lake nearby. I'll just look inside and then we can go."

He soon regretted his decision. The cat darted inside as he approached to poke his head inside the door to see the ruins of his former home. The farmhouse had been ransacked, everything of value broken or carried away by scavenging humans or goblins or whatever else had happened by.

"Not quite as you remember it," said David sadly, coming up beside him. The boy peered his head inside at the wet, warped floorboards and the frosted mold. "I'm sorry."

"It doesn't matter," said Max without much conviction. "I was stupid to hope it would be the same. I'm surprised it's still standing."

"At least we got them out," said David, referring to Isabella and the children. "We'd never have done so without Mr. Bonn. He was a funny one."

"A kind and thoughtful imp," Max mused, recalling Prusias's secretary. "Who'd have thought they exist? I hope he's okay. . . . He was a good friend. I first heard about Yuga from him. 'Patient Yuga,' he called her."

"I've heard that tale," said David. "The imps revere her. These days she might require a different nickname. Yuga's not so patient anymore. . . . Holbrymn is a wasteland."

"Have you ever seen her?" Max wondered.

"Just a glimpse once or twice through the observatory when scrying was still possible. Never in person, thank God. You think Mad'raast was big? Yuga's the size of a hurricane—a living, breathing, ravening storm that stretches to the horizon."

Max shook his head at the image's mortifying scale. Toby ambled up, chewing on a mouthful of grass from an old haystack by the paddock.

"What do you say, Toby?" said Max. "Can you do another thirty miles?"

"In thirty miles, do I get to cease my role as Shaggy the Bucktoothed Wonder?"

"For the night at least," Max assured him. "If you can go thirty, we'll reach Broadbrim Mountain and my friend will have you lounging in a wagon and eating chocolates all the way to Piter's Folly."

"Promise chocolate and you'd better deliver," sniffed the smee. "This road is hell on my hoofs. I almost miss being limbless." With a shudder, the horse spit out the hay and tossed his head. "Very well—a gulp, a trot, and then some rest. Let's get this over with."

After drinking his fill from the lake, Toby was once again cantering down the roadside. As dusk settled over the landscape, the mountains loomed ahead, their snowcapped peaks obscured by dark clouds gathering at the summits. More than once, Toby slipped on the wet road whose stones were growing icy as daylight waned and the temperature fell.

"How much farther is it?" he gasped, slowing to a hobbling walk. Leaning forward, Max saw that the smee's lips were flecked with frothy spittle, his breath coming in desperate, sputtering puffs.

"I think you've done enough for one day," said Max, swinging his leg over and helping David down. He gazed up at the sky and heard the low rumble of thunder from the mountains. The temperature was still dropping, and Max worried that they might be in store for freezing rain. Squinting ahead, he tried to estimate how far it would be to Nix and Valya's. He doubted the vyes still lived there, but he hoped their villa would be in better repair than the farmhouse. "I think it's another six or seven miles to a house I know. We can gut it out or we can make camp now."

"A roof trumps a tent," declared Toby, walking slowly in a circle.

David nodded but was rubbing his behind and looking peevish. The sorcerer was not accustomed to riding for hours at a stretch, but rather strolling along at his own pace. David was perhaps the most traveled person at Rowan, but journeys via magic tunnel were undoubtedly less taxing to his behind than hours spent riding bareback atop a cantering horse.

"I'm happy to walk for a bit," he grumbled, loosening the straps on his pack.

"Cloak-and-dagger's fun, isn't it?" Max needled, looping an arm around David's narrow shoulders. His voice dropped to an urgent whisper. "Look! I think there's our double agent at the cafe up ahead. Not the waitress—the man smoking a cigarette. *Don't stare!* I'll stake it out; you get ready to drop the briefcase. . . ."

"That's hilarious, Max. Truly."

Grinning, Max turned to address Toby when something caught his eye.

There were riders on the road behind them. At such a

distance, they seemed little more than bobbing black specks, but there were many. They were still a good ways off, but they appeared to be riding swiftly.

Max spoke sharply. "Off the road! Toby, take a smaller shape. Quick, quick, quick!"

Seconds later, Max, David, and a gray hare hurried off the road, crossing a narrow strip of dead grass and slipping into the woods. The light was already fading, and Max silently wished David would be more careful as the boy blundered through bracken and branches, cracking leaves and twigs underfoot. When they were a hundred yards in, Max brought the group to a halt.

"You two rest up here," he whispered. "I'm going back to have a look."

"Don't let them see you!" hissed Toby.

"Thanks for the tip."

David gripped his arm. "Remember your shine," he cautioned. "If they're spirits . . ."

Max nodded. He'd already thought of that and was bundled up not only to ward off the cold but also to minimize the chance that any spirit would glimpse his aura. In his cloak, he carried a mask of dark fabric whose only opening was a narrow band across the eyes. Slipping it on, Max pulled his hood down low and stole through the twilit wood back toward the road.

He selected a mountain ash some twenty yards from the roadside. Taking hold, Max climbed high enough to count the riders but stayed low enough to remain hidden by the branches of a neighboring spruce. As the rain began, Max watched and waited.

The showers were sporadic, but whenever the clouds parted, the moonlight revealed a potentially lethal minefield of watery slicks and icy stone. Max could now hear the horsemen coming.

They had not camped at nightfall as he'd hoped but continued at full gallop even as shadows fell over the land. Whatever their purpose, it was urgent. Edging forward, he peered out into the darkness to see if the riders had lit any torches.

When he saw none, Max knew they were not human. No man or woman would ride so hard in such conditions without so much as a torch to light their way. The riders were getting closer now, the ground thundering at their approach.

They passed like a wild hunt from a child's nightmare. The figures were armored, chain glinting under the moon as they hunched over swift, champing steeds whose decaying bodies revealed their sliding bones and trailing strings of sinew. There were dogs, too, rotting, ravenous war hounds that bounded alongside the horses, braying into the night. Scores of death-knights galloped by, a spectral company girded for war and racing east toward the front. Several bore Prusias's standard—a border of wheat sheaves encircling three gold coins. For an instant, Max glimpsed it fluttering in the moonlight and then it was gone—fading into the gloom as the company hurtled past and was swallowed by the mists at the mountain's foot.

Returning to David and Toby, he found them huddled behind the trunk of a fallen tree, looking cold, wet, and miserable.

"Wh-who was it?" chattered the smee, half burrowed in David's cloak.

"Soldiers of Prusias," replied Max. "They're not searching for us—they're riding too fast. I'd guess they're outriders or cavalry heading off to the war with Aamon."

"What should we do?" asked David.

"I think we should press on," said Max. "If the horsemen are outriders, there may be an army or some larger force coming up behind us. We don't want to get caught up in that. We'll stick to the woods and hike up into the mountains until the terrain gets too steep. Then we'll have to return to the road—it's the only way through the higher passes."

"So we're to have no roof?" moaned Toby. "No fire or a proper supper?"

Max shook his head. "Sorry. Not tonight at any rate. I have some jerky if you want."

"Jerky," sniffed the smee disdainfully. "I might as well chew your boot."

David coughed into his cloak, a convulsive wheeze that shook his entire body.

"Let's get going, then," he wheezed. "The ground is freezing."

For hours they felt their way through the woods, walking from one moonlit patch to another. Toby had become a lynx to better see in the dark and guide them through the close-pressed firs and spruce that blanketed the foothills. It was hard going, but Max was grateful for the forest's cover. More than once, a wind came howling through the treetops as fell spirits flew past in the night, their ghostly cries fading as they tore through the mountain passes on some unknown errand.

By dawn, the three had climbed high enough for the trees to thin. The freezing rain had departed, but a cold mist lay about the hills. The air was rich with the smell of pine and resin, the branches sagging with ice. Max stopped to check on David's progress.

Rowan's little sorcerer was leaning heavily on a walking stick as his feet stumbled along, some twenty yards back. Throughout the night, David had not uttered a peep of complaint, but anyone could see he was flagging. Max set down his pack.

"Sun's coming up," he observed, pointing at the range's golden rim. "I'd say we have another five miles, most of it road, before we reach the guardstones. We'll need energy for the final push, and I'd say it's foggy enough to risk a small fire. Get comfortable and I'll make breakfast. Are your socks wet?"

Coughing into his fist, David nodded wearily and eased down to rest his back against a tree.

"Put on fresh ones," said Max. "We'll dry the others and your boots by the fire."

Without magic, a fire would take some doing. The nearby wood was soaked through and Max had to scour for some drier sticks beneath the branches of a dense fir. Using pinches of lint as tinder, however, he soon had the wood hissing and then crackling with flame. Sitting down, Max rummaged through David's pack, finding a string of sausages and half a loaf of Marta's bread wrapped in crinkling brown paper. He soon had the sausages cooking in a small skillet. Toby practically hovered over the pan, licking his lips and sniffing at the sizzling pork until a drop of fat spattered on his whiskered chin. Yowling, he jumped back and settled by David, who was rubbing his stocking feet.

The three wolfed down their breakfast, sopping up the skillet's grease with the remaining bread. Color had returned to David's face and even Toby appeared companionable. Standing, Max gazed down at the mist-veiled road and up at the shrouded peaks.

"I think we should head downhill. The terrain only gets steeper ahead. Once we're back on the road, we need to move quickly. Do you think you can do that?"

David nodded, but glanced anxiously at the ugly blister on his instep.

"Let's bandage your feet," Max suggested, digging for a roll of clean linen. "As soon as your socks get wet or start to rub, let me know and we'll stop and change to others. It's no good toughing it out and allowing it to get worse—you'll only slow us down later. Toby, do you think you could manage a mule for a short while?"

"If I must," sighed the smee.

Minutes later, the three made their way down the precarious slope. While Toby's mule was sure-footed, David was an inexperienced rider and Max had to walk alongside and steady his friend as they navigated their way down the hill. It took the better part of an hour. When they finally reached the bottom, the sky had blushed to a pinkish blue and a sprinkling of fresh snow covered the ground.

Max kept them to the road's farthest edge so that they could shelter beneath rock ledges and leaning trees as they wound their way up the lonely passes. When they'd climbed to some new crest or vantage, he stopped and scanned the valley below with his spyglass. Snow was swirling about, weightless little flakes that danced before the lens. Squinting, Max saw no one on the road. Indeed, he saw no living thing but for a pair of circling hawks high above the vale and an elk trotting across a stream. The landscape was so quiet and peaceful; the riders of the previous night seemed naught but a bad dream.

> *"The clouds are at play in the azure space,*
> *And their shadows at play on the bright green vale,*
> *And here they stretch to the frolic chase,*
> *And there they roll on the easy gale."*

Max turned at the sound of Toby's voice. The smee was staring down into the valley, looking meditative. "Life has its moments," he reflected quietly. "This footsore misery would be worth it, if only for this moment, this view. It feeds the soul, boys. That it does."

"I didn't know you were a romantic, Toby," said David, smiling and patting his withers.

"Then you know nothing about smees," the mule retorted, flicking his ears. With a parting glance at the valley, he turned and pressed on.

For the next hour, the three pushed steadily up the mountain, following the pass as it switched back or tunneled through a narrow cleft to rise again on the other side. As they climbed, the snowfall intensified, swirling about them as mist blew past like tattered shrouds. When the road finally began to widen, Max knew they were near the goblin caverns.

"Toby," he said. "Up ahead are the Broadbrim guardstones. Do you think you can become a bird or something small and scout ahead for us? I need to know if there's a good spot where we can settle down unseen and keep an eye on the entrance."

"What do the guardstones look like?" inquired the smee.

"You can't miss them," said Max. "They're huge slabs of red granite."

"Very well," said Toby as David climbed off. The mule disappeared and Max stared down at a plump gray jackdaw, hopping about the snow and letting the wind flutter through his feathers. A moment later he was gone, flying off on his black-tipped wings.

"I hope Skeedle can help," Max muttered, well aware that the goblin might be en route to or from some distant trade destination. And goblins tended to be greedy, grasping creatures quick to exploit those weaker than themselves. What if Skeedle had lost his cheerful bloom and adopted the harsh habits of his elders?

"If he can't, we'll try something else," said David with a sanguine air. "We've traveled to the Sidh, Max. I have every confidence we can make our way to Piter's Folly and bluff our way in to see a smuggler."

Max grinned; David's spirits were reviving.

A moment later, Toby fluttered back and landed with an inexpert, skidding series of hops.

"We're in luck," he reported. "There's a small ledge across from the guardstones, some twenty or thirty feet above the road. Not an easy climb, but it should be manageable."

David glanced dubiously at his stump of a right hand.

"Worst case, I can carry you," Max offered.

"Did you see any guards?" David asked Toby.

"No," replied the smee. "Just the stones, sealed tight as a troll hitch."

"At one point I knew the password," Max reflected. "I made Skeedle and the others tell me, but that was a long time ago. I'll bet they've changed it."

"I'll bet they haven't," said David. "Let's get settled. I want to try something."

Hurrying up the road, they finally got their first glimpse of the guardstones—two gargantuan blocks of granite that were joined so tightly that the door appeared to be little more than an incongruous slab of reddish stone. Max glanced up at the ledge Toby had reported; it would be a very difficult climb for David.

But perseverance won the day. With Max giving him the occasional boost, David managed to scramble over the boulders and piled rubble, clinging to roots and rocks with fierce determination. In fifteen minutes, he reached the ledge, wheezing and coughing into his cloak. Shielding himself behind a boulder, he took a deep breath and caught a snowflake on his tongue.

"Not bad," said Max, crouching to peer at the guardstones. "You'll be scaling the Witchpeaks next."

"So what's the plan, gentlemen?" inquired the jackdaw, hopping from one foot to the other in an attempt to warm his tiny body. Giving up, he suddenly ballooned, his feathers smoothing to fur as he became a brown marmot.

"Well," said David, "we could sit here and watch for Skeedle. But that might take days and there's no guarantee we'll see him. But if Max knows the password, we might try sending him a message."

"How are we going to do that without stirring up the whole clan?" asked Max.

"A little trick," said David. "One that involves some magic, but just a very little. There doesn't appear to be anyone on our trail. I think we can risk it. . . . Speak into my hand and tell Skeedle that you want him to come outside. Assure him that he's not being haunted or going insane."

The sorcerer opened his hand and Max saw a swirling sphere of golden vapor materialize between his fingers. At David's urging, Max leaned forward and spoke into it as though it were a microphone.

"Skeedle, it's Max McDaniels. If you can hear me, I need you to come meet me outside the guardstones right away. Come alone and don't let anyone know what you're doing. Trust me; this is not a ghost and you're not going crazy. So put down your spicy faun tripe and come see your old friend. . . ."

"Perfect," said David, closing his hand about the sphere. "Now we just need you to try the password."

Leaning forward, Max cupped his hands and said, *"Bitka-lübka-boo."* He braced himself for the expected tremor.

Nothing happened.

"Maybe a little louder," David suggested. "You're practically whispering."

Max tried again, but the stones remained as they were.

Toby scoffed. "You sound like a ninny. What are you afraid of?"

"Well, I don't want to shout it," Max snapped. "There could be sentries nearby."

"When bold hearts fail, send a smee," Toby declared, brushing past Max and waddling down the steep ledge. Arriving at the bottom, he looked both ways before stealing across the road to the red slabs. Rising up on his hind legs, the marmot gingerly touched the doors.

Again, nothing happened.

Max could not hear the smee, but if his pacing was any indication, the creature was losing patience. Dropping to all fours, the marmot arched his back and bellowed.

"Bitka-lübka-boo!"

When the mountain shook, Toby panicked and came racing back, bounding up the rocky slopes to land beside them in a panting, trembling ball.

"Good work," David whispered. "Stay low."

Spreading his fingers, the boy sent the vaporous sphere snaking toward the guardstones, which were sliding apart to reveal a dark chasm beyond. It zoomed into the entrance, skimming past the head of a potbellied goblin that came clanking out in his iron-soled shoes to peer at the road. Lifting his broad-brimmed hat, the creature stood and scratched at his lumpish forehead before clutching his pelt closer and shuffling back inside. The mountain groaned as the stones slid shut.

"Now what?" Max asked.

"We wait," replied David, spreading a woolly tartan over his legs. "If Skeedle's inside, the zephyss will seek him out, slip inside his ear, and deliver our message."

"Maybe we should have sent two," said Max, imagining the twitchy goblin's reaction. "He'll definitely think he's going crazy."

"Have faith."

Within the hour, they felt the mountain shake once again. Peering over the ledge's lip, Max watched as a caravan of five wagons emerged into daylight. A pair of goblins sat in the driver's seat of each, one holding a tall spear and the other a whip. Yelling out to the mules, the drivers cracked their whips and urged the teams to turn the wagons west and head down the road from which Max and the others had come. As the stones were closing, Max saw a small figure slip outside. It paused, shielding its face from the flurries as it gazed about. Max stood and waved.

The goblin waved excitedly back, hurrying across the road and climbing skillfully up the fallen rocks until he joined them on the ledge. When Max knelt and hugged him, the hideous little creature nearly danced a jig.

"I never thought I'd see you again!" Skeedle exclaimed, struggling to keep his voice low. The young goblin had grown since Max had seen him, having added another sharp tooth and perhaps twenty pounds to his short, plump frame. "What are you doing here?"

"We need your help," Max replied. "I wouldn't ask if it wasn't important."

Settling down next to his hero, the goblin listened attentively as Max and David relayed where they were going and what was needed.

"So . . . two wagons and someone who's traded with the Great Piter Lady," confirmed Skeedle, twiddling his stubby claws as though brainstorming various options. "I've never been so far, but my cousin's been three times and once with Plümpka himself. He never shuts up about it."

"We also need trade goods," added David delicately. "Something the Piter Lady's always eager to buy."

"Kolbyt would know, but he's still passed out," said Skeedle. "He got back last night from a caravan and swore there are ghosts on the road. Went straight to the casks and drank till he dropped."

"Do you think you can wake him up?" asked Max. "I know it's a lot to ask, Skeedle, but we need you two to take us to Piter's Folly. Realistically, I'm guessing it will be six weeks for you to get us there and come back."

The goblin frowned. "Longer if the passes get snowed in," he mused. "Ravenswood Spur goes through rough country. Normally we'd need bribe money and a whole guard troop, but with you . . ."

Skeedle sat talking quietly to himself in his native tongue while flakes collected on his belly. "I think . . . I think we can do it," he said, brushing off the snow and standing up.

"Don't tell Kolbyt any more than you have to," David cautioned. "But you have to convince him to accompany us. We need him."

"Oh, don't worry about Kolbyt," said Skeedle breezily. "Give me till dusk and I'll be back with him and everything else."

"Skeedle," said Max, "I really appreciate this."

The goblin blushed. "You fought that troll for me," he said, raising his arms so Max could lift him over a particularly large boulder. "I was in a tough place and you helped me. No one's ever done anything for me." Set back upon his feet, however, the goblin glanced sideways at Max. "But just remember that as far as Kolbyt and the rest are concerned, it was *Skeedle* who took care of that troll. All by himself. *Capisce?*"

"Perfectly."

The pair shook hands before Skeedle clambered down the icy scree like a little goat, clutching his beloved hat as a gust threatened to whisk it away.

* * *

As promised, Skeedle returned just as the sun was setting, casting purple shadows that stretched across the snowswept road. Four sturdy mules pulled his wagon, a baroque-looking tank that appeared equal parts carriage and strongbox. Another team of mules followed behind, pulling a smaller wagon whose driver was nestled down between a pair of barrels. Waving to Max, Skeedle pointed east to indicate that they should meet him farther down the road.

Hurrying down from the ledge, Max led the others along the shadowed gully to where Skeedle was waiting at a turnout that offered a spectacular view of distant valleys where the faint lights of distant settlements could be seen. One by one, the stars were coming out, little jewels scattered across a sky of deepening indigo. The goblin could barely contain his excitement.

"Off to Piter's Folly with Max and his friends!" he exclaimed, double-checking the harness before hastening over to doff his hat and stow their things. When the goblin unlocked the stout wagon's doors, Max glimpsed a warmly lit, surprisingly spacious compartment, lined with crates, blankets, and pillows. He longed for a proper bite and a long nap.

"Should you introduce us to Kolbyt?" wondered Max, eyeing the squat silhouette that was waiting for them.

"Do you know how to drive a wagon?" inquired Skeedle, studiously avoiding eye contact.

"I guess I can manage, but—"

"Good," chirped the goblin, quickly tossing their packs into the back. "Just introduce yourself when he wakes up. . . ."

Horrified, Max walked over to the other wagon. An enormously fat goblin with a pronounced underbite was fast asleep in the driver's seat, his broad chest heaving like a bellows. Belching, the creature muttered something unintelligible and rolled over to scratch his patched and lumpy breeches.

"That is foul," Max groaned, wafting the odor away. "Skeedle, you said you'd wake Kolbyt up—I don't want to kidnap him!"

The goblin gave a cheerful shrug and removed the barrels that he'd used to keep his cousin propped in place. "You said you were in a hurry," he reasoned, tottering under their weight as he stowed them. "He might not stir till tomorrow or the day after. Kolbyt's a mighty deep sleeper and the cask was almost empty. Just follow me and don't drive over the edge!"

And with that, Skeedle ushered David and Toby into the back of the larger wagon where the pair stretched luxuriantly amid the fleeces and blankets. The smee was already nosing at a fat tin of chocolates when Skeedle closed the doors and the snug, jewel-like interior vanished from view like a happy dream. Unspeakably bitter, Max swung up into the driver's seat and unceremoniously shoved Kolbyt over, tossing a wolf pelt over the bloated goblin to dampen his smell and snoring. Shaking the reins, Max felt the wagon lurch into motion as the mules clopped dutifully after Skeedle's wagon, which was already descending the steep decline.

Throughout the night, Max drove the wagon down the far side of the mountain in what was one of the more terrifying experiences of his eventful life. Every ledge appeared narrower than the wagon's base; every crevasse seemed a bottomless abyss as the wagon lurched along, bouncing over fallen rocks and shattered icicles thicker than his arm. Whenever gales came screaming through the passes, Max shut his eyes while the heavy wagon seemed to roll and pitch like a storm-tossed glider. He counted eleven near-death moments throughout the night, but

Kolbyt never stirred, much less awoke to offer any expert guidance. By dawn, Max had abandoned all pretenses at driving the team. Sitting bolt upright, he merely clutched the reins with frozen hands and croaked halfhearted pleas to the oblivious mules.

At last the terrain leveled out and Max descended yet another pass to find Skeedle's wagon stopped at the cusp of some shallow foothills that fed down into another frostbitten valley. Max heard whistling and spied the goblin's absurd hat peeking from behind the bush where he was relieving himself.

As Skeedle stood on tiptoe, his face emerged. "Perfect night for driving, eh?"

The goblin's grin evaporated when he noted Max's expression. Saying nothing, Max lumbered stiffly to the other side of the bush. The doors to Skeedle's wagon burst open and Toby came hopping out, still wearing the marmot's guise.

"Fair enough, fair enough," he called pleasantly. "But next time we play by *my* rules, you knave! You saucy rapscallion!" Shaking his head, the marmot chuckled until he caught Max staring at him. "Your roommate is quite the poker player," he explained.

"That's perfect," Max muttered, staring off into the hazy distance. "While I'm teetering over chasms, you two are playing cards all night."

"Not *all* night," said the smee. "We did other things, too."

"Like what?"

"We ate chocolates," sniffed the unrepentant smee, waddling over to wash his face in a nearby stream. "And we talked. David needed my advice."

"On what?"

"Girls." Toby shivered as the icy water touched his nose. "How to woo the fairer sex. How to ply a blushing maid with wit and sweet nothings until she fairly melts with desire."

"And so he asked . . . you?"

"And I suppose he should have asked you?" laughed the smee. "Ha!"

"What's wrong with asking me?" said Max. "I've had a girlfriend—"

"Julie Teller?" chortled Toby. "Are you honestly citing Julie Teller as the basis for your expertise on love? Isn't she the very girl you were dating when you sailed away from Rowan without even saying a proper goodbye? The same young lady who was left to wonder whether you were alive or dead for over a year? I'd imagine she must be the same Julie who is now dating one Thomas Polk, a steady young man who bores her to tears and yet she still finds him infinitely preferable to you. . . ."

Turning fire red, Max opened his mouth for a furious retort. But nothing brilliant occurred to him and he shut it again. Everything the smee said was technically true. Leaning heavily on a wagon wheel, he knocked a clump of mud from his boot.

"It was complicated," he muttered. "There were lots of other factors."

"There always are," Toby observed wryly, jumping back onto the wagon's rear platform while Skeedle fed and watered the mules. His voice softened. "But don't feel too bad. Why would you know anything about courtship?"

"Well, why wouldn't I?" retorted Max, glaring at David whose face appeared inside the wagon.

"Because you're young, handsome, and inexperienced," remarked the smee. "Most girls take one look at you and swoon. You've never had to really work for someone's affection or put effort into maintaining it. In many ways, your natural gifts have done you a disservice—they've stunted your sensitivity and charm! You've never had to develop insight into what will make a girl laugh and come to love you for reasons that *aren't* handsome or heroic. That's why smees are experts on the subtle arts of courtship and seduction; nothing comes easy to us, but we do understand and live by the Lover's Maxim."

"And what on earth is the Lover's Maxim?" asked Max, feeling very uninformed.

The smee cleared his throat. *"If you can't be handsome, be rich. If you can't be rich, be strong. If you can't be strong, be witty."*

"But what if you can't be witty?" Max wondered.

"Learn the guitar."

David snorted with laughter, but Max did not. He considered these words and the unexpectedly sage marmot sitting beside him, casually grooming his coat.

"I suppose you've had a slew of relationships," Max ventured.

"Indeed," purred Toby with dreamy nostalgia. "Some lasted years; others were no more than a delightful afternoon. But all were torrid, mind you. The blood of a smee runs hot!"

"Okaaay," said Max weakly, regretting this last inquiry. He returned to his own wagon before the creature delved into details; the very idea of a lothario smee was quite enough after such a harrowing night. Skeedle had finished tending after the mules and was squinting up at the pale blue sky.

"Fair weather," he remarked. "Or fair enough. How'd the wagon handle?"

"Super," Max deadpanned, squeezing back in next to Kolbyt who was now draped across the seat and snoring to wake the dead. "How much longer do you think he'll sleep?"

"Hopefully till we're on the Ravenswood Spur," said Skeedle. "By then, he'll have to give in and go all the way to Piter's Folly. If he starts belly growling and gnawing on his lip, it means he's getting hungry. If that happens, just stuff some of this faun tripe into his mouth so he doesn't wake up."

"It just gets better," sighed Max, frowning at the dented tins Skeedle dropped onto the seat.

They drove on for the better part of two days, crossing a broad expanse of foothills and valleys. Whenever Skeedle grew too tired, they pulled the wagons over and secured the mules while David or Toby kept watch from inside via an ingenious device the Broadbrims installed in their best wagons. From the outside, what appeared to be nothing more than a small skylight was actually a sort of periscope whose system of mirrors granted those within an excellent view of their surroundings. With its surveillance, armored plating, and a plethora of hidden murder holes, the wagons were like miniature fortresses rolling their way over hills and hollows.

Thus far, however, they'd had little need of defenses. But for the occasional sight of a distant castle or lonely farmstead, the land was largely uninhabited. The endless road and Kolbyt's continued slumber provided Max with plenty of time to think. Whenever his seatmate stirred, Max merely opened one of the tins and held his nose while dangling the bulbous strip of pungent tripe above the goblin's sharp, serrated maw. Like a shark preparing to take bait, the goblin's jaws distended. With a sudden snap, the creature would snatch the flesh away and mince it about from cheek to cheek. Within seconds of gulping it down, the snoring resumed.

As the mules swallowed up the miles, Max found time to reflect upon Toby's jibes. Perhaps he had treated Julie poorly. He'd always thought of themselves as victims of circumstance, star-crossed lovers. After all, Mr. Sikes had meddled with their relationship, and his Red Branch duties often required Max to travel far away on long and dangerous missions. He had given up trying to live the life of a typical Rowan student, but perhaps he bore more responsibility for the relationship's failure. Perhaps he could have been more considerate of Julie's feelings. Max suspected this was true. But he also had to be honest with himself. When death was near in Prusias's Arena, his heart had made things abundantly clear. The person he'd longed for, the face that flashed before his dimming eyes had not been Julie's. . . .

The wagon gave a sudden jolt and nearly tipped forward as one of the mules stumbled into a ditch. Max pitched off the seat and clung to the rail as empty tins rattled about his head or clattered overboard to go bouncing down the road. Braying irritably, the mule regained its footing and the wagon righted itself. Cursing, Max climbed back into his seat and looked about for the reins.

He found them clutched in the hands of a confused and very angry goblin.

~ 7 ~

PITER'S FOLLY

Cursing, the goblin set to kicking at Max with an iron-soled shoe.

"Skeedle!" Max yelled, absorbing a heavy blow as he scrambled over the driver's railing. The other wagon continued on, oblivious, as Kolbyt lashed out with a whip that nicked Max's ear.

"*Skeedle!*" he cried again, crabbing sideways on the wagon, clinging to walls, until he could swing himself up onto its roof. Startled by the commotion, the mules snorted and trotted faster. Wheels skipped and bounced over the rough road as the wagon closed the distance on the one ahead. When they clattered past Skeedle, the little goblin offered a cheerful wave.

Upon seeing his cousin, Kolbyt tugged furiously on the reins. The wagon lurched wildly, nearly flinging Max from the roof, as the mules stumbled and slowed and finally came to a panting halt. Leaping down, Kolbyt lumbered toward the other wagon.

Skeedle met him in the middle, the two goblins smacking into one another's stomachs. The impact was such that each staggered back. Resuming the struggle, they bellowed furiously at one another in a flurry of harsh, unintelligible words while each clutched his absurd hat and sought to force the other backward with his belly.

The showdown lasted nearly fifteen minutes. By then, Max had climbed down off the wagon's roof and joined David and Toby to await the outcome. Max was amazed that Skeedle could hold his own. The little goblin was half his cousin's size, a mere peanut colliding with a pear. But he was a stubborn peanut and not in the least cowed by his more massive relation.

Occasionally, one of the goblins would jab a stubby finger at their passengers and renew their bellowing, but soon they grew too exhausted for even these demonstrations. The only word Max understood was *Yuga*, for the older goblin uttered it several times. At times, it appeared that Kolbyt's saggy bulk would win the day, but Skeedle held firm until the larger goblin tired. The final minutes were little more than the two combatants propping each other up, clutching their brims, and growling.

At last Kolbyt broke away, glowering and wiping his nostrils with a brawny forearm. Muttering something to his cousin, he shook his head disapprovingly and turned to gaze down the road.

"Well," said Skeedle, coming over and catching his breath, "everything's all worked out. He's really a softy at heart and I've always been his favorite relative."

"So he'll take us to Piter's Folly?" said David.

"Oh no," Skeedle chuckled. "He says it's much too

dangerous—not worth anywhere near what I'll be paying him. But he'll tell you what he knows about the Great Piter Lady and we'll drive you close and leave you with one of the wagons. From there you're on your own."

"That's fine," said Max. "Can I ask you what it's going to cost you, though? I hope it's not too much."

"My trade wagon for one year," replied Skeedle, readjusting his hat. "A deep bite given wartime profits, but I'll manage."

"We'll see what we can do to compensate you," Max promised. He knew the journey was already dangerous and didn't want to bankrupt the little goblin in the bargain.

But Skeedle waved him off. Grinning, the goblin lowered his voice. "Plümpka's already promised me three more wagons and choicer routes because of the troll. What Kolbyt doesn't know won't hurt him. He can *have* my old wagon; the latest models are equipped with fire spouts!"

Skeedle tittered at the mere thought of his potential wealth. Having checked on the mules, Kolbyt lumbered over. Pointing at the smee, the goblin hooked a thumb and indicated that Toby was to ride with him.

"But why me?" protested the smee. "I'm perfectly comfortable in the other wagon."

"Because Kolbyt can tell you all about the Great Piter Lady," explained Skeedle. "At Piter's Folly, you'll have to take his shape and pretend to be him. There's just one thing. . . ."

"What?" inquired the marmot suspiciously.

"Well," said Skeedle, glancing at his cousin, "Kolbyt wants you to change shape now."

"Into what, pray tell?"

"A hag," blurted Skeedle, flushing green. "A big one."

The smee looked from one goblin to the other, utterly appalled and speechless.

"I am a spy, sir!" he finally declared. "An espionage agent par excellence, a master of ruse de guerre. My duties most certainly do *not* include taking the guise of some gargantuan hag so that your depraved relations can paw at me."

"He promises not to touch," said Skeedle. "But it's a long trip to Piter's Folly; Kolbyt just wants something pretty to look at along the way. He gets lonely."

Outraged, the smee turned to Max and David for support. The boys merely shrugged.

"First a steed, now an escort," grumbled Toby. "This trip will never make my memoirs. . . ."

Before their eyes, the smee swelled into a squat hag with greasy gray skin, a tuft of auburn frizz, and a fleecy orange robe. After appraising her, Kolbyt grunted to his cousin.

"He says you look very nice," translated Skeedle. "But perhaps a little larger. He says—"

Toby exploded. "I know perfectly well what he said!"

Panting, the smee ballooned so that his flesh expanded like rising dough. When a fourth chin appeared, Kolbyt grunted his approval. Beaming, the goblin proudly ushered the enormous, petrified hag to his wagon and helped her up into the driver's seat.

They resumed their journey to Piter's Folly, Max now luxuriating in the compartment of Skeedle's wagon. As expected, the smee had devoured almost all of the chocolate, but Max found that several treats remained and kicked off his boots to savor a cherry tart and survey the scenery through the small windows. Finishing his snack, he smacked away the remaining crumbs and burrowed beneath a blanket for a well-deserved nap.

The next morning, they veered the wagons onto the smaller road known as the Ravenswood Spur. While the main highway curved away south, the new road wound north and east toward the Carpathians. Day after day, the wagons clattered toward the looming gray mountains, stopping only to rest the mules or for the goblins to snatch a few hours' sleep.

There were no human travelers on the road, but they did encounter several goblins—a small caravan of surly Blackhorns and a solitary Highboot whom Kolbyt would most certainly have robbed had they not forbidden it. The skies were growing ever heavier, ever darker as they headed northeast and began to climb again into hilly terrain.

Past a windswept hillock, Max saw the first evidence of Prusias's war. It came in the form of a caravan that had been driven off the road and into a pond of brackish water. At first Max thought it was the water's steam rising into the chill morning, but it was smoke still trickling from the charred crumble of wagons that had been incinerated down to the shallow waterline. Among the grisly spectacle, Max saw the twisted forms of burned horses and several others that were vaguely man-shaped. As Skeedle halted the mules, Max got out to scan the road as it climbed up into the mountains, winding amid the jutting clefts until it disappeared in the mist. Glancing about, he saw no evidence of the attackers; no hoof marks or even boot prints were pressed into the frosted soil. Several ravens hopped about the wreckage, eyeing Max suspiciously as he walked about the water's edge. When he stepped into the icy shallows, they cawed and flapped heavily away.

Kolbyt bellowed something in his guttural speech. Max turned to see the goblin swaddled in wolf pelts next to Toby, whose plump, haggish face looked cold and miserable.

"He says we should move on," reported Toby. "We're too exposed out here—better that we get up into the mountains."

Max nodded and took one last look at a scorched carcass before heading back inside the wagon.

David glanced up from his solitaire game. "What was it?" he asked.

"Four, maybe five wagons. All burned to a crisp and piled atop one another in a bog. No sign of survivors. No sign of the attackers, either."

"I imagine we'll see many such things before we get to Piter's Folly," remarked David, ducking to avoid hitting his head on the roof as the wagon bounced over a rut.

"I wish we were already there," Max muttered. "I've been thinking about Walpurgisnacht. Your grandfather magicked us back to Rowan in an instant—without any tunnels or the observatory's help. How did he do that?"

David smiled and lay down a final card.

"Because he's Elias Bram. My grandfather's capable of many things that are beyond my power. People like to make comparisons between us, but in truth there is no comparison."

"Well, why couldn't he have brought us to Piter's Folly?" Max wondered, calculating that they had at least another week of hard travel through dangerous country. "It would have been so much faster."

"You sound like Ms. Richter." David smiled. "She'd like nothing better than to hand the Archmage a list of miracles to perform. But Prusias and the Workshop aren't his priorities, much less some smuggler in a backwater like Piter's Folly. Imperfect as it is, my tunnel has still gotten us where we are almost a month faster than *Ormenheid* could and two months faster than an ordinary ship. Let's be satisfied with that and do our jobs so the Archmage can do his."

"And what is that?" asked Max.

"Hunting Astaroth," replied David, pushing aside the cards and pouring Max some coffee. "Not such an easy task—the Demon might not even be in this dimension, much less this world."

"You still call him 'the Demon,'" Max noted. "Even after what your grandfather said."

"If that's what Astaroth's pretending to be, then that's what I'll call him," replied David. "Knowing what something *wants* to be is very telling. Astaroth aspires to be the 'Great God' and he's masqueraded as a demon to achieve this goal. Whatever his true origins, it's clear that he really has become a demon in some respects. After all, he can be summoned against his will, and he must obey Solomon's circles if they're properly inscribed. Until I know what he truly is, he'll always be 'the Demon.'"

Sipping his coffee, Max considered this and gazed out one of the portholes. The marshy land was gone, the hardscrabble terrain growing hillier as the wagons climbed higher into the mountains. He spied a withered hawthorn clinging to life among the rocky soil. There was something vaguely unsettling about the tree, the way its limbs twitched and waved while its neighbors were still. Max shifted to keep it within view, half expecting to glimpse Astaroth peering back at him from behind its black trunk. As the wagon rumbled onward, the tree was lost from view, but Max's worries remained. He brooded upon the Demon's white, masklike face, a face that rarely blinked and always smiled.

As they crossed the Carpathians, Max asked several times if Skeedle would like a rest, but the goblin declined. He sat low in the driver's seat, his hat scrunched down upon his knobby head while he clutched the reins in his calloused hands. Max was puzzled by the goblin's taciturn mood. Given the road's sinister reputation, Max thought they'd enjoyed tremendous luck. They'd encountered hardly any travelers, much less the bandits or armies that Alistair had warned of. They'd passed several burned-out farmhouses and homesteads but seen no trace of anything on a larger scale. If war had begun in earnest, it had not trodden heavily on the region.

Descending the mountain passes, they followed the Ravenswood Spur through dark forests and shaded hills until they were a stone's throw from a snowy riverbank. Shortly after noon, Max was sitting next to Skeedle in the driver's seat when the goblin called out for his cousin to halt.

"It's too quiet," Skeedle whispered. "No birds, no foxes . . . not even a wolf has come sniffing after us and you know how they crave goblin! We're but two wagons and there have been no bandits or highwaymen. It's not natural. Th-there's something out here and it's watching us. I think it's been with us since the mountains. My mind's playing tricks—I'm seeing things in the trees and rocks. Faces." The little goblin was absolutely trembling. Mopping his forehead, he peered up at Max with an expression of shameful desperation. Tears formed in his shiny black eyes. "I—I don't know if I can go any farther," he stammered. "I thought I'd be brave enough, but the Spur's not like what I expected. The sooner I go home, the happier I'll be. Would you think I'm a coward if I turn back?"

"No," said Max gently. "I think you've already taken on more than I had a right to ask. Let's give the mules a rest while I talk to David and Toby."

While Skeedle and Kolbyt fed the mules and tinkered with the wagon, Max explained the situation to the others. Consulting his map, David glanced at the river and traced his finger on the parchment.

"I think that river's the former Vistula," he said. "We have maybe another seventy or eighty miles to Piter's Folly. We can go on alone if Toby thinks he's gotten enough information from Kolbyt."

"I know everything he knows—or at least everything he can

recall," Toby sniffed. "Broadbrim clan lore ad nauseam, their history with Madam Petra, how to enter Piter's Folly, et cetera, et cetera. I'm a certified expert on everything that rattles around that goblin's head, and I'll confess there's a great deal I'd rather not know. He's indecent."

"So Toby can bluff his way in," Max concluded. "But how are we going to get in to see her?"

"Toby's been studying Kolbyt, but I've been studying Toby," David revealed. "A smee's greatest skill is his ability to mimic another creature's aura. I think I can create an illusion that will do the same. We're going to become goblins, Max. I'll be Skeedle and you'll be our bodyguard. Choose a name."

"Hrunta, I guess," said Max, recalling a thuggish Broadbrim he'd once met. "But I don't speak goblin."

"Relax," said David. "Nobody bothers speaking to the bodyguard; just grunt. Toby, see if you can become Kolbyt."

"I shall relish the change," declared the hag.

A moment later, Kolbyt stood next to them—complete with the goblin's hat, leather armor, wolf pelts, and iron-soled shoes. Max pinched the pelt between his fingers.

"How do you do that?" he wondered. "Do you just create the clothes out of thin air?"

"Ouch!" exclaimed Toby, swatting his hand. "No, I do not—you are ruining the elasticity of my magnificent epidermis. Everything you see is smee. In fact— OH!"

The startled smee backed away from him. Max was puzzled until David handed him a mirror. Within its surface, he did not see his own face but that of a toady-faced goblin with a forelock of black hair and a lipless mouth that stretched from ear to ear. As Max smiled, the ghastly reflection did likewise, revealing several rows of sharp, mossy incisors.

"Is that really you?" Toby whispered.

"Of course it's me," Max laughed. He did not feel any different; looking down, he saw his same hand and the same Red Branch tattoo. But Cooper had taught Max that mirrors reflect all illusions, and according to this mirror, others would see Max as a barrel-chested Broadbrim with clay-colored skin and bloodshot eyes.

Toby leaned forward and sniffed him. "David," he exclaimed, "you've created an illusion that's . . . that's almost smee-worthy!"

"Yes," said David thoughtfully. "I think I have. Let's—"

A faint tremor shook the earth, causing the mules to stamp and bray. Skeedle shrieked and hurried back to them, spilling oats from his canvas sack. He stopped dead at the sight of them.

"Wh-where's Max?" he gasped. "What have you done with him?"

"I'm right here, Skeedle," said Max calmly. The goblin merely gaped. "It's just an illusion. You and Kolbyt can head back now. Which wagon should we take?"

"Th-the big one," replied the goblin, still staring suspiciously. Summoning his courage, he darted forward and poked Max on the shoulder.

"It's really me," said Max, smiling.

"You even sound . . . and *smell* like a Broadbrim!" whispered the goblin.

"Music to my ears. You'll be okay on the road back?"

"I think so," the goblin chirped. "If trouble comes, I'll run. I don't need to run fast, just faster than Kolbyt." Skeedle grinned, revealing six sharp teeth as he hugged Max. Turning, he barked out something to his cousin, who gazed over, grunted dully at the new disguises, and began transferring crates to the larger wagon. Taking Max's arm, Skeedle walked him over to the mules, explaining their individual temperaments and quirks.

"And don't hold the reins too tight," he cautioned. "Petunia has a sore tooth. When you're done with them, sell them to someone kind. Or just set them loose. They know the way home."

"Got it," said Max. He turned to Toby, who was already sitting up in the driver's seat. "Do you know our inventory?"

"To the ounce and ingot," sighed the smee. "Kolbyt might be dense, but not when it comes to what his cousin borrowed. He recited it in his sleep."

"I guess this is it, then, Skeedle," said Max, shaking the goblin's hand. "Thank you for all your help. I expect the next time I see you, you'll be sitting on Plümpka's throne."

"Maybe." Skeedle blushed, removing his hat and twiddling his fingers. "If he doesn't eat me first."

While Kolbyt turned the smaller wagon about, the rest of the group said their goodbyes. Upon seeing David take his own guise, Skeedle clapped and circled the sorcerer to assess him from various angles. Satisfied, the goblin hopped aboard Kolbyt's wagon and waved his hat farewell. Shaking the reins, Kolbyt barked impatiently at the mules and the cousins began their long, clopping journey back to Broadbrim Mountain.

"A prince among goblins," Max remarked, climbing up into the driver's seat next to Toby.

"You set a rather low bar," scoffed Toby, sounding peevish. "Your 'prince' just left us in the middle of nowhere with four gassy mules and no more chocolate. Meanwhile, the thankless smee remains steadfast after serving as a steed, masquerading as a hag, and suffering that brute's attentions."

"Don't be so dramatic," said Max. "Kolbyt said he just wanted to look at you."

"He was *not* a goblin of his word."

* * *

As they drove on, however, Max had to admit that Skeedle's fears seemed justified. There did appear to be something sinister to the landscape, a watchful silence that nipped and worried at the edges of his mind. As the afternoon waned, he found that he'd grown quiet, ignoring the smee's incessant gripes and philosophizing as the mules plodded on.

It was nearly twilight and they were coming over a barren rise when Max finally saw his first bird of the day. It streaked past the wagon, a large crow whose throaty cries startled Toby from sleep.

"Wh-what's that?" murmured the smee, blinking stupidly.

But Max was speechless.

He had never seen such an astonishing sprawl of bodies. So many corpses littered the vale below that they nearly dammed the river, forcing its waters to spill over its banks to turn half the plain into a bloody marsh. Broken bodies and equipment stretched as far as Max could see—a grisly feast for thousands of crows that flapped and hopped about the shocking carnage. When the slouching smee made to sit up, Max finally found his voice.

"Don't look. Shut your eyes and keep them shut."

Toby instantly clamped his hands over face. "What is it?" he hissed.

"A battlefield," said Max, searching for words. "A graveyard . . . a massacre. Thousands dead."

"Humans?"

"Some," said Max, sweeping the field with his spyglass. "Mostly vyes . . . ogres and ettins . . . some of those riders that overtook us on the road. A few banners are Aamon's, but most belong to Prusias. It seems things aren't going so well for the King of Blys. Most of the casualties are his."

Some movement caught Max's eye and he trained his glass on a shallow depression near the edge of a thick wood. Scavengers were there, humans dressed in rags robbing the bodies of the dead. Most kept to the fringe of the forest, stripping the fallen of their armor and weapons and tossing the spoils into great sacks that they dragged away. They were a wretched-looking lot, and Max wondered if they would attack the goblin wagon. At least they'd largely cleared the road of bodies, Max thought. Reaching back, he rapped on the wagon's front shutters.

"What is it?" mumbled David, sounding sleepy.

"Come take a look."

A minute later, David stood by the nervous, champing mules and gazed down at the valley with a sad, contemplative expression. He pointed to a distant billow of black smoke rising from hills beyond the forest.

"I'd guess that's coming from the brayma's palace," he reflected. "Prusias may have bitten off more than he can chew with Aamon."

"Let's get going," said Max, twisting about to scan their surroundings. "It doesn't do any good to sit up here for all to see."

They descended the slope, passing the first body some hundred yards from the summit. Max tried to keep his eyes straight ahead, but it was impossible not to stare at the mounds of mangled vyes and men, arrow-riddled ogres in bronze breastplates, and two-headed ettins, all half submerged in cloudy pools of river water. The crows screamed at the wagon as they passed, a shrill chorus that drove the mules into a braying panic. Gripping the reins, Max held them to the road's center as the wagon lurched and bumped along.

The living disturbed him as much as the dead. While the fallen were an appalling spectacle, the scavengers moved like hungry phantoms among them, dark shapes that stole about the battlefield, crouching over corpses and digging through the scattered wreckage of tents, chariots, and palanquins. Many of the combatants had dressed splendidly for battle—brilliant silk pennons, embossed shields, and magnificent armor of enameled plate. But the stark realities of war had stripped them of their glory; these trappings had been trampled and churned into the raw earth until they were as muddy and tattered as their owners.

I guess we know why it was so quiet.

Shaking the reins, Max urged the mules to a quicker pace as several scavengers came too close for comfort. He studied them as the wagon hurried ahead, men and women with hollow, ghoulish faces. They stared at the wagon, dully registering its occupants before resuming their work with knives and fingers and teeth.

"Can I look now?" whispered Toby.

"No."

Max did not allow the smee to open his eyes for another twenty minutes, not until the last of the bodies were in their wake. He could now make out the source of smoke and saw David had been correct. Rising from a distant hilltop crowned with charred trees was a burning castle, its bailey, towers, and parapets little more than a brittle armature as it vomited plumes of black smoke into the lilac sky.

That night they camped away from the road, hiding the wagon behind a copse of alders and willows that lined an icy stream. While Toby strapped feedbags to the mules, Max looked in on David.

He found his roommate sitting in the back, propped against a cushion and scratching a nib ever so carefully on a sheet of spypaper.

"Just a minute," he muttered. "I'm almost finished." Blowing on the ink, he held the page up to the lantern so that its warmth would hasten the drying.

"Are you writing Sir Alistair?" asked Max.

"Ms. Richter. She left us a third sheet whose twin she keeps. I updated her on our progress and told her about the battlefield."

"Any word on Cooper?"

"No. I think if there was news—good or bad—she'd have written."

Max nodded and tried to smile, but his spirits were low. The horrors of the battlefield lingered in his mind. Rubbing his temples, he stared at the lantern's golden light.

"What if there is no Piter's Folly?" he wondered aloud. "What if it's just a burned-out hulk like that castle?"

David shrugged. "Then we'll gather whatever information we can and continue the search for Madam Petra. If we can't find her, we'll go home. War doesn't come with guarantees; we just have to do our best and hope that it's enough. Get some rest, Max. You're worn out. I'll keep watch with Toby."

Max was dead asleep in a warm nest of blankets when a thunderclap shook him awake. Bolting upright, he blinked stupidly out the window as he got his bearings. He'd been asleep for much longer than he'd intended, for they were on the move again and climbing uphill. Wind howled outside, bombarding the wagon with an icy mixture of sleet and rain. Pushing aside a cask of phosphoroil, Max peered through the small shutter that was just behind the driver's seat. David and Toby were hunched low, each disguised as goblins, as the smee drove the mules through the storm.

"Where are we?" Max yelled, struggling to be heard above the wind.

David turned to him, his eyes frosted slits. "Close!" he shouted back. "Ten, maybe fifteen miles. We should be there by dawn."

"Do you want me to drive?"

"I want you to brew some coffee!"

* * *

By morning, the weather had calmed. When Toby brought the wagon to a stop, Max climbed out and gazed around. The rain had dwindled to a steady drizzle, but the storm's fury was evident in every icy pool and battered branch. Max caught the smell of cooking fires on the wind, its aroma a welcome comfort after so many days on the road. Piter's Folly was just ahead. Through his glass, Max caught glimpses of the town amid the fogbanks below.

Once David renewed Max's illusion, the three squeezed next to one another on the driver's bench and eased the wagon downhill. Training his glass on the settlement, Max made out more details as the morning mists retreated.

Piter's Folly was built upon a wooded isle in the midst of an enormous gray lake. Apparently, the settlement had outgrown these limits, for many other buildings had been constructed upon platforms and rafts that radiated out from the isle like the spokes of a wheel. Smoke trickled from makeshift chimneys, and Max even heard the lowing calls of cattle carry across the still morning. His heart beat excitedly. The town seemed relatively unscathed by the war, and there still appeared to be thousands of people living here. Since Astaroth's rise to power, Max had not seen such a large settlement of free humans beyond Rowan's borders. He had often wondered whether any existed.

Once they reached level ground, a lane diverged from the road and curved toward the shoreline. Arriving at the water's edge, they discovered a heavy bell suspended from a pole near the end of a short pier. Stretching out, Toby rang the bell with all his might. Its notes echoed eerily across the lake, drowning out the loons and the lapping waves upon the pebbled sand. Moments later, there was an answering call from out in the gray mist.

"A ferryman will come," explained Toby, settling back under his blanket. "Remember, don't act too friendly. The humans need the goblins, but they don't like them much. I'll do the talking."

Max nodded and peered out into the gloom while the loons and bitterns called in the cold, wet morning. Thirty minutes passed before a shape emerged from the haze—a flat-bottomed raft capable of ferrying several wagons across. A dozen grim-looking men stood about its periphery, leaning on long oars that dripped with lake mud. The leader squinted at the cara-van and its three passengers. He barked something irritably in a Slavic-sounding language.

"I don't understand," said Toby nervously.

"Where are other wagons?" inquired the man, his words slow and suspicious. "You ring bell three times. Three rings means three wagons. I bring more men for three wagons. You pay for three wagons."

"Oh," said the smee. "I didn't know. Three it is, then, but we're in a hurry."

The man laughed bitterly. "Aren't we all?"

Max handed Toby some coins. Once they tossed the exor-bitant fee across, the ferrymen used their long poles to position the raft against the dock. Hurrying off, the men helped lead the mules aboard and secured the heavy wagon at the raft's center with a system of ropes. The workers were brisk and efficient but offered no greetings or conversation as they went about their busi-ness. Many were badly scarred, missing fingers or limping from some past injury. Max imagined each must have survived untold horrors before arriving at Piter's Folly, where there was safety in numbers and the lake's deep waters served as an enormous moat.

"What you bring?" asked the leader, glancing at the wagon once the ferry had pushed off.

"Coffee," replied Toby. "Some sugar. Two casks of phosphor-oil and a hundred iron ingots."

"You should have brought more iron," the ferryman grunted. "Blacksmiths are busy. People want weapons before they leave."

"Leave?" asked David. "Where are they going?"

The man shrugged and lit a pipe of strong, black tobacco. "West . . . north . . . wherever they can. Aamon's winning the war, little goblin. His armies will be here soon. I hear his scouts have passed in the night. Prusias may leave us be, but Aamon will not. No humans live in Dùn. Soon none will live here."

As they sculled ahead, the town slowly emerged as a cluster of brown and gray shapes against the morning gloom. Now Max could hear hammers and saws, a woman's call. They passed moored platforms where crops were growing in floating soil beds. A small cottage loomed into view at the end of a long dock. A bundled little boy was sitting at the end, dangling a hook into the water while the mutt at his side waited patiently for his breakfast. Upon sighting the goblins, the boy stiffened. His dark eyes followed them until they had eased past and out of sight.

They passed a number of similar houses and floating gardens before they reached the town's main dock. Anchored to the island, the landing was already crowded with crates and baggage and anxious residents. It appeared the ferryman was correct and many intended to flee before Aamon's forces arrived. It was a chaotic scene, and it was clear that some were displeased with the ferryman for transporting goblins when time was scarce and many desired passage across.

Ignoring the hissing rebukes and angry muttering, the ferryman tossed ropes to his associates, who moored the raft against the pier. Clearing a path through the multitude, the ferryman and his workers led the mules and wagon down the ramp and gruffly reminded the crowd that honest travelers were to be left to their business, lest trade should wither. Cuffing a youth who was prying at the caravan doors, the ferryman repeated his admonition in a louder voice. He was apparently a person of some influence, for the throng withdrew so that the caravan now had an unobstructed path to the island's narrow lanes. Emptying his pipe, the ferryman came around to where Toby was waiting anxiously.

"I can't take you back until nightfall. If I were you, I would not haggle too hard. Watch yourself and meet me here when the bell rings for evening watch."

Toby nodded and gave the man several coppers by way of gratitude. Shaking the reins, he called out to the mules and they clopped forward, brushing past the crowd and down into the lane.

The way was relatively narrow but well maintained, encircling the island while smaller lanes branched off, leading to grazing pastures and gardens, shops and dwellings. Everywhere, there were cats slinking about in their wake or darting across their path. Toby shivered at the sight of them.

"I don't like cats," he confessed. "Don't like the way they look at me—like they know a secret."

"I wonder why there are so many," said Max.

"Keeps the rodents down," David muttered, "and some believe they drive evil spirits away."

"Now let's see," said Toby, "Kolbyt said it's the largest house at the end of the lane that runs along the shoreline. Here we go. . . ."

Max thought it a rather conspicuous address for a smuggler. The house was by far the largest and most luxurious residence they'd seen, a pale yellow Victorian with three stories, a dozen gables, and a half-dozen chimneys poking from its slate roof.

Situated on a sloping, pastured outcropping, the estate boasted its own herds and a private dock that Max could glimpse through occasional gaps in the hedge. A white fence bordered the property, and Toby drove the mules within its broad gate and down the gravel driveway to the main residence.

"I thought we'd be knocking on a door in some alley," said Max. "What's Petra's legitimate business supposed to be?"

"Furs mostly," replied Toby. "And land. You can't build anything on Piter's Folly without going through her, and she wrings out every last copper. Speaking of which, I'll need more money—at least fifty silvers' worth. Gold is better if you have some."

Max counted out the money and handed a small pouch to the smee, who weighed it lovingly before reining the mules to a halt on the circular drive. The front door opened and a young girl in a green smock slipped outside, twirling a paintbrush between her slender fingers. Leaning out over the porch, she gazed down at them disdainfully.

"What do you want?" she said, speaking English and sounding bored.

Whipping off his hat, Toby stood and bowed. "Greetings," he croaked in Kolbyt's hoarse voice. "We beg an audience with Madam Petra."

"You're supposed to go round back, you know," sniffed the girl. "The service entrance."

"Very sorry," said Toby, reaching for the reins.

"Don't bother," she scoffed. "Madam Petra's busy and cannot possibly see you. Try again in a week."

Toby seemed to anticipate this. The ensuing negotiations were swift and exceedingly expensive. When the girl had weighed Max's purse in her hand and counted every last coin, she turned on her heel and walked back to the front door.

"*Mother!*" she bellowed. "There are three goblins here to see you!"

"Don't shout, dear," came a silky voice from an upstairs window. "Take them around back and Dmitri will meet them in the rose garden. Offer them something to drink."

The girl fixed them with an acid stare. "Would you like something to drink?"

"Wine if you have it," said Toby cheerfully. "Water if you don't."

Rolling her eyes, the girl shooed them impatiently toward a garlanded gate that led around the house. Once Skeedle started the mules in that direction, she stormed back inside and slammed the door shut behind her.

"She's pleasant," muttered David, ducking a low-hanging branch.

"This isn't quite what I expected," whispered Max, gazing through the house's windows as they wound around toward the back. Inside, he saw maidservants dusting and cleaning rooms whose rich appointments evoked a tranquil estate rather than some secret smuggler's den. Passing by one broad window, Max spied the easel and canvas where the girl had been working on a still life in the style of the Dutch masters. He saw no evidence that Madam Petra's household was in a state of alarm or intended to flee before Yuga or Aamon's armies.

The lane ended in an impeccably manicured lawn that sloped deeply down to the lake and a small boathouse. Several groundskeepers were already at work, picking up broken branches and twigs and retying oilcloth covers that protected the rosebushes. They glanced up at the visitors with only mild interest. Apparently goblin caravans were nothing new.

It was almost a minute before Max observed the heads.

There were seven of them in total, each spitted on tall poles placed throughout the gardens. They were in various states of decomposition, some little more than skulls while others were jarringly fresh. Four of the heads had belonged to goblins, two were human, and the last possessed the feral, wolfish face of a vye. When Toby finally noticed them, he nearly fainted.

"Here's your wine," said a voice behind them.

The three turned to see the girl bearing a silver tray with three goblets of red wine. Setting it on a small table near the roses, she whispered something to the nearest gardener before turning to stare at them.

"My mother's secretary will be out shortly," she announced. "Make yourselves comfortable."

And with a strange little smile, she hurried back to the house, skipping over the shallow steps of the back patio to slip inside the door.

"Something isn't right," hissed Toby. "They know something. We should go!"

"Try to relax," whispered David. "Let's drink the wine and wait for our hosts."

"D-didn't you see the heads?" stammered the smee.

"Of course I did," replied David evenly. "Take a deep breath. You're going to be perfect. You know what to say?"

Nodding weakly, Toby climbed down from the wagon. Taking seats around the table, the trio sipped the strong red wine while the wind blew wisps of cool mist off the lake. They sat in silence, each watching the house and trying to ignore the seven grisly shadows on the lawn.

Almost an hour had passed when the back door opened. A young man emerged, fine-featured with a slight build and black hair that was combed back from a widow's peak. He wore an embroidered waistcoat over a black shirt and plum-colored pants that were tucked into Hessian boots. His smile was prim, his manner formal as he came to a halt before them.

"I am Dmitri," he said. "Madam Petra's secretary. And who are you?"

Toby stood and bowed. "Kolbyt of the Broadbrim clan," he announced. "I have traded with Madam Petra before."

"Yes," mused the man, plucking at his goatee. "I seem to recall your face . . . and who are the others? We do not like strangers unless they bring us very pretty things."

"My kinsman Skeedle and our servant, Hrunta," replied the smee, gesturing at each in turn. "We have brought oil and iron, coffee and sugar to please the Great Piter Lady and beg an audience to discuss a proposal."

"What is your proposal?" inquired the secretary pointedly. "You may tell it to me and I will relay it to Madam Petra. She is very busy."

"I am sorry," said Toby, shrugging. "But my news is for Madam Petra's ears alone—the great Plümpka would have my skin if we should tell anyone else."

This did not please the secretary. His eyes grew hard. "Plümpka might take your skin, but Madam Petra will have your head should you waste her time. Look about you, goblin. Better that you tell me your proposal and let me decide whether it is worth intruding upon my lady."

"Kolbyt must humbly refuse," said Toby, bowing low and offering the man a handful of silver.

"How crude," the secretary muttered, pocketing the coins nonetheless. "And why did Plümpka not come? If the proposal is so valuable, surely the chief of the Broadbrims would make the journey himself."

"He is unwell," explained the smee, bowing another apology. "And the Ravenswood Spur has grown very dangerous. A mighty battle was fought not two days' journey from here."

"Yes," mused Dmitri, frowning. "Lord Kargen's lands. He shall host no more parties, I hear. A pity, but so be it. You may see many more battles ere long. King Aamon's armies are swift." The man squinted past them at the broad lake where the sun was peeking through the haze. "Very well, you and I will continue our conversation inside. Your companions must wait here. I make no promises, but if you are who you say you are, I may be able to secure a brief audience." Gesturing for Toby to follow, the secretary flicked a parting glance at Max and David. "If we do not return within the hour, your friend will not be coming."

The smee's shoulders drooped as though he were marching to his own funeral. Clearing his throat, he ordered his companions to wait for him before following the secretary up to Madam Petra's house.

Max squirmed as he watched them go. There was something profoundly unsettling about this immaculate house with its pristine grounds and quiet, watchful servants. It set him on edge more than any of the black markets and seedy dens he'd visited in Zenuvia. Plodding behind the secretary, Toby looked so alone and helpless. Max prayed that he remembered everything Kolbyt had told him; he also prayed the brutish goblin had not played them false.

As Toby disappeared into the house, the groundskeepers set down their tools. They walked single file up the garden path, a silent procession that slipped inside after the secretary. When the last had entered, the door was closed and locked.

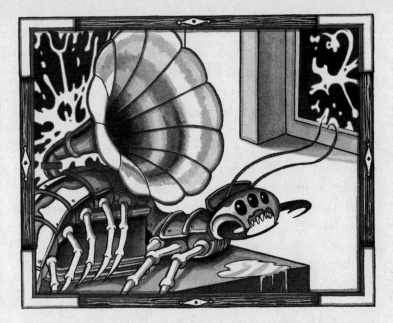

~ 8 ~

MADAM PETRA
AND THE PINLEGS

As the minutes ticked past, Max and David sat outside while the smee tried to bluff their way in to see the smuggler. The waiting was intolerable. Every so often, Max shifted uneasily in his chair and searched the many windows for any signs of activity within the huge yellow house. There were none—only the mocking reflections of the gray lake and the sun rising behind them.

"How long has he been in there?" Max muttered to David, mindful that they were undoubtedly being watched. It seemed ages since Toby had gone inside.

"Thirty minutes," David whispered, sipping his wine. "Try to relax—Toby's a professional."

"In ten minutes, I'm going in."

"You'll spoil all our plans."

"I'm not going to sit by while—"

Max broke off as the back door opened and several gardeners filed out. He craned his neck for a glimpse of Toby and exhaled as the smee emerged, a noticeable bounce to his step as he walked to the wagon with Dmitri and a pair of workers. After instructing them on which cargo to unload, Toby called out to his companions.

"Skeedle. Hrunta. Come. The Great Piter Lady has agreed to hear us."

Although the secretary was smiling, the man's eyes were spiteful. Max guessed that he either opposed his lady's decision or had hoped to wring further bribes before their interview. He did not return their hasty bows as they stepped across the threshold and entered the smuggler's house.

They followed the man through several exquisite rooms. Nightingales chirped from within gilded cages and flowers abounded: purple orchids, stargazer lilies, brilliant red tulips, and others so exotic and lush that they suggested an underlying magic or technology at work. After weeks of travel in the gray and wintry wild, the house's color and warmth were almost disorienting.

They found the daughter back at work on her still life, loading her brush with paint as she studied the arrangement.

Dmitri cleared his throat. "Katarina, your mother would like you to sit in on the meeting."

"I'm busy."

"She insists," said Dmitri, beckoning.

"Isn't that your job?"

A vein throbbed in the man's temple. "Your mother no doubt intends that you should someday replace me," he said with a tight smile. "For the young lady to do so, she must learn the family business."

"Very well," the girl sighed, wiping her brush on a rag and plunking it into a jar of turpentine. Glaring at the goblins, she swept past them and ran up a grand staircase.

"My lady indulges her daughter," remarked the secretary stiffly, leading them up the stairs where they passed yet more paintings and sculpture and palms in copper planters. As they climbed to the third floor, Max heard music playing, a tinny warbling like an old jazz recording. Reaching the third-floor landing, Dmitri led them down a long hallway that terminated at a conspicuously stout door. It was barely ajar, just enough to let the music and Katarina's voice escape into the hall.

"Have their heads and be done!" the girl hissed. "I want to finish my painting."

"I'll not ask again," replied a woman's voice, gentle but unyielding.

A stamp of a foot and then silence.

Dmitri knocked delicately. "The goblins are here, Madam Petra," he announced. "May I show them in?"

"Do."

Max and David trailed after Toby into a paneled office whose far wall was lined with enormous windows that provided a panoramic view of the misty lake. Huge artworks dominated the other walls, abstract spatters of luminescent paint on black or red canvases. To the left was a long conference table, to the right a comfortable sitting area where Katarina was pouting by a colossal fireplace. Straight ahead was a small desk. Behind it stood the smuggler.

Madam Petra was the most striking woman Max had ever

seen. She was younger than he'd imagined—midthirties, with porcelain-white skin and long auburn hair that fell in a braid to her waist. Her understated dress was in marked contrast to her ostentatious house: a simple black jacket, gray tweed pants, and black riding boots. She wore only one piece of jewelry, a diamond choker whose central stone must have been worth half of Piter's Folly. Offering a polite smile, she gestured to three chairs across her desk before returning her attention to several documents. When Max and the others were seated, Dmitri pulled up a fourth.

"We will not be needing you, Dmitri," said Madam Petra offhandedly, jotting something on the top paper. "Katarina will sit in for today."

"My lady," said the secretary, holding up his hands. "It is merely goblins—no doubt it would be better for Katarina to sit in with the Baron of Marrovia. That would be more educat—"

The smuggler glanced sharply up from her papers with eyes that flashed like emeralds. The man fell silent at once. When Madam Petra spoke, her voice was dangerously soft.

"As you say, we have several Broadbrims with us this morning. I value their clan greatly and am anxious to hear their proposal. And we must disagree; I think Katarina has much to learn from this meeting. For example, she has already seen you break a cardinal rule of our profession and compromise another client's identity. Did you intend to impart such a clumsy lesson, Dmitri?"

The man turned ashen. It was clear that he craved Madam Petra's approval on many levels.

"I—I apologize," he stammered. "With your permission, I'll take my leave."

"Very good," said Petra coolly. "Please tell the chefs that I'd like supper to be ready by eight—and no more fatty meats in pastries or boiling everything to shoe leather. Delicacy. Elegance. Subtlety. I know they object to Nestor, but ask him to lend a hand. I think he trained as a saucier. . . ."

Once the chastened secretary closed the door, Madam Petra turned to her daughter. "Katarina, come and sit by me."

"I'm fine over here. Goblins stink."

"I imagine they say the same of you. Come over here—I want your help."

At this, Katarina dragged herself up from the chaise and came to sit on her mother's lap. She was too old for such things—eleven or twelve—but the girl seemed an unusual combination of old and young, absent and present.

"How am I supposed to help?" she asked, blankly surrendering her cheek for a kiss.

"Well," said Madam Petra, "we have a problem. And I know you like to solve problems."

The girl nodded. Max glanced uneasily at David and Toby, but the two kept their attention on their hostess.

"Here's our dilemma," continued Madam Petra. "The kingdom is at war and Aamon's armies are rampaging across the land. And here comes an unguarded, solitary goblin wagon braving the Ravenswood Spur with a pittance of goods and asking for a private audience. Mind you, the Broadbrims haven't even sent anyone senior to conduct the business—just a junior trader and two others I've never met before. Now, they must have known I'd have their heads for such appalling insolence and yet . . . here they are. Why haven't I taken their heads, sweet daughter?"

The girl frowned and stared at the three visitors. "They're either crazy or something's off," she murmured. "Maybe they're acting without their leader's approval. Perhaps they've secretly brought something that we would find valuable—something they didn't want Dmitri to know about. Of course, they might not be goblins at all; perhaps they're imposters."

"Hmm," said Petra, considering her daughter's analysis. "Each suggestion seems plausible. Be a dear and flip the record for us while we talk. While you're at it, you might retrieve that marvelous little thing I showed you the other day."

"I don't want to touch that. It frightens me."

"Do we always get to do what we want?"

"No, Mother."

Easing her daughter off her lap, the smuggler turned her eyes on Toby as the smee cleared his throat.

"We hoped to speak alone, my lady," he said, glancing at the girl. "Our proposal is sensitive. It would not do for this information to go beyond this room and, as you know, children are prone to talk."

"Your proposal is safe with us," replied Madam Petra, sounding bored. "Let's have it, then."

Toby edged forward in his seat and spoke as Katarina flipped the record and placed the needle at its edge. Music issued from the antique, pouring into the room from a polished horn that resembled an enormous silver flower. The recording evoked a powerful flood of memories; Scott McDaniels had often listened to this very album whenever he sat at the dining room table to do his taxes. Max blinked; it was such a strange image and triggered such a jarring, incongruous jumble of emotions. No wonder tyrants often outlawed music; it was a shortcut to the soul. Max wondered how Madam Petra managed to have such forgotten luxuries and realized it must have been a gift from the Workshop. The smee's words snapped him from these thoughts.

"We have found gold down deep beneath our burial halls," Toby explained. "Ullmach says it is a rich lode, the richest we have found for many generations. But we cannot reach it without disturbing our ancestors, a blasphemy Plümpka will not permit. He suggested that the Great Piter Lady might have friends with tools—*machines*—that could mine gold more carefully than picks and shovels and fire-rock."

"And what would I get for introducing you to these friends?"

"Twenty percent of the gold."

The smuggler gave an utterly charming laugh and walked to a small bar by the sitting area. She moved like an athlete, every step fluid and graceful. Max now recalled why her face seemed so familiar—he had seen it many times on magazine covers and television. Madam Petra had been a very famous person in her former life. Unlike most humans, it was a life she seemed to remember, even as she carved out her own little empire in the new order. She now offered the goblins another drink. When they declined, she poured herself a glass of champagne.

"You want me to introduce you to my friends for twenty percent of an unknown sum?" She laughed again and sat down. "What a preposterous notion. I won't even broach the subject with them for less than fifty."

"Fifty is too much," Toby countered. "Your friends will want their share as well."

"Which is better? Fifty percent of something or one hundred percent of nothing?" she inquired, blinking innocently. "If you're concerned with my friends' share, then we can agree to a seventy percent commission and you let me worry about compensating them."

"And what do we get for such generous terms?"

"Your gold will be mined, processed, and stamped into forms of your choosing without so much as disturbing the dust on your ancestors' tombs. Your people can oversee the operation and we'll even let you keep one of the machines once the business has concluded."

"That sounds good," piped up David enthusiastically. "But we would need proof such machines exist."

"Oh, they exist. My friends really do design some marvelous things," she replied, sipping her champagne. "And I can acquire just about anything they make. For example, look at this little prototype they've just concocted. Bring it here, Katarina."

The smuggler's daughter brought over a cylindrical tube. It looked like the sort of thing an architect might have used to carry his drawings, except that it was made of polished silver and engraved with runic symbols. Setting it on her mother's desk, the girl unfastened a series of clasps and removed the top. Max leaned far over in his chair to peer inside the tube's dark interior.

Something was peering back.

There was a scratching sound within, faint and metallic as though dozens of legs were pricking and tapping at the tube's interior. Slowly, cautiously, a pair of long silvery antennae extended from the opening, flicking the air like buggy whips. An instant later, a three-foot centipede spilled forth and scuttled onto the desk.

At first, Max thought it was a machine. Its pincers resembled retracting steel hooks while its body segments were a metallic blue-gray with two ridges of tiny green lights that ran along the length of its back. But as Max looked closer, he noticed something very much like saliva moistening the creature's maxillae, and its many semitranslucent legs seemed wholly organic. The creature was some sort of revolting hybrid of insect and machine, a Workshop abomination now splayed upon the smuggler's desk. Toby was the first to find his voice.

"Is . . . is that *demonic*?" he wondered, his jaw hanging slack.

"Remarkable intuition," said Madam Petra, removing a pair of slim spectacles from a compartment within the tube's top and slipping them on. "How unusual for a goblin. My friends call this a pinlegs. And when I wear these glasses, it understands and obeys my thoughts. For example . . ."

In a heartbeat, the pinlegs leaped off the desk and clambered up Toby's leg. Clinging to his chest, it spread its mandibles wide so that their razor tips were poised on either side of his throat.

"No sudden movements," the smuggler warned. "Its bite is highly venomous."

The smee was trembling like a leaf. "Wh-why do you threaten us?" he stammered.

Madam Petra shook her head. "Oh, I don't threaten," she laughed, allowing Katarina back on her lap. "Those who threaten are simply indecisive. We're either partners or we're not. And if we're not, you die. But before we make that decision, my friend, we need to know who or what you really are. My eyes are only human, but this little pinlegs allows me to see what it sees. And it sees quite a lot. . . ."

Every muscle in Max's body was tensed. He could have a knife to the smuggler's throat before she could blink, but that might mean Toby's death. Sitting absolutely still, he studied the woman—the tiny muscles at the corners of her mouth, the furrow of her brow, the dilation of her pupils. Cooper would have known her intentions before she did; Max hoped he could do the same. Long seconds passed while the smuggler appraised them. At last the pinlegs released Toby, its legs retreating down his chest as it turned and scuttled to the floor. The smee exhaled and mopped sweat from his gray-green brow.

"It appears you really are a goblin," said Madam Petra politely. "But what are your friends, I wonder? They look strangely out of focus. Have a look, Katarina. You see things I don't."

The girl slipped the glasses onto her slender face while the pinlegs wove in and out of the goblins' legs. Max remained still, ignoring the nauseating brush of its metallic body and clicking legs as it stopped and peered up at each, its mandibles aquiver.

"I still see goblins," reported the girl. "They're still there, but there's something else flickering behind . . . flickering like your projector machine. It's a boy, Mother! He has blond hair and he's very pale. And . . . and he's missing a hand!"

Madam Petra raised her eyebrows. For the very first time, Max saw a glint of fear in her cold green eyes. "And the other?" she asked, her voice taut.

"He's a boy, too," the girl whispered. "But a light is shining through him. He's so bright I can hardly see his face. But it's beautiful . . . like something in a dream."

"I see," said Madam Petra. "Katarina, my sweet, you are looking at David Menlo and Max McDaniels. They come from Rowan. Max is the very Bragha Rùn you cheered for in King Prusias's Arena. Do you remember that day?"

The girl nodded, both frightened and fascinated as she stared at them. Removing the glasses from her daughter's head, the smuggler folded them carefully and set them on the table.

"This is unexpected. If you intend violence, kindly leave my daughter out of it."

"We intend nothing of the kind," said David, dissipating their illusions and letting her see him plainly. "We've been told you're a person worthy of great respect. I apologize for the disguise, but surely you understand our need for secrecy."

"Why didn't you announce yourselves to Dmitri?"

"Because we don't trust him," replied David. "Your servants inform on your activities to Prusias, as you know full well."

"Ah," said Madam Petra, tapping her chin as though searching her memory. "I see that Sir Alistair is more than the foolish little popinjay I'd taken him to be. And you're quite a clever fellow, David Menlo, although I suppose I shouldn't be surprised. Do you see what he got me to do, Katarina?"

"He made you greedy," observed the girl, scraping paint from her fingernails. "He made you boastful. You admitted you had friends at the Workshop and even showed him their new invention. Now he knows you *still* have friends there. He learned a lot from you, Mother."

Madam Petra clucked her tongue. "Yes, he did," she allowed. "They might not trust Dmitri, but I wonder why they trust us? With the price that's on their heads, I could set up as a duchess. Think of that, Katarina—no more tedious affairs with smelly goblins or witches or penniless refugees. We'd be the richest women in the land!"

"I thought you said you didn't threaten," said Max, ignoring the woman's playful smile.

She merely shrugged. "My boy, nine automatic weapons have been targeted upon you since you sat down. Is that a threat or merely a fact? I've seen how quick you are, Max, but I doubt your companions could even rise before they were cut to ribbons."

"We aren't here to quarrel with you," interjected David. "We traveled a long way to speak with you in the hope that you can deliver a message to someone senior at the Workshop—preferably Jesper Rasmussen."

"Jesper's irrelevant," said Petra, dismissing the man with a wave. "He's a figurehead. The chief engineers run the Workshop. Unless you count concessions, Jesper hasn't made anything in decades. What is it you want from them?"

"I'm going to be as direct as I can," said David, leaning forward and staring hard at her. "We believe Prusias means to attack Rowan even if we meet his demands. We believe the Workshop is developing something special for him—some sort of secret weapon. We want an alliance with the Workshop. If

the Workshop cannot join with us, we want you to share whatever information you can about their activities and this weapon
they're developing. Is that direct enough?"

"Admirably so," said the smuggler. "What you want is impossible, of course, but you did lay it out nice and neatly. And you
have made me curious. . . . Why on earth would the Workshop
jeopardize its existence and technologies to join with little Rowan
on the eve of her destruction? What is possibly in it for them?"

"Freedom," replied David simply. "A chance to help humanity and reunite with old friends. This might be their last chance
to break free unless they intend to serve Prusias and his kind
forever. Is that what they intend?"

"They intend to survive," said Madam Petra frankly. "Even
with Elias Bram's return, an alliance with Rowan is the shortest
path to their own destruction. Candidly, I'm amazed that Rowan
would make such an absurd proposal, much less preach to others
about helping humanity. While your Director was sipping tea
and hiding behind her walls and treaties, the rest of civilization
faded away. Do you remember what the world used to be like?"

"Of course."

"No," said Madam Petra, rising to pace before the broad
window. "I mean do you *remember*? Not some foggy, pleasant
haze about life before Astaroth, but how things really used to
be? Do you remember governments and cities, skyscrapers and
television . . . Elvis! Do you remember Elvis and Andy Warhol
and Star Wars and satellites?"

"Yes," said Max, realizing that almost anyone else would
think the woman was raving mad. "And I remember Miles
Davis. My dad used to listen to this album. And I remember
you. My mother would buy any magazine with your picture on
it; she said you had style."

The smuggler gave a rueful smile and glanced at her

daughter. "Katarina remembers, too. I wish she didn't. We were living in Paris when they announced that the government had been dissolved. The authorities told us to paint Astaroth's sign on every door and window, lest the Demon's interrogators come knocking. You should have seen it—bankers, lawyers, doctors, and officials all weeping in the middle of the night and painting that terrible symbol on anything they could reach. And for most of them, it didn't even matter. They were still sent to prisons or reeducation camps; they still died in plagues and fires or fell to whatever came scratching at their windows once the city really fell into chaos. The things I've witnessed . . ."

The woman fell silent at this and turned to gaze out at the placid gray lake.

"When my husband was dying, we used every contact and pulled every string to gain admittance to the Rowan field office. Niels had been bitten by a vye, you see. He was infected. Each day, his sanity ebbed and he became more dangerous. We had to tie him down . . . I couldn't let Katarina near him. I begged your Agents for aid, but they had no more antidote and cited 'other priorities.' In the end, I had to kill Niels myself. So you can imagine I find it a little difficult—a little *amusing*—that Rowan should presume to make appeals based on duty to one's fellow man. But your people did teach me a very valuable lesson—when things go dark, you look after your own and adapt as best you can."

"I can't argue with anything you've said," replied David. "When Astaroth rose to power, the world was falling apart. Rowan couldn't help one in a thousand who needed and deserved their help. But Piter's Folly is an outlier, Madam Petra. Whatever free humanity exists is seeking shelter at Rowan—hundreds are arriving every day and the harbor towns and inland settlements are growing. Whether you love Rowan or despise it, our realm represents the best chance for humanity to survive and maintain some semblance of freedom. Surely the Workshop doesn't want to play a role in its destruction."

"Katarina," said Madam Petra, leaving the window and smoothing her daughter's hair. "Dmitri will be wondering why this meeting has run so long. I want you to go downstairs and ask the chefs to make you some lunch. If he pesters you, say that we're discussing a possible gold-mine partnership. The Broadbrims are afraid of anyone else knowing their discovery and thus we don't want to be disturbed. If he seems impatient, make him sit for a portrait. I want him occupied. Can you do that?"

"Yes," replied the girl, slipping out the door and closing it firmly behind her.

Madam Petra turned back to her guests. "My sources tell me that there are over eight hundred thousand people living within your realm and almost ninety thousand sheltered within Rowan's outer walls. How many of those can you muster to defend it? How many of those are old men and women, or children too young to heft a sword or stand a watch? Prusias has over twenty million subjects; his main army is nearly bigger than your entire population and there are no crones or quaking boys among its ranks. The King of Blys doesn't need the Workshop to conquer Rowan; he just needs an excuse. And you gave him one when Bram destroyed Gràvenmuir. . . ."

"Perhaps Prusias is getting ahead of himself," said David. "We passed the remnants of his forces on the road. It looked like Aamon is winning."

Madam Petra gazed about the room, at its rich décor and strange luminescent paintings, before shrugging at David. "Does it look like I plan to flee from Aamon?"

"No," said Max. "But the docks of Piter's Folly are filled with others who aren't as optimistic."

"Of course they are," laughed Petra, returning to her seat.

"Who do you think is feeding the rumors? The only thing I like better than a frantic buyer is a desperate seller. The sheep are selling me their homes and property for a pittance. And when Prusias wins this war, they'll come skulking to my door and buy them back at thrice the price. War doesn't destroy fortunes; it makes them."

"How do you sleep at night?" asked Max, incredulous at her callous pragmatism.

"Like a baby," she purred, finishing her champagne. "It's a hard world we live in. If others aren't smart enough to play the game, it's better that I have their chips."

"What makes you so certain that Prusias will win?" asked David.

"Now, that's valuable information," replied Madam Petra, examining her nails. "What will you give me for it?"

"Some valuable information in return," said David.

The smuggler flashed the very smile that had once charmed the world. "Oh, I like this," she said, rubbing her hands together. "Dazzle me, David Menlo. What little tidbit is worth Prusias's big secret?"

David gestured toward Toby. "My friend here is not a goblin."

Madam Petra blinked. Her smile faded. "Of course he is," she scoffed. "I saw him through the pinlegs."

"And the pinlegs was mistaken," retorted David. "Allow me to present the illustrious smee. Toby, if you'd be so kind as to take your natural shape."

A moment later, Madam Petra was staring at the smee's mottled, yamlike body slouching in her expensive chair. The woman's lip curled.

"Charmed," said Toby, dipping his twisty head.

"Er . . . likewise," she muttered, glancing quizzically at the creature before returning her attention to David. "And you think *this* is worth information about Prusias's war machines?"

"Tut-tut," chided David. "You're not seeing the possibilities, my dear Madam Petra. Our associate just fooled your pinlegs. He—"

"Fooled the pinlegs," she repeated, sitting up. "His aura wasn't detected. . . ."

"Our particular talent," declared Toby proudly. "I must confess I was somewhat pleased to see my companion's illusion fall a smidgeon short of the smee standard. You see, many have tried to replicate—"

The smuggler cut him off with a pointed question. "Do you ever work on commission, my fine fellow?"

"I—I haven't," stammered the smee. "But I . . . well, I suppose we could arrange something. Perhaps we could discuss it over dinner?" he added hopefully.

"Very well," said Madam Petra, sitting back. "One interesting tidbit deserves another, and your friend *is* most interesting." Once again she put on the spectacles and called the pinlegs over from where it had been lurking by the fireplace. It responded at once, clicking over the rugs and hardwood floors and climbing atop the desk like some hideous remote-controlled toy. Coming to rest by its tube, the creature settled down in a twitching, salivating jumble of legs, segments, and pincers. The smuggler gazed down at it.

"Prusias will win this war whenever he chooses," she said softly. "His initial losses to Aamon and Rashaverak are merely drawing them in. Aamon has committed almost all of his forces to the eastern front and Rashaverak has done the same in the south. When the time is right, Prusias will send in his little pinlegs and victory will be his."

"How is that going to defeat an army?" asked David, peering closely at the creature.

"I don't know precisely," replied Madam Petra. "My contacts

gave me this prototype as a curiosity, but they said it isn't 'paired.' I haven't the slightest idea what that means, but my contact joked that if I ever see those little green lights flash red, I'd better run for the hills and never look back. Apparently, it has something to do with the demon that would normally be trapped inside it, but they gave no particulars. In any case, I hear that Prusias is amused by his enemies' early victories; they're allowing him to test the loyalty of his braymas and purge his own ranks of traitors. But whenever he chooses, this war will be brought to a swift conclusion. And once Queen Lilith sees the others' fate, she will race to make a deal and cling to whatever lands and power she can. That will leave only Rowan. My advice is to submit to whatever terms Prusias demands and hope that he indulges Rowan as a vassal state."

At her command, the pinlegs crawled back inside its tube, whereupon she closed and carefully fastened the lid.

"But the Workshop—" said Max.

"The Workshop cannot help you, dear," interrupted Madam Petra, removing the glasses. "Without Prusias, they lose their technologies and they would never risk such an outcome. You're trying to appeal to their sense of humanity, but do you understand that most of their population has *never* been above-ground? Most have never felt real sunlight or swum in the sea or even met anyone from 'topside.' From their perspective, we might as well live on a different planet. You want them to help save the world, but their world is a different one than ours. Furthermore, they recognize and understand something that you do not."

"What's that?" asked David.

"You cannot win," replied Madam Petra matter-of-factly. She gestured at the huge paintings. "Do you know what these are?"

They gazed about at the enormous canvases and their

strangely beautiful patterns and splatters of luminescent paint. Max shook his head.

"They're demons," said the smuggler, gazing up at each. "Or at least, the remains of demons. Minor ones, of course—gifts from a generous brayma following a médim. If you've ever attended such a gathering, you know the demons engage in three types of contests: *alennya, amann,* and *ahülmm.* The first two are pleasant enough—beautiful, violent, and familiar. But the *ahülmm* is like nothing I've ever seen before. It's a performance, gentlemen—the ritual suicide of one who sacrifices his life for the sake of entertaining the audience. As the demon recites its death poem, it spills its life and essence onto the canvas. The demon perishes, but the canvas remains behind as art. If the *ahülmm*'s performance is admirable, one can almost see the poem and hear the words in the painting. As you can imagine, such works are priceless."

"And what does that have to do with Rowan's fate?" asked Max.

"Sometimes a demon will perform *ahülmm* to honor a debt, but the vast majority are voluntary," explained Madam Petra. "Think about that for a moment: an immortal spontaneously choosing to end its existence for the sake of an artistic gesture! I've seen a four-thousand-year-old rakshasa—a lord of immense standing and influence—perform *ahülmm* for no other reason than to surprise and entertain his guests. Do you really think you can win against such beings?"

She was smiling at them, sad and bemused as if they were already dead. From far off, they heard a bell ringing faintly in the town. The sound was harsh, a discordant clanging that caused Madam Petra to rise again from her chair and walk to a window along the southern wall. Brushing aside some drapes, she leaned close and gazed back toward the town.

"Good God," she muttered. "The docks are on fire.

Storehouses, too; all that bloody silk going up in flames. What the hell is going on?" Frowning, she strode over to the door and flung it open.

Smoke billowed into the room, thick and noxious. The door must have been soundproofed, for as soon as the smuggler opened it, Max heard shouts and commotion below—a frenzied din of footsteps and shattering glass as though a terrible struggle were taking place on the stairs and landings. Katarina's voice sounded from the hallway, terrified beyond all reason as she screamed for her mother.

"Where are you?" the girl cried. "I can't see!"

"Here!" exclaimed Madam Petra, racing into the hallway and snatching her daughter. The child's hair was singed, her face streaked with soot and tears. Dashing up, Max took hold of the door, peering out into the hallway only to see it filled with oily smoke. There was an appalling crash and a gurgling shriek followed by the sound of rapid footsteps coming down the long hall. Through the smoke, Max glimpsed a hazy, man-shaped form running at the door. He slammed it shut, bracing it with his shoulder as automatic locking mechanisms slid into place. The door trembled as the intruder crashed against it.

"How strong is this?" asked Max, glancing at Madam Petra.

"It should withstand even a pulse grenade," she said.

Max eyed it doubtfully as it gave a groan and a crack appeared above the frame.

"Is there another way out of here?"

But the smuggler didn't answer; she had rushed back over to her desk and was pressing a number of hidden controls. As Max watched, the fireplace revolved away, revealing a spiral staircase hidden inside the chimney. Rushing to a small portrait, Madam Petra flung it aside and began working the combination to a hidden safe.

"Take Katarina!" she shouted, gesturing at the secret passage. "I'll be right behind. I can't leave my jewel—"

She broke off, coughing as smoke and hot ashes started pouring into the room from various vents. Several of the drapes began to catch fire. Katarina screamed as the door shook again. Plaster cracked and fell from the walls to shatter on the floor.

"Grab that!" Max yelled to David, pointing at the metal tube. Snatching up Toby, David hurried over to Madam Petra's desk and scooped up the pinlegs. "Can you put out—"

The room erupted in machine-gun fire.

Hundreds of bullets sprayed the chairs where Max and the others had been sitting only seconds earlier, splintering the chairs and embedding themselves in the floor and walls. Several struck a metal sculpture and ricocheted about the room, shattering lamps and tearing canvases. At first Max thought they were under attack, but he realized the guns were part of the room's defenses.

"The controls are malfunctioning!" yelled Petra. "Stay down!"

Max dropped flat to the floor as guns continued to belch forth a stream of bullets. Every second or two, he heard a lethal *ping!* as a bullet struck metal and ricocheted. Beside him the door trembled, groaning and shaking as their assailants tried to bludgeon their way in. Its reinforced frame was bending, warping inward and allowing great torrents of heat and smoke to pour in. It would not hold much longer.

The firing stopped as quickly as it had begun; they heard a staccato *click-click-click* as the hidden weapons ran out of ammunition. Max was up immediately, rushing over to Madam Petra, who had abandoned the safe to shield her daughter.

"The passage leads to the roof," she gasped. "There's a—"

Katrina shrieked as a grappling hook shattered a nearby window and snapped back to anchor in the sill. Max rushed over and peered down the window to see a hooded figure scaling the wall. Grabbing a bronze bust from a nearby pedestal, Max hurled it down. The heavy sculpture smashed into the attacker's head with a sickening sound, sending him crashing down to the flagstones. Max wheeled to find his friends.

"David!" he shouted, but it was Toby who answered.

"Max, I need your help!"

Dashing across the room, Max found David sprawled unconscious at the base of Madam Petra's desk. He'd been shot in the thigh and shoulder. At a glance, Max could tell that the shoulder wound was superficial, but the leg was bad. Blood pumped steadily from the wound, spreading over David's hand where he'd pressed against it.

Max glanced at Toby. "Take the pinlegs and follow Petra out the fireplace," he ordered. "If we don't get out, you're to get that thing to Ms. Richter. Do you understand?"

The smee understood perfectly. In an instant, he changed into a red-capped lutin that snatched up the pinlegs case and raced nimbly across the room to where Madam Petra and Katarina were already escaping up the secret passage. Swinging David onto his shoulder, Max stumbled after through the smoke.

But the staircase was already disappearing, its steps rotating away beneath the mantel as the fireplace revolved back into view. Cursing, Max hastened across, ducking low and scurrying as fast as he could with David. It was only twenty feet away, a dwindling gap no larger than a suitcase.

Panting, Max pulled up. It was no good. There was no way to dive or squeeze through without running the risk of being crushed to pulp between the sliding masonry. The door was on the verge of giving way. Setting David down, Max toppled a heavy bookcase and slid it in front of the door before bracing it with the metal sculpture. It might keep the intruders at bay for another minute, maybe two. Running to the grappling hook, he wrenched it out of the sill. Max leaned as far out of the broken window as he could, swinging the heavy grapple and letting it fly up and over the roof.

Twice the hook came clattering and careening back, but on the third toss, it held. Once he checked that the rope was secure, Max dashed back to retrieve his roommate. Slinging David's arm around his neck, Max seized hold of the rope and hoisted the two of them up, up to the steep pitched roof. Once he'd navigated the overhang, Max flipped over and dug his heels into the slate tiles, pushing them up the steep incline while he pulled on the rope. From inside, he heard a crash. Smoke billowed out the window below; the door had given way. Gritting his teeth, Max cut away the excess rope and redoubled his efforts. He heard the smee's voice above, yelling at Madam Petra to wait.

"We're coming!" Max shouted.

Releasing the rope, he rolled onto his side, gripping David's collar with one hand and feeling for a handhold with the other. Sliding over to an attic gable, he braced against it and pushed himself up to a crouch. Half dragging, half carrying David, he scrambled up the roof to its peak.

Just beyond the ridge was a landing pad, hidden from below by the house's many gables. A hot-air balloon was floating there, straining at the tethers that anchored it. Shuffling and sliding down the roof's back slope, Max took the last few steps at a run and grabbed hold of the balloon's swaying basket.

Taking David from Max, Madam Petra helped the boy aboard. Max dove in afterward, almost landing on Toby as Madam Petra stood and swiftly cut the cables.

Slowly, the balloon caught the wind and drifted lazily, bumping several chimneys until it was finally free of the house and rose unfettered into the sky. Scrambling to his feet, Max gazed down at the dwindling landscape. Madam Petra's house was an inferno, flames crackling from every window as a smoky pall settled. Skeedle's poor mules had dragged the wagon down to the water's edge and stood braying in the shallows while dark figures raced about the house's perimeter. One caught sight of them and apparently called out to the others, for they all stopped what they were doing and watched as the balloon carried east over the enormous lake. Max turned his attention back to his injured friend.

David's pants were sopped with blood, but the flow was diminishing. Feeling about, Max found the exit wound and breathed a sigh of relief; the bullet seemed to have passed through and to have missed both bone and artery. Unfortunately, however, David's pack and all of their supplies were down in the wagon. Tearing strips of fabric from his tunic, Max bound David's leg and shoulder to staunch the bleeding.

"How is he?" asked Toby anxiously.

"Okay for now, I think," Max gasped, realizing his lungs were seared from all the smoke and superheated air. He felt David's pulse and pushed his hair back from his eyes. His roommate was pale and breathing fitfully, but breathing nonetheless. "Let's get him warm and keep his feet up. He might be in shock."

"There are some blankets in that bag," said Madam Petra, adjusting the burners. "Please put one on Katarina—she's not dressed for the cold."

Max glanced at the girl. She was crouched in the corner, huddled in the fetal position and staring dully ahead. Tears streaked her pretty face, pale channels through the soot. Toby retrieved two blankets from a small duffel and draped them over David and the girl. Neither stirred. As the balloon pitched and rocked on the breeze, the pinlegs tube rolled about the basket.

Max picked it up, running his hands over its polished case and inspecting the symbols etched about its periphery. Inside was a part of Prusias's clicking, crawling war machine. If they could get the pinlegs back to Rowan, perhaps someone could make sense of its purpose and turn it to their advantage. If not, the mission was a failure. He gazed down at the gray waters, listened to the creak of the wicker basket and the low roar of the burners jetting hot air into the balloon. Already Piter's Folly was far below and far behind—a dwindling trail of smoke in the vast expanse of lake.

Flexing his fingers, Max glanced down to see that his hand had been rubbed raw and bloody from the rope. Shaking his head, he wedged the pinlegs beneath the duffel.

"Your secretary," he muttered. "He was the one who betrayed us?"

"It must have been," replied Madam Petra. "I've suspected Dmitri for some time."

But Katarina tried to speak. Closing her eyes, the child clutched at her throat and winced from the pain. She had been downstairs and Max guessed that her lungs were damaged worse than his. When she found her voice, it was barely audible over the wind.

"D-Dmitri's dead," she whispered. "They killed him. They killed everyone."

"Who were *they*?" exclaimed Madam Petra, crouching beside her daughter. "Who attacked us?"

"Most wore masks," the girl whispered. "I only saw one of their faces."

"Who was it?" pressed her mother, clutching Katarina's hand. "What did he look like?"

The girl pointed a shaky, soot-stained finger at Max.

"He looked just like him."

~ 9 ~

HUNTED

The blood drained from Madam Petra's face. "Are you certain, love?"

Katarina nodded.

"Clones," said Max quietly. "I fought one in Prusias's Arena, but there are others."

"Two others," said the smuggler knowingly. "I saw them once at a reception. They're the crown jewels of the Workshop's genetics program. But the rumor is that things went amiss. The Workshop attempted modifications and something went wrong. The clones became too dangerous, impossible to control. Homicidal. They killed several engineers and destroyed half the creatures in the exotics museum. I'd heard the Workshop had given up and were trying to find a buyer. The Atropos must have acquired one—perhaps the pair."

"So you know about the Atropos," said Max.

"Of course I do," replied Petra coolly. "There's quite a price on your head, my dear. And if I'd had the good sense to alert someone as soon as I knew you were in my home, I might be sitting on a mountain of gold instead of fleeing from my burning house in this ridiculous balloon. You owe me a new estate, Max McDaniels."

But Max's mind was working too quickly to address her lost fortune. That Madam Petra could not be trusted was plainly evident; she had even greater incentive to betray him than before. He glanced at the pinlegs. It was imperative to transport the mysterious creature and David back to Rowan as soon as possible. David had mentioned another tunnel in Raikos, and they were drifting toward that eastern province, but he also considered Sir Alistair and Kolbyt's warnings. Yuga might have reduced the area to a wasteland. David's tunnel might not even exist anymore.

"What's the date?" he wondered.

"December eighth," replied Madam Petra. "Why?"

"Prusias expects an answer by solstice," said Max. "That leaves just a few weeks. We're relatively close to a place that might magic us to Rowan, but it's near Yuga. What have you heard about her?"

"Aamon certainly gave her a wide berth," replied Madam Petra. "His armies abandoned the Iron Road altogether and invaded Blys over open country. Supposedly she's in Raikos, but whether she's near Taros or Bholevna, I don't know."

At the mention of these cities, David stirred. Grimacing, he tried to sit up and fell back against the wicker basket. Despite the cold, his face was hot with fever.

"Bholevna," he murmured weakly. "My pack . . ."

Max knelt by his friend and inspected the bandages, which were already damp with clotted blood.

"We left your pack in the wagon," said Max. "It's back at Piter's Folly. What about Bholevna?"

"Tunnel . . . ," David whispered.

"The tunnel's near Bholevna?"

David nodded and gestured weakly for Max to come closer. The boy's bloodstained fingers plucked at Max's sleeve, fumbling about until they caught hold of his hand.

"Hold it tight," David whispered.

Max did so, wrapping both of his warm hands around David's cold one. The sorcerer's lips twitched, mouthing silent words over and over. Max began to feel light-headed. His head swam as David slowly leeched energy from his body like some sort of vampire.

A sudden surge of energy departed Max, pumping through his fingertips like waters bursting from a dam. David's hand seized up as though he'd touched an electrified fence. The boy's legs kicked against the pinlegs case, harder and harder. Max tried to tear his hands away, but he was weakening rapidly.

"Pull him off!" he wheezed.

Instantly, Toby changed from a lutin to a chimpanzee. Max felt the primate's powerful hands grip his and pry them from David's. Baring his teeth like a wild animal, David kicked and struck out at Toby, thrashing about the balloon's compartment as though possessed.

"What's the matter with him?" shrieked Toby, pulling. "He's—"

Max toppled heavily onto his side. The motion and the smee's efforts finally broke the connection, and David collapsed back against the wicker basket, struggling for breath. Smoke rose off the sorcerer's clothes as though they'd been thrust into an oven.

"I'm sorry," he gasped. "I—I should have known . . . my God!"

The boy lost consciousness, his nose whistling as it often did whenever he was deeply asleep. Madam Petra crept over to Max, crouching over him and peering at him closely.

"Are you all right?" she asked tentatively.

Max nodded blandly. His wits were wandering, but he was profoundly wary of betraying any weakness to the smuggler. The woman had just lost a fortune; should she deliver Max McDaniels and David Menlo to the Enemy, she might regain it tenfold. Gathering himself, Max stood on shaky legs.

"I'm fine," he lied. "David used me to strengthen himself. It caught me by surprise."

The smee changed back to a lutin and examined his hands. "I didn't know David was so strong!"

Max said nothing, seizing the opportunity to gather himself. Leaning over the basket's rim, he allowed the cold gales to clear his mind while he gazed out at the gray clouds and the faint, gray-green landscape far below.

The winds howled at such heights, whipping through the balloon's rigging with a stinging mix of ice and sleet. Katarina was sitting quietly, curled next to her mother, who was ministering to her burns and soiled face. Gazing back down, Max tried to estimate their speed as the balloon carried them east over a series of small lakes and hardscrabble hills. For the moment, they were traveling in the proper direction, but the winter winds were capricious. He hoped whatever David had done, whatever energies he had sourced from Max, would enable a swift recovery. They might need Rowan's sorcerer to summon a breeze to blow them toward Bholevna. Easing down, Max rested his back against the basket and closed his eyes to think.

Are my own clones working for the Atropos?

What should we do if Yuga has destroyed David's tunnel?

How did our enemies know we were at Madam Petra's?

His next realization was that someone was shaking him.

Night had fallen. The burners' golden light danced on the smuggler's face as she crouched above Max and tugged at his cloak.

"Wind's changed," she said. "We're drifting north. Something's happening below."

For several seconds, Max merely blinked at the woman and tried to piece together where he was. His face was numb from the cold and he was disoriented not only from ordinary exhaustion, but also from the aftershocks of David's spell. Nodding dumbly, he pushed himself up.

Below was a sea of clouds. In the moonlight, they appeared like herds of soft, silvery cattle drifting over the slumbering earth. Peeking here and there through the gaps was the edge of a great city, a sprawl of twinkling lights in clusters and spokes and patterns. Above the winds and the creak of cordage, Max heard droning calls, as if the clouds were lowing in their dark pasture. Was he still dreaming?

"What city is that?" he murmured.

"That's not a city," breathed Madam Petra. "It's an army."

Rubbing his eyes, he peered again, reminded suddenly of Mina's accounts of the many worlds, half veiled within the summoning circles. The lights might have been such a place, thousands of fireflies hovering over some dark, primeval marsh. They were so tiny, so distant that Max imagined the smuggler was joking until he heard the lowing again. Slowly but surely,

his wits returned as the freezing winds cleared away the cob-
webs.

The sound was not lowing cattle; it was the call of war horns.
There must have been hundreds of them—perhaps thousands—
all blowing in unison far below. At ground level, the volume
must have been deafening, a din to herald an End of Days. As
Max watched, many of the lights began to move, creeping north.

"Can they see us?" he wondered.

"I doubt it," said Madam Petra. "We must be a mile or more
up, and there's cloud cover. The burners are small . . . even if
they saw us, we'd probably just look like a tiny star."

"A tiny star that's moving," said Max.

"An army that size isn't concerned with a moving star; it's
concerned with other armies."

Madam Petra snatched Max's spyglass as soon as he produced it. Leaning out from the balloon, she scanned the landscape below. She was silent for several minutes, sweeping the
glass across the lights, which were converging into distinct patterns and formations. Focusing on a shimmering cluster, she
shook her head and returned the glass to Max.

"Prusias is here," she said grimly. "That's his palanquin in
the central column. Do you see it?"

Max spotted it right away, a section where many lights
were crowded like honeybees congregating around their queen.
The rolling palanquin must have been enormous, but still it was
dwarfed by the surrounding sea of banners and torches. There
must have been a quarter million troops below, not even counting the siege engines and supply wagons, cooks, engineers, car-
penters, blacksmiths, servants, and God knew whatever else
accompanied an army of such size. Max's initial impression had
been correct. This was indeed a city—a creeping city bent on
conquest. The horns had ceased, replaced now by the tolling

boom . . . boom . . . boom of drums to set the march. As they sounded far below, the columns tightened and the army curved to the northeast, following the line of a river as it stretched toward Dùn and the border with Aamon's kingdom. The smuggler's voice tickled Max's ear.

"Still believe Rowan can win?"

Max said nothing but watched Prusias's legions coursing north like streams of glowing lava. Leaning against the basket, Madam Petra brushed against him.

"The king still bleeds, you know," she said. "His wounds won't knit. My contacts say you carry a blade that nearly took Prusias's heads, one by one. Rumor has it the malakhim have to replace his bandages thrice a day lest they soak through and frighten off all his little concubines. Can you imagine? The King of Blys sullen on his throne while those wraiths attend him like anxious nursemaids!" The smuggler laughed like a mischievous girl. "Poor Prusias, no wonder he's grown so ill-tempered! I should like to see the weapon that could hurt one such as he. Do you have it here?"

She was standing very close, beautiful and wicked by the light of the burners. The others were asleep, snoring beneath piled blankets while Toby dozed as a luxuriant ermine. When Max did not respond, Madam Petra gave a nostalgic smile.

"It's so strange to think that you were Bragha Rùn," she reflected. "I saw three of your victories in the Arena. You fought like a god—so strong, so quick. Your matches were poetry. The whole kingdom was dying to know who was beneath that frightful mask." Leaning close, the smuggler searched his face. "There's something in you that isn't in those clones," she concluded with a whisper. "Something immortal . . ."

She stared at Max as though he were a piece of art, a prized jewel she'd salvaged from her smoldering safe back in Piter's Folly.

Max's tone was sharp. "I'm not some moonstruck politician or Workshop admirer."

The smuggler's smile vanished. "You misunderstand me, Max."

"I think we understand each other perfectly, Madam Petra. I'm taking my friends and the pinlegs back to Rowan. You and Katarina will be welcome if you choose to come with us. At Rowan, you'll have land of your own and whatever protection we can provide."

The smuggler gave a wry laugh. "And if we choose *not* to settle in a doomed realm?" she inquired, blinking sweetly.

"You can do what you like," replied Max. "But until we're on our way home, you and Katarina are staying with us. I won't have you running off and raising the alarm."

"You think I'd betray my own kind to the demons? How uncharitable."

"You were fleecing your own people on Piter's Folly. I don't pretend to know what you'd do or who you'd sell. But you won't sell us."

"So Katarina and I are hostages?" she asked, obviously bemused. "Let's see if I understand this properly. You sneak into my home, bring assassins to my door, steal my pinlegs, and hold us against our will, but *I'm* the criminal?"

"Yes, ma'am," said Max, returning the smile. "You can lodge a complaint with the Director."

"You know, I met her once at a party," recalled the smuggler. "Beautiful woman; terrible shoes—"

Just then, something heavy struck the basket, nearly upending it. Stumbling at the impact, Madam Petra toppled out, catching its rim with her fingers. She clung to the bucking balloon as if it were a life raft.

"Get it off me!" she shrieked, her face white with terror.

Lunging over the side, Max seized the smuggler by both

wrists and wrenched her up. Something dark was clinging to her lower legs. A screeching filled the air as something else collided with the balloon from above.

Heaving Madam Petra back into the basket, Max saw what had been clinging to her. At first he thought it was a baka, for the creature also had batlike wings that scratched and snared on the wicker. But as it raised its bloody, raptorlike face and hissed, Max saw that it was a Stygian crow—a rare breed of evil creature he'd read about in one of David's books. It was three times the size of its natural namesake and had a fiery core that shone through thin, membranous patches along its rib cage. Its talons were enormous, and these had raked the smuggler's legs cruelly. The creature had released the woman, however, and was now hopping about the basket like a ravening vulture, stabbing its beak at Katarina, who screamed and kicked at it. More screeches sounded in the air.

Max's first swing of the *gae bolga* sheared cleanly through the creature's neck. The headless body spun away from the girl and staggered toward Toby. The smee was now wide awake and hysterical, shielding David and pleading with the creatures to go away as they swarmed about the balloon like moths around a flame. Some rocketed past while others swept up to seize hold of the ropes and rigging. Slashing at those within reach, Max had slain half a dozen of the creatures, but he could hear others atop the balloon, their claws pinching and scrabbling for footholds on the slick material. Already the wind was howling through a score of tears and punctures. The balloon was losing altitude.

Down, down the balloon swept and spun toward the earth, curving away north as it was buffeted about by the icy gusts. Max could see stars through holes in the balloon's fabric as it strained to hold together. The crows screeched and struggled to hold on, their belly fires burning like bright furnaces.

"Hold on to anything you can!" Max shouted, skewering another crow and stumbling back to seize several ropes. The balloon was impossible to steer, but Max had glimpsed a lake glittering below and prayed that they might reach it. Thrusting the ropes in Petra's hand, he stumbled as the balloon bucked in a sudden gale and nearly sent the pinlegs tube skittering over the side. Max snatched out his hand and caught it, cradling it under his arm and peering over the basket's edge. The army was much closer now, individual torches visible to the naked eye as they plummeted down. They would end up crashing into its midst, unless . . .

"Toby!" Max yelled, cutting away the ballast of sand bags. "Become something big—something with wings that can slow down our fall!"

"What do you want?" cried Toby. "There's only so much—"

"ANYTHING!"

The smee leaped out of the balloon, hovering momentarily with a look of terror upon his ermine face. They quickly left him behind, spinning like a top as the ruptured balloon plunged to earth. The Stygian crows had now abandoned their crashing quarry, their silhouettes turning lazy circles against the bright moon. The balloon had drifted a mile or two east of the marching army, but the ground was already racing up to meet them, a blur of snow-sprinkled terrain that was dotted with lakes and pine forests. One of the lakes was just ahead, but their altitude was dwindling rapidly. By now, the balloon was no more than a charred and torn sail dragging against the wind. Across the basket, Petra was huddled around her daughter. Max did the same with David, propping the unconscious boy up in his arms and praying that they struck water.

And then, almost imperceptibly at first, they began to slow. Above them, Max beheld a pair of wings, stretched as wide and taut as a glider's. A gargantuan albatross had snatched up the remains of the balloon and ropes in its talons and was breaking their fall. The bird's wings were twenty-five feet across, and yet it could only dampen the speed of their descent. The smee squawked with the strain, his voice warbling as the balloon's trajectory smoothed and they were skimming twenty feet above the lake Max had sighted. Just a little slower and they could safely—

With a screech, the albatross abruptly dropped the balloon and they crashed into the water.

The initial shock of impact was replaced by brutal cold, needle stabs of pain as Max tumbled about in the shallows of the icy lake. He saw stars as his head struck something, a log or fallen tree. He groped for air, felt it rush into his lungs as he finally broke the surface. A hand brushed his and he glimpsed David sinking back below. Seizing his friend, Max raised his head out of the water and began swimming toward shore.

It was hard going. The chain shirt was an anchor about Max's neck, pulling him ever down into the reedy depths. He kept his eyes fixed on the stars, glittering beyond the billows of his sputtering breath. Gasping and straining, he towed David to shore.

Madam Petra and Katarina were already there, shivering on the banks and sorting through the wet baggage they'd managed to salvage.

"The p-pinlegs?" asked Max, chattering in the frigid cold.

Petra could not speak but merely pointed out toward the lake.

"Get in the woods," said Max, nodding toward the nearby trees. "Start a fire."

"The army," gasped Petra. "They'll be coming. We have to hide!"

"It w-won't matter if we die of cold," said Max. "Can you carry David?"

The smuggler nodded, buckling only slightly as Max slung the boy over her shoulder. She walked briskly to the woods, Katarina staggering along in her wake. There was a coughing sound near Max's feet. A beaver was waddling out of the shallows, looking cold, wet, and miserable.

"Toby," said Max. "Are you all right?"

"I think I broke something," the smee groaned, limping.

"Petra's gone ahead to start a fire," said Max, quickly pulling off cloak and hauberk. "I'm going back for the pinlegs."

Before the smee could respond, Max dove back into the lake, stretching out for the ruptured balloon that was floating atop the icy waters like a lily pad. The cold was like an iron vise clamped about his chest, each stroke squeezing the life out of him. At last his hand touched the balloon, fumbling about until he found a rope. Taking hold of it, Max filled his lungs and dove straight down.

The basket was swinging slowly in the depths like a pendulum suspended by the balloon on the surface. Max felt frantically about the basket's interior, swimming around inside and groping blindly for the pinlegs tube. After several minutes, his lungs were afire. He abandoned the dive and raced back to the surface.

A glimpse of stars, the rush of oxygen into his lungs, and he dived once again, feeling his way down the ropes to the basket. Once there, he gazed desperately about the water and saw nothing—not even a trace of moon or starlight that filtered through the surrounding blackness.

With frantic concentration, Max enveloped his hands with witch-fire. He'd never tried to do such a thing underwater and wasn't certain that it would work, but sure enough the eerie blue flames kindled from his fingers, a swirling, incandescent blaze that sent bubbles hissing up toward the surface. Battling the cold, he paddled through the lake's depths, his hands like two ghostly flares as he searched the weeds and wreckage.

On his fourth dive, Max found it. The pinlegs was peeking out from a nest of reeds on the lake's bottom, a dim glint of metal at the very limits of the witch-fire's radiance. Even as Max seized it, he felt the strange creature kicking and scrabbling against the tube's interior. Clutching it tightly, he rocketed to the surface and swam for shore.

Had Petra not called out to him, Max might have wandered about the woods until he collapsed. He was delirious with cold, his skin blue and his mouth frozen into a horrid grimace as he stumbled about in search of his companions. Taking his hand, the smuggler led him to a small hollow, shielded from the wind by a close stand of pine trees. Some dead wood had been heaped in the hope of a fire, but the fuel was wet and they'd been unsuccessful.

Max was so desperate for warmth he dropped the pinlegs tube and promptly seized hold of two logs. Again, witch-fire coursed from his fingers, bathing the wood with flames. Seconds later, they were hissing and popping, fully ablaze as he stood holding them.

"They'll burn you!" exclaimed Madam Petra, swatting the wood out of Max's hands. They fell onto the other logs, catching into a small fire as Katarina fed them with strips of bark and kindling. Max stood right next to the pile, even as it grew to a crackling blaze that sent plumes of sparks and embers cascading over his legs.

Slowly, warmth returned, seeping into his bones to chase away the mortal cold. Gazing down, he saw the others gathered about the fire. Madam Petra and her daughter had undressed down to their underclothes, drying their other garments on an array of rocks and logs that they'd dragged over. Toby was sniffing gingerly at his injured leg, inching ever closer to the heat. David was still unconscious but breathing evenly. Madam Petra had removed his wet clothes as well, and Rowan's sorcerer lay in naught but his underwear, the firelight dancing on the shiny ten-inch scar that ran down the center of his chest.

Max stood staring at the flames for another five minutes. When life finally returned to his fingers and limbs, he squeezed the remaining lake water out of his clothes and threw them directly on one of the smaller logs. When they began to smoke, he removed them and slipped them on.

"Look after them," he said, buckling the *gae bolga* to his side. He nodded to the longsword lying by the smuggler's boots. "Do you know how to use that?"

Madam Petra nodded.

"Good." He nodded. "If I'm not back by dawn, strike out for Bholevna. There's a shortcut near there—a way to get home. David knows where it is and how to use it."

"But where are you going?" asked Katarina, sounding frightened.

"Back to the lake. They'll be coming soon."

Indeed, they were already on the scene when Max emerged from the wood. He saw the riders milling about the lake's shoreline, a score of dark figures seated on horseback while one waded into the moonlit water and cast a hook at the balloon. When the hook caught, the soldier tied it to his saddle and swatted his horse's flanks. It trudged forward on the icy banks, dragging the balloon and basket into the shallows. The riders' attention was fixed on the lake; none were watching as Max slipped from the woods and stole closer, keeping to the brush and bracken.

He was now within twenty feet of the closest, an armored vye sitting atop a destrier bred to handle the creature's weight. In his taloned hand, the vye held a long spear. He shifted uneasily in his saddle, gazing back toward the trees.

"They've fled into the woods," he growled. "We should be after them already!"

Another turned his dark face at his comrade and bared his jagged teeth. "They've fled on foot, fool!" the vye sniggered. "We'll have them soon enough. You heard the captain; he wants the humans *and* the flying machine. Start the chase alone if you're so eager."

"But the battle—"

"Can start without us. We get a lucky plum of an assignment—one that whisks us from the front lines—and you want to get it over with? Slow and easy, friend—a bit of luck and we'll rejoin ranks after Aamon's crushed. You want to be in the thick when those scuttlers are set loose?"

"No."

"Then shut it. A nice long chase over wild country is just the thing."

With a grunt, the vye turned back to watch the balloon as it was dragged to the water's edge. Once his back was exposed, Max stole forward and slipped the *gae bolga* between the vye's ribs. The blade hummed in Max's hand, growing warm as Max quietly tipped the vye back off his saddle. The attack was so smooth and quiet that the vye's horse hardly stirred. Such mounts were used to the din and clamor of battle; the scent of blood did not spook them.

But the scent did spook the vyes. Max had silently slain three more before the wind changed and carried the smell of death to their comrades. They whirled about just as Max smacked the flanks of the closest horse and sent it cantering into their midst.

As the vyes charged, Max met them head-on, a lethal blur of motion nearly too fast for the creatures to see, much less strike. He evaded each spear point and cavalry saber with fluid ease as the Morrígan's blade struck home time and time again.

It clove metal in two, shearing through helmets and hauberks in a scream of red sparks. The hunters had become the hunted and the battle devolved into a massacre. When only four vyes remained, they tried to flee.

Max raced after in pursuit, desperate to let none escape and return with greater force. The last made it no farther than the other side of the lake before Max ran its destrier down, tearing the vye from the saddle and ending his life with a savage stab through the heart. It was all over in minutes.

Panting, Max stood and scanned the surrounding country. Every sense was electric and terrifying; his fingers twitched as the Old Magic howled within him—always pushing, straining for total control. The *gae bolga* burned in his hand. It whispered to Max, urging him to hunt down Prusias and finish what he'd started. He could destroy the King of Blys and save Rowan this very night. Who cared if he ultimately fell in battle? People would sing of Max McDaniels for a thousand years—the boy who slew the Great Red Dragon.

What are you about? Answer quick or I'll gobble you up!

The wolfhound's challenge echoed in Max's mind.

"I'm a god," he whispered, steam coursing off his body. "A god of war and blood and victory. Every day I grow stronger. I'll drive every army before me. My enemies will know fear like they've never known it before. . . ."

Visions appeared before him: Prusias's palace engulfed in flames, the marids' crystal towers crashing down into the sea. One by one, Max would conquer the other kingdoms. And when he had broken all resistance and sent all evil things slinking back into the shadows, David would set things aright. David would pick up the pieces and govern and heal the hurts of the world. The Great War could start tonight. Prusias was so . . . very . . . close.

* * *

Night was waning when Max finally put the visions and whispers to rest. He had remained absolutely still throughout this silent battle, a brooding statue locked in a struggle to master the forces within him. The Old Magic wanted so desperately to break free, to purge Max of everything human and mortal, weak and loving. He had struggled all his life to keep it bottled up, to divert these energies and control them until they subsided. But the Old Magic was growing stronger . . . and in the *gae bolga*, it had a new and potent ally. Unless Max discovered new reserves of will, this was a battle he would someday lose.

But he would not lose it tonight. Max gazed down at the blade in his hand. It was such a grisly weapon, and now there was blood frozen on its blade, lacing the metal like red syrup. For the moment, the Morrígan's presence was subdued, but Max knew it was forever lurking, forever poised for its next victim and opportunity. Looking down, Max stared at the body of the last vye. His teeth were bared in a death grimace, the yellow eyes staring blindly at a barren elm. His mount was nearby, quietly nosing about for grass and nettles as its hooves scraped through the crusted snow. Gazing about, Max saw a score of dark, motionless shapes scattered about the shoreline.

He dragged the vyes into the lake, letting the water buoy the bodies until he could shove them farther out. Their armor sank them to the bottom, burying each in a grave of silt and reeds.

The sky was growing light by the time he rounded up two of the great black horses. He had hoped to bring more, but the animals were trained for war, for attacking another's mount in the midst of a chaotic battlefield. Without a rider to control them, they grew aggressive whenever another stood too near. Max could only manage two. Holding their reins at arm's length, he led the gigantic horses back into the woods.

Madam Petra was pacing anxiously when Max returned. Their hasty camp was packed and most of the embers were buried beneath dirt and snow. David was bundled in blankets, lying next to the beginnings of a travois so they might drag the injured boy over the snowy ground. The smuggler glanced up, looking utterly spent.

"I'd almost given up on you," she muttered before eyeing the horses. "They only sent two?"

"Twenty."

"And they are . . . ?"

"Dead," replied Max curtly, bending down to inspect Toby. The smee had taken his native shape and was warming himself by a pyramid of embers.

"Don't fret," declared the smee bravely. "I'll be all right and war stories work wonders with the ladies. I can tell them all about how I saved you from going squish!"

Max grinned and crouched over David.

"You changed his dressings," he observed, examining David's wounds.

"Did you think we'd leave an injured boy to die in the wild?" the smuggler snapped. "Katarina tended to him all night."

Max thanked the girl, who merely stared at Max with a glassy, curious expression.

"You killed them all?" she wondered.

Max looked away. "More will come," he said. "We have to be off and quickly. We're still much too close to that army. Bholevna's north of here?"

Madam Petra nodded.

"Well," said Max, "these horses might be big, but they're still just horses. You and Katarina can ride one and I'll take David on the other."

"So I don't have to be a steed?" said Toby, audibly relieved.

"No," said Max, scooping him up. "You've earned a ride in style."

Within ten minutes they were packed and mounted with Max balancing David on the saddle in front of him. The Kosas were clearly expert riders, sitting easily on the great horse and stroking its braided mane. Max noticed Madam Petra staring curiously at him.

"Letting us ride together?" she wondered, a faint smile on her lips. "Not afraid we'll gallop off?"

Max nodded toward the travois. "Not anymore," he said, taking up the reins and spurring his horse ahead.

They rode throughout the morning and into the afternoon, the horses picking their way through forests and along snowy streams, cantering whenever it was possible. While David dozed, Toby nestled in the folds of Max's hood and bombarded him with reflections about casino odds, the meaning of life, and his fondness for baked potatoes.

"But I have to enjoy them on the sly," the smee reflected sadly. "Otherwise everyone looks at me like I'm some damned cannibal. Why, that goose Hannah once caught me feasting on one and practically—"

"So, what's the matter with you?" interrupted Max, growing weary of these ramblings.

"There's *nothing* the matter with me, sir!" thundered Toby. "Potatoes are an entirely different species!"

"No," said Max. "What's injured?"

"Oh," sniffed the smee, lying back. "It's my latissimus nub. The right one can flare up whenever I carry something heavy. Nothing a hot bath and some Epsom salts can't cure. Perhaps Madam Petra can give it a deep tissue massage. I don't want to boast, but the woman can't keep her eyes off me."

Max sighed. The smee persisted.

"Oh, I know what you're thinking," he declared. " *'Come off it, Toby old chap—the woman's merely staring out of revolted curiosity.'* And perhaps you're right. But I've seen that look before, my boy, and it almost always precedes a scandal."

"Dear Lord . . ."

The smee was still telling tawdry tales when Max reined their horse to a halt. Madam Petra and Katarina had dismounted up ahead and were standing where the forest opened onto a broad valley dotted with little lakes. The sun was already setting, flooding the west with brilliant bands of pink and orange. But in the east, the sky was strangely, unnaturally dark. There, above the distant hills and river valleys, an amoebic mass was floating like some vast cloud of volcanic ash. It might have been fifty miles away and still it dwarfed the landscape, a roiling storm that flickered with glimmers of heat lightning as dust clouds and debris swirled beneath. A sound carried to them on the wind, a faint but unmistakable moaning.

The storm was Yuga.

~ 10 ~

KNIFE, SPEAR, AND STORM

The demon filled the eastern sky, so massive it seemed that one could touch her or trail their fingers through her nimbus of black vapors. Despite the fact that she was airborne, there was something uncannily dense and ponderous about the demon's form and the slow-moving tendrils that protruded here and there like the hungry, searching arms of an anemone. Max wondered if the inky nebulae were the demon's basic essence or if they shrouded something else within. It was a horrifying and alien creature whose amorphous shape and blind hunger reminded Max of the grylmhoch he'd encountered in the Arena. But the similarities ended there; *millions* of grylmhochs would not have equaled her appalling size. Yuga eclipsed anything Max had ever seen by such a stupefying margin that a mountain would have seemed infinitesimal by comparison. The demon was bigger than a small country, forever moaning as she devoured all life and energy in the lands beneath her. She was entropy itself.

Max glanced at Madam Petra and her daughter. Holding hands, they simply gaped at the far-off demon. There was not even fear stamped upon their faces, but rather a blank, uncomprehending emptiness. The mere spectacle of Yuga had overwhelmed their senses.

"D-dear God, what a monster!" stammered Toby, peering out from Max's hood.

"Don't look at her," said Max gently. "Yuga's far, far away yet."

"Can she see us?" whispered Madam Petra, retreating back into the wood.

"I don't think so," replied Max, projecting a calm that he did not feel. "She is still very far from us, Petra. Miles and miles and miles. The sooner we go on, the sooner we find David's tunnel and get away from her. Katarina?"

The girl only responded on the third call, tearing her attention away from the demon.

"Katarina, have you ever stared at an eclipse?"

The girl blinked. "No," she muttered. "It would hurt my eyes."

"That's right," said Max. "There's something in the eastern sky right now that's like an eclipse. It's far away and it can't hurt you unless you stare at it. You look at your mother instead, okay?"

When the girl nodded, Max turned to Petra. "Do you have any idea where we are relative to Bholevna?"

She scanned the land ahead, the fields and farms that had

been trampled by Aamon's armies. There were no landmarks, nothing but a few burned-out and abandoned farmhouses.

"I don't know," she confessed. "Bholevna may be farther north or perhaps east. I can't say for certain."

"Toby," called Max. "How's that 'latissimus nub' feeling? Could you become another bird?"

"A small one, perhaps," replied the smee, wriggling like a grub. "Let's see, let's see."

Seconds later, a sparrow hopped out of Max's hood and tentatively fluttered its wings.

"Perfect," said Max. "Can you fly up and have a look around for a landmark, a river, a road—anything that might give us a better sense of where we are?"

The smee zoomed from Max's shoulder, spiraling up into the winter sky until he was almost lost from view. Once Toby was gone, Max checked on David.

His roommate was asleep, his cheeks flushed with fever, but his condition did not appear to be deteriorating. Peering beneath the bandage, Max saw that Katarina had done a good job cleaning the wounds, which were already mending.

"Can you hear me?" said Max, reapplying the bandage. "David?"

The sorcerer's brow furrowed with irritation. He grunted.

"You can sleep again in a minute," Max assured him. "Is the tunnel in Bholevna itself?"

The reply was so faint, it was little more than an exhale.

"East," whispered David wearily. "A mile. Farmhouse . . . stream."

"The tunnel is a mile east of Bholevna in a farmhouse by a stream?"

David nodded.

"Good," said Max, patting his friend. "That's good. We can't be too far away."

Toby returned a few minutes later, swooping down into the forest to settle onto Max's shoulder.

"There's a brayma's palace perhaps ten miles to the north beyond that strip of forest," he reported, gesturing with his wing. "Magnificent, really—reminds me of St. Basil's Cathedral—but it looks like it's been sacked. All the surrounding farms have been burned. It appears that Aamon's armies have already been through this land."

"I know that palace," said Madam Petra. "It belongs to Baron Hart—Katarina and I attended a hunt there last spring. Bholevna's just another ten miles or so northeast of there."

"Let's make for the palace," Max decided. "If the horses aren't spent and we feel up to it, we can push on to Bholevna tonight. If not, we can take shelter and see if there's any food about. Agreed?"

The Kosas nodded, and even David managed a weary grunt. Reminding them not to look east, Max swung back up into the saddle, checked to see that the pinlegs was secure, and led the ride north.

The moon had risen high by the time they neared the palace. The journey had been slow going, for the horses were exhausted and the land grew rough and rocky in places, requiring them to pick their way carefully amid the trees and outcroppings. To the west, Max heard the faint blare of war horns. Periodically, there was a flash in the western sky as though lightning rippled through the clouds.

But it was Yuga that occupied Max's attention.

He had said nothing to the others and hoped they had not noticed, but the hollow moaning was growing louder. The demon was so enormous that it was difficult to gauge her direction or speed—her motions seemed as slow and deliberate as the Earth's rotation. But she *was* moving, and it sounded as though she was moving west, drawn perhaps to the warring armies and the vast feast they represented. Despite the darkness, she was still visible—a gargantuan void among the stars as though a huge, ragged patch had been torn from the night sky. Max wondered if Bram, or even Astaroth, could destroy such an abomination.

The dismal truth was that they were caught between terrible forces. He prayed that David's tunnel still existed. If not, they would have to flee north to the Baltic and rely on *Ormenheid* to carry them home.

"These horses will keel over if we don't rest them," panted Madam Petra, shivering in the cold. "And I'm falling asleep in my saddle. Do you think it's safe in the palace? We can water the horses and see if there's food. Just an hour or two of sleep," she pleaded.

Toby flew off to scout. When he returned and pronounced the palace abandoned, they led their weary mounts across its trampled fields and orchards.

The smee had been correct; the place really did resemble St. Basil's Cathedral with its painted towers and voluptuous domes glinting beneath the moon. Before its fall, it must have been a wonder. But much of the palace was damaged, its gatehouse a charred ruin while several of the towers had collapsed into the inner bailey, obliterating a handful of smaller buildings in the process.

Much had been destroyed, but there was an uncontaminated well. While the horses drank and the others rested, Max went searching for food. He wandered about the empty palace, stepping over fallen stones and peering into ashy chambers that had been stripped of tapestries and furniture and anything else of value. Crunching through broken pottery, Max climbed a spiral staircase to a rampart connecting two of the towers. Perhaps there would be food in a guardroom.

But the upper levels were little better. They had suffered less damage, but the wind was stronger at these heights and went whipping through the open corridors and broken windows like a troop of lost and lonely spirits. There was an oppressive emptiness to the place, reinforced by the surprising lack of bodies. Someone had either buried the dead or taken them for some other purpose. Max declined to speculate.

He climbed to the top of the tallest tower, an immense rounded structure capped by an onion dome. The doors to the uppermost chamber had been wrenched off their hinges, revealing what had been a luxuriant bedchamber or seraglio. The arched walls were adorned with charred frescoes and mosaics and windows set into the curving walls so that the tower commanded a view in every direction. Most of the windows had been broken, however, and the wind swept through, glittering with snowflakes that settled on the inlaid floor.

Stepping to one, Max gazed down at the central courtyard hundreds of feet below. Madam Petra had started a fire, a tiny flicker no bigger than a candle flame amid the shadowed wreckage. Max could not help but admire the woman's spirit and resilience. She had just lost everything and already she was coping, adapting, surviving. He half hoped she would decide to settle at Rowan—they could use such a capable person.

Something flashed in the west, an enormous light that filled the sky with a sickly green light. The sound came after, a rumbling chorus of horns and drums that was soon eclipsed by something else . . . a keening, wailing sound akin to an air-raid siren. Max rushed to another window and gazed out.

The west was ablaze, its skies exploding in wild flashes of light and pluming fire as though the clouds themselves had ignited. Horns sounded from afar, and a tremor ran through the earth, shaking the tower. Down in the courtyard, Petra was calling his name.

"What's happening?" she cried.

Max cupped his hands. "A battle!" he shouted. "The armies have met!"

More flashes and the earth shook again, the tremors as slow and rhythmic as a battering ram. Far off, there was an explosion, and then a brilliant fireball rose in a mushroom cloud against the night sky. The tremors continued.

Max watched, spellbound, as the battle raged on. The armies were too far away to make out many details. But for the incandescent flashes, it might have been a forest fire, a haze of flames and smoke that stretched all along the horizon. Occasionally he caught glimpses of the army columns gleaming like molten gold. The tremors continued, a percussive *thump, thump, thump* that shook the remaining shards free from the windows. They fell about the room's perimeter, shattering like little icicles.

Something to the southwest caught Max's eye.

He trained his glass on a number of small lights glimmering in the surrounding woods. At this distance, he could not be certain if the lights were torches or lanterns, but they were now converging swiftly on the palace.

Max ran from the room, leaping down the stairs and yelling for the others to pack up. He hoped the appearance of these horsemen was coincidence, that they were merely deserters or refugees seeking shelter. But in his heart, Max knew otherwise. These riders were hunting for them.

Arriving at the courtyard, Max saw the Kosas hastily gathering up their things. Over the din of the distant battle and Patient Yuga, Max could now hear the sound of galloping hooves. He ran to the gatehouse and peered outside.

The riders had passed the orchards and were now racing over the fields. Looking wildly about, Max saw that the outer gates had been broken, but one of the inner portcullises was still intact. Racing into the guardhouse, he found the winch that controlled its chains and spun it about as quickly as he could. With a reluctant groan, the heavy iron grill slid down its grooves and fell into position. From outside, there were several shouts and the hoofbeats slowed. Max ran to Madam Petra, who had hidden the others behind the ruins of a fallen tower.

"What are you doing?" she hissed. "We haven't seen another way out—you'll shut us in!"

"No," he panted. "Sneak the others and the horses back into the keep. Go as far back as you can, as close to the eastern wall as possible. There must be some other exit, a postern gate or something. Start searching."

"Yes, but how—"

"Just trust me. If I can deal with these riders on my own, I will. If not, the portcullis will delay them long enough so we can find the door and get away. If there is no exit, I'll make one."

"And what if they kill you and we're still trapped inside?"

Max unsheathed the longsword and handed the weapon to the smuggler.

Taking the sword, Madam Petra lifted David and led the others into a dark archway that opened into the main keep. Stealing across the courtyard, Max saw the riders assembled beyond the portcullis, dark silhouettes against the moonlit countryside. Spurring his horse, one of the hooded figures approached the gatehouse, brandishing a torch.

"You can't outrun the Fates!" the figure called out. "Cease this cowardice and show yourself. Embrace the death that comes for you."

When Max heard that voice, his heart nearly stopped. From

far off, the war horns blared and the western sky flashed with light. Another tremor shook the palace, knocking debris from the walls in little avalanches of rubble and broken masonry.

Smiling grimly, Max walked to the gates and unsheathed the Morrígan blade. He had been mistaken after all. That was no troop of Prusias's soldiers waiting outside the gates.

The Atropos were here.

And the voice that challenged Max was his own.

The clone leaned forward in his stirrups and studied Max through the heavy bars of the portcullis. He might have been Max's mirror image, but for his close-cropped hair and more powerful build. The Workshop had evidently tinkered with the source material, as though they had melted Max down and recast him into a form that was bigger and stronger than the original. Beneath his cloak, the clone was armored with a breastplate of polished black steel. Golden runes were traced upon the metal and gleamed like pale fire by the light of his torch. Behind him sat a dozen of Prusias's malakhim. They formed a horseshoe around the gate, silent executioners whose faces were hidden behind darkly beautiful masks. One rode forward to take the clone's torch and hand him a heavy, ancient-looking spear. The clone tested its weight and gazed across at Max. His handsome face was composed and cruel as he urged his horse toward the portcullis.

"I was afraid you wouldn't answer," he said calmly. "The buyer said you were a coward, that you'd run again and again until we finally caught you. But I told him you were better than that. You and I come from the same place, after all. And I don't run."

"So what now?" asked Max.

"I kill you."

The response was chillingly flat, no emotion.

"We'll see." Max shrugged. "Did you murder those people at Piter's Folly, too?"

The clone's eyes glittered like dark jewels. "The world's at war. There is no such thing as murder. Just obstacles and accidents."

"I'm sorry you think so."

The clone smiled and steadied his horse. "Prusias said you were weak," he sneered. "Said his imp had to make up stories about your Arena opponents so you'd fight angry. Pathetic. You're lucky you fought Myrmidon. I'd have had your head, brother."

Walking closer to the portcullis, Max stared through the bars at the brazen youth sitting astride his coal-black courser. "You're not my brother," he remarked. "I don't know what to call you. You're just an experiment that didn't work . . . a Workshop castoff scooped up by the Atropos to nip at my heels."

In unison, the malakhim drew their swords, red-hot blades that smoked like hearth irons. The clone merely gave a venomous smile and laid the spear across his saddle.

"I don't nip at heels. I bite at throats. Open the gate and find out."

Max recalled his battle with Myrmidon. At several points, he'd overwhelmed his clone and struck what should have been a conclusive blow. And yet Myrmidon always recovered; the gladiator had advanced again and again as though nothing could hurt him. The encounter was seared into Max's memory, its imprint as painful and poisonous as anything he'd experienced. This clone was far larger than Myrmidon had been. The Workshop must have conducted different experiments on each of its three prototypes. The assassin sitting astride the courser looked as though he could tear through the portcullis with his bare hands. Max wondered why he didn't. Perhaps the clone was curious—intrigued about the original from which he'd stemmed. That curiosity might give Petra enough time to find another exit. Assuming there was one.

"Do you have memories?" Max wondered. "Or do they implant false ones?"

Talk of pasts and memories apparently displeased the clone. His face darkened momentarily before relaxing into a faint smile.

"There is no past; there's only now. Memories are nostalgia, and nostalgia is for the weak."

"The Workshop took my blood three years ago," Max reflected. "You're awfully big for a three-year-old. Did they grow you in a little tube or some giant machine? Did they have to train you, or did you just pop out, ready, willing, and able to kill?"

The clone's smile became dangerous. "No big machines," he replied. "Just a cozy little incubator with nanobots, accelerants, and neural feeds. It didn't sing me lullabies, but it did make me strong . . . far stronger than you, brother. I've fought a million hyperbattles in the simulations and I've never lost. You want to think of me as a copy, as a cheap imitation. But you're wrong. I'm an original. And you can stall or run for as long as you like, but you can never escape us. . . ."

As he said this, the clone held up something tucked inside his breastplate. At first glance, Max thought it was simply an ornament on the chain that fastened his cloak. But as the torch-light danced upon its gleaming case, Max recognized the object.

It was a magic compass.

Cooper had used the very same device to locate Max when he'd been imprisoned deep in Prusias's dungeons. David had made it. Instead of pointing toward magnetic north, its needle always pointed toward Max.

"So that's how you tracked us," he said heavily.

The clone slipped the compass back inside his armor. "Your name has been written into the Grey Book," he said. "Your life is over. Submit and we might spare your companions before Yuga devours them. Do you submit?"

As he said this, the sky rippled with a wash of incandescent light. Its brilliance cast a host of shadows that stretched through the gatehouse tunnel. Max glimpsed shadows of torches and chains . . . and a figure stealing up behind him. He whirled to face the assassin. When the sky flashed again, it revealed a familiar face.

The assassin was the second clone.

While Max had been speaking to one, the other must have scaled the high walls. Silent as a wraith, the nimble clone bore down on Max with a long dagger in each hand. Sparks flew as Max caught one blade on his cross-guard. But the other blade struck home, piercing his mail shirt and cutting along his ribs as he twisted aside. Seizing the clone's wrist, Max turned and hurled him against the portcullis.

The clone crashed into it, his knees buckling from the impact and bending several bars. Backing away, Max saw him clearly for the first time. This clone barely resembled the one outside the gate. He was a good fifty pounds lighter, as gaunt as a week-old corpse, with tangles of black hair that hung past his shoulders. Like the witches, every inch of his pale skin was covered in tattoos. But the runes and hieroglyphs were not made with any ink; they were carved into his flesh by a knife or scalpel. The clone was panting, handling each blade with terrifying expertise. Gazing at Max, he grinned and revealed a row of razor-sharp teeth.

Max gasped. "What the hell did they do to you?"

The clone began sniggering like a madman. "Everything," he whispered. *"Everything . . . EVERYTHING!"*

The clone was a blur as he leaped, a frenzied assault of knives

and teeth as he lunged at Max like a rabid animal. Driving Max back into the courtyard, he gave a primal howl as the pair circled one another beneath the flickering sky. The clone was a quick-twitch nightmare with animal instincts far superior to anything human. Every time Max thought he had an opportunity to strike, the clone sprang away or slipped just out of reach. It was like trying to stab smoke. Even worse, the *gae bolga* felt heavy and leaden in Max's hand. It was uncharacteristically silent and seemed little more than an unwieldy length of metal. Perhaps the blade was reluctant—even unwilling—to harm its own flesh and blood.

Blood trickled into Max's eyes from a cut across his forehead. Backing away, he feigned a stumble over a fallen block. As the clone lunged in, Max twisted aside and cracked his opponent's cheekbone with the *gae bolga*'s heavy pommel. Howling, the clone bounded away on all fours, leaping onto one of the squat guard towers and scuttling sideways into the tunnel like a great black spider. A moment later, Max heard the winch being spun as the clone raised the portcullis.

An eerie dance took place as the malakhim galloped through the gate and rode about the courtyard's perimeter with their torches and swords. They hemmed Max in, surrounding him and drawing the noose ever tighter as they leaned from their saddles and swept their swords in long, lethal arcs. Max fought defensively, careful to vary his patterns and keep an eye out for the clones. His only hope was to whittle down the odds and capitalize on rare opportunities.

And while such opportunities were rare, they did exist. The Morrígan's blade might have balked at the clones, but it had no misgivings about the malakhim. The weapon roared back to life, keening for the cloaked spirits and cleaving through their swords and mail with frightful ease whenever one ventured too close.

Four of the malakhim had fallen when a fist-sized rock struck the back of Max's head. He stumbled forward, catching himself on one knee. Another smashed into the base of his skull and he crumpled onto the snow-swept courtyard. Blood now trickled from a dozen wounds, stinging his eyes and fingers, hissing whenever it touched the *gae bolga*. Dazed, Max scrambled to his feet and staggered sideways, tripping over icy stones at the base of a fallen tower. With a jubilant howl, the savage-looking clone dropped the rock and rushed forward with his knives.

The other joined him, leaping down from his saddle and racing at Max with his spear. The *gae bolga* fell silent as they closed the gap, leaping over scattered stones and converging like a pair of hounds closing on a wounded quarry.

The spear struck first, a screeching blow aimed right at the heart. Max turned the point aside, but the blunt force of the collision cracked his collarbone and sent him staggering back against the well. Turning, he evaded another thrust and just managed to duck as the other clone came leaping after him, brandishing his knives.

As Max battled the clones, the remaining malakhim cut off any escape. The fighting was the most frenzied and brutal Max had ever experienced, skills and strategy devolving into a desperate, savage contest of wills.

At last Max saw an opening. With a roar, he downed the knife-wielding clone, striking him a blow to the temple with the *gae bolga*'s pommel. But when he made to finish him, the other clone darted in, dropping his spear and seizing hold of Max from behind. Before he could counter, Max's feet were wrenched off the flagstones.

With appalling strength, the clone squeezed tighter and tighter, driving the steel rings of Max's hauberk clear through the tunic to bite the flesh beneath. Max nearly lost consciousness. He was only dimly aware of his captor's voice shouting above Yuga's incessant moan and the din of the distant armies: "You fought well. But your time has come."

Rising on unsteady legs, the other clone pushed his long hair back from his face. One eye was swollen shut and his jaw appeared broken. Spitting blood through a jigsaw of shattered teeth, he nevertheless grinned at Max and offered a soldier's salute. The grisly smile remained, but the clone's eyes went as cold and dead as a shark's. Stepping forward, he raised the knife high and brought it screaming down.

But no blade struck Max.

Instead of a dagger, the clone now held a wriggling asp by the tail. Its body thrashed wildly about, but its fangs were sunk deep into the other clone's cheek. Howling with pain, he released Max and scrabbled at his face, prying the venomous snake free and flinging it away. For a surreal instant, the three looked from one to the other in stunned confusion. Across the courtyard, Max glimpsed a small figure on horseback steadying his frail form against the keep's great archway.

David!

Rowan's sorcerer was trembling with anger. The night grew colder as he rode from the keep, the atmosphere twitching and crackling with an electric charge. As David approached, Max felt energies emanating from him, sluggish ripples of Old Magic that seemed to warp and buckle the air. The remaining malakhim and even Max's clones backed away from the boy as if he were radioactive.

Crack!

The masks of the malakhim shattered.

They fell in a tinkling shower of obsidian shards, revealing the ghastly faces beneath. In the moonlight, they were milky and translucent, a swirl of features that bubbled like melted wax, ever seeking to assume a beautiful visage. But as soon as one was formed, it instantly liquefied and curdled into something grotesque. The spirits turned away, covering their naked faces as though each held some secret of their shame and fall.

The sorcerer's attention locked onto the clones. They were rooted in place, but every muscle and vein now shone as though they each were straining furiously against some invisible binding. Trembling uncontrollably, the larger one managed to raise his spear. Glowering, he spoke through clenched teeth.

"You're not strong en—"

With a backhanded gesture, David blasted the clones off their feet. They flew as if they'd been shot from a cannon, somersaulting through the air like rag dolls until they struck the courtyard wall in an explosion of stone and debris that knocked the malakhim from their horses. From the palace wall, there was a groan. A moment later, a vast section collapsed inward, sending a cloud of dust rolling across the dark courtyard. The clones were entombed.

David turned to Max, his face weary and spent.

"Can you ride?"

When Max nodded, David called out for Madam Petra. The smuggler emerged cautiously from the keep, leading the other horse by its bridle. Katarina was ashen-faced, clutching the reins as she stared at the broken malakhim. Slumping against his saddle's pommel, the sorcerer gestured toward the eastern sky. He struggled to make himself heard over the coming storm.

"Max and I are hurt—we have to make for Bholevna. Yuga is getting closer; it might be very dangerous. Do you understand? You can come with us or go your own way."

Mother and daughter gazed into the east, at the consuming blackness that blotted out the stars. Then they looked at each other and reached a silent agreement. Handing the smee back to Max, the smuggler swung up into the saddle behind her daughter.

"We're wasting time."

The group fled northeast beneath the moon, cutting across sparse forests and empty homesteads as they raced toward Bholevna. Max rode with David, holding the reins as the exhausted sorcerer struggled to remain conscious. He slumped back against Max, holding his injured shoulder and wincing whenever the horse jumped over a ditch or clambered up a hill. Max tried to keep his friend awake, but he was having difficulty himself. He was badly wounded, and despite his remarkable powers of recovery, he'd lost a tremendous amount of blood.

"Don't nod off!" cried Toby, nestled once again in Max's hood. "You've got to keep riding, boy. There's medicine and good food and soft beds at Rowan. We've got to get that pinlegs to the Director! We've come all this way and now we're going home, so stay with me. Both of you!"

Max was dangerously dizzy by the time they glimpsed Bholevna. The demon city was a sprawl of Gothic buildings and small palaces that straddled a wide river and was knit together by a series of bridges and causeways. In the moonlight, the river looked like polished silver, but the city itself was dark. No lights peered from windows; no smoke trickled from chimneys. In the path of Yuga, Bholevna had been utterly abandoned.

Riding down a series of shallow hills, they merged with the main road that fed into the city. There were no guards posted at the western wall. They galloped through the open gates and onto cobbled streets where freezing gusts whipped papers and debris about in little windstorms. The main avenue through the city led directly east toward where Yuga filled the sky like a spreading pool of ink. Her moaning was deafening now; it filled the air and shook the very earth. Max shouted to David, but he couldn't even hear his own voice. A flock of birds sped past, fleeing the ravenous demon.

Riding out the opposite gate, they veered off the road, galloping over snowy wheat fields and open country toward several farms that bordered a fir wood. In the east, the landscape had become a churning vortex of dust, soil, and trees that swirled about in gargantuan funnel clouds that rose thousands of feet before disappearing into the demon's roiling bulk.

When viewed from a safe distance, Yuga was truly frightening. Up close, her presence simply overwhelmed all sense and sanity. Max had never experienced such terror. Every instinct screamed frantically at him to turn around, to flee, to hide, to pray, to beg, to do *anything* that might spare him from such a monster.

It was far too much for the horses. They shied at the same instant, as if they'd crossed some invisible threshold that broke the poor creatures' minds. Max managed to roll from the saddle, pulling David with him before their mount sidestepped and collapsed. It stared dully ahead, steam rising from its flanks as it lay in the snow. From what Max could tell, the animal wasn't injured; some insidious force or perhaps sheer horror had compelled the horse to succumb, to lie still and wait for the demon to devour it.

Madam Petra was huddled on the ground, shielding Katarina as the wind and snow whipped about them. Max yelled to her, but she did not hear him. Lifting David onto his shoulder, Max grabbed the pinlegs tube and stumbled over to the smuggler. He screamed and tugged at her arm, but the woman could hardly respond. She merely gaped at him as he gestured furiously at the distant cabin. The entire earth was shaking. Max feared his eardrums might rupture.

Pulling the Kosas to their feet, Max seized Madam Petra's wrist and started running, half dragging the woman and her daughter toward the cabin. Their first steps were mechanical, as if the pair were drugged. But soon they came to and began running on their own, sprinting ahead as Max staggered behind with David and Toby.

The cabin was some two hundred yards away and set on a little hill. Glancing east, Max saw no stars—only a wall of darkness that stretched to the horizons. He ran harder, tapping every last reserve of energy and will. Petra reached the cabin first and tried the door before using his sword to smash through a nearby window. As her mother scrambled inside, Katarina reached the porch and turned back to look for them. Glancing east, the girl's knees nearly buckled. She screamed at them to run, but Max could only see her mouth moving, frantically forming the word over and over.

Max refused to look east or heed any pain as he stumbled along. Petra flung open the door, and soon mother and daughter were exhorting them, pleading for Max to run faster. Spots appeared before his eyes, teasing lights that danced in his peripheral vision. Was he dying? He'd lost so much blood; his entire body felt like ice. Just a little farther . . . just a little faster.

Staggering toward the cabin door, Max practically tackled the Kosas, knocking the entire group down to the floor. He was losing consciousness, clutching the pinlegs to his chest. David's face was anxious but calm as he took Petra's hand and she took Katarina's. Max could no longer hear; he stared at the ceiling while the others huddled close. The cabin was shaking violently, but he felt strangely peaceful. When the windows blew in, he closed his eyes and waited for the stinging shards to fall.

~ 11 ~

RECKONINGS

Tap, tap, tap . . . tap, tap, tap. The sounds formed a soft, rhythmic melody that cut through the fog in Max's mind. There were other sounds, too: the squeak of a chair, the crystalline notes of metal striking glass, but always the soft *tap, tap, tap* returned. Max imagined they were tiny miners, sounding out spaces with their little hammers and digging deep into the earth.

Wherever he was, it was light. And warm. His whole body was swaddled in warmth, in a smooth coverlet that tickled against his chin. He stirred. A bandage crinkled and there was a low throb of pain throughout his side. Max groaned. To his right, another squeak of a chair followed by a soft swish of fabric. Max felt a welcome coolness upon his forehead, the tender dabbing of a damp cloth tinged with a sweet-smelling herb. Moments later, the melody returned.

Tap, tap, tap . . . tap, tap, tap . . .

It was the aroma of coffee that finally woke him. It wafted over, strangely out of place amid the smells of linens and soap and herbs. Opening his eyes a crack, Max glimpsed the blurry form of David Menlo sitting in a bedside chair and sipping from a mug. Slowly, the image came into focus. David was studying the top paper from a pile upon his lap. His brow was furrowed and he rocked slightly as was his tendency when deep in thought. Max made to speak, but his throat was too dry and he merely grunted.

Glancing up, David urged Max to lie still.

"Rest easy," he said gently. "Your injuries were severe. But they're healing now. The moomenhovens are taking good care of you."

Raising his head, Max saw that he was in Rowan's main healing ward. One of the moomenhovens was sitting in a rocking chair by a table laden with roots and herbs, glass jars, and ceramic bowls. The plump, rosy-cheeked woman was patiently grinding ingredients for medicines, swishing her cow's tail in time with the soft tapping of the pestle in the mortar.

"The others—" croaked Max.

"The others are fine," David assured him. "The Kosas have settled into an apartment in the township, and Toby's crowing about his heroics at the roulette tables. Of course, Madam Petra's already demanding better accommodations, but everyone's safe and on the mend. As for me, my wounds are healing nicely. Some scars and I'll be using a cane for a few weeks, but I've had much worse."

"I owe you my life," Max muttered hoarsely.

David instantly dismissed such sentimentality. "And I owe you mine many times over. If you hadn't pushed yourself beyond the brink, we'd all be in Yuga's belly. It was a near thing and we scraped by thanks to you, so let's not speak of debts and honor. I think you and I are well past keeping score."

Max smiled weakly and gazed up at the ceiling where sunlight was streaming through gauzy white curtains. "How long have I been here?" he asked.

"Six days," David replied. "At first, the healers despaired of saving you, but I assured them that you're just about unbreakable."

Max glanced down at his sling and the many bandages covering his person. "Could have fooled me."

"On the contrary," retorted David. "Do you have any idea how much damage you withstood? The clones' weapons were coated with Workshop poisons. Very nasty stuff. What we finally leeched from your system was enough to kill *hundreds* of men, Max. You suffered thirteen wounds, a broken shoulder, a fractured skull, a lacerated kidney, and I'll still wager that you recover within the week. Unbreakable, indeed."

Memories seeped in of the battle in the courtyard, the panic of being hunted and trapped.

"The Atropos have your compass," Max rasped. "The one Cooper used to find me in Prusias's dungeons."

David's smile faded. "I suspected as much. They were on our heels too quickly for it to be mere coincidence. With any luck, Yuga has consumed it and them. But it was very careless of me to permit that compass to fall into enemy hands. I should have had Cooper destroy it once it served its purpose."

"Did Miss Boon and Grendel find him?" asked Max, trying to sit up.

Looking down, David took another sip and set his coffee

on the nightstand. "They did," he replied cautiously. "The Cheshirewulf tracked him to an Atropos hideout north along the coast. There was a battle . . . some casualties. Fortunately, Miss Boon's unharmed and they managed to rescue Ben Polk. But the Atropos still have Cooper. Miss Boon's been taking it very hard."

"But he's still alive, then," said Max, relieved.

"Yes," said David. "But . . ."

Max grew wary. Ignoring his throbbing shoulder, he propped his back against the headboard. David's uncharacteristic loss for words was strangely unnerving. The sorcerer abandoned several explanations before settling on something simple and direct.

"Things started well," he began. "Apparently, we surprised them and Grendel had cornered the leader when Miss Boon and the others rushed in. We were winning and winning handily until the Atropos set Cooper loose."

"I don't understand," said Max, puzzled. "Cooper fought for *them*?"

"Yes," said David quietly. "He'd been confined in some chamber. When they let him out, the tide turned. Xiùměi is dead. Matheus is badly wounded. He's over there—behind that curtain near Ben Polk. Fortunately, Agent Polk is coming around. We're hoping he can give us more information about the Atropos and what they've done to Cooper, but it doesn't look good. Miss Boon's devastated—says Cooper's not really human anymore. Every outpost and sentry has been informed. We won't let him get close to you."

Max said nothing for some time. *Cooper killed Xiùměi?* She had been the oldest member of the Red Branch, a wizened woman who had survived countless battles and world wars only to fall at the hands of her own captain. Max would miss her toothless grin and irreverent humor. Sorrow aside, there were practical matters to consider: The Red Branch was growing thin. Only seven of the twelve were now in commission and war was coming. Poor Miss Boon. He grieved for his old Mystics teacher. Hazel Boon was not the sort who loved quickly or easily, but she had loved William Cooper.

Sitting up, Max gazed about the infirmary at the many beds and patients. Some he recognized, Agents wounded on other missions. Others were hidden behind curtains. Max watched a moomenhoven pull a curtain aside and glimpsed a man whose skin had been burned away. He was suspended by a system of silken nets and pulleys, blinking stoically while the healer applied some salve.

Despite such grisly sights, the ward was peaceful. It was clean and quiet, sunlight streaming through the high windows as the moomenhovens made their rounds and tended the wounded with herbs and draughts and shy little smiles.

"Patching us up for the war," Max reflected.

Sipping his coffee, David smiled. "Cynical already. You *are* getting better."

"What about the pinlegs?" Max wondered, turning around. "Where is it?"

"Down in the Archives. The scholars are studying it, as is Peter Varga. We're hoping he might be able to use his prescience to foresee its full capabilities. I'm giving it some attention, too." He patted the documents on his lap.

"What have you figured out?"

"Let's see, let's see," David muttered, lowering his voice and glancing at the topmost papers where Max glimpsed diagrams of the creature and the various runes and markings that were found on its case. "Strange little creature. It's some sort of genetically engineered centipede, but it has mechanical elements fused to the organic—sensors, transmitters, cloaking devices. On its own, it'd be a neat little spy or assassin, but that's not what's got everyone worried. It's these. . . ."

David held up one of the sheets of paper on which several intricate diagrams had been drawn. Max saw that each was purposefully left incomplete, lest it inadvertently trigger some sort of unintended consequence.

"These inscriptions were almost invisible," said David, scooting his chair closer. "They've been etched onto the pinlegs' segments in lines so fine we almost missed them entirely."

"Summoning circles," Max breathed, squinting at the diagrams.

"That's right," David confirmed. "But we don't know for what kind of spirit. I've never seen anything like these diagrams before. They don't make any sense."

"What's so weird about them?"

"In some ways, a proper summoning is like a math equation; you're specifying particular terms and operations according to established principles. One of those principles is that the thing you're summoning is . . . a thing. It is whole. It is a complete being—with a truename and a spirit or soul. But these diagrams imply a different sort of operation. They're designed to call *half* a being."

"Half of what?"

"I don't know," remarked David, frowning and staring at the diagram. "That's what we're trying to figure out. But I don't like the idea that the pinlegs could be tethered to something else—something it can summon at a moment's notice. We don't yet know what it is, but we know the Workshop and Prusias believe it will tip the balance in their favor."

Max remembered back to the vyes he'd overheard by the lake. He told David of their dread of "scuttlers" and what might happen when they're set loose.

"Do you remember those strange lights in the skies above Raikos?" said Max. "And that sound . . . like air-raid horns followed by earthquakes and tremors. We didn't see or hear anything like that when we floated over Prusias's army. I'll bet Prusias unleashed the pinlegs when we were holed up in that palace. I'll bet those lights and tremors were made by whatever they summoned."

David nodded and jotted several notes in the paper's margins. "I was too out of it," he lamented. "Did you actually see anything?"

"No," replied Max. "The horizon was filled with fire and smoke and lights flashing across the sky. The entire palace shook. Whatever made those sounds and tremors must have been huge."

"And arrived *instantaneously*," added David. "That's the real worry. If Prusias can have these pinlegs instantly call in some sort of monstrous cavalry, his army's nigh invincible. He must have found a way around the energy requirements."

"What do you mean?" asked Max.

"Teleportation requires an ungodly amount of energy," said David. "Even I can't teleport on my own. I can only do it if I find a wormhole or construct a tunnel from our room, and those take me months to craft. But summoning achieves much the same effect as teleportation—it instantly transports a being vast distances to a specified place. It just uses a different, more efficient means."

"Am I going to get a headache?" Max moaned. "Why do I always get a headache when I talk to you and Mina about these things?"

"No headaches," David promised. "This is a simpler concept. In teleportation, the caster has to do all the work himself. He has to metaphysically transport a large mass over a vast distance in a tiny period of time. That requires colossal sums of energy.

But in summoning, you're simply teleporting the being's soul. A soul by itself has almost zero mass and thus the process requires only a tiny fraction of the energy."

"But then how does a summoner also transport the body if that's so hard?" asked Max.

"He doesn't," replied David. "The *soul* does. You see, the bond between a soul and its body is very strong—atomically strong. They do not like being separated. During a summoning, the connection between the two has not been fundamentally broken, but it has been stretched almost infinitely thin—like the thinnest, strongest rubber band you can imagine. While the soul is anchored in place by the summoning circle, the body is free to move. And move it does! They reunite almost instantly. But in this scenario, the energy was provided by the bond between soul and body—not the summoner."

"But why would the pinlegs want to summon half of something's body?" Max asked.

"Why indeed . . . ," mused David, gazing out the window. He reposed in silence for several minutes, staring off into space with a blank, abstracted expression. At last the sorcerer blinked and clucked his tongue. Glancing at Max, he rose from his chair and bowed. "*Some people without possessing genius have a remarkable power of stimulating it.*"

"And what is that supposed to mean?"

"Forgive me," said David, smiling. "A quip from Mr. Sherlock Holmes. The truth is that you've just given me a very good idea—one I need to investigate right away. I'll look in on you later. Ms. Richter's posted guards to the ward entrance, the *gae bolga*'s beneath your pillow, and you have your ring. Pay attention to it, Max. I don't want to frighten you, but the Atropos may be close. Until I return, here are some letters that have been piling up. They've already been screened for anything insidious.

You might have your enemies, but it also seems that a few people care about you. Shocking, I know. I promised Mina she could look in after supper, so steel yourself for some highly intelligent and periodically trying company."

"You're good practice," Max retorted, accepting a stack of letters and bidding David farewell. Taking up a slim wooden cane, David hobbled out of the ward with his mug and papers stuffed into the crook of his free arm. He resembled an absent-minded professor late for a lecture.

Max glanced at the letters and notes. They were in a small pile, an array of paper sizes and colors and handwriting. The first was from Hannah.

Max! The minute I heard you were home and hurt, the goslings and I came to see you. They wouldn't let us in, if you can believe it. Some officious boob suggested we might be assassins. Ha! You poor honey—I hope you're getting better and that the moomenhovens are taking proper care of you. One of them is transcribing this letter for me, and if she doesn't write down every single word, I'm going to show her the business end of my beak. Oh, I guess she really is writing everything down. Good. Where was I? Oh! Honk misses you terribly. He's a sweet little thing, but he really needs a strong male influence in his life or he becomes unmanageable. Unmanageable! There's a new gander strutting about the pond and I have to get my bosom feathers tufted. Hmm . . . "bosom" isn't really spelled like you think it would be. Anyway, here's a big smooch from the wee ones and me. SMOOCH! —Hannah

Smiling, Max laid the letter aside and opened others from Nigel Bristow, Cynthia Gilley, Mr. Vincenti, and Nolan, and a brusque note from Tweedy that a manuscript on siege warfare was "shamelessly overdue" from the Bacon Library. Max promptly incinerated this reminder and turned to a letter from Sarah Amankwe. Events had transpired so swiftly the night of Rolf's death that he had never had a chance to check on her. Unfolding the stationery, he gazed at his classmate's graceful script.

Dear Max,

The rumor is that you're in the healing wards, but access is restricted and I can't visit. You and David had already left on some secret mission, but Ms. Richter came and spoke to me the night that Rolf died. She said that he'd been possessed and that Umbra actually saved your life. That's some comfort, I suppose, but it was still a terrible thing. I miss Rolf very much. His funeral was tasteful—Monsieur Renard and some of the other teachers spoke. They talked about what a fine student he was . . . capable and considerate . . . always willing to help. Ajax, Umbra, and the others wanted to attend, but I asked them to stay away. I know it's not their fault, but I didn't think Rolf's family would have wanted them there. I've been training with them like you suggested and have to admit that it's made me better. Umbra's speed and technique are like nothing I've ever seen. She sparred against one of the Vanguard Agents and it wasn't even close. They have her training some of our own students now. I'm trying hard not to hate her. Come find me when you're up and about. Some say the Enemy will be coming for us soon. I'm going to be ready.

Love,
Sarah

"Poor thing," he muttered, folding the letter and placing it atop the others. There was one remaining—a brown envelope containing a folded sheet of faded stationery. The writing was cramped and jittery, and Max had to read each line twice to decipher it.

Dear Max,

They tell me that this letter may not be welcome and that you may likely toss it aside. I will consider myself fortunate if you read through to the end. My name is Byron Morrow and I once taught you humanities here at Rowan Academy. I am retired now and live in a cottage near the Sanctuary dunes—any teacher can tell you where it is should you choose to visit. I would like that.

I am writing because my health is declining and I'm afraid I will not see the spring. At such moments, one wants to reflect upon their life, about the person they ultimately became . . . the decisions they have made. While I remember my Elaine and my son, Arthur, I fear that my recall is not what it was. The nurses tell me that many people have such holes in their memories. They assure me that its a common problem in this new age, but I cant help but feel a little silly.

You're probably aware of this, but did you know that you're a living hero? I have often seen you at a distance and wanted to introduce myself to the great Hound of Rowan, but my caretakers never allowed it. One day I insisted (I can be stubborn) and they informed me that I had once betrayed you. It took some doing to get the whole story, but they claimed that I had given information to the Enemy that put you and many other children at risk. Of course, I told them they were mistaken. But they insist that it is so, and I cant argue back with any facts or certainty. It has been a difficult thing to bear.

This is not the first time I have tried to write you. I don't know entirely what to say or how to express myself properly. If what the nurses say is true, then I am so very sorry. I am sorry for everything. I would prefer to tell you in person, but I do not know if I will have that chance. Time and your own feelings may preclude such a meeting. In any case, I'm not certain that I'd deserve it.

I've never been the religious sort—never been certain of what to expect once my time comes to an end. But as that day approaches, I find myself rooting selfishly for reincarnation. Life is such a wondrously complex and tricky game. The notion that one might have another go and make amends is wildly tempting for anyone who's made such mistakes as I have. I don't know if such a magnificent thing really exists, but if it does, I hope our paths will cross again. I will do better by you.

With respect and admiration,
Byron Morrow
Instructor of Humanities, retired

Max glanced at the letter's date and found that it had been written some three weeks ago. Calling over the nearest moomenhoven, he pointed to Mr. Morrow's name.

"Do you know this man?" he asked.

The healer squinted at the letter and nodded.

"Is he still alive?"

All moomenhovens were mutes, but no words were necessary. With a sympathetic smile, she shook her head and reached with a soft hand to take Max's pulse. He waited patiently until she had finished, clutching the letter as Old Tom chimed three o'clock. Once she had taken his temperature and checked his bandages, the healer set a glass of water by his bedside before returning to her mixtures. Sipping the water, Max read the letter again, refolded it, and gazed distractedly across the room. The afternoon light was streaming through the high windows, forming shapes and rectangles that shimmered on the folds of a faded tapestry. Max watched the rectangles grow dimmer as the afternoon waned. Soon, the moomenhovens padded about the ward, lighting its candles and lanterns.

The letters were stacked on the nightstand and Max was drowsing to the familiar *tap, tap, tap* when the pattern was broken by the patter of excited footsteps and the soft swish of a robe. Very gently, a hand took hold of Max's. It was small and hot and wonderfully full of life.

For three straight evenings, Mina visited Max after she'd finished supper. Sitting by his bedside, she tinkered with her mage-chain and chattered about the doings at Rowan since he'd been away. There was a great deal to share, and Mina endeavored to relay it all in eager, breathless, disjointed accounts that might have lasted all night if the moomenhovens did not see her off once Old Tom struck ten o'clock.

Did Max know that Mina had added eleven masteries to her chain?

Did Max know that Emma Bristow had been scolded for riding Nigel's piglet, Lucy?

Did Max know that Claudia and the others had painted Bob's cabin yellow?

Did Max know that Circe had given birth to seven baby lymrills?

This last statement brought Max's drifting thoughts to a screeching halt.

"What did you say?" he asked, halting Mina in midpirouette. Grinning, she hopped up onto the bed and plucked at a stray thread on her sleeve.

"Circe had babies," she repeated. "Seven little lymrills all squirmy and warm. They're smaller than my hand, but their claws are sharp! There are two coppery ones and a goldeny-yellow one, three silvers, and one that's so black you can hardly see her until she opens her eyes. They're so precious! Circe won't hardly let anyone touch them, but she lets me! I remember your stories of Nick, but I never thought I'd get to hold a real lymrill!"

"Maybe one will choose you to be its steward," Max mused thoughtfully.

"I would like that—a lymrill of my very own. But that is not to be. Did I not tell you that my charge is coming, Max? When the gulls cry out and the waters run red, he'll rise from the sea to find me."

"And when will that be, Mina?" asked Max, disturbed by her manner.

But the girl would not reply and merely turned her attention to the torque about his neck.

"That's from a lymrill, isn't it?" she asked, running her fingers over the coppery metal. "That's from your Nick. I can tell."

"It is," said Max, slipping it off and letting her handle it. "His final gift."

"It's unbreakable," she said, as though divining its properties at a touch. "A Fomorian made this for you. I can hear his song in the metal. What was he like?"

"The Fomorian? Well, he was as big as a house and he had ram's horns and several eyes and he was very strong and old and . . . sad. He's been living a long time, Mina, and I think he's been very lonely on his isle and in his caves beneath the sea."

"We could invite him to live here," she declared. "Then he wouldn't be alone."

"You are very thoughtful," said Max, letting her scoot next to him. "But I don't think he would come. The Fomorian belongs to another age. He's like a living fossil and follows older laws and customs than we do. It could be dangerous to have someone like him at Rowan."

"But he made this for you," she remarked, turning the gleaming torque over. "And your sword."

"Reluctantly," Max replied. "David almost lost his head in the bargain. Speaking of which, how is he?"

"Busy," she replied a bit sullenly. "He's working with Agent Varga and studying that crawly pinlegs. They both use canes, you know. I followed after them with a stick of my own to play Three Blind Mice, but David told me it was bad manners and wouldn't let me past the runeglass." She sighed. "I've had to take my lessons with Ms. Kraken. She's always cross and she smells like an old lady."

"She is an old lady," Max pointed out, "and that's not very nice. But what about the Archmage? I thought he was giving you lessons."

"Uncle 'Lias is worse than you and David," she pouted. "Much worse. Always running off, disappearing in a blink and reappearing in the middle of the night. He makes such a racket when he returns—clomping in his boots, lighting lanterns, and digging through old books. It scares Lila half to death. But by the time she peeks out the door, he's already gone. She thinks his room is haunted."

"What's the Archmage doing?" asked Max.

The girl leaned close. "Hunting for Astaroth," she whispered with something like real delight. "Always hunting, never sleeping. I should not like to be the Demon. When Uncle 'Lias gets an idea in his head, he doesn't let go. He's wild like you and wise like David."

"Has he had a look at the pinlegs?" Max wondered.

"No," she replied. "He says it's our job to save Rowan. He must save everything else."

"You know, Mina," sighed Max, "I don't entirely know what to make of our Archmage."

Old Tom struck ten o'clock. Placing the torque around Max's neck, the little girl grinned. "He says the same thing about you."

With a farewell kiss, Mina scooted off the bed and scampered out of the room, waving farewell to the healers and dashing past the door wardens.

The moomenhovens released Max the following morning. Four of them had gathered around his bed to unwrap his bandages. Curious faces peered, unblinking, at the many wounds, pausing now and again to give shocked and covert glances at one another. One consulted a chart, jotting furious notes while her sister healers poked and prodded and gauged to see if any of their tests caused Max any discomfort. They did not. The tests were nearly complete when one of the kindly creatures gestured at a scar on Max's face, a thin pale line that ran from cheekbone to chin. It was the only scar that remained, the only blemish on an otherwise perfect specimen of health, strength, and vitality.

"I got that years ago," Max explained.

What he did not explain was that he'd received the wound from Scathach, the warrior maiden who lived in the Sidh and who had instructed Max in the greatest arts of combat. He had been slacking late one afternoon on the battlements of Lugh's castle when she had whipped her blade across his face in a sudden, stinging reprimand. The scar had never faded. Whenever Max looked into a mirror, he saw the thin white line and remembered beautiful, deadly Scathach. He wondered if she ever thought of him.

The moomenhovens brought Max his clothes, cleaned and folded. Rips had been sewn, boots cleaned and polished, and even the hauberk's rings had been repaired so that no tear or rent showed when he held it up to the window. Dressed, Max thanked the healers for their kind care and buckled on the *gae bolga* when he turned to look at his fellow patients.

There were at least fifty other beds in the main ward, and each was occupied with an Agent or Mystic who had been wounded in the line of duty. To Max's knowledge, none had been released during his stay. He imagined each must be badly injured.

For the rest of the morning, he walked down the line of beds and visited quietly with those who were awake. He knew relatively few of the patients, but they all knew him. Those who could manage it sat up or shook his hand with whatever vigor they could muster. Max smiled, looked into each face, and tried not to stare at the appalling wounds that each had suffered. It was such a strange realization that they would look to one so young for strength or assurance, but the fact was undeniable.

"I didn't think you'd make it," croaked one aged Mystic through her bandages. "This whole place was in a panic when they brought you through here. You should have seen yourself, child. So bloody, so broken. And here you are . . . tall and straight as a sapling. You give me hope, boy. Not for me, but for Rowan. They'll never break us while we have our Hound. *Sol Invictus.*"

He had many such conversations. Some wanted only to meet him and hear a bit of encouragement. Others wanted to share their stories. Throughout the morning, Max listened to tales of smuggling weapons, infiltrating witch camps, sabotaging Prusias's shipyards. . . . The scope of Rowan's espionage and intelligence operations was enormous, and Max soon realized that his and David's efforts were but one slender thread in a complex web of activities. Some initiatives were grand and others were small, but all were engineered to slowly, methodically tip the

scales in Rowan's favor. Whether recruiting well-placed informants, intercepting critical shipments, or sowing false information to mislead the Enemy, Rowan was already fighting a secret
war with everything she had.

It was past noon when finally Max left the healing ward. He
strode out of one of the Manse's side doors, inhaling the scent of
evergreens and wood smoke as he gazed out over the Old College and the academic quad. It was cold, but the sky was blue
with thin, nacreous clouds drifting above. The pathways were
shoveled and glistening, the walkways crowded with students
hurrying off to lunch or some final class. Max smiled to see
garlands of holly strung about the streetlamps.

Purchasing some minced pies from a vendor's cart, Max
walked along the shoveled walkways toward Maggie. Wolfing
down the warm pastries, he nodded hello to passersby but was
ever mindful of his ring. When would it grow hot, he wondered.
When would the Atropos make another attempt?

It was wearing to view everyone with suspicion, to maintain constant vigilance even among one's friends. Aside from
the physical toll, a state of perpetual caution cast a miserable
pall on life.

*You're not going to tiptoe about in a state of constant fear, Max.
Live or don't live.*

He had resolved to live when the sight of an approaching
figure made him question his decision. Julie Teller was coming up the path. She had not yet seen Max but was listening
attentively to her companion, a slight man of about twenty with
curling blond hair, a fringe of beard, and ink-stained fingers.
Max thought about veering off onto a side path or even turning around when Julie's brown eyes flicked up and met his own.
Max felt his cheeks flush scarlet.

"Hi, Julie."

She stopped dead in her tracks, gaping at him as though he were a ghost. Brushing a strand of auburn hair from her eyes, she walked calmly forward.

"Why, it's you," she observed wryly, clutching her companion's arm. "Celia said you were here—at Rowan, I mean. But then one hears so many rumors about Max McDaniels. I never know when you're here or away keeping us safe or 'finding yourself' or whatever it is you do."

The barb found its intended target and burrowed deep. Julie's tone was cool and reserved, but her eyes had grown very bright. Her bottom lip was trembling, but every other aspect was poised for confrontation.

Max cleared his throat. "It's nice to see you," he said. "I'll be going."

"Of course you will," she said tightly. "That's what you do."

Max stopped in midstride. Julie gazed back at him, angry and defiant, her eyes now brimming over with tears. The young man leaned close and whispered to her.

"C'mon, Julie," he muttered. "Let's go."

"This is Thomas Polk," she announced, her eyes never leaving Max's. "We've been dating for over a year and we're engaged to be married."

A pause. Max only hoped his shock wasn't painfully apparent. "Congratulations," he said. "Your parents must be very happy."

"Not really," said Julie casually. "They think nineteen's too young for marriage. But they'll get over it. Ultimately I think they're just thrilled that I'm not dating you."

"Julie," said Thomas, tugging at her arm. "You're getting upset. We should go."

"I'm not upset!" she declared hotly, pulling away. "I'm running into an old friend and filling him in on all my exciting news. What's *your* exciting news, Max? Been off killing things for the Red Branch? Maybe Thomas can run a piece on your adventures. His family owns the *Tattler*. They're always looking for good stories."

"Maybe some other time."

"Ha!" she laughed, tears flowing freely down her cheeks. "Some other time? And when will that be, I wonder? See you in a few years, Max. If you're still alive, perhaps you can meet our children."

"Julie!" exclaimed Thomas, glancing nervously at Max. "That's a terrible thing to—"

"It's okay," said Max quietly, holding up his hand. "I had it coming. Congratulations on your engagement, Thomas. Congratulations to you both."

Max left the pair behind, staring at his boots and listening to the wind in the trees, the distant drum of cold surf crashing on the beach. He walked past Old Tom and Maggie, glancing momentarily at the broken cliffs where Gràvenmuir had stood. The ocean was gray and dotted with whitecaps and the sails of merchant ships. The harbormaster's bell rang and he watched as a goblin carrack from Svalbard eased past the watchtower. The ship looked as stout and weathered as an old boot, pushing through the icy water and giving the Blyssian xebec a wide berth as it steered toward one of the loading docks.

The ambassador's ship had not moved since its arrival. It was still moored in the harbor, tethered to the main pier by heavy ropes. Smoke drifted lazily from open hatches and stovepipes. The witch had disappeared from the deck, but the pillar of witch-fire remained near the prow. Max imagined the ambassador coiled behind runeglass in some luxuriant cabin, waiting for Rowan's reply to his king's demands. The solstice was just a few days away. Prusias would have his answer soon.

As he stared out at the xebec, Max tried to take Julie's words and consign them to some safe place within his heart or mind. But they resisted. It was not that she'd said anything unjust or unfair; he knew he deserved what she'd said and more besides. It was her hardness that lingered, the hurt and disdain that surfaced as soon as she'd seen him. His Julie had been playful and mischievous, a vibrant and loving soul who was always seeking some new adventure. The sad truth was that this new Julie seemed diminished. It was not a physical decline—she was still as beautiful as ever—but her inner radiance had dimmed. Life and circumstance had worn down her youth and sapped something in her essence, some spark of fundamental optimism or joy. Max hoped that it was merely surprise and righteous anger at running into an ex-boyfriend, but that was a lie. The painful truth was that he had sensed the change before she ever laid eyes on him.

Turning, he left the bluff and its broad view of the harbor and the wide world beyond. At his back were Prusias's armies; ahead loomed Maggie and the pinlegs deep down in its Archives. Max gazed up at the venerable gray building with her shale roof and squat chimneys puffing white smoke into the wintry air. With a sigh, Max kicked a stone and trotted up the path to her door.

It was a long walk down to the Archives, a twenty-minute descent down winding staircases that plunged deep into the earth. The trip always reminded Max that much of Rowan was alive. Old Magic had created the school, and something of these wild, primal origins still pulsed within the hollowed stone and arches. As Max descended, the walls became damp and almost seemed to aspirate as breezes from below sent the torches sputtering. Visiting the Archives felt like climbing down into the ribbed belly of a whale or dragon.

Where the stairs ended, they opened upon a tall vestibule

whose double doors were guarded by a pair of shedu. At first glance, the enormous creatures looked like mere statues of man-headed bulls with great stony wings. But the eyes blinked and followed Max as he approached.

"Max McDaniels requesting access to the Archives," he said, holding up his Red Branch tattoo.

The creatures stared implacably at the tattoo and at his face with fire-opal eyes. Shedu were bred to guard, to detect deceptions and illusions of all kinds. They were so effective that Max was not entirely surprised to hear an indignant sniffle behind him.

"You're looking very well."

Max turned to see Toby sitting dejectedly on a small bench that had been placed for visitors.

"How long have you been here?" asked Max.

"Oh, a day or so," replied the smee glumly. "I tried to follow David down here—to help with the analysis. I tried to change into one of the scholars, but it was no go. I forgot about the ban. Instead of becoming a scholar, I just turned fire red like I was . . . like I was *relieving myself.* Well, the shedu slammed the doors and threatened to squish me like I'm just some common busybody!"

"Hard to believe," replied Max. He turned back to the guardians. "Would it be all right if he comes in with me? He was involved in a DarkMatter operation for the Director."

The stolid shedu glanced doubtfully at one another, but at last the massive doors opened.

"I told you I was someone important!" roared Toby, twisting about to glare at each as Max carried him through the great archway.

"How on earth did you make it down here?" whispered Max once they were inside. "There must be a thousand steps."

"Twelve hundred," grumbled the smee. "And each a grueling

humiliation . . . inching to the edge of each stair and flipping myself over like some acrobatic gourd. There should be a slide!"

"Shhh!" whispered Max as several scholars glanced up irritably from their tables.

"Well, I want to be able to change shapes at Rowan!" hissed Toby. "They should lift that silly prohibition. Promise me you'll put in a word with the Director."

"Okay," said Max. "But keep your voice down. You have to be quiet down here—it's like a big library."

Indeed, the Archives were like a library, but one that was larger than any cathedral. It was a vast, arched space with many levels where millions upon millions of manuscripts were housed behind archival glass. Vaults were spaced along the main level, gargantuan steel doors set into the stone and protected with various runes and spells. One of these belonged to the Red Branch and housed their greatest treasures, but some belonged to different orders, including the Vanguard, the Minstrels, the Promethean Scholars, the Bloodstone Circle, and many other esoteric groups from Rowan's early days. Light was provided by witch-fire lanterns and from pale shafts of daylight that filtered through translucent stone high above. Despite the crowded tables on the main level, the atmosphere was quiet and this reverential hush—even more than the space's grandeur—reinforced the impression that one was in a holy setting, a temple of sacred antiquity.

A domovoi directed them to David, who was hunkered down in one of several top-secret laboratories housed in a restricted wing. Cupping Toby, Max walked past many windows behind which Mystics were peering at various objects or even creatures suspended within glass orbs that held swirling vapors or shimmering lights of every color. He stopped at one, peering at an evil-looking creature that turned about in its orb, glaring at its captors. At Max's knock, one of the Mystics glanced up, did a double take, and hurried over to open the door.

"Hi," said Max. "Sorry to bother you, but is that a Stygian crow?"

"A very nasty one," confirmed the Mystic, a graying middle-aged woman wearing glasses. "We captured a sortie from one of Prusias's detachments."

"What are you doing with it?" asked Max as the creature gave a furious shriek that shot flames from its membranous blowholes.

"Testing its sensitivity to various concentrations of Blood Petals and Zenuvian iron," replied the Mystic. "Most promising."

Max nodded and took another gander at the hideous creature before leaving the Mystic to her work. David's laboratory was at the end of the corridor, conspicuous among the rest with its circular iron door set into a wall of smoky runeglass. Max knocked.

Miss Boon answered, looking tired and careworn.

"Max," she said, embracing him. "What a wonderful surprise to have you up and about so soon."

"Is that really him?" rasped a voice within the chamber. It was a heavy, Balkan accent and belonged to a man who had played a strange but instrumental role in Max's life.

Stepping across the threshold, Max saw Peter Varga sitting on the edge of a chair and leaning forward on his cane. His black hair was now flecked with gray, but his face was less gaunt and harrowed than it had been when Max first saw him on a train in Chicago. Then, the man had been an outcast from Rowan—hunted and pursued for making unauthorized overtures to the witches and the Workshop. Having rescued Max from Marley Augur's crypt, Varga had earned his way back into Rowan's good graces, but it had come at a terrible price. Marley

Augur's hammer had broken his back and he'd never fully recovered. Even now, he refused a wheelchair and relied instead upon a cane to get about with ungainly, stumbling steps that invited inconsiderate stares.

Few stared for very long, however. Peter Varga's most arresting trait was not his injury, but his eye. While one was green and unremarkable, the other was entirely white and possessed a ghostly, sentient quality that seemed to latch on and study its subjects with chilling intensity. No one lingered long under the eye's prescient gaze, and it, combined with the man's lurching gait and notoriety, made him a popular subject for rumor and gossip. Even after Cooper invited him to join the Red Branch, few people trusted Peter Varga and many shunned his company.

Max was among these, but his feelings had nothing to do with the man's appearance. When it came to Peter, Max's feelings were confused and deeply personal. Agent Varga had once protected Max and saved his life, but his prescience played a role in the disappearance and untimely death of Max's mother. Gratitude, guilt, and anger were difficult feelings to reconcile, and Max did not try. Since his mother's passing, he simply ignored Peter Varga and rebuffed every attempt at friendship.

But he could not ignore him now. Pushing up from his chair, Peter hobbled toward him, smiling faintly as he took Max in. He stopped several feet away, uncertain whether a handshake would be welcome. It was an awkward moment. Max thought of Byron Morrow's letter and the sad absence of any closure or reconciliation.

"I envy your powers of recovery," said Peter, shaking the proffered hand appreciatively. "David said your wounds were very serious. At least they were not in vain."

The man gestured toward a large, levitating orb of runeglass in which the pinlegs was scuttling about like a hamster running on a wheel. As the orb turned, its inscriptions changed, ranging from the most basic Solomon Seal to intricate pentacles involving hundreds of tiny runes and sigils. Every so often, there was a spark and the pinlegs jumped to avoid a particular rune or section of an inscription. When this happened, enchanted quills recorded the details upon a huge roll of parchment like a sort of seismograph. Several sheets had been torn away and hung upon the far wall, where David was appraising them, studying the dense symbols and patterns like an astronomer trying to identify one particular star among the infinite heavens.

Sipping his coffee, the sorcerer spoke in a weary voice. "Did Mina charm you into bringing her? She's been trying to sneak in."

"No," said Max. "But Toby's here. He was waiting in the vestibule."

"Toby," chided David, his pale eyes never leaving the patterns. "What did I say?"

"You said this was top secret," recounted Toby, uncoiling as Max set him upon a table.

"Exactly," said David.

"But I helped you acquire the awful thing!" the smee protested. "I—I'm part of the team!"

"You are part of the team," David assured him. "But you're also an inveterate gambler who is willing to do or say just about anything to impress your audience. For example, did you not boast to a certain faun how your timely actions saved us above Piter's Folly?"

"I don't recall," sniffed the smee.

"I do," said David calmly. "It was three nights ago in Cloubert's casino. You were at the roulette table and were already down four lunes and eleven coppers."

"H-how do you know that?" sputtered Toby nervously.

"I bribed that faun to inform on you." David shrugged. "A

single lune was all it took for her to report everything you'd said throughout the evening. She didn't even know—or care—who I was or why I wanted the information."

A beat of mortified silence as the smee swelled up with indignation. "That was an unconscionable assault upon my privacy!"

"Very true," David confessed. "It is also an invaluable reminder to you that we are on the threshold of war. Rowan welcomes refugees and new arrivals every day. Most are simply seeking shelter, but there are doubtless many spies and saboteurs among them—even in Cloubert's. We cannot trust you with confidential information if you're going to blab secrets to every faun that catches your eye at the roulette table. The stakes are too high."

The smee drooped. "You're right," he sighed. "I've been indiscreet. I will be silent, David."

"Very good," said David, turning to join them. He smiled at Max, but there were deep circles beneath his eyes and he was still wearing the clothes from his visit to the healing ward. Limping toward the sphere, he stopped to peer in on the pinlegs and tap the orb with his finger. As soon as he did so, the pinlegs whipped about and attacked the very spot, its legs and pincers scrabbling madly for a hold on the enchanted glass. Venom dribbled from its mandibles, and for just an instant, Max caught faint flashes of red designs on the creature's segmented body. When David stopped touching the sphere, the creature returned to its mindless, undulating trek.

"Did you see it?" he asked, turning to them.

"The symbols," put in Max. "They flashed red when it attacked."

"That's right," said David. "The pinlegs is trying to arm itself. Miss Boon has gotten the thing to cycle through its operation settings. There's a whole range: dormant, stealth, even the fairly terrifying seek-and-destroy mode you've just witnessed. On this setting, it will attack anything that comes near it, and this is the mode we've been trying to study."

"What's the flash designed to do?" asked Max.

"It's to summon something," answered Miss Boon. "We believe the intermittent flash indicates that it's not working properly. In this mode, the pinlegs is trying very hard to establish some sort of connection, but the connection is failing almost instantly. Madam Petra said this one was not 'paired.' We have several theories on what that might mean, but we also think some trigger component is missing from this specimen. Perhaps another symbol or inscription is required to complete the cycle and let the creature sustain the necessary elements for a proper summoning."

"And so that's why the runeglass is cycling through inscriptions," said Max. "You're trying to identify what the proper symbol is. You're cracking a safe."

"Trying to," said David. "But the Workshop's people are very smart. There's a lot of cryptography at play, and while we're trying to optimize the testing, it's very slow going. Theoretically, it could take years to play out the permutations. I'm trying to accelerate things, but we're hoping Peter has a breakthrough."

"What David means is that we're trying to cheat," Varga chuckled. "I've been trying to concentrate on Prusias's army and see if I can glean any information about these creatures or what they summon. I get glimpses, but they're hazy. Little more than impressions."

"What can you make out?" asked Max.

"Not enough," muttered Varga, closing his eyes. "I can hear the pinlegs scuttling all around. There's light and sound. So much sound! At first it's like thunder, but then there are horns—they grow louder and louder. It's hard to endure them. The earth shakes. I'm looking up, but something's blotting out the sky. I can't see it clearly, but it's huge. And then darkness." The man opened his eyes and cleared his throat. "There's death in those visions."

"And we'd like to avoid it," remarked Miss Boon. "The plan is to deconstruct this thing's operations and find a way to sabotage them if we ever encounter them on our shores. We're not there yet, but we're hopeful that some of Sir Alistair's intelligence will yield another prize. He's identified several of the Workshop engineers who worked on the pinlegs project. Only two live above ground, and Agent Kiraly's tracked one to his estate outside Prusias's capital. We hope to have him shortly."

Max nodded his approval. Natasha Kiraly was also in the Red Branch, an exceedingly capable Agent whose stealth and swiftness were legendary. If the target was accessible, Max had no doubt she'd get him.

"One of my tunnels is near that location," said David. "Agent Kiraly's using spypaper to communicate with Ms. Richter each day. Once we confirm she has the target, we'll give her the tunnel location and I'll go retrieve them. With any luck, we'll soon have a valuable prisoner."

"But won't the Workshop know he's gone missing?" asked Max.

"We plan to install a replacement," replied Varga. "To delay suspicion."

"Brilliant!" exclaimed Toby. "Who's the decoy?"

All eyes turned to the smee.

"B-but, I'm injured," he protested. "My latissimus nub—"

"Will be fine," interjected David. "You won't have to do anything strenuous. You just have to pretend to be an elderly man who's fighting a cold. The engineer's a widower, semiretired with no children or regular visitors. With any luck, you can lounge in bed, putter about the grounds, and just keep up appearances. The malakhim were watching him, but apparently they've been reassigned now that the project is complete and the war has begun."

"And if I do this, I presume the unseemly ban on my shape-shifting would be lifted?"

"You presume correctly."

"Well, then. I'm your smee!"

"But what about the war?" asked Max. "What's the latest news from Blys?"

Rubbing at her eyes, Miss Boon poured more coffee from a silver carafe. "Lots of news," she sighed. "Almost all of it bad. The Director's office is practically covered with spypaper and updates from contacts all over the kingdoms. Prusias is now running roughshod over Aamon and Rashaverak. His initial losses drew their armies well within his borders and he is now grinding them to dust. He's already won major victories in Raikos, Acheral, Lebrím . . . all the major duchies. His ships have cut off Rashaverak's retreat, and we hear Queen Lilith is already making secret overtures for a treaty. Wherever the pinlegs have gone, victory has followed."

"So what does Ms. Richter intend to do?" asked Max quietly. "Solstice is a few days away. Prusias's emissary will demand his answer."

"I don't know precisely," said the teacher. "The Director's exceedingly busy these days and it's not easy to get a word. I won't speak for her, but I highly doubt we're studying pinlegs and kidnapping Workshop engineers because she intends to surrender."

Max smiled and looked around the room, at his friends and the pinlegs crawling about the spinning sphere. More symbols, more flickers, and the quills copied down the outcomes. As daunting as the prospects seemed, it was a comfort to know that there were so many capable people scattered about the globe doing everything in their power to keep Rowan free.

"Is there anything I can do here?" he asked. "My handwriting's awful, but I can jot down symbols if you like."

"Very kind, but unnecessary," replied Peter. "I'm confident the Director will have many things for you to do, but for now it's best if you rest and recover."

"I'll head back up, then," said Max. "Are you coming, Toby?"

"Staying. I need to study up on this Workshop chap—marinate in the character, so to speak. Tell that domovoi at the reference desk to bring me a ham sandwich and a pot of warmed honey. My tonsils are a wee bit tingly."

Ignoring the smee's demands, Max turned to Miss Boon. "Could I have a word with you outside?"

The teacher followed him out into the dim corridor. When she closed the door, Max cleared his throat, uncertain of just how to begin.

"I heard about Cooper," he said. "The raid . . . the casualties. I heard he was involved and I just wanted to say I'm sorry. I know how much he means to you."

Closing her eyes, Miss Boon simply stood quietly with fingers clasped. She looked almost like a chastened schoolgirl awaiting a reprimand. Tears ran down her cheeks while she struggled to control her emotions. Max feared he'd made a terrible mistake until she finally exhaled.

"Bless you," she said, removing her glasses and wiping her eyes. "No one wants to talk about what happened—they just tiptoe around it or concoct euphemisms like 'unfortunate outcomes' and 'compromised assets.' Thank you for having the courage to speak plainly and acknowledge my feelings. It means the world to me, Max."

She gave a sad smile and looked at him, no longer a teacher but simply a person in pain.

"Do you know what breaks my heart?" she said. "To most, William comes across as such a hard man—so grim and sinister. A professional killer. I called him that once when we were aboard the *Erasmus*. Do you remember?"

Max nodded.

"You'd never have known it then," she continued. "But that little gibe wounded him. He knew that's how people saw him—a scar-faced brute and nothing more. Rowan's attack dog. For years, I think he even believed it—he withdrew into himself and became the role. But there is such nobility in that man," she said, shaking her head. "There is such warmth and love. And what have the Atropos done? They've stripped it all away and turned him into the very monster he feared he was. . . ."

"What can I do?" asked Max, feeling helpless.

She blinked. Her mismatched irises returned to focus squarely on him. "Nothing," she said sharply. "You are to do nothing, Max McDaniels. You are not to go looking for him. He is no doubt looking for *you*, and we're expending many resources to ensure that William Cooper—or whatever he has become—stays far away from your person. Do you understand me?"

"But—"

"*No,*" she snapped. "I love very few people on this planet and I'm not going to lose them all to the Atropos. Grendel is on the hunt again and the Cheshirewulf is better equipped to track his steward than anyone else. If we need your help, we'll ask for it."

"Fair enough," said Max, anxious to change the subject. "Are you teaching again?"

"Just two classes." She sniffed. "Third and Fourth Year Mystics. I'd like to say my personal life hasn't affected my work, but those students just took the hardest exam I've ever written."

"Well," said Max, "just grade it on a curve."

She glared at him, simultaneously shocked and appalled. "Do you honestly believe in such ridiculous measures?"

Max winced, feeling as though he'd violated some academic commandment. He made to speak, but she raised an authoritative finger and began pacing.

"Tell me," she demanded. "Are we to lower our standards and applaud a student's mediocre efforts because it's simply *less* mediocre than his or her peers? On the same basis, shall we admit an Agent to the Red Branch because he can do three whole sit-ups while his fellows only managed two? Are these the utterly absurd standards that you would impose upon the world's greatest school of magic? Well, I submit to *you* that . . ."

With a hasty bow, Max retreated.

He left the Archives, climbing up the many steps and passing a handful of winded scholars along the way. Emerging from Maggie's front doors, he beheld a campus that was settling into late afternoon. Above, the sky was azure; to the west was a thin band of orange as the sun dipped behind the Manse and the hedge woods of the Sanctuary. The air was colder and a light snow was blowing in off the ocean.

Wrapping his cloak about him, Max walked through the woods behind the academic buildings, winding his way among the birches and oaks, conscious of the distant shouts and ring of steel from the refugee camp. But he drifted away from the noise, content to let his boots sink through the crusted snow and let the smell of pine tickle his nose.

At last he came to the clearing where Rose Chapel stood.

The sun had set and the snow was falling harder now. The chapel was conspicuous in the darkness, an elegant building of white stone whose open doors spilled warm yellow light onto the graveyard's headstones. Poking his head inside, Max saw an elderly chaplain and several domovoi laying out prayer books for the Sunday service. The chaplain spied Max in the doorway, lingering at the threshold.

"Can I help you?"

Max cleared his throat. "Would it be all right if I sat in here awhile?"

"Of course," said the chaplain, gesturing toward the pews.

Max slid into the nearest row, leaning back and staring up at the ceiling. It had been two years since Scott McDaniels's death. The funeral had been held here; Max could still picture the man who raised him lying in a coffin by the altar. This very chaplain had spoken. Max wondered if the chaplain knew who he was. He almost certainly did, but at least he had the decency to let Max be—not to preach or pry but to simply let him sit in this quiet space of wood and glass and stone.

When they'd finished with their work, the domovoi filed out. The chaplain followed behind, stopping only to set a lantern by Max's feet.

"Stay as long as you like," he said. "No need to lock up."

Max lingered for another hour, savoring the silence and the warm glow of the yuletide candles set within the alcoves and windows. At last he rose and left the chapel, closing the door gently behind him and gazing out into the dark churchyard. Snow was still falling, the flakes settling softly onto the gravestones.

Holding the lantern, Max walked the rows of the dead, shining its light upon each headstone until he found the one for Scott McDaniels. It was a modest slab of pale granite with the proper letters and numbers chiseled into the hard stone. Kneeling, Max brushed away the snow and wiped away the bits of dirt and grass that had accumulated upon the foundation.

Rolf's grave was easier to find. There were still flowers propped against the headstone, half-frozen roses and lilies left over from the funeral. As Max arranged them, he found a medal buried in their midst—an award the boy had won in Mr. Vincenti's class. Polishing its surface, Max hung it around the headstone so that it dangled next to Rolf's name.

There were no flowers at Byron Morrow's grave. It was a small plot near the woods that ran along the churchyard's boundary. He'd been buried next to his wife, Elaine. Her headstone was weathered, the corners worn smooth by many rains and winters. But Mr. Morrow's was new, its edges clean and sharp as Max knelt to brush the snow away.

He had just finished when he noticed that someone was watching him.

The figure was standing in the woods, just beyond the lantern's light. It did not move, but there was something unsettling and sinister about its quiet surveillance. Drawing the *gae bolga*, Max hoisted up the lantern.

"Who is that?" he hissed. "Show yourself!"

The figure glided smoothly forward, emerging from the dark wood so that the lantern shone full upon his white and smiling face.

It was Astaroth.

~ 12 ~

A WATCHER IN THE WOOD

Max stared, disbelieving, as the Demon came forward. The last time Max had seen Astaroth, he had been radiant and white—a luminous image of terrible power. Now his raiment was less glorious, more subdued. He wore a simple black robe and leaned upon the very staff he'd been carrying when he pursued Max and David in the Sidh. The Demon's face was the same—a gleaming white mask of patrician, almost genderless beauty framed by smooth black hair that hung past his shoulders. His fathomless black eyes crinkled into cheerful slits as he spoke in his honeyed tenor.

"Now it is the time of night
That the graves, all gaping wide,
Every one lets forth his sprite
In the church-way paths to glide.

"Are we communing with the dead?" he inquired pleasantly.

"I'm imagining this," Max murmured, watching the Demon's image grow translucent and flicker in the lantern light. "You're not here—you're skulking, lurking, hiding from Bram. You're just some mischievous spirit, some watcher in the woods."

The Demon gave a knowing smile. "I'm the watcher in all the woods," he replied softly. "And I am here. Not in the flesh, alas, but then I can't risk getting close to that awful blade. What a crime to craft such a weapon. You will never be free of it. You've made a bargain with the Morrígan, my boy, and blood is the only coin she takes."

Frowning at the *gae bolga*, the Demon's expression became thoughtful, almost melancholy.

"Dismiss your silly thoughts of violence," he said. "When I'm in this form, we cannot harm one another. I've merely come to talk with you, Max, to appeal to your good senses and save you from the path you're on."

"Of course," said Max scornfully. "You're here to save me."

"Yes, I am," replied Astaroth. He gazed about the church-yard and the falling snow and sighed. "You and David and all the rest have done such foolish things," he lamented. "It tries even my patience. I resurrect this beautiful world, give you a veritable Eden scrubbed clean of mankind's mistakes, and you're determined to throw it all away."

Max's face darkened. "This is your Eden? A world of war and death and fear?"

"Tut-tut," Astaroth chided. "Where is your vision? I suppose it's not entirely your fault—it's the human in you. But try to have some perspective. We're merely baby steps into a grand project, but already the old cities and governments and even memories are gone, cleared away so that a new and better world can take their place. Will death and heartbreak accompany such massive upheaval? Of course they will. When a farmer tills his fields, the ants must scatter or perish. But very soon, new life is created. The land *and* the ants are better for it."

"Tell that to everyone who lost their families and their freedom."

Astaroth sighed. He glided past to examine the headstones, stooping to read aloud several names of the deceased and how long each had lived. The Demon raised a slender eyebrow.

"Has it ever occurred to you that humans are dreadful at governing themselves?" he said. "Their lives are short but their appetites are large. It's an almost comic recipe for greed and discontent. Most care nothing for future generations of their own kind, much less other beings and creatures. The rare specimens who strive to live in peaceful balance are quickly exploited or conquered by those who do not. They are punished for their virtue while the rest of the species cultivates and rewards its very worst traits. Moral man and immoral society, indeed!"

Chuckling, Astaroth shook his head.

"If humans are such a cancer, why not simply destroy them?" Max mused. "You have the Book of Thoth. You could strike humans from the record, make everyone fade away like everything else you've changed."

With a shrug, the Demon rose and turned from the headstone.

"It is tempting," he confessed. "It would be dishonest to pretend I have not weighed such a measure—a chance to wipe the slate clean and begin things anew, refashion the species and purge it of its lesser qualities. But I have not yet given up hope for humans. Within them exist the divine and the profane. Did you know that Isaac Newton published his *Principia* in the very year a sailor slaughtered the last dodo bird?"

"What's your point?"

"My point is this. The genius who produced *Principia* is worth saving; the lout who bludgeoned the last of a helpless species is not. Such baffling extremes exist within mankind. Forgive me, Max, but such extremes exist within *you*. It's why you intrigue me. And while it is periodically tempting to obliterate humans, I entertain the hope that they can be taught to nurture and embrace their better nature. It won't happen overnight, but I'm optimistic that within a few centuries, we might see real progress. Perhaps we'll see the same with you."

"So we're all just living in your little garden," Max scoffed. "Some pruning here, some planting there, and wondrous things will grow."

"You say it like it's a bad thing," teased the Demon.

"People want to make decisions for themselves."

"Oh, I know they do," the Demon purred. "They're just not any good at it. How could they be when they lack the necessary vision, wisdom, or patience? You curse my name, but the painful truth is that mankind was already teetering on self-destruction. Would you prefer a nuclear holocaust, laboratory plague, or technological singularity to my ascendancy? You shed tears for the fallen, but my intervention has saved humanity. A benevolent dictator is best, as Plato himself realized."

"If you're so wise and benevolent, why did the demons turn against you?"

"Because they're as greedy and shortsighted as the humans. I believed that Prusias and others would be content with what

I'd given them. I was mistaken. I shall not make such an error again; Prusias will learn the error of his ways."

"What are you waiting for?" Max laughed. "His armies are rampaging all over Blys. Go punish him. Or have you grown too weak?"

The Demon's smile waned. "Let us understand one another. This is not about strength or my capacity to impose my will. I can destroy almost anything upon this planet the moment I choose. Shall I incinerate the earth's atmosphere? What if I melt down the ice caps or turn every drop of water into dust? The Book of Thoth gives me that power. If my ambition was merely to crush my enemies and rule as a tyrant, I could do so. That is Prusias's aim, not mine. Any brute can become a tyrant if he stumbles into enough power. That holds little interest for me."

"So what does interest you?"

The Demon gazed up at the stars. "Creation," he murmured. "To bring forth something whole and lasting from something diseased and broken. To design and build something that has never existed. I am older than you imagine, Max McDaniels, and I have seen countless worlds. None rival this for its beauty or sheer possibilities. In a few thousand years—a mere heartbeat of the cosmos—this could be paradise."

"Not if Prusias destroys it," remarked Max. "Why don't you stop him?"

"There's elegance in economy," replied Astaroth. "Why should I expend the energy to humble Prusias when he will do the job for me? Even if he conquers the other kingdoms and little Rowan, Prusias and the Workshop have broken Nature's laws and birthed horrors that will inevitably spiral out of control. When that happens, whatever survivors remain will beg for my return. Really, I should be grateful—nothing could illustrate my value more than greedy, savage Prusias. Does the prospect of his invasion frighten you?"

"I'd rather fight Prusias than bow to you."

"Touché," replied the Demon. "That's the very choice man has always faced—the king on the hill or the wolf at the door. A just king will protect you from the wolf, but he demands loyalty and service. You can choose to face the wolf alone, of course, but that is a risky proposition. And we're not even talking about a wolf, are we? We're talking about a Great Red Dragon. . . ." The Demon gave him a sharp look. "When Prusias comes, do you think Elias Bram will save you?"

When Max did not reply, Astaroth laughed soundlessly.

"Your silence speaks volumes. Already you sense what I know. The Archmage cares little for Rowan or its people. His real concern is hunting me and achieving vengeance. He may cite grand causes and ideology, but it's really just his ego. It always has been. Look no further than how Elias won the hand of the lovely Brigit. Do you know that laughable myth?"

"No."

"I'm surprised," replied Astaroth. "It was very popular once upon a time. You see, Brigit and Elias were hardly childhood sweethearts. In fact, her father had already given his blessing to another suitor and did not approve a match to the brazen young sorcerer. But Elias was exceedingly stubborn and far too danger-ous to simply dismiss out of hand. When Bram proclaimed that he would meet whatever demands Brigit's father cared to set, the shrewd patriarch saw his chance. He devised a list of tasks so perilous that few believed Bram would even survive, much less fulfill them. Of course, they were mistaken. The Archmage not only completed the tasks and won his bride, but he also multi-plied his fame in the bargain. Who could resist the story of the smitten sorcerer defying death time and again to win the hand of his truelove? The bards ate it up with a spoon and spread the tale to every shore. . . ." The Demon paused and tapped his chin. "Can you tell me what's missing from the minstrels' songs?"

"Brigit's former suitor," said Max, frowning.

Astaroth inclined his head. "Like myself, you have an instinct for justice," he remarked. "What indeed happened to her betrothed? The bards never delved into such details because I daresay it complicates things. It just might make you consider your Archmage in a less flattering light. As you know, Brigit honored her father's oath and married Elias Bram. But was she happy with this turn of events? Did she ever grow to love the arrogant young Archmage? Only she could say. Some have surmised that she was not pining for Bram when she waded into the sea but rather for this former suitor . . . the man she was *supposed* to marry."

Max cleared his throat. "Well, what happened to him? The other suitor, I mean."

"Sad stuff," sighed the Demon. "Ironically, this fellow had been Bram's closest companion. And despite this man's many virtues, Elias still dominated and outshone him in every conceivable way. There was nothing the poor boy could have or achieve that Bram could not take or surpass. However, that all changed when this friend found love. Until that day, Bram had no interest or use for such sentiments, but nevertheless it galled him that this associate—this *inferior*—should possess something that he did not. And thus the spiteful Archmage resolved not only to take a wife, but also to take the very woman with whom his friend was smitten."

"That's terrible," Max said.

"Yes, it is," concurred Astaroth. "But you must understand that winning was never enough for Elias Bram; others also had to lose. And so you see, the famous tale of Bram's heroic courtship is actually one of history's great betrayals. Shall I tell you the name of Brigit's suitor or can you guess?"

"Marley," concluded Max stiffly. "It was Marley Augur, wasn't it?"

"Correct," Astaroth hissed. "You've always thought of Marley as a villain and a traitor, but aren't those labels better suited for Bram? Be very careful of trusting Rowan's fate to the Archmage, Hound. One might say that those who know him best, love him least."

It was an uncomfortable revelation and Max wondered if David knew these allegations about his grandfather. Max did not doubt that they were true. For one, Astaroth never lied. For another, Max had also read some of Bram's own papers and had to admit that nothing the Demon said ran counter to the tone or tenor in the writings. Elias Bram *had* been an arrogant young man; he *had* been consumed with his own achievements and advancement. And then there was Marley Augur . . . the blacksmith's loathing of Bram, his desire for revenge, had staved off death itself and turned him into a revenant. The hatred was real and its origins were deep.

Still, Max gave a bitter laugh. "Should we look to you, then?" he wondered. "Will 'the Great God' come to Rowan's aid when Prusias storms our gates?"

The Demon's smile vanished and he glided almost within arm's reach, hovering like a phantom.

"You have but to ask," he whispered solemnly. "You have but to ask and I will come to you. Do you remember how to call me? *'Noble Astaroth, pray favor thy petitioner with wisdom from under hill, beyond the stars, and beneath the deepest sea.'* Utter these words, Max McDaniels, and you shall have an ally in your hour of need."

"How generous," Max observed. "And what would you expect in return?"

"One minor service," replied the Demon.

"And what would that be?"

"You must slay Elias Bram."

Max smiled in disbelief before simply shaking his head.

"Don't assume my motives are purely selfish," Astaroth cautioned, leaning close. "It may be in *your* interest to destroy the Archmage."

"What are you talking about?"

"He does not love you, Max McDaniels. You frighten him. You are a demigod and your lineage is very great. The Archmage's powers are in full bloom, but yours are in mere infancy. Bram knows there will be a day when he cannot stand against you. Given the man's past, do you really believe he will let that day come?"

Once he'd posed the question, the Demon stopped and awaited a response. Max gave a rueful smile.

"Your words are always poison."

The Demon sighed and leaned upon his staff. "Truth is a bitter draught, but the wise man swallows it. Consider what I've said, Max. Sleep on it. Should the wolf come scratching at your door, know that you have an ally in waiting. Speak the proper words and we have a contract. Speak the proper words and I will aid you."

"That will never happen."

"As you will," replied Astaroth softly. "But never is a long time and Rowan's hour draws near."

As Astaroth spoke these words, Old Tom struck ten o'clock. The notes rang clear and cold as the Demon backed slowly into the woods. And as he did, his ghostly form seemed to fade and dissipate. At last it unraveled into a wisp of vapor that scattered on the wind.

Following this strange and unsettling proposal, Max returned to the Manse. Once there, he retired to his room and remained there for two days. He did not share news of the Demon's visit with anyone. A part of his consciousness—a hopeful sliver—wanted to believe that he had imagined the whole affair. Besides, what was he to say—that *Astaroth* was willing to save them in exchange for Elias Bram's murder? Such an awful temptation might bitterly divide Rowan's leadership when unity was needed.

Max regretted the conversation extremely. The Demon's offer was an immense burden upon a mind and conscience already laden to capacity. He brooded over the many facets of their discussion, pacing about his room and gazing up at the starlit dome. While Astaroth never lied, he was often selective about what he shared and was perfectly willing for others to draw their own conclusions. He rarely relied on direct confrontation or brute force; his were more subtle schemes of leverage and manipulation. The Demon was notorious for moving allies and enemies about like chess pieces. Max did not fool himself that he could divine Astaroth's grander game, but he did not have to be a pawn.

When in doubt, keep things simple.

He had no sooner resolved to speak with David when his roommate entered the observatory carrying Toby.

"Here you are," said David, sounding distracted. "How are you feeling?"

"Fine," said Max. "What's up?"

"We've heard from Natasha Kiraly," replied David, heading toward his bed. "She has the Workshop engineer and is waiting at the safe house. We're going to make the switch."

"Farewell, friend Max!" cried Toby. "As I set forth into peril, I do so with a full heart and no regrets. Was it Tennyson who once said—"

"Yes, it was," snapped David, silencing the melodramatic smee. Sitting on his bed, he touched the headboard and glanced up at the stars. When Andromeda appeared, he muttered the constellation's name and the pair promptly vanished.

Walking over, Max stared at the bed as though expecting it to perform another trick. But it disappointed him. Uneventful minutes passed until he grew bored and went down to the lower level to make a fire. Spreading a blanket upon his lap, he sat and gazed into the crackling hearth.

Twenty minutes passed before David reappeared. Max saw him rounding the upper story's ledge and leading a confused-looking man by a slender, glowing cord. The engineer blinked and gazed about, his silvery hair standing straight up as though he had been electrocuted.

"I'd have been back sooner, but Toby needed to 'get into character,'" sighed David. "Let me take Dr. Bechel down to Miss Boon and I'll be back. Our guest won't have anything useful to say until the effects of the passive fetter wear off." He paused and looked attentively at Max. "Are you all right?"

"We need to talk."

"Give me an hour and I'm yours."

David made good on his promise. Before the clock struck six, he eased into the armchair across from Max and kicked off his shoes.

"Ah," he sighed, wiggling his toes. "Much better. Now, what's the matter?"

"Astaroth visited me," replied Max. "Two days ago, by Rose Chapel."

David raised his eyebrows but said nothing as Max relayed every detail he could recall. When he had finished, David gave a bemused smile.

"Well, I have to applaud his generosity," he reflected. "That's a far better proposal than the one Prusias made. In exchange for one life, we save thousands and our realm besides. We don't even have to surrender the *gae bolga* or suffer another embassy on our lands. It's very tempting." The sorcerer chuckled.

"David, I'm being serious."

"So am I." He shrugged. "Or at least half serious. I may despise Astaroth, but I pity him, too."

Max glanced at David's wrist, the puckered stump where the Demon had bitten off his hand.

"Why would you of all people pity him?"

"Your conversation with him was very telling," said David, rubbing his eyes. "To reiterate Astaroth's point, he still holds all the cards. With the Book of Thoth, he can destroy this world—wipe the slate clean anytime he chooses and yet he doesn't! Instead, he visits you and makes a personal appeal. Why should he do such a thing?"

"To use me as a weapon against your grandfather," Max brooded, staring at the fire.

"Possibly," David allowed. "That's undoubtedly part of his objective, but I think there's more. Astaroth could have stated those terms far more directly. Instead he tried very hard to justify himself to you, to convince you that he's not a mere tyrant or mass murderer. He tried to persuade you that his vision is grand and worthwhile—that it will benefit all once it reaches fruition."

Max nodded, uncertain where his roommate was going.

"But why should he remotely care whether you or anyone else approves?" laughed David. "Why should Astaroth entertain *any* objections or resistance when he has the means to obliterate them?"

"I have no idea."

"Perhaps I do," mused David, tapping the armrest. "Astaroth doesn't want power for its own sake—he finds that juvenile and crude. And despite his stated interest in creation, we know that creation alone doesn't satisfy him. After all, he already possesses the means to destroy or create almost anything he wishes. Strange as it sounds, I think what he really craves is consent . . . consent and admiration. Astaroth *believes* in his vision, and he desperately wants us to believe as well. And to love him for it."

"Well, at least he's insecure," Max quipped. "That's a comfort."

"Cold comfort," remarked David, shaking his head. "I far prefer an enemy like Prusias. He's cunning, brutal, and greedy, but he's also pragmatic. Prusias wants what he wants, and he'll gladly bash you over the head until you give it to him. The King of Blys is content with slaves, but Astaroth demands followers."

"What's the difference?"

"Oh, there's a big one. A tyrant like Prusias doesn't really care *why* you obey him; he only cares that you obey. But Astaroth is a fanatic. He wants true believers who share his ideals. Fanatics are scary, Max. Ultimately, they'd rather burn the board than let someone else win the game."

"Astaroth said the same things about your grandfather," Max reflected.

"He's not wrong," said David. "Astaroth and my grandfather have more in common than they'd probably care to admit. The Archmage may be family, but I harbor no illusions about him—I know he is a dangerous man. And given this, I think you should tell him about Astaroth's offer. It will be best coming from you."

"I wasn't going to say anything," said Max sheepishly. "I don't want him to be suspicious of me."

"It's your choice," said David. "But have you considered that my grandfather may already know about the Demon's proposal? In fact, I would guess that Astaroth has already told him."

Max had been tapping the profile of a raven engraved upon

the *gae bolga*'s scabbard. He stopped and glanced at David, who was eyeing him thoughtfully.

"Why would Astaroth warn the very person he's trying to kill?"

"Because he's a strategist," David replied. "Astaroth knows the chances of you acting upon his offer are slim—it's simply not your nature to murder someone in cold blood, no matter what the reward. Now, if you do and say nothing about it—as is likely—Astaroth has not gained anything by making the offer. But if my grandfather *also* knows about the proposal, many more possibilities unfold. At a minimum, the prospect of your treachery is a considerable distraction to the Archmage. In the best case, the information triggers a violent confrontation between the two of you. So long as Elias Bram knows about the offer, Astaroth is guaranteed an outcome with some value. It's basic game theory. And so I think you should tell my grandfather, Max. The more forthcoming you are, the less suspicious he will be."

"I don't see why Astaroth doesn't just do the job himself," said Max. "If he wants Bram dead so badly, I would think he could do it whenever he wishes."

"Not with the Book," said David mildly. "In this world, the Book of Thoth has no power over my grandfather or anyone else in my family. If it did, Astaroth would have destroyed me long ago."

"But why can't it affect you?" asked Max.

"There are three basic requirements for the Book of Thoth to have power over something," David explained. "First, the Book's pages must contain the thing's truename. Second, the Book must be in the same world where that truename originated. And finally, the thing itself must also be in the world where it's truename originated. For example, do you remember Folly and Hubris, those birds I created in the Sidh?"

Max nodded.

"Well," said David, "the Book has no power over them while they're in this world. If we were to take them and the Book back to the Sidh, we could do whatever we wished—modify them, make them the size of ostriches, or negate their existence altogether. But while they're in this world, the Book has no power over them. The same holds true for my grandfather and thus for my mother and me."

Max considered this and arrived at a bizarre conclusion. "So . . . Elias Bram is from another *world*?" he gasped.

"Technically, yes," said David, smiling at Max's astonishment. "You can pick your jaw up off the floor. Elias Bram was born in this world, but he no longer has his original truename. Long ago, he gave himself a new one."

"How did he manage that?"

"As you know, he once possessed the Book himself. Before he hid it in the Sidh, he studied its pages and realized just how powerful it could be. It disturbed him that someone could control, change, or even destroy him using his truename. My grandfather is not the sort to leave himself so vulnerable and thus he removed his own truename from the Book."

"But wouldn't he cease to exist if he did something like that?" Max wondered.

"I'll spare you the alternate-universe theories, but yes—if he had removed his own name in *this* world, he would have effectively destroyed himself. Instead, he used the Book to create another tiny world—no more than an extradimensional pocket. And once inside this new world, he gave himself a new truename, one that tied his origins to this little place of his own creation. Once he had achieved this, he removed his former truename from the Book of Thoth. Because of these precautions, he is effectively beyond the Book's reach. Since my mother's and my truenames stem partially from him, we inherit this immunity. The Book can only manipulate those whose origins are tied *wholly* to one world. That is why you are also immune from its direct control—your truename has roots in this world and the Sidh. If Astaroth wants to destroy us, he'll have to do the job himself . . . or get others to do it for him."

"Which is why he's bribing me to turn on your grandfather," Max concluded.

"Precisely. Max McDaniels might be able to destroy Elias Bram with the *gae bolga*, but the Book cannot. And at the moment, I don't believe Astaroth can either."

"You think Walpurgisnacht weakened him?"

"I do," said David with evident satisfaction. "Alas, he's not weak enough for someone like me to tackle him, but I believe Astaroth is legitimately afraid of my grandfather. I think he is waiting . . . biding his time for the wars to play out and to see who survives. He is nothing if not patient."

Max stood, feeling as though a great weight had been lifted from his shoulders. Stretching, he walked to a washbasin to splash some water on his face.

"Thanks for listening," he said. "I do feel better—it's no good to keep a secret like that, and I'm glad to hear there are some things beyond the Book's reach." He glanced at the fire. "Should we throw on another log or do you want to get something to eat?"

"I'm meeting Cynthia, Sarah, and Lucia for dinner," replied David. "They've just finished up exams. Why don't you join us?"

"Okay," said Max, rubbing uncertainly at his sandpapery chin. "We can go to the Hanged Man. It's nice and quiet in there."

"Normally I would be in full agreement," sighed David. "But Lucia laughed me down when I proposed it. Apparently the Pot and Kettle's the place to be."

Judging by its overflowing crowd, the Pot and Kettle was indeed the place to be. It was located on a corner of the township's main avenue in a handsome building of pale stone with a wraparound porch and sky-blue shutters. The porch was already teeming with people when Max and David arrived, bundled up students and teachers and wealthier refugees enjoying hot cider or a pipe while waiting for their tables. As they stepped onto the porch, Max thumbed his ring. The metal's coolness was reassuring, a reminder that no evil spirits or possessed servants of the Atropos were lurking nearby. David craned vainly about to find their friends among the crowd.

Max saw them almost immediately. The three girls were standing on the porch near a far pillar, a trio of viridian robes as they laughed and sipped their ciders. Cynthia Gilley was the tallest of the three, a round-faced English girl with reddish-brown hair and a friendly, earnest bearing. Spying Max, she grinned and waved them over.

"Look at you!" she crowed, giving Max a sisterly hug. "All we hear is that you're injured, knocking on death's door, and you show up looking like Prince Charming. Shame on you! And, David, might I say you look very elegant with your cane. Dashing, even."

David beamed and stood on tiptoe to give Cynthia a shy kiss on the cheek. She blushed and he did the same, causing Max to raise an eyebrow. Resisting a strong temptation to comment, he instead leaned over to Sarah.

"Thanks for the note," he said. "I was afraid you'd be angry at me for . . . for what happened."

"Nonsense," said Sarah, squeezing his hand. "Rolf's death was not your fault. It's not even Umbra's. I blame the Atropos, and when I'm an Agent, I'm going to put them out of business. You mark my word. Lucia's going to help me."

"Assolutamente!" declared the Italian beauty, her dark eyes fierce and resolute. Turning to Max, she leaned forward and kissed him in the distracted European fashion, a peck on each cheek, but her hands were clutching something boxy beneath her robes.

"What is that?" asked Max, careful not to knock it.

Lucia hissed at Max to be quiet while rearranging her robes and glancing about to see if anyone at the restaurant had noticed.

"It's Kettlemouth," whispered Sarah, referring to Lucia's charge, an enormous red bullfrog from a magical breed known as Nile Croakers. "He's been sick and Lucia won't go anywhere without him. She's been sneaking him into classes, exams, the dormitory showers. You can imagine how that went over. I told her to leave him at home, but she wouldn't listen."

Max gave Sarah a knowing look. Lucia Cavallo was not only a paragon of Mediterranean beauty and a gifted Mystic, but she was also haughty, opinionated, and notoriously demanding of her friends. Fortunately, these less desirable qualities were offset by a deeply loyal and protective nature. Lucia might drive her friends to an early grave, but no one would weep harder at the funerals.

Eyeing the crowded porch, Max gave a worried glance at Sarah.

"What if he sings?" he whispered nervously. Kettlemouth was often drowsy and seldom made a peep, but on rare occasions he suddenly burst into song. These ballads were infused with a love enchantment so powerful they didn't merely reduce the listener's inhibitions but eliminated them altogether. A quiet library might suddenly turn into a madhouse of breathless smooching and stammering sonnets as every unspoken crush or budding attraction suddenly flared into full, unrestricted bloom. The Pot and Kettle was bursting to the gills; an untimely performance would be pandemonium.

"Sing?" scoffed Lucia, wheeling on him. "My baby can hardly eat, much less sing! I knit him silly hats, I massage his toe pads, and still he just puffs his gorgeous cheeks and blinks."

"Didn't he just kind of do that before?" Max wondered.

Lucia almost erupted into a frenzy of Italian when Cynthia headed her off.

"What does Nolan say?" she inquired delicately.

"Oh, what does he know?" grumbled Lucia, patting the carrying case. "The dryads suggested some oysters to perk up my dumpling. We will see. Anyway, nothing is going to spoil my big surprise."

"You should just tell them," said Sarah impatiently.

"Over dinner," demurred Lucia, rolling her eyes at an admiring Sixth Year.

Fortunately, they did not have to wait very long for a table. Handing Kettlemouth to Cynthia, Lucia promptly knifed through the crowd to beg a word with the busy proprietor. Max saw her flash a singularly winning smile even as she pointed back to their party and at Max and David in particular. The gentleman nodded, a waiter was summoned, and the five were promptly whisked to a choice banquette in a candlelit corner. Many of their fellow diners eyed the party as they crossed the room. Some appeared awestruck, some discreetly curious, and still others looked vaguely hostile—as though the presence of Max and David boded ill. While Max was highly conscious of the stares, he was even more so of his ring. Its metal remained cool. Pushing it from his mind, he tried to relax and enjoy the company of his friends.

"How did you manage this?" hissed Sarah, taking her seat. "I thought we'd wait forever."

"They are celebrities," said Lucia, nodding at the boys while slipping Kettlemouth beneath the table. "Celebrities do not wait. I told the owner they would sign some menus."

"Marta will never forgive me," sighed David, passing the bread.

Lucia ordered for the group, perusing the menu with an authoritative air and inquiring about several dishes before making her final choices. Max did not recognize half of the selections. The only sticking point occurred when she flagged down the sommelier and requested a wine list.

"But the young lady is not eighteen," sniffed the sommelier, nodding at her viridian robes.

"My parents always let me have wine," she declared indignantly.

"Perhaps the young lady should have brought her parents."

With an irritated wave, Lucia transformed her robes from viridian green to a blazing scarlet—a Sixth Year's colors. "Is this better?" she asked, gesturing for the list. When he declined to hand it over, she sprouted a luxuriant mustache and raised her eyebrows inquiringly. Max almost spit out his roll.

"An impressive addition, but alas I must say no," replied the sommelier, smiling. "I will send over some sparkling cider . . . on the house."

"Puritans," grumbled Lucia, returning both her robes and facial hair back to normal.

"That's quite a trick," said David. "Are you specializing in Illusion?"

"Firecraft," replied Lucia, tapping the concentration of red stones and copper links among her magechain. "Illusion's just a hobby."

"Well," said David, raising a flute of cider, "you're very good at it."

"Hear, hear," said Max. "I'm only sorry Connor didn't see his beloved Lucia with a handlebar mustache. How he'd have laughed!"

"Well, if that's not a sign to share your news, Lucia, I don't know what is," remarked Cynthia.

"Okay, okay," sighed Lucia. "Twist my foot, why don't you?"

"Arm," said Sarah stiffly. "She's twisting your *arm*. You've been speaking English for years, Lucia. I think you do that on purpose."

"So what if I do?" she said innocently. "Anyway, here is what Cynthia is twisting my leg about. I let you read it yourself. Some parts are for you. But not all!"

She smiled in spite of herself, her cheeks turning rosy as she handed over a pouch of oiled silk containing folded sheets of thick parchment.

My Lucia,

Sending this letter is like wishing on a star. Each day I think of you and the life I left back at Rowan. Each day I think of our friends, grouchy Miss Boon, Old Tom's chimes, and even—God forbid—my homework! Kyra must be cursing my name, and I don't suspect my family thinks much of a son who sold his soul for a spot of land and a fancy title across the sea.

That's behind me now, but try as I might, I can't forget about a certain long-lashed beauty

who struck me dumb the first day I arrived at
school. How'd she win my heart? Every way a girl
could.

Enlyll is what they call my little province.
Lord is what they call me, although you may
laugh to hear it. Down on the docks, they give
me other titles—Baron, Master, Jester, and some
other things that aren't fit to print. Enlyll's a
coastal province, you see, and trade's what keeps
my subjects in food and wine, silks and servants.
Rowan's a fair place, but it's got nothing on our
golden hills and wineries, forests and orchards.
Someday, I'll show them to you.

Enough of all that. I hope you'll share this
letter with David and Max and the rest of our
friends. I miss the lot, particularly David and his
way of always seeing things for what they are.
Funny bloke—I've heard tales of him and Max all
the way out here. Sounds like they pulled quite
a job last April. They've got all of Blys stirred up.
Saw Max fight an early match in Prusias's games.
Still can't believe he was Bragha Rùn. You should
have seen him, Lucia! If you ever read this, Max, I
hope you know I actually commissioned a painting
of Bragha Rùn after the tournament. Serves me
right for trying to act all lordly. What a tosser—for
a whole month there I am eating my breakfast
beneath a life-sized oil painting of my new hero
only to find out he's actually my mate. I was red
for a week. Sorry, but my shame demanded that
I give you the boot from the castle. You're hanging
in one of the gardener cottages, where I hear

you're supervising the shears and doing a stellar
job. Well done.

I know Rowan's in a bind these days and wish
I could help, but I'm sworn to Prusias. Could be
worse—his imp pretty much lets me alone so long
as I meet my quotas and keep trade lively. No one
looks to wee little Enlyll for soldiers—the braymas
come here to relax, drink good wine, hold médims,
and conduct some business. Happy to say the war
hasn't really touched me yet, but for Rashaverak's
ships prowling beyond the harbors. They're trying
to barricade, but he doesn't have enough ships and
his spies and sailors are a sorry lot. Don't catch
one in ten of my cutters and soon it'll be one in
twenty. They can kiss my behind—doubly so if
they're reading this letter. (Honestly, where's your
respect for privacy?)

You know where to find me, Lucia. You say the
word and I'll send a ship. Your face could launch
a thousand, but I don't yet have that many. Give
me a year or three and I just might. Anyway,
that's my attempt to dazzle you with some
Homeric charm. Did it work? I bloody well hope
so. Be sure to tell Morrow I remembered my Iliad;
he'll drop that pipe and turn a cartwheel.

With love and an affection that burns really,
really hot!

Connor Lynch, Lord of Enlyll

Max read the letter twice, grinning as he imagined his
friend's Dublin lilt bouncing over each word and syllable. When
Connor had departed for Blys, he was in many ways a broken

person, a boy whose naturally buoyant personality had been smothered by a sense of guilt and thoughts of vengeance against his captors during the Siege. But that was over two years ago, and it seemed that both time and a change of scenery had been wonderfully therapeutic. It was the old Connor that Max heard in the letter—the cocksure, mischievous boy with a mop of brown curls and an irrepressible spirit.

"Isn't it wonderful?" said Lucia, practically swooning.

"Yes, it is," said Max, leaning back as the waiter set a plate before him.

"David," growled Cynthia, waving her hand before his blank, glassy expression. "Don't you think it's wonderful, too?"

"Sorry," said David, blinking. "Yes . . . yes, it's a wonderful letter. Very romantic and all that. But do you notice anything unusual about its beginning?"

"What about it?" asked Lucia, snatching the papers away from Max. Her eyes raced across each line until she declared. "He loves me. It is beautiful!"

"Yes," said David, sniffing eagerly at a bowl of mussels. "I don't doubt that's true, but wouldn't you say that the first few paragraphs are a little . . . stilted? The rest flows naturally, as though Connor were here talking to us, but the beginning seems off. And then the fourth paragraph begins 'Enough of all that' as though he were shifting to another topic entirely."

"Are you *grading* my magnificent letter?" inquired Lucia, clutching its sheets to her chest and looking outraged. "Are you marking him down for grammar?"

"No," replied David calmly. "On the contrary, I think Connor may have written an even more impressive letter than you suspect. May I see it again?"

Slowly, reluctantly, Lucia allowed Cynthia and Sarah to pry the letter away and slide it over to David. The sorcerer glanced at it for a mere instant before asking if anyone had a quill. Fortunately, the waiter obliged, bringing one to David along with a bottle of ink and a clean sheet of parchment.

"Score one for the Pot and Kettle," he murmured. "Marta would have tossed me a can of bacon grease." Studying Lucia's note once again, he quickly jotted down a seemingly random sequence of letters. "These are the first letters of each sentence in the first three paragraphs," he announced. "If I group them by their respective paragraphs, they spell out three words." The Little Sorcerer held up the paper so all could see.

SEEK THE ELDERS

Cynthia wrinkled her nose. "Who are the Elders?"

"Vyes," Max breathed, staring at the letter. "I met two Elder Vyes in Blys—Nix and Valya. They were good friends. They said the Elders hail from the original stock, direct descendants of Remus."

"You mean Remus . . . as in Romulus and Remus?" wondered Sarah. "The babies who nursed from a wolf?"

"Not a wolf," Max corrected. "A wild spirit in the guise of a wolf. The Elder Vyes go back a long time. The goblins steered clear of them. They can use magic. The ones I met were almost admitted to Rowan until the Potentials test revealed what they were."

"Pshaw!" scoffed Lucia. "How could a vye attend Rowan? And besides, my Connor would never have anything to do with such vile creatures."

"I don't know, Lucia," Max mused. "If you heard Nix and Valya talk about their lives on the run from Agents, you might think differently. In any case, not all vyes are evil. Nix and Valya certainly weren't. And in his new life, Connor might have encountered quite a few."

"Why do you think Connor would want us to seek them?" whispered Cynthia, beckoning for the letter.

"Perhaps he's met some and thinks they can help us," reflected David. "After all, I don't think the vyes are happy that they've been pushed aside by the demons. Elder Vyes are an old legend at Rowan. During the eighteenth century, a group of Agents based in Prague argued that they existed in larger numbers than anyone imagined. They theorized that the Elders had started their own schools of magic and might have even infiltrated our ranks."

"So what came of those theories?" asked Sarah.

"Nothing." David shrugged, flagging down a waiter for coffee. "Some investigations, a few minor discoveries in Eastern Europe and central Asia, but nothing to suggest a population of real scale or significance. Maybe Connor's found something. . . ."

Max was going to respond when he noticed a number of hushed and urgent conversations taking place throughout the dining room. Several tables called for the maître d', quickly settling their checks and gathering their things. In the corner, a faun was playing a sonata upon a grand piano, its soothing melodies strangely out of sync with the rushed and hurried departures.

"What's going on?" asked Cynthia, putting the letter aside.

"I don't know," said Max, just as a waiter set down an ice bucket and a bottle of champagne. "What's this?"

"The sommelier has finally come to his senses!" declared Lucia.

"Compliments of the lady in red," announced the waiter, popping the cork and pouring five crystal flutes. "She would like a word when Master McDaniels has a moment."

Scanning the room, Max spied a splash of scarlet and found that Madam Petra was leaning casually back and observing them.

The smuggler was wearing an embroidered gown of brilliant red silk along with a creamy stole of arctic mink. Her hair was up and adorned with an obscenely large jewel she had not possessed when she'd arrived at Rowan. Her companion was a well-dressed portly man who exuded a jowly air of self-importance. Max recognized him at once; he had been a wealthy industrialist before Astaroth's rise to power. Inclining her head, Madam Petra gave a knowing smile and raised her glass.

"Who is that?" asked Lucia suspiciously.

"I told you about her," hissed Cynthia. "That's Petra Kosa. She came back with Max and David."

"She's very pretty," Lucia said with the steely, subdued air of a competitor.

Max slid out of his seat. "I'd better see what she wants."

Taking his champagne, he walked over to the table and gazed down at the smuggler, who smiled and sank down luxuriantly into her stole.

"Max," she cooed, "meet Victor. In our former lives, he was a *somebody*. I'm happy to say he still is. He's been helping Katarina and me get settled after our harrowing arrival. Victor, this is Max McDaniels."

The man grunted, but his eyes never left Madam Petra.

"I'm glad to see that you and David are keeping a cool head, my dear," she observed. "It would seem the news has everyone else in a panic."

"What news?"

The smuggler gave him a skeptical look over the rim of her wineglass.

"You honestly don't know?" she asked, sounding pleasantly surprised.

The industrialist grimaced, swirling and staring at his port as though it held his fortune.

"Prusias has won, boy," he declared flatly. "Devoured Aamon and executed all of his officers. Rashaverak's to surrender tomorrow. Lilith's already sworn fealty."

Max glanced about the nearly empty restaurant. "So that means—"

"War."

The word rolled off Madam Petra's tongue like some dark prophecy. The industrialist stood and pulled out her chair. With a wistful smile, the smuggler stood and clinked glasses with Max.

"Savor the champagne, my dear. You might not taste any for a very long time."

~ 13 ~

The Aurora and the Polestar

War was declared the next afternoon.

No grand gestures accompanied the news. There were no crowds or trumpets or defiant proclamations. Hostilities were announced with no more than a letter. The Director delivered it herself to Lord Naberius's ship, descending the cliffs alone and bracing herself against the ocean gales as she walked the long dock. One of the ambassador's servants accepted the slim envelope and brought it inside. Within the hour, the sinister black xebec weighed anchor and sailed out of Rowan Harbor, navigating around Gràvenmuir's treacherous remains.

The rejection of Prusias's demands triggered a firestorm

of controversy. Many labeled the Director a fool; others questioned her authority to make such a monumental decision. She was skewered in the press and hanged in effigy by frightened mobs that marched upon the Manse demanding explanations. Ms. Richter met them on the steps and calmly explained that Rowan was a haven for free peoples and that it would fight for that freedom. Any who lacked the necessary courage or conviction to make such a stand was welcome to leave. The choice was theirs.

In the weeks that followed, thousands took the Director at her word, packing their families and possessions onto carts and wagons and heading west into the continent's vast interior. Max was not sorry to see them go. With war on the horizon, Rowan would face her greatest challenge; she needed stalwart volunteers, not halfhearted conscripts.

This very thought occurred to Max very early one February morning as he hurried across the campus. Some hundred yards ahead, a lone wagon was making its way down a cobbled lane toward Rowan's massive Southgate. *Skulking out while everyone's asleep,* Max mused, eyeing a lean man walking alongside the horse. When the wagon passed beneath a streetlamp, the eerie light illuminated a blond and familiar head. Max quickened his pace.

"Nigel!"

Halting, Nigel Bristow turned and peered back through the murk. When he saw who it was, Max's old recruiter smiled and shook him warmly by the hand, standing aside so Max could say hello to Emily Bristow and their toddler, Emma. The pair was sitting in the wagon's driver's seat, bundled up against the chill.

"And where are you off to at such an ungodly hour?" asked Nigel.

"The Euclidean Fields," replied Max. "I've got my troops training there."

"At five in the morning?" exclaimed Emily. "It's a wonder anyone shows!"

"Oh, they'll show," said Max, smiling. "If not, we'll start training at four."

"From student to slavemaster in a few short years," quipped Nigel. "And which troops are so unlucky as to have you as a commander? I confess I'm behind on the assignments."

"The Trench Rats."

Nigel looked puzzled. "But that's basic infantry," he said. "Some might say remedial infantry. Surely the Director offered you other options."

"She did," Max admitted. "But I turned them down."

"Why on earth would you do that?" said Nigel, incredulous.

"What's the matter with the Trench Rats, dear?" inquired Emily delicately.

"Well," said Nigel, stalling for something politic, "they're . . . I suppose one should say . . ."

Max put him out of his misery.

"They're the dregs," he stated flatly. "They're the leftover refugees no other regiments wanted."

"Why not?" wondered Emily. "What's wrong with them?"

"Too old." Max shrugged. "Too young. Too inexperienced. Too unruly. Take your pick."

"Yes, but why are you leading them?" pressed Nigel. "It's very noble of you, but surely another Agent can teach them to shoot an arrow or hold a pike. Forgive me, but it seems a poor use of Rowan's finest warrior. I'm surprised Ms. Richter allowed it."

Max posed a question of his own. "If I train and fight

alongside the Trench Rats, what message does that send to the rest of the refugees?"

Nigel pondered this before clucking his tongue appreciatively. "Very clever," he admitted. "Our greatest warrior serves alongside the least, thus improving morale, unity, and discipline throughout the battalions. No wonder I'm not Director. . . ."

"You can't be Director if you leave," said Max, glancing pointedly at the wagon.

"I'm not leaving," sighed Nigel, taking his wife's hand. "Just the girls. They're going to live with Emily's sister in Glenharrow. I'm merely seeing them off."

Max had heard of the place, a thriving settlement that was a two-week journey west.

"But wouldn't the cliffs be safer?" he suggested, referring to the high series of caves deep within the Sanctuary. "Glenharrow's far and the roads are getting worse."

"I've sheltered in those cliffs before," said Emily stubbornly, her tone suggesting Max had broached a well-worn topic. "If the Enemy scales those walls, there's no other place to go. I can't— *I won't*—trust my daughter's life to such a death trap."

It was no use arguing. Max would rather defend a strong place, but he could see Emily's point. Glenharrow and the inland settlements were no threat to Prusias; perhaps they would escape his attention entirely. A bell sounded faintly from Rowan Harbor.

"We'd best be going," said Nigel gently. "Other families are waiting for us outside the gate."

Nodding, Max leaned into the wagon to hug Emily and pat Emma's shoe. The child grinned at him, ruddy-cheeked in the cold as her father took up the horse's reins.

"Be safe, dear," said Emily, wiping away a tear.

"You too."

Max watched the Bristows go, the old mare clopping slowly toward the looming walls of Rowan's Southgate. As they vanished into the mist, he trotted off to meet his troops.

There was less fog upon the Euclidean Fields, but it was also colder as the wind channeled through breaks in the forest to sweep across the broad, open space. The enchanted grounds had once been used for a unique brand of soccer where matches took place on an undulating pitch whose shifting hills and gullies added new dimensions and challenges to the game. Since the declaration of war, however, Max had claimed and repurposed the fields to capitalize upon its unique properties.

Spectator stands had been cleared away to accommodate trenches along the perimeter while Monsieur Renard's beloved turf had been trampled into a muddy morass. The fields no longer bore any resemblance to an elegant array of soccer pitches. With their trenches, barricades, and bonfires, the fields resembled a war zone, and that was just the way Max wanted them.

There had been three pitches and his troops now covered all of them, twelve hundred men, women, and children standing about in clusters and blowing on their hands. They were a sorry spectacle, a veritable sea of mottled leather and quilted vests holding longbows or spears or whatever else they'd made, salvaged, or stolen on their travels. An unspectacular group, but a willing one. For the most part, they'd done as asked, submitting to orders and doing so with more spirit and energy than Max might have hoped. Thus far, only a score had been dismissed for various acts of fighting, drunkenness, and insubordination.

A well-ordered mind was required to manage so many people efficiently, and Max knew that his talents did not lie that way. He'd considered asking Miss Boon for assistance, but her time was taken up with analyzing the pinlegs. The more experienced

Agents had commands of their own, and, of course, Ms. Richter was busy beyond all comprehension. In the end, Max had turned to Tweedy—a Highlands hare with a sharp brain and sharper tongue who worked in Bacon Library. The gruff hare accepted at once, demanding the title of aide-de-camp, an officer's commission, and the freedom to organize the battalion's administration as he saw fit.

And organize he did. The battalion met three times each day—at dawn, midday, and dusk—for physical exercise, weapons training, and combat simulations. Tweedy ensured there were cooks on hand, an officers' mess, and a medical tent where a moomenhoven named Chloe tended the innumerable bumps, bruises, and cuts that came from hard training. Throughout the days, Tweedy hurried about with his clipboard, taking note of progress and barking orders to Jack, the scrawny refugee who the hare had designated as a messenger.

Tweedy was not the only Rowan regular to join the Trench Rats. Sarah, Lucia, and Cynthia had signed up, too. Sarah took command of an entire company while Lucia and Cynthia served as the battalion's Mystics. Rolf's charge, Orion, had also joined, the massive shedu bringing along a pair of centaurs whose skills at archery made them an invaluable resource when it came to teaching those who were ill-suited for hand-to-hand combat.

The battalion's greatest asset, however, was Bob.

He'd reported the very first morning the Trench Rats had assembled, standing at attention with a notched cudgel. As Tweedy took roll, the ogre recited his name and stared dutifully ahead with only the merest twinkle in his pale blue eyes.

Max was delighted to have him. Bob was not only formidable, but also his steady presence and calm, natural authority did a great deal to settle any arguments or bickering before they flared into outright brawls. Of greatest importance, however, was the simple fact that Bob was indeed an ogre. Very few refugees had ever witnessed an ogre's battle charge and lived to tell the tale. The fact that their battalion boasted a live specimen who gamely demonstrated such horrors was exceedingly valuable. No simulation—not even Lucia's illusions—could wholly capture the experience of having to hold one's ground against the onrush of a ten-foot, five-hundred-pound monstrosity. Time and again, Bob would smash through formations of anxious soldiers until they learned to stand as one and level their pikes in unison.

In all, Max was pleased. The Trench Rats were not the Red Branch and would never be, but he took comfort knowing they were no longer lambs being led to slaughter. They were acquiring discipline and proper technique, and—most importantly—they learned that Rowan valued them. As Max arrived at his command hill, he looked upon faces that had been purged of hostility and skepticism.

There was one conspicuous exception. Tweedy came bounding up the slope, his whiskers twitching with indignation.

"Having a comfy snooze, 'Commander' McDaniels?"

"I thought we were on for five o'clock," said Max, confused.

"Correct!" chuffed Tweedy, noting something on his clipboard.

"Then why are you upset? I'm five minutes early."

"Are you to be congratulated, then?" exclaimed the hare in his rough burr. "A battalion commander sidling up at the appointed hour like some slack-jawed delinquent. For shame! What kind of example are you setting for your troops, sir? Shall they mimic their commander and dillydally about their duties with casual indifference? Even that Swedish monoglot arrived twenty minutes early!"

"You're right," Max sighed, recognizing the folly of argument or explanation. "It won't happen again. How would you like to begin?"

"Humph," said Tweedy, simmering down and consulting his notes. "I think we should get back to basics. The troops are overly pleased with their progress of late and have taken to boasting. Unbecoming, undeserved, and un—*what is it, Mr. Cochran?*" The hare whirled on the refugee boy Jack, who promptly froze midstride.

"Er . . . begging pardon, but some of the troops are wondering when we're going to begin. It's awful cold just to be standing about."

Tweedy glared up at Max. "I rest my case!" he cried before turning upon his cringing messenger. "You tell those fidgeting miscreants that they will stand in place all morning until it pleases me to acknowledge them. You tell them—"

Max shouted a command. Instantly, the troops gave a unified reply and quickstepped into their review formations. It had taken them weeks to stop bumping into one another, but they finally seemed to have it down, Max reflected as he strode down the hill to review them. They stood at rigid attention, forty soldiers to each platoon, pikemen in front and bowmen in back, along with six troops assigned to operate a wheeled ballista that could fire enormous bolts at a rate of two or even three per minute. He stopped before a middle-aged soldier whose pock-marked face was missing an eye.

"Name?" he asked.

"Sameer," replied the man, clearing his voice. "Pikeman, right flank."

"What's our turf?"

"Trench Nineteen."

"What's our job?"

"To hold the line," he said fiercely. "Nothing gets past."

"Are you the worst pikeman in your unit?"

"Hell no," spat Sameer before recovering himself. "I mean, no, *sir*."

"Who is?"

The question was met with a blank, reluctant expression. The man had no wish to inform on his fellows. When Max repeated the question, however, Sameer relented.

"It's Richard," he said, nodding toward a gangly, reddening youth two spots over. "Sorry, boy, but you know it's true."

Richard nodded glumly but kept his eyes straight ahead.

"From this day forward, you're responsible for Richard," said Max. "It's your job to help him get better. Is that understood? By week's end, Richard will lead a demonstration with Bob."

Richard looked ill.

Max turned to Tweedy. "Have the commander of each unit submit a list ranking their troops by midday."

Tweedy made a note and Max continued his inspection, finishing with the Rowan specialists who were not assigned to any one unit. These included his former classmates, Bob, Orion, and the centaurs, along with Umbra. The refugee girl stood apart from the rest, leaning upon her formidable spear and staring at Max.

"Umbra, I want you to focus on training the best troops from each of the commander's lists. They'll be responsible for working with the next four and so on. Is that understood?"

She nodded.

"Lucia and Cynthia, can you spend the morning working on a simulation for tonight? Ideally, there will be a surprise or two. I want to see if they can stay calm and maintain discipline in a crisis. Got it?"

The girls looked knowingly at one another. Lucia flashed a wicked smile.

"I take it that's a yes," said Max. "Unless there are questions, we'll have Sarah and Ajax lead the conditioning."

Max stepped aside as Sarah and the refugee leader took command and started barking orders at the troops. There was a stamp and clash, the clink of mail and the thump of boots as the units fell into single-file lines and began to jog about the field's perimeter. Max and Umbra joined the last, trotting behind the gasping pikemen even as the enchanted terrain began to shift beneath their feet, forming deep ditches and wheeze-inducing hills.

He could not help but glance at Umbra as they ran alongside one another. The girl remained a mystery. She was often the first to the fields and the last to leave, but she rarely spoke or consorted with the other soldiers unless absolutely necessary. Even Ajax—ever haughty and irreverent—treaded carefully around her. It was not just Umbra's skill that checked him, but her air of simmering, watchful intensity. She forever reminded Max of a viper, coiled and poised to strike.

"Where are you from?" he asked, quickening his pace at Sarah's whistle.

"Far."

"Ajax says you fell in with them as they came down the coast."

She nodded, breathing easily as they climbed a steep hill.

"Where did you learn how to fight?"

"Here and there," she muttered, shifting her spear to the other hand.

"Why'd you choose the Trench Rats?" Max wondered. "I heard the Vanguard offered you a place."

"I'm not here for the Vanguard."

"What are you here for, then?" asked Max with a laugh.

"You."

A chill raced down Max's spine. Umbra did not look at him when she said it; she stared stoically ahead, running with a doe's effortless grace. He let her go on without him, falling back and watching the troops clamber up a hundred-foot rise while Sarah and Ajax barked encouragement.

What on earth did Umbra mean that she was here for *him*? The word and its strange delivery had so many possible interpretations. Had she joined the Trench Rats because of Max's formidable reputation? Had she enlisted because he might have something to teach her? Did the word imply some sort of threat or was it just the opposite—the awkward admission of a crush?

By midafternoon, this last possibility seemed absurd and Max reddened at his vanity. If their conversation had embarrassed Umbra, she gave no indication. While the troops rested and ate with their units, Umbra sat alone beneath a tree, sharpening her spear and glancing occasionally at Max as he collected the lieutenants' lists. There was nothing shy, friendly, or even familiar about the way she looked at him; he simply seemed to be an object of ongoing curiosity.

Putting her out of his mind, Max was enduring another Tweedy harangue about those running the armories and storerooms ("Base thieves and charlatans!") when he happened to pass Tam, Kat, and the other refugees who had confronted him when he'd returned to Rowan the previous fall. The group was huddled around one of the many firepits, resting before weapons training and eating hot porridge and bread. They looked absurdly young sitting there with their round faces and eager expressions as one girl regaled the group with an amusing story. Their weapons were strewn about them like discarded toys—bows, quivers, a long knife, and a dozen pikes along with Tam's prized sword. Catching sight of Max, Tam nearly choked out her porridge and stood at attention.

"At ease," said Max, motioning for her to be seated. "I just wanted to see how you're doing."

Reddening, the girl wiped porridge from her chin and nodded. "Pretty good," she said. "The running's hard and we're nervous 'bout tonight's simulation, but no complaints. You ain't giving out any hints, are you?"

"I don't know what it will be myself," said Max. "But if you stick to your training, you should be able to handle it. What should you do if it's vyes?"

"Assume a spread formation to protect our archers."

"What about ogres?"

"Wedge formation to resist a charge, and the archers should use fire arrows."

"And what about demons or deathknights?"

"Zenuvian iron treated with Blood Petals," she replied. "But each archer only has three of those."

"Then I guess they'd better hit the mark," said Max.

The girl nodded and picked absently at a scab. "You really think we got a chance when Prusias comes?" she asked, cocking her head.

"I heard his army's huge," put in Kat. "I heard he's got a secret weapon!"

"His army is big," conceded Max, "but don't assume he's going to send the whole thing. It's not easy to move an army, and Prusias's kingdom is all the way across the sea. And don't forget that his weapons aren't so secret anymore. We've got some very smart people studying them right now, not to mention a hundred other battalions that are training just as hard as we are. Everyone at Rowan these days has chosen to be here, chosen to fight. I like our odds."

The girl grinned and Max left them on that hopeful note, continuing to his command tent, a roomy pavilion where he could consult with his officers, plan exercises, and review Tweedy's innumerable reports. Stepping inside, he splashed some water on his face and fairly collapsed into a pelt-covered chair. Tweedy hopped in after, directing Jack to deposit a heap of documents on a small writing desk. When the boy had departed, the hare hopped onto the opposite chair.

"Did you really mean that?"

"Did I mean what?" replied Max wearily, rubbing his eyes. He found the responsibilities of command—the endless decisions, the posturing, the need to project constant optimism—to be absolutely exhausting.

"That bit about liking our odds," Tweedy clarified. "Do you believe that?"

"Yes, I do."

"You don't need to put on a brave show for me, son," said the hare. "Prusias can send a mere fraction of his forces and outnumber us ten to one. If he leverages—"

Max cut him off. "It's not your job to worry about Prusias," he snapped. "It's your job to supply twelve hundred troops who are assigned one mile of trench between the outer walls and Old College. You should be worrying about the fact that my archers have only three Zenuvian arrows."

"And they should be grateful for even that meager allotment," retorted the hare. "Some shipments have gone missing and the iron's being rationed out on a miser's scales. Most has been allocated to the archers on the outer walls."

"Where there's war, there's black markets," Max reflected. "I'd bet the lutins know where to find some. Sniff around Cloubert's and see if you can turn anything up."

Tweedy was appalled. "You want *me* to descend down into that godforsaken den of vice? I won't—"

"—let your battalion down," Max interjected. "If you need

help stealing some, get Ajax to help you. I'm guessing he has plenty of . . ."

"Plenty of *what*?" grumbled Tweedy, jotting down the order.

Max sat up abruptly. "Madam Petra!" he exclaimed. "If she hasn't already laid her hands on some, she'll know where to get it. Do you know who she is?"

"A woman whose striking appearance corrupts our young gentlemen by mere proximity?" the hare said disapprovingly. "Yes, I believe I do. And how shall we pay for these illicit goods—assuming she can acquire them on our behalf?"

"I'll pay for them out of my own wages," said Max.

"Very generous of you. But I don't believe your wages could buy more than a wee ingot or two. Even without a smuggler's rapacious markups, the stuff's more valuable than gold."

Max frowned. "Just make the inquiry," he sighed. "We'll figure out how to pay later."

"Very well," replied Tweedy, "but I should not think the lady will extend you any credit. For one, black markets are a cash business. For another, it's my understanding that you already owe the lady an estate on Piter's Folly."

"How did you hear about that?" asked Max, reddening.

"A certain smee," remarked the hare with an amused twitch of his whiskers. "And now, with your permission, we shall turn to the lists. . . ."

This they did, reading through the lieutenants' rankings and strategizing how best to train the troops in the least amount of time. Max did not delude himself that they had much to spare; there were already reports that Prusias's forces were massing near Blyssian harbors and that its shipyards were working at a feverish pace. At best, Max guessed that they had two months, maybe three, until they came under attack. Whether that would be the main assault or merely feints to assess Rowan's strength remained to be seen. In any case, he wanted his troops to be prepared.

The best gauge of the battalion's readiness was the combat simulation at the end of each day. It was nearly five o'clock when Max and Tweedy emerged from the tent, rounding the fields and climbing to the top of their observation hill.

"I wonder what the young ladies have concocted," mused Tweedy, looking down upon the trenches where the units were settling into position.

"Something devious, I hope," said Max, breathing deep and letting the crisp air fill his lungs. It was a fine evening, the moon a slim crescent in a darkening sky. In the distance, Max heard Old Tom and the faint clamor of another battalion—one of the shoreguard, no doubt—engaged in an exercise of their own. Gazing at a neighboring hill, Max saw Cynthia and Lucia conspiring beneath an oak, making their final preparations.

The attack began with a convoy of Stygian crows. Once Max signaled for the simulation to begin, the demonic horrors came flapping from the southern treetops to swoop down at the entrenched battalion. There were hundreds of them, their screeches filling the air as they wheeled and dove at the troops, leaving bright trails of smoke and flame.

The attackers were met with volley after volley of virtual arrows, slender shafts of green or red light that issued a golden burst whenever they scored a hit. The green shafts represented a normal arrow while red represented those tipped with Zenuvian iron and Blood Petals. While Max was pleased at the flurry of gold flashes, the troops were using far too many of their special arrows. They might well need them for—

The field began to tremble and shake as though an earthquake were occurring. Even as the Stygian crows were dissipating, a hundred ogres came barreling out of the woods. The phantasms were terrifyingly lifelike, bearing down upon the troops at terrific speed with maces and clubs that could crush bone to powder.

But even as archers redirected their fire and the pikemen hurried into formation, another threat appeared. From the woods, a rakshasa emerged—a tusked, tiger-headed demon—wreathed in flames and leading a troop of mounted deathknights. The archers wavered, uncertain whether to direct their fire at the ogres or the hellish cavalry. All semblance of order disappeared; arrows were fired at will with many targeting the fearsome rakshasa. Even worse, most had spent their special arrows on the Stygian crows and thus those that struck the rakshasa and deathknights had little effect. When it appeared that the enemy cavalry would reach the trench before the ogres, the pikemen panicked and broke formation, realizing only too late they had been tricked. At the last moment, the rakshasa and his knights parted ranks and wheeled away from the trench, letting the ogres come roaring through the gap like runaway trains. There were no massed pikes to meet them, only individual weapons at ineffectual angles. The hulking attackers crashed right through the battalion's line, hardly breaking stride as they stormed through the trenches.

The illusions dissipated and Max groaned. Had the exercise been real, his battalion would have been utterly overwhelmed. When one considered that the units would be spread far thinner over the actual ground they were to defend, the outcome was even more depressing. Shaking his head, Max summoned the officers to his tent.

They crowded inside, sweaty and stinking as they pushed wet hair from their eyes and exchanged glances that spanned the spectrum from angry to sheepish. More than a few glared at Lucia and Cynthia.

"So," said Max, scanning the group, "what did we learn?"

"That a pair of witches get their jollies by humiliating us," seethed one hotheaded lieutenant.

"I'm a Mystic, you idiot," retorted Lucia proudly.

"What's the difference?" muttered the man darkly. "You should all be strung up."

"That's enough," said Max sharply. "Lucia and Cynthia are here to help us. The exercise tonight was difficult, but not unrealistic. There's no point to mastering easy simulations—they'll only get people killed. So, let me ask again. What did you learn?"

"We've got to save the special arrows for the true demons," said Ajax. "Can't be wasting them on those crows when a regular one will do the job."

"Good," said Max. "What else?"

"When that demon came screaming out of the woods, I didn't know what to do," confessed a lean, gray-haired woman. "I ordered my archers to fire at it, but maybe they should have kept at the ogres."

"Same thing with my infantry," said another. "Pikes pointing every which way and I'd say half were about to flee, illusion or no illusion."

"Which is why you should be thanking these two," said Max, gesturing toward Cynthia and Lucia. "If and when the Enemy comes, your soldiers won't be seeing these things for the first time. Our job is to hold the line, and the only way we'll do that is if we keep our heads. . . ."

For the next hour, Max discussed tactics and how to prioritize their targets and subdivide responsibilities among their units should they face intense and varied opposition. Sarah was particularly helpful, drawing diagrams on large sheets of paper and soliciting input from each so that even the surliest lieutenants were soon volunteering their mistakes and voicing suggestions for improvement. Only Umbra remained silent, keeping to the rear where she listened and watched.

"We won't do it all in a day," Max said, ignoring Umbra's implacable stare and rising to dismiss the rest. "Tomorrow we'll match the soldiers with their new training partners based on your rankings. The simulation will emphasize using Zenuvian arrows on the proper targets. If we're all very nice, perhaps Lucia won't send another rakshasa."

"I make no promises," she replied, eliciting a general laugh.

"All right," said Max. "See that your troops are fed and get a good night's rest. We'll reconvene tomorrow morning. Dismissed."

They filed out, but Max's friends remained. They sat on three of the many cushions piled about the tent. Lucia retrieved Kettlemouth, who had been lounging in his little cage covered by a silk kerchief. She let him climb out, and he settled sleepily on her lap.

"That was quite a simulation," said Max, pouring himself lukewarm coffee. "Next time, warn me if there's going to be anything like a rakshasa."

Lucia gave an indifferent shrug. "You said you didn't want to know."

"Did the arrows work properly?" asked Cynthia. "I was concentrating on the illusion." It was Cynthia who had devised the spell that allowed the soldiers' ordinary weapons to shoot the tracer bolts of light, an ingenious mixture of enchanted phosphoroil that was dabbed on the front of each bow before the simulations. Other battalions had already borrowed the recipe and incorporated it into their own training.

"They were perfect," said Max.

"We're going to need more Zenuvian arrows," said Sarah pointedly. "Three per archer just aren't enough."

"I take it that's my cue," muttered Tweedy grumpily. Giving Max a halfhearted salute, he hopped out of the tent.

"We're also going to need more Mystics," Sarah added, looking puzzled at the hare's sudden departure. "I know we'll have these two, but we have a mile of trench to cover. Sarah and Lucia won't even be within hailing distance of one another."

"Mystics are in high demand these days," said Max. "We're lucky we have these two."

"You should ask David to enlist with us," said Lucia.

Max laughed. "Don't you think every battalion would love to have David Menlo?"

"I'm sure they would," said Sarah. "But we have Cynthia. If *she* asks him . . ."

Cynthia's broad, pale face flushed red as a tomato. "I—I have asked," she confessed. "He's busy studying that creepy-crawly thing. And besides, the Director's asked him to be our navy."

"How is David going to be our navy?" asked Sarah.

"By destroying every Enemy ship that approaches these shores," said Cynthia proudly. "And don't you think he can't. My David can do anything."

"*Your* David?" Max clarified.

"Yes," said Cynthia, steadfastly ignoring Lucia's giggles. "He wrote me a poem that told me how he felt. He's absolutely wonderful and we're now a steady item."

"A steady item," repeated Max, blinking.

"Yes," she said, lifting her chin. "Don't look so astonished."

"I'm not," he said. "Scratch that—I am. Not that he's with you, of course, but I . . . I didn't know David wrote poetry!"

"He doesn't, but the smee helped," explained Cynthia. "I

don't mind. David said that smee was very helpful at getting him to sort through and acknowledge his special feelings."

Max's mouth fell open.

"That's a winning look," she remarked. "And if you . . ." Cynthia trailed off, her attention drifting to the tent's opening where Julie Teller was poised, looking awkward and hesitant. Julie was dressed for travel, wearing a gray overcoat and a white cap that showed her auburn hair to great advantage.

"I was wondering if you had a moment," she said, looking at Max.

He nodded, ignoring his friends as their eyebrows lifted in unison. Easing up from their cushions, they slipped discreetly out of the tent. Only Lucia paused at the exit.

"Should we send for the smee?" she inquired innocently.

Max glared at her.

Even when they had gone, Julie hovered at the tent's entrance, gazing about at the maps and diagrams, battered shields, and muddy pelts strewn upon the floor.

"Do you want to come in?" he asked.

"I—I shouldn't," she stuttered. "People will gossip. Maybe we could take a walk instead?"

Grabbing a lantern, he followed her outside into the crisp night, pulling his cloak about him and inhaling the wood smoke that drifted across the campus. The Euclidean Fields were smooth once again, the trenches having been leveled so that the whole field looked like an enormous slab of damp clay that gleamed beneath the moon. The bonfires were still burning, however, and many of the Trench Rats still lingered by them, roasting sausages, gambling, or singing along as one of them played a fife.

Staring at the scene, Julie shook her head with mild disbelief.

"So much has changed," she said wistfully. "I watched you play soccer here on All Hallow's Eve when you were just a First Year. You beat the Second Years almost single-handedly. Do you remember?"

Max smiled and nodded.

"And now I hardly recognize this place," she said, gazing about. "It's all been swallowed up by mud and blood and everything else. No one plays soccer anymore."

"Did you come here to talk about soccer?" prodded Max.

Shaking her head, she took the lantern from his hand and made for a path that wound along the woods. Max fell into step beside her.

"I—I came to say that I'm sorry," she said. "I want to apologize for my behavior when I last saw you. I said some awful things . . . inexcusable things."

"Please don't worry about that," said Max gently. "I deserved it, and I know you didn't really mean them."

"I appreciate that," she murmured. "I also wanted to say goodbye."

"Where are you going?"

"Glenharrow," she answered. "Tonight. Thomas and his family are coming with us. It's too dangerous for us to remain here with my little brother. And my parents aren't soldiers, Max. They're too frightened to stay, and they need me to protect them."

"I understand," said Max. "Glenharrow sounds like a good choice. Nigel sent his family there this morning."

"At least I'll know someone," she sighed. "How are things with your troops? Everyone's talking about Max McDaniels and his Trench Rats."

"They're coming along," he said. "A work in progress."

"I was proud when I'd heard you signed up with them." Her voice choked with emotion. "Those people have had a hard go of it. They need someone like you, something bright on their side."

She stopped and gazed up at the stars, shining far above.

"When I was six, my grandmother told me a tale about a maiden who was courted by both the Aurora and the Polestar and had to choose between them," she recalled softly. "The Polestar was constant; every evening she could find him in the night sky, twinkling at her from the very same spot. Plain, but predictable. But the Aurora was simply *spellbinding*, a swirl of mysterious lights and mists that made her ache with longing. Utterly smitten, the maiden spurned the Polestar and chose the Aurora."

"And did she choose wisely?" asked Max.

"Of course not," said Julie. "While the Aurora was beautiful and glamorous, he was inconstant. Unlike the Polestar, the Aurora never stayed for long—he was wont to disappear and the maiden could never be certain if and when he would return. Eventually she withered away from loneliness, forever staring into the heavens and hoping the Aurora would return."

With a teary smile, Julie took his hand.

"I'll never forget the day I fell in love with you," she said. "It was during that very soccer match. You were like a god, so swift and dashing—almost radiant. When I looked at you . . . it was like fingers running through my soul. But something in you changed after you went off to the Sidh. Something had awakened, something grand and terrible and far too great for little Julie Teller. And when your father died . . . well, I knew I'd lost you forever."

Max began to speak, but Julie squeezed his hand.

"I won't be that girl in the story," she insisted. "Thomas is not a hero, Max, but he's smart and kind and constant. I'm the most important thing in his life and always know just where I stand. I've come to learn that there's real value in that—a value greater than any infatuation."

"Thomas is a very lucky guy," said Max. "I suspect he knows it."

"He does," she said, fumbling for a handkerchief. "He knows I'm here with you. He encouraged it, told me I should say my piece and put things to rest. I guess I've done that."

"I guess you have," said Max, hugging her. "I wish you both all the joy and happiness in the world."

She thanked him, staring up into his face and wiping away her tears. "Did you ever love me?" she wondered.

"I think I did," said Max. "At the very least, I wanted to."

"Fair enough," she said. "I was never sure. I was always afraid that you'd fallen in love in the Sidh. With the girl who gave you this."

With her finger, she traced the thin white line that ran from Max's cheek to his chin.

"Why do you say that?"

Standing on her tiptoes, Julie kissed his cheek and held him close. "Because young lovers are foolish," she whispered. "They always go for the ones who hurt them."

Releasing him, she placed the lantern back in his hand and backed away. For a second or two, she gazed at him, as though trying to fix the moment in her mind. And then, with a farewell wave, Julie Teller turned and strode briskly up the path. Moments later she was gone.

Max returned to his command tent, setting the lantern upon the desk and sitting at his chair. He was flooded with conflicting thoughts and emotions: regrets, grief, and a sincere hope that Julie would find happiness. He reflected on what she had to say, her thoughts on love and her intuition regarding Scathach.

Max wondered if she realized the irony of her tale. While Max might have been Julie's Aurora, Scathach was his. The warrior maiden lived in the Sidh and Max lived here: in this tent, this time, this world.

When he'd left Lugh's castle at Rodrubân, Scathach had given Max an ivory brooch and a reminder to remember that he was the son of a king. Unclasping it from his cloak, Max studied the object, tracing his finger over the image of a Celtic sun and the curving arcs of its rays.

An hour passed, maybe two with Max sitting quietly and musing on his life. His thoughts were not only of Julie and Scathach, but also of his parents and Nick, the many people whose lives had intersected his and were no more. His mind had drifted far away when something abruptly brought it back.

The tent flap had rippled open. Max caught the movement from the corner of his eye, a slight but undeniable disturbance as though a breeze had brushed the canvas apart. Normally, he'd have paid this little mind, but tonight the wind was in the west. Casually, he set the brooch down upon the desk. A second later, his worst suspicions were confirmed.

Max's ring was scalding hot.

~ 14 ~

A SHADOW FROM THE SIDH

As the ring blistered his finger, Max focused on the strewn cushions. Even now, one of them moved, as though brushed aside by something circling the tent's perimeter. Reaching slowly for the *gae bolga*, Max heard a throaty gurgle that made his hair stand on end. The sound reminded him of his clone, the grinning, emaciated assassin he'd last seen buried beneath a mountain of rubble.

Had the clones survived?

There was no time to wonder. With a snarl, the invisible intruder attacked. But even as Max drew his sword, he sensed another presence behind him. He ducked, twisting away just as a sharp blade sheared across his throat. At the same instant, something slammed into his shoulder, knocking him over the desk. He fell heavily to the ground, losing his grip on his sword just as the entire tent went black. A heavy boot kicked him squarely on the chin. Dazed, he fell back, only dimly aware that a wild animal was atop him. It felt like a vye, huge and matted, its claws scratching his limbs as it growled and scrambled for position.

There was a shout as someone else rushed into the tent. The animal rolled off of Max, snarling like a rabid dog as the clash of steel rang in Max's ears. Blood was gushing from his wound and he sensed a powerful poison already at work. Disoriented, he gazed helplessly about, unable to see anything until an arc of brilliant light suddenly tore through the darkness. Sparks flew as it struck something metallic. There was a gasp, staggering footsteps, and Max heard the growling animal rush past him. A furious din ensued of snapping teeth and tearing fabric until at last Max heard the grisly sound of hard metal striking soft flesh. A sharp yelp gave way to a whimper. A voice spoke in the blackness.

"Ignis!"

The unnatural darkness vanished as the tent burst into flames. A great surge of heat washed over Max, scorching his eyes as the tent's walls curled and collapsed inward like the petals of a dying flower. Through the billows of smoke, he finally glimpsed his attacker.

William Cooper stood ten feet away. He was breathing hard, standing astride a mound of dark, twitching fur. He held a long knife in each hand, but one had been broken, its blade sheared cleanly in half. Firelight danced upon his grim, pale features as he scanned about for his target. When his eyes settled on Max, the man raised the unbroken blade and spoke in a hoarse, alien voice.

"Atropos *a-kultir veytahlyss. Morkün i-tolvatha.*"

Max could not even raise a hand to defend himself. The poison had numbed his limbs and he was rapidly losing consciousness.

But even as Cooper went to finish his victim, something stepped between them.

It resembled a lithe and living shadow. When Cooper sprang, it rushed to meet the attack. There was a blinding flash and a sharp crack as of lightning splitting a tree. A howl erupted, so hideous and resonant it could not have been human. From outside there came screams and a stampede of boots as though onlookers were fleeing.

Max felt someone take a firm hold of his arm. He was dragged outside, away from the flames and smoke and into the welcome cold. The stinging in his eyes subsided and Max found himself gazing dazedly up at the stars. They seemed to be descending, growing ever larger until they were radiant jewels, every facet polished to an astounding, unearthly gleam. Max was weakly aware of a pressure at his neck. At first, the sensation was comforting and warm. But then it intensified. He moaned, but the person only held him tighter, sucking and worrying at his throat like a vampire.

The agony became horrific. Every nerve and blood vessel seemed to be fraying, splitting down the middle. He writhed, but the vampire refused to let go. The pain was unbearable. It invaded Max's being, rousing the Old Magic so that its vast, dreadful power came roaring forth in answer. Instead of pain, Max was soon transfixed and horrified by the forces amplifying within him. He was becoming a bomb, a mass of energy that might suddenly ignite and incinerate everything for miles. His hands shook uncontrollably. Surely his body must burst, shed its mortal coil and explode. . . .

And then the pressure stopped.

The Old Magic retreated, surging away like a riptide. With a sputtering gasp, Max exhaled and felt his sensibilities return. He heard frightened voices nearby and tried to glimpse those around him, but everything was hazy. A coarse blanket was draped over him, smelling faintly of lanolin and tobacco. Once again the stars were their proper size, sharp and scintillating against the wintry sky.

A larger crowd had gathered by the time Max could sit up. A score of the Trench Rats were in a perimeter about him to keep curious onlookers at bay. Reaching tentatively for his throat, Max felt nothing but smooth, unblemished skin. The cut Cooper made had disappeared. Pushing the blanket off, he rose unsteadily to his feet.

"You should be dead," muttered a voice.

Max turned and saw Ajax. The battle-scarred captain was crouched within the guard's perimeter, leaning on his sword and eyeing his commander warily.

"I didn't know she was a witch," Ajax breathed.

"What are you talking about?" said Max.

"That girl Umbra," replied Ajax. "We came running when we saw the tent go up in flames. She was already here and dragged you out of the fire. One look at that wound and I wrote you off as dead, but she did something to you . . . some sort of blood magic." He gestured at something on the ground. "She left those for you. Said we weren't to touch 'em."

Looking down, Max saw the *gae bolga* and his ivory brooch lying on the bloodstained grass. He gathered them up, pocketing the brooch and sheathing the deadly blade.

"Where did she go?" he asked.

"Dunno," replied Ajax. "Hunting that assassin, I think. Scariest guy I ever laid eyes on. Would have opened me up like that beast if I hadn't backed off."

Max nodded. His wits were returning slowly. Everything had happened so fast, but his mind began to piece events together.

"Wait," he muttered. "What beast? Where?"

Ajax hooked a thumb at the smoldering remains of the tent where a smaller crowd had gathered. Max slipped between his guards and hurried over.

Grendel was lying on his side, breathing slowly and bleeding from a gash across his belly. The Cheshirewulf's powerful form faded as he breathed, growing translucent with each inhale. No one had dared come to the animal's assistance; a glance at his jaws explained why.

"He'll have your arm!" cautioned a woman.

Ignoring her, Max crouched down to examine the injury. It was a grievous wound, but perhaps only one of Cooper's blades had been poisoned. Pressing the tear closed, Max scanned the surrounding faces. Most were his own troops, but he spied one delicate face peering from between a pair of archers.

"Kellen!" Max cried. The faun stepped hesitantly forward, gazing with a mortified expression at Grendel's wound. "Do you know any healing spells?"

"Non," blurted Kellen, reverting to his native French. *"Mais YaYa est de retour—elle se repose au refuge!"*

"Go get her," Max ordered. "Right away!"

Dropping his basket, the faun dashed off. Max gazed down at Grendel's broad muzzle and bloody snout. It had been the Cheshirewulf he spied slipping into the tent. He thought it had been attacking, but it had been trying to protect him from its maddened steward.

"Hang in there, Grendel," Max whispered, stroking the animal's ruff.

But as the minutes passed, Grendel's low growling subsided and finally ceased altogether. The wound was no longer bleeding, but Max grew anxious as the Cheshirewulf's brilliant yellow eyes began to dim. Max spoke quietly to him, but the animal's breaths came ever more slowly.

From the growing crowd there was a shout, followed by a parting of bodies—some in awe and some in alarm—to make way for YaYa.

The ancient ki-rin slowed to a walk as she approached, oblivious to the surrounding press of humans. A dim radiance outlined her, a dusting of moonlight that shone upon her black fur and illuminated each plane of her noble, leonine face. YaYa stood taller than a man at the shoulder, but her massive paws barely made any impression upon the snow and grass.

The Cheshirewulf responded immediately to her presence, whining in his throat and straining to rise. Dipping her head, the ki-rin nuzzled Grendel still and then settled her bulk alongside him. He looked a mere kitten by comparison.

Turning to Max, YaYa gazed at him with a pair of blind, milky eyes. "You may leave us," she said gently. "I will look after him."

"It was Cooper," said Max, shaking his head sadly.

"I'm aware," replied the ki-rin, turning back to Grendel. "I know when any steward has harmed their charge. William Cooper must answer for this."

There was an ominous edge to the ki-rin's words. Max remembered the day when he and his classmates had been matched to their charges. On the occasion, each student had signed a book in YaYa's presence and pledged to always honor and care for their creatures. Max tried to explain that Cooper was possessed, that he was not responsible for his actions, but the ki-rin was unmoved.

"You may leave us," she repeated calmly.

This was not a request, but a command. Max stood, gazing down at the Cheshirewulf as YaYa cleaned his wound and brushed her ivory horn against it. A ki-rin's spiral horn was known to have wondrous healing properties, but YaYa's had been broken during the Siege of Solas centuries earlier. Max gazed dubiously at its chipped and jagged remains. He prayed it would be enough.

Leaving YaYa to her task, Max turned to Ajax. "Which direction did that assassin run?"

The youth pointed toward a nearby strip of wood that stretched east to the sea and extended almost all the way to Rowan's wall and Southgate.

"We'll go with you," he offered, but Max shook his head.

"That'd only get people hurt," he said. "I'll have a better chance of finding him if I'm alone."

"I've done my share of tracking," insisted Ajax. "I can help you hunt him."

Max gazed at the wood, a dark labyrinth of tangled trunks and branches.

"I won't be hunting him. He'll be hunting me."

As the night deepened, Max stole through the forest. He made no sound as he wove through the trees and underbrush, scanning every tree and shadow and listening for any telltale sounds. His ring had grown cool, but the wood was eerily quiet, as though the wild creatures sensed a predator.

He searched far and wide, bending toward the sea and then back along the crenellated walls and watchtowers that guarded Rowan's southern flank. As he padded west along the forest's edge, Max noticed that an unusual number of guards were posted at Southgate and that they were searching not only those who wished to enter Old College, but also those who wished to leave. A quiet alarm had been raised.

The William Cooper Max knew would never leave a job unfinished much less flee by a main gate. Now that he had infiltrated Rowan's campus, the Agent would remain close—patient and hidden—until another opportunity emerged. Max recalled the many times he had trained with the man, matching wits and skills in the Sanctuary. While the Agent was no longer Max's equal in direct combat, he was far more experienced when it came to deceiving and stalking a target. Unless Cooper was apprehended, there would be another attack and Max knew—with dreadful certainty—that it would be planned with chilling, lethal precision.

These unsettling thoughts occupied his mind as he prowled about the woods. Max did not delude himself that he could track Cooper or penetrate his illusions, but his ring would warn him if the possessed man was nearby. To his knowledge, the Atropos did not know about the ring and Max hoped that Cooper—finding his victim alone and seemingly vulnerable—might be tempted to make a sudden, spontaneous attempt.

He hoped in vain.

It was well past midnight when Max finally abandoned the effort. He had searched from the sea cliffs to the Sanctuary wall, traversing every wood and field in the stretch along the southern borders of the Old College. His ring had remained cold throughout, and Max guessed that Cooper had probably doubled back and escaped in a different direction to throw off pursuit. Perhaps Umbra had had better luck. In any case, he needed to speak with her, and it could not wait until morning.

* * *

The refugees' main camp had improved greatly since its earliest days. The sprawling slum of shacks, tents, and refuse had been cleared away, replaced by long barracks and small cottages that lined the broad clearing, small gardens, and grazing pens. Most of the windows were dark, but some dozen figures were huddled by the fires still burning by the training pits.

Max recognized none of their faces. Even with so many departures, there were still tens of thousands of refugees living within Rowan's walls. Judging by their blank stares as he approached, they did not recognize him either. Max imagined they must be newcomers. Sipping from a flask, one of the women gestured at his bloodstained clothes.

"Where'd ya bury the poor bugger?" she laughed, passing the flask.

"The blood's mine," said Max. "I'm looking for someone."

"I'll bet you are!" she exclaimed, getting a chuckle from the others.

He asked them several questions, but they merely shrugged until one thought to elbow a dozing man who was using his grizzled mutt as a pillow. The man woke with a start and glared at his neighbor.

"What gives, Jim?" he demanded irritably.

"You been here longest, Sam," said the other. "Boy's asking after someone named Umbra."

"Umbra who came here with Ajax and his bunch?"

"That's right," said Max. "Do you know where I can find her?"

"Shoot," said the man, beckoning for the flask. "I can't be steering chaps to a young lady's door at such an hour. For one, I'm a gentleman. For another, that lady'd feed my nose to Pepper here." The dog wagged its tail. "Besides, how do I know she ain't the one who bloodied ya?"

"She's the one who rescued me," Max explained.

"He wants to thank her properly," laughed Jim. "C'mon and tell the boy, Sam! You were young once, weren't ya?"

A sigh. "So they say."

"Please," said Max. "It's important."

"Well, you didn't hear it from me. I don't need no trouble and least of all from her. That Umbra doesn't live in this camp. She sets up in that gypsy caravan by the big oak just north of here. . . ."

Max had seen the caravan before. It sat alone on a shallow rise at the edge of the woods, shaded by the boughs of an ancient oak and rooted to the spot by many brambles that twisted and twined through its spokes. Its door faced east, its planks worn and weathered by sun and sea. No lights peeked from inside. Climbing the first step, Max reached up and knocked. When there was no answer, he walked around and stood on tiptoe for a peek through its curtained window.

"The last one to try that lost six teeth," said a voice behind him.

With a start, Max turned and saw Umbra leaning on her spear.

"I just wanted to talk with you," said Max, holding up his hands.

"Funny. That's what the last one said."

Max studied the girl's hard, unyielding face before speaking. "Ajax says I should be dead," he said simply. "He says that you saved me."

"The Cheshirewulf saved you," she said. "I just pulled my commander from the fire and drew poison from his wound."

"There is no wound," Max observed, touching his neck. "That's quite a trick."

"That's your magic, Commander, not mine."

Max stepped toward her slowly. "It wasn't Grendel that drove that assassin off," he said. "It was a shadow."

"Poisoned people see all kinds of things," she remarked, raising her spear to keep him at a distance.

"Fair enough," said Max, stopping at its point. "I just have one more question."

The girl stared at him, both cautious and curious.

"I understand why you'd retrieve my sword," Max mused. "But I don't get why you'd bother with the brooch. All that commotion, an assassin on the run, and yet you run back into a burning tent to find it?"

Closing her eyes, Umbra bowed her head in silent self-reproach.

"Only one person would do such a thing," Max continued.

"And who's that?" she muttered, her voice quiet and forlorn.

"The one who gave it to me."

Smiling bitterly, the girl raised her head and met his gaze.

"Greetings, Scathach."

Even as Max spoke the name, Umbra's appearance began to change. She grew taller, her features shifting in the moonlight to reveal a young woman with pale skin, raven hair, and eyes that gleamed like gray pearls.

Brushing past him, she climbed the caravan steps. "Come in out of the wind."

Lighting a lantern, Scathach hung it from a chain. The caravan must have belonged to a fortune-teller once, for upon the walls were faded images of towers and chariots, hermits and hierophants, matched lovers and a fool hanging upside down at the gallows. The caravan was old, but it was snug and neat with a small bed and tiny table with a single chair. Offering the chair to Max, Scathach reached for a towel and wiped the grime from her face. All the while, she stared at her shadow as though it were grimly fascinating.

"You're a long way from the Sidh," said Max.

She nodded, absently handing him the towel and sitting on the edge of the bed as though wrestling with a host of conflicting emotions. At length, she simply shook her head and stared at the worn red rug.

"I came here for you," she said, smiling sadly. "Lugh first sent me after your father was murdered. When you sailed to Blys, I followed. It took me a year to catch up. When I finally found you in Prusias's Arena, you were cloaked in a metal skin and a demon's mask, but it made no difference. Bragha Rùn fought just like my Max; he had the same style and genius. I'd have known it was you just by listening."

"I remember," Max breathed, recalling his bloody contest with Myrmidon. "I was nearly finished when I saw you in the stands. You inspired me to get up. And I remember the woman in a black veil at my father's funeral. She slipped away before I ever saw her face. Why didn't you just come to me directly?"

"I was forbidden to speak to you," she replied. "But I could not help myself at the funeral. You were so broken, Max. I had to touch you, embrace you, and remind you who you are. Lugh was angry. He was angrier still that I let you see me in the Arena."

"Why?"

"You are the son of Lugh the Long-Handed," she answered, gazing at him. "You are a prince of the Sidh. But I am not a princess. I was born a mortal, and it is only by the High King's grace that my spirit was ferried to his lands and I was blessed with the life eternal. My lord believes I disobeyed him because my interest in you is personal. He would never approve of such a match. As punishment, he banished me from Rodrubân for one year. But even as I went into exile, I heard disturbing rumors, whispers that the Atropos had risen anew and that your name had been written in the Grey Book. I returned to Rodrubân and petitioned the High King to let me protect and watch over you as best I could. He agreed, but insisted on one condition."

"What is it?" asked Max.

Scathach stood from the bed and walked toward her shadow, gazing at it as though it were a stranger trapped within the painted planks.

"The condition was simple," she said, her fingertips touching the shadow's. "If you ever discovered my identity and addressed me by name, I would forsake eternal life. This has happened and I am mortal once again."

"But that's ridiculous!" said Max, standing up. "You didn't mean to reveal your identity. You didn't do anything wrong!"

She gave a rueful smile. "It does not matter. The rules are the rules, and this shadow says I have broken them."

"I don't understand."

"My name means 'shadow' in my native tongue," Scathach explained. "When I was reborn, the High King declared that I had left the mortal world behind and must therefore relinquish a part of my mortal identity. My name puzzled him; he thought it was strange—even unlucky—for one person to possess two shadows. Thus he offered me this choice: I could keep my name or my shadow, but not both. I chose to keep my name, and from that moment I cast no shadow . . . until now."

She turned and examined Max's stunned and downcast face.

"Do not grieve for me," she said sternly. "I knew the risks and accepted them."

"But it's just a brooch," said Max, aghast. He pulled it from his pocket, tempted to break the thing in two.

Scathach smiled. "Do you really believe I'd delay pursuing that assassin just to recover some bauble? The High King himself made that brooch for you, and it is very special." Coming over to him, Scathach took the ivory ornament and held it on her palm as though it were an exquisite, even living thing. With a finger, she traced its Celtic sun.

"It is not an easy task to travel between this world and the Sidh," she remarked. "There are few paths and their gateways are rarely open. Many years may pass before one appears, and even then its presence is fleeting, a precious hour or two before it fades."

"My mother used one," said Max, remembering. "She left us without even saying goodbye. When I found her again, she said she'd had no time for explanations; the gateway was her only chance to help me in the future."

"She was right," said Scathach. "For most, the gateways are the only way to cross from one realm to the other. But other means do exist. The *Kestrel* was one. This brooch is another. It is very precious, Max, for it can open a gateway to Rodrubân. Should you receive your death wound, this will spirit you to the Sidh and the halls of your father."

Max's face darkened. "The Sidh is not my home," he muttered. "And Lugh is not my father. He barely even acknowledged me when I came to Rodrubân. I'm just his offspring, Scathach, not his son. And my mother was nothing more to him than a broodmare. You're the only one from the Sidh who has ever tried to help me, and how does the 'High King' reward you? He takes your immortality away!"

"I understand your anger," said Scathach gently, setting the brooch down and taking Max's hands. "But the Sidh is your home. The old gods keep their own counsel, Max. Their minds can be hard to fathom and they do not always show affection as mortals do. But the High King does love you in his way. He has done more for you than you guess."

"Not as much as you," said Max bitterly. "You've sacrificed everything."

Scathach's eyes flashed. "I've sacrificed nothing!" she said proudly, releasing his hands and pacing about. "I regret only the foolish way I broke my bargain, not the bargain itself. Am I to mourn my mortality? What is death to me? A warrior craves honor and excellence, not a measure of mild years. Those who cringe at death are half dead themselves; they forever keep to the shallows of life!"

Following this outburst, Scathach fell silent. She was breathing hard and looking more fierce and beautiful than Max had ever seen her. He was deeply moved and went to kiss her, but she backed away like a skittish foal.

"Don't," she warned.

"But why not?" asked Max, blinking. "I—I thought you had feelings for me."

"I do," said Scathach, closing her eyes as though the confession pained her. "But I saw you. I saw that girl come to your tent tonight and the two of you holding hands. She kissed you. You embraced her. And I will never surrender my dignity, not even for you."

"But you don't know what it is you saw," Max pleaded. "Julie and I, we're not together. She loved me once and I tried to love her back, but my heart was someplace else. Julie's getting married, Scathach—she's leaving Rowan. She only came to say goodbye."

Anger and indignation faded slowly from the warrior maiden's face. She looked away. "You say your heart was elsewhere," she murmured. "Where was it?"

"It was with you!"

A tear ran down Scathach's cheek. Exhaling, she took Max's hands once again and contemplated him with a look of such open, sincere affection that no words were needed.

"It's not easy for me to love or trust," she said at length. "You must be patient with me. I have trained many great warriors, and to a man, they were fierce and strong. They were also haughty, brutal, and selfish. It was never enough that I taught them the feats that made them legendary. They wanted more, expected more as though I were some awestruck girl from their homelands. Many knocked at my door and I turned each away, but I learned a bitter lesson in the bargain."

"What was that?"

"The proudest men are the least secure," she replied. "And many are apt to turn private failures into public boasts. Some of the warriors returned to their comrades and kingdoms and claimed many things. When I first heard the stories, I was furious. I named them liars, but no one cared. Eventually, I stopped caring, too. The stories were told and the damage was done. I thought my heart had closed forever.

"And then you came to Rodrubân," she said, her eyes twinkling. "And you were a revelation. You had all of Cúchulain's skill and beauty, but not his arrogance. Loving people raised you, Max, and I am forever grateful for their influence. You might have become something else entirely. You were not the first hero I trained, but you were the first gentleman."

Reaching for the brooch, she fastened it to his tunic.

"And this gentleman should return to the Manse," she sighed. "It is late and many worried people must be looking for you. You should report back. Sarah and Ajax can lead the battalion today."

Max's mind raced back to training and formations and twelve hundred rough-and-ready troops. "I shouldn't be leading the battalion," he reflected. "You should. You have more experience than I do."

"No," said Scathach decisively. "The soldiers know me as Umbra. They respect me—even fear me—but you are the Hound of Rowan. They believe in you and that's far more important than any tactics. Can you imagine their faith now that they've seen you rise up from such a wound?"

"Then maybe I should appoint Umbra to be my official bodyguard," said Max, half teasing. "She'd have to stay by me at all times. It would be her job."

"Umbra would like that very much," replied Scathach, smiling. "But it's best if she remains your unofficial bodyguard. That makes her a far less predictable obstacle for the Atropos, and we need every edge we can get. Tonight's attack frightened me. That assassin was far better than the last—better than any I've ever encountered."

"That assassin is the commander of the Red Branch."

"That would explain it," muttered Scathach. "Max, that man is very dangerous. I have never failed to track or overtake an enemy before tonight. He's not just skilled, he's also smart. The timing of his attack was too perfect to be a fluke."

"What do you mean?"

"I sensed danger tonight," she replied. "I saw nothing, but the woods were too quiet. After you dismissed the lieutenants, I circled back and kept watch from the forest. When Julie came to see you, I followed."

"To protect me, I'm sure," said Max.

"No. It was to spy," admitted Scathach, unabashed. "In any case, when that girl kissed you, it wounded me. I was angry— I almost threw a pinecone—but I kept still and out of sight. When you returned to your tent, I followed and kept watch from outside. Eventually, my emotions got the best of me. I kept picturing you embracing that girl, kissing her. I grew spiteful and left. Fortunately, I regained my senses and returned, but you were already under attack. I'll never forgive myself for leaving my watch."

"It's not your fault," said Max reassuringly. "The timing was coincidence."

"You don't believe that any more than I do," laughed Scathach bitterly. "The fact is that when I was watching you, the assassin was watching me. And when the opportunity arose, he struck. It's a miracle you weren't killed."

"Not a miracle," said Max. "Grendel told me danger was near. And so did this." He showed her David's ring and explained its properties.

"That provides a warning, but it is not a shield," she remarked. "You cannot trust your safety to it alone. I was foolish to leave you, but you were foolish to leave yourself so vulnerable. Until I find and kill that man—"

"No!" Max exclaimed. "He is my friend, Scathach. I owe him my life."

"He seems eager to take it."

Shaking his head, Max paced despondently. "You don't understand," he sighed. "Cooper's a good man . . . he . . . he's not in his right mind."

Scathach would have none of it. "He is possessed," she asserted firmly. "You see your friend, but he does not see you. He only sees what the Atropos have told him to kill. And I won't allow that to happen. I will capture him if I can, but I'll take no foolish risks to do so."

"You might not have to do anything," said Max, considering. He told Scathach about stewards and charges and the sacred bond between them. "Cooper violated his oath tonight," he reflected. "As you said yourself, the rules are the rules. I've never seen YaYa so upset. She's not so young anymore, but I wouldn't want her coming after me."

"Nor would I," said Scathach. "Ki-rin were messengers from the gods themselves. It would never do to provoke one."

"So try not to worry," said Max, pulling her toward him. "Cooper may be hunting me, but he'll have an angry ki-rin hunting him. In the meantime, I have my ring and the fearsome Umbra watching my back. I like those odds."

Scathach tried to smile, but it faltered. "I won't rest until he's taken," she said gravely. "And you must promise me you'll always keep Lugh's brooch with you. You must never take it off."

"Never?" asked Max, flashing a mischievous grin.

Rolling her eyes, Scathach took up her spear and pointed to the door. "The only thing worse than a haughty hero is one who thinks he's funny."

~ 15 ~

THE WANDERER

Assuming Umbra's face and form once again, Scathach escorted Max home. They avoided the refugee camps, keeping to the dark woods until they reemerged along a garden path that wound behind Old Tom and led toward the Manse. Dozens of people were gathered near the Manse's front steps. Some were armored and mounted on horseback; others wore Mystics' robes and were positioned in a perimeter around the illuminated fountain.

"Here is where I leave you," whispered Scathach. "Wish me good hunting."

With a squeeze of Max's hand, she backed away and faded,

blending like a wraith into the landscape. Turning, Max stepped onto the path and beneath the bright halo of a streetlamp. He had not walked three steps before he was sighted.

"Halt!" cried a harsh voice by the fountain. "Hold where you are!"

Max stopped as three glowspheres converged, circling about him like three great spotlights. He raised his hand to shield his eyes from the glare.

"It's me!" he yelled, taking a step forward. "Max McDaniels."

"Stay put or you will be shot!"

Squinting, Max saw a dozen archers rise from positions upon the Manse roof, their silhouettes interspersed among the many chimneys.

"What's Sarah Amankwe's charge?" called the voice.

"A Cantonese Huang named Su," Max yelled.

The glowspheres dimmed and zoomed back to their Mystic.

"Come inside, son," called the voice, sounding anxious and relieved. "Hurry."

Trotting ahead, Max saw that the speaker was Nolan. Max had never seen Nolan in armor or even carrying a weapon, and their effect was strangely unsettling on such an inherently peaceful, good-natured man. Nolan was smiling, but he also looked careworn and tired. His smile died when he saw Max's clothes.

"Is that *your* blood?" he gasped.

"It is," said Max. "But I'm okay."

"My god," muttered Nolan. "I'd heard the attack was bad, but I . . . I didn't imagine anything like this. I don't even see where all that blood came from."

The man's jaw dropped when Max drew a finger across his throat.

"There's more to this than I want to know," said Nolan,

steering Max up the steps. "But I swear that if I ever get my hands on William Cooper . . ." His mouth tightened. "That man is in for a reckoning," he said, pushing the doors inward. "If Grendel doesn't make it, I won't be able to talk any sense into YaYa. She'll swallow Cooper whole."

"Nolan," said Max, "if anyone should want revenge, it's me. But it wasn't Cooper who attacked me—it was the demon controlling him. We can't forget that. He needs our help, not our anger."

Halting in the foyer, Nolan sighed and rubbed his eyes wearily. "You're right," he admitted. "Of course you're right. But to see Grendel like that and you covered in all that blood . . . I guess I'm just tired."

"How is Grendel?"

"Hanging in," replied Nolan. "He wasn't poisoned, but that knife went awful deep. YaYa brought him back to the Warming Lodge. We'll just have to wait and see, but I'm hopeful. Cheshirewulfs are tough as old tree roots. Anyway, the Director has been awful anxious for any word of you. Do you want me to tell her you're okay, or do you want to tell her yourself?"

"I'll go," said Max. "Is she in her office or at Founder's Hall?"

"The Director's always in Founder's these days," replied Nolan. "C'mon, I'll take you. We've tripled the guards on post, but I'll sleep better if I've seen you there myself."

Following the declaration of hostilities, Founder's Hall had been transformed into Rowan's war room. Almost every square foot of its vast space had been converted to some useful purpose. Upon its curving walls hung enormous maps, lists of regiments, crop inventories, architectural drawings, astronomical charts, and one vast section that was covered with sheets of Florentine spypaper. Despite the late hour, the hall was brightly lit and teeming with activity.

It was difficult to locate the Director amid the hundreds of people and creatures bustling about: Promethean Scholars, Mystics of various specialties, Agents, older students, innumerable domovoi, and a sandstone shedu boasting four unblinking faces. At last Max spotted her at the far end of the hall, leaning upon a table and conversing with an anxious-looking domovoi.

Most everyone was busily occupied, but as Nolan led Max through the hall, people began to notice not only his presence, but also his appearance. Conversations ceased, the silence spreading so conspicuously that the Director glanced up. When she spied Max, initial shock was replaced quickly by an expression of profound relief.

"This must wait, Zimm," she remarked absently to the domovoi. "Question the lutins and scour the lower vaults. Zenuvian iron doesn't just walk away."

As the domovoi and Nolan took their leave, Ms. Richter came around the table to give Max a maternal hug and flick a stray leaf from his shoulder.

"Well," she sighed, looking him over, "it's been a long night and you're a mess, but you're here on your own two feet and that's all that matters. I'd jump for joy if Directors were allowed to do such things. Let's have a private chat."

He followed her into an adjoining conference room and sat at a table while several apprentices quickly brought coffee, a basin of water, and a clean shirt to replace Max's bloodstained horror. Sipping her coffee, Ms. Richter grimaced and set it down.

"Who would have imagined that a bawdy, incorrigible hag could be so irreplaceable?" she said. "For all of Mum's foibles, she didn't mistake sludge for coffee." The Director chuckled. "My days are consumed by war—its awful scale and grandeur—and yet the littlest things make such a difference. Now, tell me what happened. . . ."

Max relayed what he could remember of Cooper's attack—the ambush, Grendel's intervention, and Umbra finally driving Cooper off and pulling Max from the fire. He did not mention Umbra's true identity.

"And you're certain it was William Cooper," said the Director.

"Yes," said Max. "The tent was smoky, but I saw him clearly enough."

"I'm curious," mused Ms. Richter, stirring her drink. "This Umbra is the same refugee who slew Rolf Luger. I find that very odd. Unless I'm mistaken, she has now sabotaged two assassination attempts, outdueled the commander of the Red Branch, and promptly healed a poisoned victim with a slit throat. That's quite a girl. And yet you maintain that you know nothing else about her?"

"Um . . . yes?"

"Max McDaniels, you are the least competent liar I've ever encountered," said Ms. Richter. "It's a good thing, too, because you're not terribly forthcoming. Who is this Umbra? And don't you dare tell me she's just some random refugee."

Reddening, Max gave in and told Ms. Richter that Umbra was none other than Scathach who had crossed over from the Sidh to protect him. The Director raised her eyebrows.

"Well, well," she muttered. "That is a surprise and a pleasant one. I'll send word that she should be allowed access to the Manse and anywhere else you happen to be. If she's your bodyguard, why wasn't she in your tent to begin with?"

"I didn't know that Umbra was really Scathach until tonight," replied Max. "She was forbidden to reveal who she was. It's . . . complicated."

"I see," said Ms. Richter, looking shrewdly at him but letting the matter drop. "Well, just so you know, we've got Ben Polk and some others searching for Cooper. I also hear that YaYa may join the hunt, so rest assured that we're doing everything we can to track him down. While they're hunting him, perhaps you can explain this. . . ."

Removing a sheet of spypaper from a folio, she pushed it across to Max. He glanced at its single line of bold black script.

Send the Hound to my chambers at midday.

"Who's that from?" he asked.

"Elias Bram," replied Ms. Richter coolly. "Our illustrious Archmage rarely emerges from his chambers, ignores nearly all communication, and has contributed nothing to Rowan's defense, and yet he suddenly wishes to speak with you. As Director, I want to know why."

"I have no idea," said Max.

"And here we go with another transparent fib . . . ," she observed with thinning patience.

"Well," said Max. "I—I mean I have *some* idea. But I've already tried to go speak with him several times without any luck. He's never there—or at least Mrs. Menlo never admits he's home."

"And why have you gone to speak with him?" asked Ms. Richter.

Max glanced at the Director, wilting under her penetrating gaze. At length, he sighed and drummed his fingers on the table. "Because Astaroth came to speak with me."

"What?"

Max had never heard Ms. Richter exclaim in such a fashion or register such open shock upon her face. It was several seconds before she composed herself.

"When did this occur?" she asked quietly.

"The day before we declared war."

"And what did he want?" she asked. Before Max could reply, she raised a finger in warning. "Do not omit *anything*. You will share every word of this conversation and then you will explain why you never reported it to me."

Max did as he was told, repeating his conversation with Astaroth and the Demon's offer to save Rowan in exchange for Bram's murder. He also shared his subsequent discussion with David, including his roommate's theory that Astaroth might also have told his grandfather about the proposal. By the time Max had finished, Ms. Richter looked ashen.

"And you never thought to share this with me?" she wondered, aghast.

"I almost didn't even tell David," Max replied sheepishly. "I wanted to forget about it . . . pretend it never happened."

Ms. Richter closed her eyes and rubbed her temples in weary frustration.

"There are times I have to remind myself that you are still very young," she murmured. "You are a young man at the epicenter of enormous happenings and may not always see things in their proper perspective." Opening her eyes, she gazed at him. "Max, you cannot simply pretend that such monumental events 'never happened.' Did it ever occur to you that I might need to know about this? Do you understand that right now we are *at war* against a vastly superior force and may come under siege within a matter of days or weeks? You have been withholding information that could not just influence this war's outcome, but absolutely determine it!"

"But you would never—"

"Sacrifice Elias Bram to save our realm and all of our people?" she interrupted testily. "To be perfectly honest, I'm not certain. I'd like to think I'd rise above such temptation, but as

Director I still need to know our options. All of them! Even those that may be repellent. Aside from everything else, the fact that Bram might already know of Astaroth's proposal puts you at enormous risk. Did you ever stop to consider that?"

"David did," said Max heavily. "I've tried to meet with Bram, to explain and clear the air, but he was never at home."

"I'm glad he wasn't," remarked Ms. Richter. "You should not meet with him alone. I will be at that meeting later today. We are going to clarify where Elias Bram stands on a number of topics, you not the least of them. Now, as long as I'm hearing confessions, are you certain there isn't anything else you'd like to share?"

Max was mortified. "You mean like . . . impure thoughts?"

"No," said Ms. Richter. "I was thinking more along the lines of Zenuvian iron. Your face assumed a rather knowing, hangdog expression when you overheard Zimm and I discussing it."

"Oh," said Max, flushing a deep scarlet. "I might have asked . . . er, *ordered* Tweedy to see if he could acquire some on the black market. My archers have only three arrows apiece."

"Well," said Ms. Richter, slipping the spypaper back into her folio, "I suppose I can't fault a commander too badly for trying to get his troops what they need. If nothing else, it shows enterprise. I won't have Zimm pursue the matter too strenuously, but next time let's go through the proper channels. In any case, I've been thinking about your battalion. . . ."

As Max followed the Director back into the hall's commotion, he saw that there were many people waiting to speak with her. She asked them to be patient as her eyes followed a distant glowsphere drifting toward the mosaic of spypaper. When it settled by a particular section, the sphere began to pulse.

"What's happening?" asked Max.

"An intelligence update," explained Ms. Richter, squinting. "From this distance, I couldn't say whose report that is, but it's from someone stationed in Blys. We're getting news from all over—troop movements, naval estimates, Workshop rumors, counterintelligence, and everything else you can imagine. My hope is that there are names attached to this particular update. We suspect Prusias has several well-placed spies in the refugee camp, and we mean to ferret them out. . . ."

She trailed off as an apprentice hurried over and handed a transcription to the Director.

"Very good," she murmured, scanning its contents with a decoding glass. Motioning for a nearby Agent, she showed him the names and offered a significant look. The man departed and Ms. Richter returned her attention to Max, leading him to stand before an enormous map of Greater Rowan that included not only the Old College, but also its outermost fortifications and all the lands in between.

Craning his neck, Max saw that it was marked with colorful labels that included the number, nickname, and standard for each of Rowan's battalions and special regiments. There were hundreds of them. Some were old and storied companies—the Vanguard, the Wildwood Knights, the Bloodstone Circle—but others were new and the names they chose for themselves sounded more like street gangs or goblin tribes than military units. Among the many, Max spied Southgate Jackals, Tin Squires, Jawbreakers, Death Cheats, Rough and Tumbles. . . . His eyes drifted to the map's northeast quadrant, where they settled upon the now-familiar standard of a black rat set against an ivory background.

"As I said, I've been thinking about your battalion," said Ms. Richter. "How are your troops coming along? Tweedy's reports are meticulous, but they read more like a purser's list. I'd like to hear your candid assessment."

"They're improving," Max allowed. "Some are very good fighters—tough, experienced. Others are totally new at this. They're a work in progress."

"Admirable. But can they hold that line?"

She pointed to a numbered trench set halfway between the outer curtain that protected Rowan's outlying homesteads and the citadel walls that enclosed Old College as though it were a single massive keep. Three miles of open country and farmland separated the outer walls from the inner fortifications. The Trench Rats were one of the battalions responsible for defending that territory and preventing the Enemy from besieging Old College.

"That's a critical stretch of ground," she continued. "Your battalion's close to Northgate and the sea. It's conceivable that the Enemy could breach the cliff defenses and attack along your flank. I assigned it to the Trench Rats solely because of you, but in retrospect that might have been a mistake. I'm tempted to reassign it to a battalion that has more experience and Mystics support."

"That's your decision," said Max. "But they're a determined group. We'll have more arrows, and don't forget about Scathach. She's worth a company by herself."

Ms. Richter considered this. "Very well," she said. "We'll leave you there for now, but I'd like to see a demonstration of their readiness one week from today."

"Can we have two?" pressed Max.

"One," repeated the Director. "We may not have two weeks. One week to show me they're ready or I'm reassigning them and you."

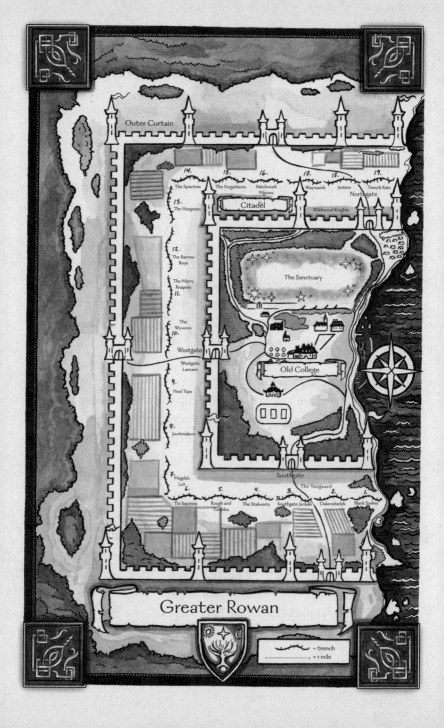

Greater Rowan

"We'll be ready," said Max.

"I know you will," she said. "Now go get some sleep. I will be waiting for you outside the Archmage's chambers tomorrow at noon. Do not be late."

Indeed, the Director was waiting outside the Archmage's door at the appointed hour. But the Archmage did not answer when they knocked. Instead, David's mother opened the door, looking sleepy and disheveled as Lila trailed at her skirts. Recognizing them, Emer smiled dimly and took Max by the hand, leading them past the stacks of books and maps.

"Is your father here?" asked Max. "He wanted to see me."

The woman did not answer but merely shooed Lila away from a canister of tea leaves. Setting the kettle above the hearth, Emer sat in her rocking chair and the amiable cat settled in her lap.

"Is that Max?" called an excited voice from inside one of the bedrooms. Its door flew open and Mina came racing out, wearing an embroidered blue robe and clutching something against her chest. She came to a sudden halt when she saw the Director.

"I thought you were alone," she murmured shyly.

"Oh, don't mind me," said Ms. Richter kindly. "What have you got there?"

Mina's enthusiasm rekindled. "Sit down and I'll show you!"

The little girl practically bulldozed them back onto the bench beneath the window. Once they were seated, she laughed gleefully and ordered Max to lean back and close his eyes. Once Max complied, he felt something warm being placed delicately on his chest.

"Mina, what is that?" he asked, as its surprising weight settled on him.

"Shhh," she hissed, "just a minute."

The weight was repositioned and Max felt something move and issue a tiny mewl. Reaching up, he touched something both soft and sharp, as though a million hairs were each tipped with a razor-sharp needle. Opening his eyes, Max looked down.

A baby lymrill was clinging to his chest.

It was no larger than a newborn kitten and yet the shockingly dense creature must have weighed more than Lila. Its quills were a glossy blue-black, but the claws that clung to Max's tunic were red-gold and gleamed by the firelight. The animal peered at Max with a pair of coppery eyes just as Nick had done when he'd chosen Max to be his steward years before. Almost immediately, a lump formed in his throat.

"Why are you sad?" asked Mina, looking concerned.

"I'm not," Max insisted, taking a deep breath. "It's just that this is how I said goodbye to this little guy's daddy. Does he have a name?"

"*She* is called Nox," corrected Mina.

"The Goddess of Night," said Ms. Richter. "A fitting name for such a beauty. But should she be away from her mother?"

"They don't nurse anymore," replied Mina, scooting between them on the bench. "Nox is a huntress now. She gets all the mice Lila's too lazy to chase. Just yesterday, she killed a rat that was three times her size!"

"Just like Nick," said Max, grinning as Nox nipped his finger and grazed his chin with her velvety muzzle.

"She likes you," Mina observed. "And she doesn't like anyone else but me. I think you should keep her."

"I'd like that," said Max, gently easing the lymrill's claws away from his neck. "But I'm too busy these days to look after a charge. Nolan will match her with someone else—a younger student."

"No, he won't," said Mina knowingly. "They've already

tried. Her brothers and sisters have all been matched, but Nox wouldn't choose anyone."

"Perhaps she's chosen you," suggested Ms. Richter.

"No," sighed Mina. "I love squirmy little Nox, but she's not my charge. She's meant to be with fierce Max. She's Nick's last gift."

Max said nothing but cupped the little creature in his hands. Closing her eyes, Nox retracted her claws and lay on her back, so dark and glossy she might have been a scoop of volcanic glass. From beneath the study's door, Max glimpsed a faint pulse of light, followed by the sound of heavy boots.

"The Archmage is home!" Mina whispered.

The door opened and Elias Bram walked into the room. His face was ruddy, his gray robes wet and fringed with melting snow as was his tangled beard and crown of curls. He looked like he'd just been out in a heavy blizzard, yet it hadn't snowed at Rowan in days. Leaning down, he kissed Emer on the forehead and asked Mina what she would be preparing for supper.

"I'm going to make stew!" the girl declared, hopping up from the bench.

"Very good," said Bram, removing his cloak and tossing it to dry by the fire. "But follow a recipe, child. No more experiments."

At last the man's piercing eyes fell on Max and Ms. Richter. He looked briefly from one to the other, as though he'd just registered their presence.

"You're both here," he observed. "Well and good. Come in."

Pushing the door wide, the Archmage beckoned Max and Ms. Richter into his study, a long and cluttered room whose bookcases and tables were laden with manuscripts, odd bits of amber and stone, and what appeared to be the skeleton of a humpbacked homunculus. There were several chairs scattered about, but these, too, were piled high with books and papers. Clearing two of them off with an unceremonious grunt, Bram urged them to sit while he went back out to fetch the tea.

It was only when the Archmage returned and shut the door and settled into another chair that Max experienced the room's strangeness. Once the door closed, he began to see double. It seemed as though his eyes registered more than a cluttered study, but also an alternate version whose planes were constantly folding and warping to form bizarre, almost incomprehensible spaces as though it were simultaneously collapsing and expanding. The effect was extremely disorienting, and there were instances when Max could have sworn that he was upside down. Apparently, Ms. Richter noticed it, too.

"I wasn't aware you had configured this room," she said.

"I haven't," replied Bram, gazing about with mild interest. "It's merely *trying* to configure and I won't it allow it to complete the process. This room is more useful to me if it's dimensionally unstable. But I'm fairly certain Rowan's Director hasn't visited to discuss my living quarters. Would you like to tell me why you are here?"

"Are you aware that Astaroth made a proposal to Max?" she asked pointedly.

"I am."

"And are you aware of its particulars?"

"I think so."

The Archmage betrayed no surprise or emotion as he answered Ms. Richter's questions. His face was a mask of granite stoicism.

"Well," she said, leaning forward. "I'm here to ask if you intend to harm this fine young man."

Stoicism vanished. The Archmage's eyes twinkled, as though her frankness amused him.

"I believe the question is whether or not he intends to harm me," he replied.

"Of course he doesn't," snapped Ms. Richter. "This is nothing more than Astaroth's attempt to sow dissension in our midst. Surely you can see that."

Turning to Max, Bram calmly appraised him. "I see many things," he reflected. "And I see not only Astaroth whispering in his ear, but also the Morrígan. The Hound is bound to that perilous blade and she is a part of it. The Morrígan lusts for war; she craves the blood of gods and kings, and she is very strong. Does Max possess the will to resist such powerful voices?"

Even as the Archmage spoke, Max recalled Astaroth's plying words from the churchyard: *He does not love you, Max McDaniels. You frighten him. . . . Bram knows there will be a day when he cannot stand against you. Given the man's past, do you really believe he will let that day come?*

"I don't know," said Max quietly.

Ms. Richter grew pale, but Bram nodded his approval.

"It's wise to admit as much," he remarked. "Against such forces, fear and humility are better shields than hubris."

"Astaroth said you're afraid of me," said Max. "He said that someday I will become stronger than you and that you would never allow that to happen."

"Ah," replied Bram, touching his fingertips together. "Astaroth's wordplay is at work. As we know, he never lies, but he is very clever in how he presents his statements. He is only sharing those facts he chooses, and even these are carefully framed to shape their interpretation. Did Astaroth actually state that I would attack you?"

"No," said Max, considering. "He said that you did not love me and that I frightened you. He had told me stories—awful stories—about your past. Then he asked me if I thought you would ever let the day come when I could threaten you."

"That sounds like the Astaroth I know," replied Bram, smiling grimly. "He states a truth or two, arranges a clever context, and leads his audience to draw conclusions that suit his purpose. If his listeners are not careful, they may later convince themselves that Astaroth put forth their own conclusions as established fact when really such things are no more than their own manipulated assumptions. He never lies, but he is the most devious being I know."

"So you have no intention of harming Max," Ms. Richter clarified.

"Do I *intend* to harm him?" replied Bram. "Of course not. Max McDaniels is a 'fine young man' to use your term, Director. But he is also quite a bit more than that, which you seem unable—or unwilling—to grasp. The Hound of Rowan *does* frighten me, and my younger self would never have endured such a threat to my person. Long ago, I would have taken matters into my own hands. However, I am now a bit older and wiser and understand that Rowan needs its Hound."

"In the days ahead, Rowan will also need its Archmage," replied Ms. Richter pointedly. "Why have you done nothing to aid us? When Prusias comes, can Rowan count on your help?"

"Tell me, Director," mused Bram. "How many soldiers do you have to defend this land?"

"One hundred and eleven battalions," she replied. "Some hundred and thirty thousand troops."

"And how many Mystics scattered among that number?"

"Roughly two thousand," she replied.

"Firecrafters, aeromancers, spiritwracks, phantasmals,

enchanters . . . ," muttered Bram, ticking off various schools and specialties.

Ms. Richter nodded uncertainly.

"And how many creatures and spirits from the Sanctuary have pledged themselves to Rowan's cause?" continued the Archmage.

"Eleven hundred, give or take a few," she said.

"Centaurs, dryads, domovoi, Cheshirewulfs, fauns . . . even a roc and a reformed ogre, if I hear rightly."

"Yes, but—"

"And of course there is my grandson and the Hound, and let us not forget little Mina. In this dire hour, Rowan boasts no less than *three* children of the Old Magic, along with a massive host to contest the armed might of Prusias. But tell me, Director, who is contesting the might of Astaroth?"

Ms. Richter said nothing.

"There is but one," continued Bram grimly. "And as I've said before, I believe that Astaroth poses the greater danger. As long as he possesses the Book, it is not just Rowan's sovereignty that hangs in the balance, but the fate of this very world. I do not have the power to destroy Prusias's army, Director. Only the Book of Thoth is capable of such a feat. If your current forces are not enough to stave off Prusias, Rowan's independence is ultimately doomed whether or not I come to your aid. Astaroth has made far less noise than Prusias, but he has not been idle. He is lurking, Director—watching and waiting for a chance to turn things in his favor. He and I are like two kings on a chessboard, locked in a stalemate. If I divert my focus and energies to oppose Prusias . . ." He shook his head as though the consequences were too terrible to contemplate.

Max leaned forward. "What *is* Astaroth?" he asked. "You said yourself that he isn't really a demon, that he only masquerades as one. If that's so, then what is he and where does he come from?"

"That remains a fundamental question," said Bram, rising and brushing past them to sort through a stack of ancient parchments and manuscripts. "Astaroth has always tried to hide his past from me, but there have been glimpses, impressions that I gained while he was my prison. He is a profoundly alien entity. Most demons are corrupted stewards—spirits of Old Magic that rebelled against their given purpose. But Astaroth is far older than they are. I believe he comes from another universe altogether. I have been trying to discover his origins, how he came to be in this world and—most importantly—why he stays."

The Archmage handed Max a small stone carving whose chips and cracks spoke to its ancient origins. Turning it over in his hands, Max gazed upon a grinning figure with its hands clasped together.

"What is this?" asked Max, finding the figurine oddly disturbing.

"That is Astaroth," remarked Bram, staring at it. "It was made by the Olmec people thousands of years ago." He handed Ms. Richter a piece of tortoise shell on which mysterious characters had been carved. "And this is from China. It was recorded by one of the emperor's magicians and tells of a day when they tried to summon a river spirit to quell a flood, but something else appeared . . . a 'Smiling Man' who caused the waters to recede and showed them how to improve their plantings and their harvests. He was soon admitted to the royal court. The pharaohs told similar accounts; so did the Mesopotamians, the Nubians, and the Aborigines. Astaroth's presence on this earth predates recorded history."

"And so is that where the investigation ends?" asked Ms. Richter.

"No," replied Bram. "Fortunately, there are means of digging further. In this regard, the witches hold the key. Rowan boasts its Archives, the Workshop has its museums, and the witch clans have their ossuaries."

"What is an ossuary?" said Max.

"A place for keeping human remains," answered Ms. Richter, studying the tortoise shell.

"Indeed," said Bram, "grave robbing has long been practiced by various professions—physicians, artists, and, most infamously, necromancers. But the witches are the most prolific. Over the centuries, they have pried into coffins, crypts, burial mounds, tombs, and mausoleums of every kind and from every culture to amass their collections."

"And what exactly are they collecting?" asked Max.

"Mostly dirt and dust," said Bram, smiling, "bones if any remain; canopic jars and urns. *What* they find is not as important as *who* they find. The witches have been studiously collecting the remains of every mystic, shaman, and sorcerer they can get their hands on—the remains of anyone they believe has trafficked with the spirit world or possessed knowledge that they value. They have collected many thousands of specimens and organized them as meticulously as Rowan's Archives."

"But I thought the witches were all about the wild and living things," said Max. "They worship nature. I've never heard they practiced necromancy."

"They don't," said Bram. "At least, not necromancy as it's usually defined. The witches are not interested in animating corpses to serve some dark purpose. They use the remains to communicate with the dead and gather wisdom from the past.

According to their beliefs, the practice is not a desecration but a great honor—the deceased's counsel is sought and valued even after their spirit has left this world. The witches see themselves as communing with nature, not violating it."

"How are the ossuaries aiding your pursuit of Astaroth?" pressed Ms. Richter.

"They allow me to communicate with shamans and spirit guides from many thousands of years ago—people who lived before any cultures kept written accounts," explained the Archmage. "And some of the oldest recall a pale being that followed their tribes at a distance and watched them as they huddled by their fires. Many years might pass between its appearances, but its coming was always viewed as an evil omen. Whenever they saw the pale being, women were wont to miscarry, brothers quarreled, and the hunt became scarce. But there was one shaman in the far north who finally mustered the courage to approach it. He asked what it was and where it came from. He asked why it was bothering them and driving all the animals away. The shaman's people meant it no harm. It should leave them alone."

"What did it say?" asked Ms. Richter, spellbound.

"It pointed to the stars and tried to emulate the shaman's speech, but struggled to do so. Abandoning the effort, it pointed again at the sky. The shaman decided that it was trying to show him where it came from. Interestingly, the shaman also sensed that it was *afraid*—not of him, but of something out among the heavens. The shaman smiled, named him Wanderer, and tried to indicate that he understood. The Wanderer mimicked his smile and then seized his hand. When the shaman shrieked and tried to flee, the being released him and simply walked away. The next morning, the tribe awoke to find dead caribou arranged and heaped about their camp. It seemed the Wanderer had left the animals, but the tribe would not touch the meat and never returned to that place. The unfortunate shaman grew ill and died within the month."

Max found that he was holding his breath. He exhaled, his mind fixated on the primitive but eerie similarities between Astaroth and this ancient Wanderer of the shaman's tale. He envisioned Astaroth's ever-present, masklike smile and wondered if it was a sort of ingrained mannerism that stemmed from his early interactions with people: *Humans do this to put other humans at ease and be welcomed.* This thought made Astaroth seem even stranger and more alien to Max than before.

"What do you make of this?" asked Ms. Richter quietly.

"I still have much more to learn," replied Bram. "But I do not doubt that this 'Wanderer' from the shaman's account was Astaroth, as he is now known. And I do not doubt that the 'Smiling Man' and the Olmec carving are also him. It was not until the Middle Ages that he even assumed the identity of 'Astaroth' and that dreadful name began to appear in the scholars' lists and grimoires. By that time, Astaroth had essentially *become* a 'demon' as we tend to think of them: He assumed their aura, he could be summoned, and, despite his great powers, he was bound by certain rules and strictures. Scholars believed that he was one of the greater corrupted stewards and fit him into their hierarchies. Even other demons took Astaroth for one of their kind and served him out of devotion or fear until his humiliation on Walpurgisnacht."

Finishing his tea, Bram sat back down and gazed into the cup with a dark, melancholy air.

"And this strange being," he muttered. "This imposter—this 'Wanderer'—who has masqueraded for millennia as both demon and man possesses the Book of Thoth. Nothing—not even Rowan's fate—is more important than recovering the Book and destroying Astaroth once and for all."

Setting down her tea, Ms. Richter gave a nod and stood. "These revelations about Astaroth are disturbing," she said. "A part of me—a childish part—wishes I'd never heard them. Thank you for your explanations. I suppose it was my greed. Despite all the forces we've arrayed against Prusias, Elias Bram is a mighty weapon and I wanted him in my arsenal. Now I understand. . . ."

"You are not driven by greed," said Bram gently. "It is your love of Rowan and all who shelter here that drives you, Director. I admire you. You're a far better leader than I ever was."

She bowed appreciatively. "Well," she said, "I'm overdue in Founder's Hall. We will leave you to your labors, Archmage. Do I have your word that you will leave Max McDaniels to his?"

"You do," he promised. "But we never even discussed why I originally sent for him." Bram glanced beneath the door to make sure Mina wasn't eavesdropping. "I know about the attack by the Atropos," he said gravely. "A very ugly business, and I don't want Mina to hear about it. It would upset her terribly. In any case, my own charge has asked my permission to serve Max for the time being."

"YaYa?" said Max, confused.

The Archmage smiled. "It's been many years since YaYa carried a rider into battle, but I don't think you will be disappointed. The Enemy fears her, for good reason, and your soldiers may find greater heart and courage in her presence. Will you accept her service?"

Max nodded, speechless at this unexpected boon. When Bram opened the door, the study's disorienting effect ceased and Max felt like his feet were planted firmly on the floor once again. In the common room, they found Emer dozing in her chair, Lila scratching at the door, and Mina stirring a large pot and peering at its contents with an anxious, irritated expression.

With a groan, the Archmage strode across the room and flung open the windows.

"It just needs more basil," Mina assured him.

"No, it does not," Bram declared. "It needs *less* garlic. Didn't I tell you to follow a recipe?"

"I did follow a recipe!" shouted Mina, defiantly flinging the rest of the basil into the pot.

"Show it to me, then."

"I threw it in the fire!"

"What have I told you about lying, child?"

"To get better at it!"

~ 16 ~

IN THE DRAGON'S COIL

One week later, Max sat astride YaYa and surveyed the
Trench Rats as his battalion stood at attention. While the afternoon sun may have caused the soldiers to squint, its rays also
imparted a coppery gleam and pleasing uniformity to the rows
of dented helms and mismatched armor. Max was grateful for
that sun. He was grateful for the weather in general. On dark
days when it was bitter cold, the troops could not stand still for
long; they tended to fidget and stamp, appearing less like a crack
battalion and more like kindergartners during an assembly. But
not today, reflected Max proudly. Today they seemed content to

stand at attention, bask in the warm breeze, and allow the sun to work its ennobling magic.

"I think they look every bit as good as the Wildwood Knights," Max remarked, unable to contain himself. Standing taller in his stirrups, he cocked his head at the formations. "And those lines are pretty straight!"

Tweedy glanced up from his perch on a neighboring stool. "One cloud and the whole effect will be ruined," he sniffed. "You think a bit of sunlight and boot polish is going to fool the Director? Ha! Look at her! She's only drawing out this charade to punish me for my . . . my moral implosion!"

Looking out, Max spotted Ms. Richter trailed by a dozen aides and advisers as she inspected the companies and platoons. As a rule, she did not allow commanders to accompany her during reviews; she liked to question the rank and file directly and believed that a superior's presence stifled candor. At present, the Director was speaking earnestly with a young refugee whose longbow was as tall as its owner. In response to an apparent request, the archer slung her quiver off her shoulder and presented it to Ms. Richter.

Tweedy nearly fell off his stool. "Do you see that?" he exclaimed. "She's inspecting their arrows! She *knows*!"

"I've already told you that she knows," said Max wearily.

"Well, that's it, then," moaned the hare. "My reputation is officially ruined. The Director thinks I'm a degenerate. She probably lumps me in with that loose and saucy crowd at Cloubert's, and why shouldn't she? Evidently, I *am* the sort of hare who lurks about casinos and wharves giving significant looks to passersby in the hope that they'll stop and say, 'Hey there, old fellow, how'd you like to get your paws on some Zenuvian iron?'"

"I thought Madam Petra invited you into her sitting room and offered you tea?"

"Well, she did," the hare admitted. "But I had to do lots of investigating before it came to that. Aside from sullying my own paws, you're now drowning in debt to a person of questionable character. For all her charm—perhaps because of it—I do not trust that woman. She says she only took your property for collateral, but do you realize she's probably already sold it for fifty times what you owe her?"

"We've been over this, too," said Max. "Bartering was the only way to get the iron. I can't do anything else with it, and she promised not to sell it for a year. I'll get it back."

"What was this treasure you bartered?" asked YaYa, shifting beneath him.

"My torque," said Max, touching the bare space at his neck. "The Fomorian made it from Nick's quills. Do you think I was wrong?"

"You used it in the hope of saving lives," replied YaYa. "What better use is there?"

A cloud passed before the sun and the battalion's splendid gleam died a slow, flickering death.

"Well, that's it," sighed Tweedy. "We'll be assigned to guard a pumpkin patch."

"Don't be so dramatic," replied Max. "This isn't the part I'm worried about."

He gazed at the neighboring hill where Lucia and Cynthia were making final arrangements for the upcoming simulation. The Director had personally dictated the simulation's parameters, and Max had no idea what they would be. Over the past week, he'd ratcheted up the intensity immensely—conditioning, weapons practice, and the execution of various maneuvers and formations. The formations ensured that the battalion's firepower could be directed at critical targets and that its defenses—or even retreat—would not devolve into a mad scramble in the midst of battle. Without training and discipline, the Trench Rats would be no better than a mob.

Fortunately, the battalion was not merely willing but eager to put in the additional work. They seemed to take a perverse delight in the fact that Max not only survived assassination, but also showed no trace of the attack. The more superstitious troops considered this a magnificent omen; their commander was apparently invulnerable and naturally they must be, too. When they also learned that YaYa would be joining their ranks and that Zenuvian iron had been procured for arrows and pike tips, confidence spiraled up to the stratosphere. Now, instead of naming their battalion with an apologetic shrug, many were sporting homespun patches with sinful pride. While no two were exactly alike and some of the "rats" were not readily recognizable as such, they still had the intended effect. A black rat—or blob—on an ivory background signaled that its wearer was a member of the Trench Rats. And this had become a very good thing.

Fortune could be fickle, however. Max knew that if they failed this review, the Trench Rats' station and spirits would sink very low indeed. It would be humiliating to be reassigned. If this occurred, the troops would no doubt find themselves inside the citadel, protecting a building in Old College or perhaps joining civilian patrols about Rowan Township. Necessary work, but the Director would undoubtedly put someone else in charge and redeploy the battalion's prized and unique assets to more critical functions at the front.

Something caught Max's eye. A bannerman was waving his standard to signal that the commander could rejoin the group. YaYa descended the hill at a slow, heavy walk. It was an adjustment getting used to her; the ki-rin was far more massive than the biggest destriers and moved with an entirely different gait. And she was a truly ancient creature. Max would never have voiced his misgivings (her offer to serve him was a tremendous honor) but privately he worried if YaYa was really up to this task. Her body was powerful, but it was also arthritic. She grew tired easily and he had yet to urge her beyond the meager trot with which she covered the last fifty yards to where the Director was waiting.

"So, Commander McDaniels," said Ms. Richter amiably, "shall we see a few demonstrations?"

Max nodded and wheeled the ki-rin around to face his troops. When he blew his horn, the entire company broke apart like the pieces of a machine, each company and platoon jogging to their assigned positions in the practice trench while the ballistae were wheeled into place behind them. They faced a broad field where numbered targets had been set up at various distances and intervals.

"All archers," said Ms. Richter. "Their nearest target."

The signal was relayed to the company commanders and lieutenants. Seconds later, six hundred bowstrings were drawn in unison and held until Sarah gave the command to fire. They did so in a single whistling volley that thudded into their targets with a truly satisfying sound. A few had missed, but the vast majority struck their mark.

"Company two, target eleven," said Ms. Richer calmly.

Ajax relayed the order to his company and gave the command. Within ten seconds, arrows were nocked, bows raised high, and a volley arced toward a target some hundred yards away. About half hit their mark at such a distance: decent if not outstanding. One of Ms. Richter's aides jotted down the result.

"Company four is under attack by vyes," said the Director. "They are to fire two arrows apiece as fast as they can. Starting . . . now."

The ensuing arrows flew with considerably less uniformity and precision than previous volleys. Max was less concerned with the speed than he was with target selection and accuracy. The Director was clearly probing to see if the archers knew the proper distances at which to fire at a charging vye. One had to take into account the creature's speed, and conventional wisdom held that even an expert bowman would only be able to get off two shots on a closing vye before it was upon them. The optimal distances were at one hundred yards and twenty-five yards. Gazing out, Max exhaled as most fired at the proper targets. Some missed, some plunged into the wrong haystacks, but the general performance was respectable.

For the next hour, the Trench Rats' bows, ballistae, and pikemen were put through their paces. The results were mixed, but there had been no gross embarrassments.

That could change in a heartbeat, thought Max, gazing uneasily out at the wood.

"Very good," said Ms. Richter. "Let's see a live demonstration of an ogre charge with Company Three, Platoon Six."

Inwardly, Max groaned. The Director had chosen the worst pike unit in the entire battalion. He doubted this was an accident. Max could practically see the boy named Richard droop when the unit had been named. Swapping out their weapons for padded training pikes, the unit assumed a proper wedge and faced the woods.

Bob emerged. Hefting his cudgel, the ogre wore a steel breastplate and a horned helm whose fearsome grating obscured his kindly face. He looked nothing like his typical self, and it was unnerving to see him standing there some hundred yards away. When the ogre broke into a trot and then an all-out clanking sprint, it was downright terrifying.

As Bob charged, Max watched the soldiers closely. Thus far they were maintaining a tight formation and digging in their heels. A few pikes were trembling, but no one simply threw down their weapon and fled as had happened on several occasions. Everything depended on timing, on the unit's ability to stand firm and deliver a single, concentrated blow. Should they fail, they would not have another opportunity. If an ogre managed to invade a trench, all nearby could expect a sudden and savage death. Each group of pikemen had to hold their ground; a single weak link could mean ruin.

The earth shook. Lowering his head and giving a hoarse roar, Bob crashed into the formation at full speed. The impact was tremendous. One of the pikes shattered outright and its owner was thrown back. But the rest held, striking Bob's breastplate as one and jolting him upright so that he staggered backward and toppled onto his behind. The pikemen were ecstatic, flinging their weapons into the air and rushing to help Bob up. Climbing wearily to his feet, the ogre removed his helmet and caught his breath.

"I think you must pass them, Director," he croaked, wiping sweat from his knobby forehead. "Bob not do that again. . . ."

An hour later, Max was feeling almost giddy as he strode down the dormitory hallway toward his room. The corridor was fairly crowded with Fifth and Sixth Year boys, leaning against the walls in their academic robes and chatting before they would all head down to supper. Max nodded hello as he swept by, highly conscious of his ring but oblivious to the mud he was tracking with each long stride.

Max stopped, however, when he saw Omar Mustaf. The boy was technically Tweedy's steward, which Tweedy interpreted to mean that he had been granted legal authority to function as Omar's official guardian, tutor, and scold. While other students were off playing with their charges in the Sanctuary, Omar was forced to endure Tweedy's heavily advertised, sparsely attended lectures on everything from Greek architecture to the exhaustive works of David Hume. Omar had not merely approved Max's request to speak with his charge about serving as aide-de-camp; he had given his enthusiastic blessing.

"How did it go?" inquired Omar cautiously.

Laughing with pleasure, Max lifted the boy three feet off the ground.

"We passed!" he exclaimed, spinning Omar about. "The Director has 'every confidence' that we're the group to hold Trench Nineteen. Tweedy's brilliant!"

"He'll be the first to tell you," said Omar, grinning as Max set him down. "But I'm glad—Tweedy's been such a nervous wreck."

"Oh, that reminds me," said Max, regaining his senses. "Bob's whipping up a late supper for the officers up at Crofter's Hill. Tweedy will be there. You should come!"

"I'd like that," said Omar, "but I've got to wolf something down and get back to my own unit. We're doing night exercises beyond Southgate."

Max glanced at Omar's magechain and blinked at the brilliant aquamarine at its center.

"A full-fledged aeromancer!" he exclaimed. "Look at you!"

Reddening, Omar gazed down at the glittering stone. He downplayed its significance, joking about "battlefield promotions" and the recent spate of advancements, but he nevertheless looked pleased. Very few Fifth Years could claim official

Agent or Mystic status, and the honor was far greater than the ever-humble Omar would admit. With a promise to stop by Bob's if he could, Omar departed and Max entered his room.

To his surprise, David was home. His roommate was occupying one of the armchairs on the lower level, scratching at his severed stump and staring at the fire. He glanced up as Max descended the stairs, muttered something about "muddy boots," and returned to his thoughts.

"We passed!" Max crowed, padding back down in his stocking feet.

"I heard," David groused. "I'd imagine everyone in the dormitory heard. So the troops have 'won' the right to occupy a muddy trench in harm's way. An odd thing to celebrate, but I guess people will jump at anything so long as they're convinced it's prestigious."

"Nice to see you, too," said Max, plopping down in the opposite chair.

Slumping back, David gazed wearily up at the stars beyond the Observatory's glass.

"I'm sorry," he muttered, closing his eyes. "That was rude. Truly, I'm sorry . . . I'm just tired and more than a little frustrated."

"What's bugging you?"

"Oh, just that thing," he sighed, gesturing absently beneath Max's chair.

Leaning forward, Max spied a pair of large, undulating antennae between his feet.

The ensuing shriek—both its pitch and volume—were unprecedented, as was Max's Amplified leap to the upper level. Clinging to the railing, Max shouted furiously at his roommate while the pinlegs scuttled out from beneath the toppled chair and meandered about in a state of apparent confusion.

"Why didn't you tell me it was under my chair?"

"I'm sorry," yelled David, also in a state of apparent confusion. "I forgot!"

"What's it even doing in our room?"

"I needed a break from the Archives!"

"Why didn't you tell me it was under my chair?" Max roared again, his rage and revulsion coming full circle.

Pleading with his friend to come back down, David righted the chair and picked up the pinlegs to demonstrate that there was really nothing to fear as the creature was on a docile setting. This did not have the desired effect, as the pinlegs flailed its many limbs about while clicking its maxillae and issuing a high-pitched chittering. Max groaned and clutched the railing tightly.

But reason—or at least a willingness to conquer rational terror—prevailed and Max crept back down the stairs. By now, David had released the pinlegs, which promptly moved away to settle on the fireplace mantel like some glistening Jurassic horror. Even as Max inched forward, he saw that the chitinous plates along its back were covered in faint, glowing pentacles.

"Why did those appear?" he asked suspiciously.

"Heat illuminates them and the hearth is warm," replied David, settling back into his seat. "Nothing to worry about. Again, I'm very sorry I didn't say anything."

"Neither did Ghöllah," muttered Max, glaring at his ring and easing back down.

"Remember that this is just a prototype," said David. "There is no demon—or any part of a demon—inside. It hasn't been paired with a dreadnought."

"What the heck is a dreadnought?"

"That's what Varga calls the creatures that the pinlegs summon. He's had glimpses of them in his visions . . . says they're bigger than Old Tom. I'd love to speak with someone who's seen one in person, but we can't find any. Nobody who has seen a dreadnought summoned has survived to tell about it."

"What about that Workshop engineer we kidnapped?" asked Max. "He must know something."

"Unfortunately, no," replied David. "The Workshop partitioned the project so that only one or two people have detailed knowledge about all the components. Dr. Bechel only worked on the pinlegs. He knows very little about the dreadnoughts or the process by which the Workshop splits an imp's spirit in two. . . ."

Unscrewing a nearby coffee thermos, David sniffed at its contents, sighed, and set it back down.

"Honestly, Max, I've never been so frustrated. I feel like I've been handed a big jumble of knots to unravel, and every time I manage one, I find that three more have appeared. The Director, Ms. Kraken . . . everyone's counting on me to solve this, but I just don't know. I've hit a dead end."

"Impossible," said Max, trying to cheer him up. "You're a genius!"

"Charitable," said David. "Even if that's true, I'm not alone. The Workshop has more than its fair share. For example, I have tried everything I can think of to confuse this pinlegs' settings—block incoming signals, manipulate outgoing signals. . . ." He trailed off, looking utterly worn and dejected. "Miss Boon is beside herself. Varga too. Dr. Bechel says that they incorporated a slew of poison pills to guard against tampering."

"What's a poison pill?"

"A clever defense tactic," replied David wearily. "Every time we try to crack the pinlegs' symbolic code, that code becomes twice as complicated to break. We're now at a point where it could literally take *millions* of years to run through the current permutations and we'd only be digging ourselves a deeper hole.

I'm ready to scream. We're all so close to the problem that we're not even thinking clearly anymore. I came up here to get away from the Archives, sit by the fire, and clear my head. I'm tired of staring at runeglass."

"How's Miss Boon doing?" asked Max delicately.

"Better now that it looks like Grendel's going to make it, but I'm not certain anyone took the attack on you harder than she did. Ms. Richter has absolutely forbidden her to go searching for Cooper. Miss Boon's been trying to help with the pinlegs, but it's hard for her to focus. Any sign of Cooper?"

"No," said Max. "Umbra goes out searching every night, but no luck."

"*Umbra* goes out searching," David repeated with peculiar emphasis.

Max had not yet told David of Umbra's true identity. He'd only seen his roommate once since the attack in the tent. There had been so much happening that Max hadn't had the opportunity to speak with his friend in private. And thus he wondered at the wry twinkle in David's pale, almost colorless eyes.

"What do you know?" asked Max, shifting uneasily in his seat.

"Well," said David, betraying a ghost of a smile, "I don't know anything for certain. I can only say that Max McDaniels has been trying very hard to compose some poetry and has been struggling to come up with anything to rhyme with *Scathach*. He does seem to have the 'roses are red, violets are blue' part down pretty well. It's appeared in every draft."

Max turned fire red. "I was just using that to get the ideas flowing," he snapped, before turning about to find that his waste-basket had been moved. "Did you go through my garbage?"

David looked sheepish. "I did," he admitted. "I didn't mean to, but the pinlegs knocked it over and all these papers spilled out. I was cleaning them up when I glimpsed a few lines. I knew it was wrong to read them, but . . ." He winced. "Not my proudest moment."

Digesting this, Max settled slowly back in his chair. "Oh, it's all right," he sighed. "I've snooped in your stuff plenty of times. I guess the real question is whether you think there's anything I can use?"

"I'd say you're building a strong foundation for future success," replied David diplomatically. "Anyway, tell me about Scathach."

Max did so, unable to keep the grin off his face. "It's hard to concentrate when I'm around her," he confessed. "But it's even harder to pretend she's Umbra in front of everyone else."

"Well, I don't think I've ever seen you so happy," David reflected. "Perhaps love does conquer all—or at least fear of the Atropos and the threat of invasion. I always suspected there was something between you two."

"Please," Max scoffed. "I hardly ever talked about her."

"*Exactly,*" said David with a knowing grin. "Anyway, I look forward to meeting her. I only got a distant glimpse of her at Rodrubân. Is she the reason behind the Trench Rats' recent success?"

"One of them," said Max. "But lots of people have made the difference."

"And how are the Mystics in your battalion?" inquired David, casually examining his fingernails. "I'd imagine they must have done some good things."

"Lucia and Cynthia have been fantastic. During tonight's simulation, Lucia created an entire troop of deathknights that were so realistic you'd have sworn we were hiding back in the woods near Broadbrim Mountain. Amazing detail!"

"Hmmm," said David, frowning. "Lucia's got undeniable

talent, but I find her magic—ooh—a little temperamental. Cynthia's work might be a little less flashy, but every outcome is rock solid and reliable. Utterly dependable in a pinch. There's real bottom there."

Max gave him a sidelong glance. "I'll take your word."

"It's just refreshing to know someone like that," David continued dreamily, swinging his legs up onto the ottoman. "Someone who's always cheerful, always willing to laugh or listen."

"She's a good friend," Max agreed, thumping his armrest. "A real *steady item.*"

It was David's turn to blush. Blinking rapidly, he opened his mouth, but evidently words failed him and he merely stared at the fire in mortified silence.

"We agreed to keep it a secret," he finally whispered.

"But why?" said Max gleefully. "Love should be shouted from the rooftops! I think it's great that Toby helped you sort through your *special feelings. . . .*"

David moaned, slouching ever lower until his eyes were level with his knees. "Who else knows?"

"Just Sarah and Lucia," replied Max. "And the *Tattler* gossip columnist . . ."

"You are a very witty person."

"I *am* very witty," Max agreed, rising from his chair to stretch. "Not everyone can come up with these little gems and also make a battalion work. It's not enough to focus on each platoon or even a whole company; *all* the pieces have to fit together perfectly. If they don't, you'll have a weakness, and if you have a weakness—"

"Shhh!"

"You're much too sensitive."

"No," said David, waving him off. "Be quiet—I need to think." And think he did, curling into a ball and staring ahead with a preoccupied air that Max knew all too well. The sorcerer glanced occasionally at the pinlegs and then back at the fire, as though they were two separate equations he was trying to reconcile. At length, he got up and began to pace. Max knew he would be late for Bob's supper, but he could not leave. David seemed poised on the cusp of something truly momentous. Twenty minutes passed before he finally stopped and stared at Max with an expression of profound wonder.

"You're a genius."

"I could have told you that in half the time."

"No," said David, pacing again. "It's what you said about all the pieces having to fit together perfectly." He absently made to knit his fingers together, recalled that he had but one hand, and abandoned the demonstration. It did not diminish his enthusiasm. "The Workshop has somehow split the soul of an imp and embedded one half in a pinlegs and the other in a dreadnought. That's what allows the pinlegs to instantly summon its other half."

"Okay," said Max, trying to follow where David was going.

"We've been totally focused on trying to identify the pinlegs' vulnerabilities so we can prevent it from summoning its dreadnought. But as we're learning—and as Dr. Bechel confirmed—there are a million safeguards to prevent anyone from sabotaging it. As an individual component, it's almost impossible to crack. But what happens *after* it's summoned its dreadnought and the pieces are put together?"

"Everything gets destroyed," said Max.

"True," David allowed. "And it's a terrifying prospect, but I wonder if the dreadnought is actually more vulnerable than the pinlegs. Not physically, of course, but . . . Well, how *does* a soul function once it's been split in half and is then reunited? Is it really whole and seamless, or is it compromised in some way?"

"I have no idea."

"Neither do I," said David excitedly, grabbing the startled pinlegs from its apparent slumber. "But it's promising. Come with me to Founder's Hall. I have to speak with Ms. Richter!"

"But Bob's making dinner—"

"Leftovers are delicious!" cried David, hurrying up the steps. Flinging open the door, he rushed out, clutching the hideous pinlegs to his chest as though it were his firstborn.

David was wheezing by the time they reached Founder's Hall. It was as crowded as ever and David was half stumbling as he wove through the many analysts and scholars and domovoi. A shriek went up as someone spotted the pinlegs and a path soon opened. Barging through the crowds clustered around the Director, David plopped the pinlegs right on her table.

"I need to borrow all the Promethean Scholars," he gasped. "Right away!"

Ms. Richter merely stared at the revolting creature splayed before her. She had not flinched or even blinked at its sudden appearance, but when its long antennae brushed her chin, she spoke with unnerving calm.

"David Menlo, be so good as to explain why I should not have you pilloried."

"Can we speak in private?"

"Will this thing be joining us?"

David nodded, coughing hoarsely as he scooped the pinlegs up. The Director rose, muttered an apology to the rest, and stepped into the adjoining conference room. She glanced up at Max as he followed them inside and shut the door.

"McDaniels," she observed. "I believe we already had your review. I hope you rewarded your battalion for a job well done."

"They have the next two days off," he replied. "They need it."

"Good," she said. "Hard work should be rewarded. Now,

what has David Menlo in such a state of excitement that he's determined to startle me into cardiac arrest?"

Catching his breath, David summarized their difficulties with the pinlegs and his theory that the dreadnoughts might present a different sort of opportunity.

"The dreadnoughts are huge," he said. "But it's just an imp's mind and soul that's controlling it. I'm sure they'd rather use a more powerful demon, but it's probably much more difficult to split their soul in two. I think—and it's just a theory at this stage—that it might be possible for us to take control of a dreadnought by possessing the imp inside it."

"You'd need the imp's truename," reflected Ms. Richter.

"You would if its spirit is intact," replied David. "But these spirits have been damaged; they've been torn in two and the halves reunited. Perhaps they're weaker in some way."

Glancing at the pinlegs, Ms. Richter considered David's words.

"So what is it that you need from me?" she said. "And be very specific. I have no uncommitted resources. Anything you request must be taken from something else."

"I understand," said David. "I'm asking for all the Promethean Scholars for the next two weeks."

Ms. Richter shook her head. "David," she replied. "The latest intelligence estimates that Prusias's main fleet will be here in two weeks. Meanwhile, the Promethean Scholars are working on a dozen initiatives that I *know* have value. Your pinlegs project is the most critical, but there's been no real progress in over a month. I realize that you're excited about this new theory, but it's still in its infancy and may well come up empty. I simply cannot redirect all of Rowan's best minds to help you research your hypothesis at the expense of everything else they're doing. It's too big a gamble at the eleventh hour unless you can prove to me that Prusias's force is more than two weeks away. Have you been able to use your observatory for scrying?"

"No," David admitted, pacing once again and looking irritated. "Scrying hasn't worked at all since the demons went to war with one another. I think the Book of Thoth is behind it; otherwise I might be able to break the spell."

"So you think Astaroth is causing it?" asked Max.

"No," replied David. "I think Prusias is causing it—creating his own fog of war to blind his enemies. Don't forget that Prusias has a page from the Book embedded in his cane. I think that would be enough."

"So you can't tell me when Prusias's armada will arrive," said Ms. Richter pointedly.

David shook his head.

"If that's the case, then I have no choice but to rely on intelligence reports," she said. "And my most reliable sources say that Prusias is due here sooner than we could wish. So let's negotiate."

The pair went back and forth in rapid succession, making offers and counteroffers until Ms. Richter finally agreed to let David have three Promethean Scholars along with four spiritwracks of his choice.

"Names?" she asked, retrieving a slim notebook.

"Smythe, Oliveiro, Wen, and Olshansky."

"Done," she muttered, jotting them down. "Now, you must excuse—" She broke off as someone started knocking furiously upon the door. Raising an eyebrow, Ms. Richter strode over to the door where she found Ms. Kraken looking like she'd seen a ghost.

"Come outside, Gabrielle," hissed the aged teacher. "Something's happening!"

Suspicious at this urgent intrusion, Max touched his ring,

but it was cool. Glancing uneasily at one another, Max and David followed the Director back into Founder's Hall. The huge room was eerily silent. All eyes were fixed on the wall that displayed the Florentine spypaper. A dozen glowspheres were converging at a section whose larger, unencrypted sheets were used to correspond with distant Rowan settlements. One sphere settled above a sheet marked for Grayhaven. Another halted at Sphinx Point while others slowly came to rest by Blackrock, Fellowship, North Spit, South Spit, Cold Harbor, Anvil . . . every coastal township within two hundred miles. All of the spheres began to pulse, their collective radiance filling the hall with a sickly yellow light. Max heard gasps as the messages started to appear. Ms. Richter called for silence, walking briskly through the crowd with Ms. Kraken, Max, and David trailing in her wake.

Even from a distance, Max could read the messages. They appeared simultaneously, and each contained but two words scrawled in heavy black ink.

SAVE US!

Quickly scanning the other parchments, Max found the sheet for Glenharrow and saw that it and most of those for the inland settlements were still blank. Just as Ms. Richter was about to speak, drips and smears of black ink appeared like pattering raindrops to muddy and obscure the pleas from the coastal towns. Recognizable patterns soon emerged, as though fingers were dragging through the wet ink and tracing a common design: three circles set between opposing sheaves of wheat.

It was the seal of Prusias.

"That's impossible," muttered Ms. Richter. "Alistair insisted that they wouldn't land for at least two weeks. They're supposed to be in the middle of the ocean!"

Flipping open a portfolio where she kept highly classified correspondence, the Director riffled through several pages of spypaper before removing one and reading it through her decrypting lens. From where Max stood, its grisly message was perfectly clear.

ALISTAIR DIED BADLY

As Ms. Richter crumpled the sheet, Old Tom's bell began to toll in deafening peals that shook the very hall.

The Enemy had been sighted.

~ 17 ~

TRENCH NINETEEN

When Old Tom's ringing ceased, Ms. Richter strode to the head of Founder's Hall and raised her arms for silence. Her voice was admirably calm.

"The Enemy is here," she announced, surveying the room. "Rowan needs us and I know she will not be disappointed. Each face I see fills me with that confidence. There is no time for long speeches or debate. I will say only this. Rowan is not merely our home; it is a haven for all humanity. Prusias is strong, but I remind you that Rowan has stood for nearly four hundred years and has never been more prepared to meet such a foe. He has underestimated our strength and our resolve, and he will pay dearly for it. Do your duty and may God be with you. *Sol Invictus.*"

Everyone present responded in kind before setting out for his or her assignments. A surreal energy permeated the hall—brisk professionalism tempered by fear and excitement. There was no wasted discussion, no cries of anguish or despair, and no evident panic. Striding to her table to retrieve her most critical papers, Ms. Richter glanced at David.

"I'll send who I can, but don't wait for them," she said sharply. "Can you look to see if ships are landing? We may need you to do what you can there."

Clutching the pinlegs, David nodded and hurried out, joining the rapid exodus of Agents and Mystics.

Ms. Richter's eyes snapped to Max. "You are the Hound of Rowan," she said. "You are our champion, and Prusias fears you like nothing else upon this earth. Do not forget that."

Before Max could even respond, the Director was already engaged in other matters. He hurried out of Founder's Hall as Old Tom sounded the alarm anew.

It was pandemonium in the Manse's corridors, a crush of people hurrying out to their stations or rushing to the dormitories to retrieve some needed item or weapon. Max also needed to retrieve something, but it was not in his room. Squeezing past a cluster of anxious-looking students, he crossed the foyer and spilled out with the others into the clear, cold night.

YaYa was already waiting by the fountain, humans streaming past her like floodwaters parting at a great rock. The ki-rin's eyes were glowing, her breath pluming from her nostrils in white billows. Hurrying down the steps, Max slid a foot into a stirrup and swung high up into the saddle.

"We have to go to the smithy!" he shouted, straining to be heard over Old Tom's clanging and the incredible din as thousands hurried across the quad. At the slightest pressure from Max's knee, YaYa wheeled and lumbered heavily toward the township.

The ki-rin could do no more than walk as they swam against a tide of people. It was fifteen minutes of impatient agonizing until they could get through the Sanctuary tunnel and YaYa could manage a lumbering trot. A great heat was coming off the ki-rin, and periodically she shivered as though growing feverish.

At last they arrived at the smithing shop owned by the brothers Aurvangr and Ginnarr. The upper windows were dark and shuttered, but Max saw a gleam of light peeping from beneath the door. Swinging out of his saddle, he ran up the front steps and knocked urgently. Something crashed within and he heard someone curse before another angry voice cried out, "Closed!"

"It's Max McDaniels!"

The door opened and Max looked down to see the dvergar—a dusky, dwarflike creature with pale eyes and beard—half dressed in armor of overlapping scales.

"It's in the workroom," muttered Aurvangr, waving Max toward the back. "By the quenching tubs. Not pretty yet, but it works. There's something else on the table. We decided your need is greater. Close the door behind you. We're due at Westgate."

Ducking inside, Max hurried into the back room where the dvergar kept their forge and anvil. Max found what he was looking for propped against the wall next to a trio of water barrels. It was a spear shaft some seven feet long, fashioned of roughened steel and devised so that Max could use it with the *gae bolga*. He'd commissioned it from the brothers after his first day supervising the battalion from atop YaYa. The *gae bolga*'s limited reach was poorly suited for mounted combat and was impractical to wield on a horse, much less a ki-rin standing eight feet at her shoulder.

Keeping the blade sheathed, Max pressed its pommel to the top of the spear shaft. Like a ravenous snake, the shaft swallowed up the hilt, clamping tight at the cross-guard so that the short sword was transformed into a long-bladed spear. Hefting it, Max tested its weight and balance before turning to the object folded neatly on the neighboring table. It was an exquisite corselet of fine gray mail, the very armor Max had bartered to the dvergar in exchange for the *Ormenheid*. The shirt had once belonged to Antonio de Lorca, Max's predecessor in the Red Branch, and no ordinary weapon could pierce it. Quickly, Max stripped off his tunic and hauberk, swapping the heavy, cumbersome rings for a garment more supple than linen. Pulling the tunic back over his head, Max checked that Lugh's brooch was in place, took up the *gae bolga*, and hurried out of the shop.

As YaYa picked her way through the winding lanes back to the main avenue, Max witnessed the very best and worst of humanity. Many companies of troops and militia were hurrying to their posts, but there also were brawls, untold looters, and some who chose to greet Prusias's arrival with doomed, drunken revelry. Rounding a corner, Max stopped as he saw a half-dozen Trench Rats carousing with a group that had broken into the Pot and Kettle and were rolling its wine barrels up the cellar ramp to break them open in the street. Upon seeing their commander, one promptly retched while the others snapped to some semblance of bleary, blinking attention.

Max glared down at them. "It's a thirty-minute march to Trench Nineteen from here. If you're not there in twenty, I'm going to find each and every one of you."

"We were on leave," said the one, sullenly wiping his mouth. "You got no right to judge!"

"When does leave give you the right to loot and steal?" Max

growled. "Stay and sit in your filth. You're discharged. Rip off his patch."

The man's companions did so, tearing the patch off his shoulder while he swore and protested. Seconds later, the other five were running as fast as they could toward the Sanctuary tunnel and their distant post.

"Bravo, bravo!" called a voice from the restaurant's elevated porch.

Madam Petra was lounging between the industrialist and Katarina. She was sipping a glass of wine without an apparent care in the world. Around her neck, she wore the coppery torque made from Nick's quills.

"Oh, don't worry about us," she said, swirling her wine. "We're not looters. We paid for our drinks. You look very dashing, by the way."

"Going to sit things out here?" said Max, gazing at the smuggler with unfeigned disgust.

"Yes, I am," she said, smiling sweetly. "That's the nice thing about having friends on both sides. You don't really care who wins."

"You think Prusias will just leave you be?"

"I don't see why not." She shrugged, stroking her daughter's hair. "I've been invited to many parties at the royal palace. Why should he be angry with a Rowan hostage? In any case, I hope the Zenuvian iron serves you well. You certainly paid for the privilege."

Max stared hard at the woman. "You had better pray that we win," he said quietly. "Because if Rowan falls, there will be no one left to forgive you. And if that happens, you'll have to live with this shame forever."

"Well, I've heard that good wine can drown sorrow *and* shame," she replied lightly, checking the bottle's label. "And if that fails, I'm sure this torque can buy whatever forgiveness I might require. Run along now and keep us safe."

Swallowing his loathing, Max wheeled YaYa away and rode south. Once back at Old College, the ki-rin set a slow, steady pace as she wove through the mass of soldiers and civilians. Passing the Manse, Max rode toward the cliffs so that he could see what might be happening at sea.

The waters of Rowan Harbor were choppy as those assigned to the beaches and cliffs were busy preparing their defenses. Far to the north, Max could make out a few points of light hugging the coast, probably warships with witch-fires burning at their prow. The night sky had been clear, but the weather was changing. Most apparent was the wind, which was now howling in off the ocean as Rowan's Mystics summoned and gathered it to them.

Max and YaYa rode north along the cliffs, past Maggie and Old Tom, past the refugee camps and over the windswept tussocks until he reached the massive Northgate archway. The archway was forty feet from cobble to keystone and still dwarfed by the walls, which rose a hundred feet above even the tallest trees. Max could see hundreds of figures hurrying to man the towers and anchored trebuchets that could rain heavy projectiles upon an approaching enemy.

YaYa cantered through the arch, her shadow huge upon curving walls that tunneled through eighty feet of solid stone. It was teeming with soldiers and carts bringing supplies out to the trenches and outposts that would sorely need them. The crowds cheered when they caught sight of YaYa and made a lane so that she and her rider could pass.

They exited the other side, over the moat's causeway and into the dark, open country that lay between the citadel that sheltered Old College and the outer curtain that protected outlying farms.

Torches were moving urgently about the countryside, carried by messengers on errands to the trenches or outer defenses. Above Old Tom's ringing, Max heard the low boom of signal drums and saw a distant flare arc like a tiny red star.

YaYa made for a cluster of fires burning at intervals along Trench Nineteen. There, at the base of their fluttering standard, the Trench Rats were gathering and grouping into their platoons. Some grinned as Max rode up, but most looked frightened. Many were frantically putting on pieces of armor or rummaging through packs whose contents had been gathered in haste. Scanning the group, Max saw that only a third of the battalion had already reported. There was not yet any sign of Lucia or Cynthia or many of the officers who had presumably been at Crofter's Hill when the alarm was raised. Ajax was there, however, sitting astride a heavy bay stallion and berating several boys who had cracked a water barrel while unloading a supply cart.

Max called him over. "Assemble the companies and keep them here," he said over the wind and distant horns. "Don't let them rush or forget something they need. Once we're settled in, we won't be moving, so send riders to fetch anything that's missing—food, medicine. They won't close Northgate unless the Enemy advances within a mile. I'm riding to the outer walls to see what's happening."

As Ajax turned to carry out his orders, Max saw Scathach ride up on a spotted Appaloosa. She was in Umbra's guise but now wore a shirt of silver chain and carried a small round shield strapped to her back. Her hair was tossing wildly in the wind as she slowed the horse to a walk and gazed at Max.

"I'm going to the wall," he said. "Come with me."

She nodded, spurring her mount ahead. The two rode alongside one another, covering the distance as swiftly as YaYa could manage in her lumbering trot. The outer walls rose before them, less massive than those that surrounded Old College but still a formidable defense. Eighty feet high and half as thick, with guard towers twice as tall that commanded a wide view of the lands beyond.

They reached the battlements by riding up the broad ramps that doubled back and again until they arrived at the top. Hundreds of people were busily engaged—Mystics gathering atop casting towers, refugees heating iron shot and cauldrons of pitch, archers setting up their quivers behind stone merlons. Dismounting, Max and Scathach walked up a short staircase to a platform that would permit a glimpse of Prusias's forces.

At this distance, the approaching army resembled a forest fire, an eerie, distant flickering light that was closing upon Rowan. Max guessed that the outriders were three, maybe four miles away. Peering through his spyglass, he could clearly make out war galleons sailing down the shoreline as the army approached over land. "Can you guess their numbers?" asked Max, surveying the distant lights. Even now, he could hear the faint sounds of distant drums and horns. They reminded him sharply of his escape from Piter's Folly on Madam Petra's balloon. He had heard these drums before and witnessed the awful devastation that accompanied them.

Frowning, Scathach scanned the horizon. "Impossible to say," she muttered. "But many, many thousands. There are no breaks in those torches. They'll reach these walls in three hours... maybe two."

Max was about to reply when he heard cheers go up from a host of archers, who were pointing beyond the wall to the countryside where moonlit runes and sigils were forming on the hills like luminescent brands.

"What are those?" asked Scathach, peering out at them.

"Glyphs, signs of protection," Max explained. "They're being cast by the spiritwracks." He pointed to one of the tall octagonal towers where the specialized Mystics could be seen linking hands in an open chamber at the top.

Just then, a hurricane-force gale came screaming in out of the east. It tore through the forests beyond the wall like a wailing spirit, bending the trees in a sweeping arc before doubling back and dissipating out over the ocean.

"Aeromancers," said Max, pointing to another tower, where Mystics were summoning the wild winds from the sea and directing them like orchestra conductors. "Prusias is going to find that there's more than arrows and pikes waiting for him here."

Scathach was impressed. "Perhaps we won't be needed."

But even as she said this, hundreds of horns blared in the distance, followed by the louder, deeper *boom, boom, boom* of kettledrums. The pace of the drumming increased and her smile faded.

"We should ride back," she reflected. "Your soldiers will want to see their commander."

Max nodded and the two left the wall, descending the ramps to the rutted road that led back to Trench Nineteen. As Max settled into YaYa's gait, he gazed across a vast landscape of shadowy blues and grays, a backdrop of dark farmland and sparse forests in which thousands of torches were flickering as battalions and companies took up position along the trenches. The citadel walls and fortifications protecting Old College loomed behind them, white and gleaming beneath the moon. They reminded Max of castles he'd seen in the Sidh.

Most of the Trench Rats had assembled by the time they'd returned. They stood at attention, some unsteadily from interrupted celebrations, but the majority appeared clear-eyed and anxious. Max found his friends among them. While Lucia and Cynthia were wearing Mystics robes, Sarah was dressed for combat. Like the other company commanders, she rode a charger and was armored in gleaming half-plate with the Rowan crest chased in silver upon the cuirass. She carried the *naginata* she favored, along with the battalion's horn that would signal an advance, cease-fire, or retreat back to the Northgate. Standing behind Cynthia was Bob, cradling his great helm and leaning upon his cudgel. Calling out to the lieutenants, Max had them bring the troops closer so that they could hear him as he shouted over the wind.

"The Enemy is marching upon us," he announced. "Umbra and I have seen them from the outer curtain. In a few hours they'll reach those walls. We're going to take up our positions now and settle in. We might be here for days."

He scanned the faces, many still dirty and dusty from their review. They were trying to pay attention, but many could not keep from gaping about as signal flares screamed overhead like shooting stars. Drills and training were well and good, but they were still a far cry from taking a real field against a real opponent. Max's gaze fell upon one face in the crowd, a young pikeman named Joshua. The boy was shivering, standing on tiptoe to follow a troop of centaurs as they galloped toward the outer wall.

"I know you're frightened," said Max, his eyes moving from Joshua to the multitudes surrounding him. "Every good soldier is frightened before a battle. Those who deny it are liars or fools. Even Bob is afraid."

Necks craned to glimpse the ogre, who smiled and nodded.

"Don't fight your fear—embrace it," Max urged them. "Let it sharpen you and give you strength. Most of you have never fought in a battle like this. But when the call was sounded, you answered. You have the courage and will to overcome your fear and do what's required. There isn't a person here who hasn't cheated Death to make it to Rowan."

Max paused as grim nods passed among the many refugees.

"You're survivors. In the past, many of you had to do it alone. But you are not alone anymore. I am with you. Everyone you see, everyone in this battalion, from Ajax to Umbra, is with you. War is big. Make it small. It's not your job to defeat Prusias. Let others worry about that. Your only job is to defend those on either side of you. You do that and they cannot break us. Nothing passes Trench Nineteen!"

A wild cheer went up from the battalion. Some embraced while others shouted angry oaths at Prusias or demons or whatever else they fancied. Those who were closest to YaYa touched the ki-rin's broken horn for luck. At Sarah's signal, the troops spread out along the trench, marching behind their lieutenants and company commanders until they reached the fluttering pennants that marked their assignments. Behind them, ballistae were being wheeled into place, healing tents had been pitched, cooking fires were lit, and soldiers were filling their canteens from the water barrels.

Max heard a harrumph from below and gazed down to see Tweedy looking up at him.

"All the arrangements have been made," he reported. "There's more water on its way, Chloe recruited another moomenhoven to tend the wounded, and Jack's fellows are seeing to the cooking fires. Where should I take up position?"

"Tweedy, we talked about this," said Max. "You don't have to stay out here. Once everything's situated, you can go back inside the citadel. It will be safer there."

"And I told *you*, Max McDaniels, that I'm a member of this

battalion and won't be sent off for milk and cookies like a puling wee one. So where shall I go?"

"By Bob," Max sighed, figuring that if anyone could keep the hare safe, it would be the battalion's ogre and his iron-banded cudgel. "But don't talk his ear off, Tweedy. Bob gets quiet at times like this. Leave him be."

Turning to Cynthia and Lucia, Max sent them off to their posts—Lucia to support the right flank nearest the cliffs while Cynthia held the middle. It was an emotional moment. Even Lucia had tears, embracing Cynthia like a sister before hurrying off toward the cliffs and the roar of the churning surf below. Only Scathach remained, sitting easily on the Appaloosa with her spear laid across the saddle.

"Your father would be proud," she said, her eyes glittering.

"Which one?"

"You know the one I mean," she replied. "Command comes naturally to you."

"Where will you take up position?" asked Max. He'd given Scathach the freedom to go wherever she thought she was needed.

"For now, I'll stay by you," she replied. "The Atropos care nothing for this war; their only concern is you. That assassin is still lurking."

Max held up his hand so she could see the silver shining on his finger. "I'll know if he's close."

"If Prusias storms the outer walls, these lands will be riddled with demonkind," she replied. "That ring will scald whether he's close or not. You must not trust it."

"Then I'll have to trust you," said Max, smiling.

"As you should."

Even as she spoke, her features shifted and Umbra's guise fell away to reveal the proud, beautiful face of the warrior maiden. Her expression was solemn as she took his hand. "No one knows what battle may bring," she said, gazing at his brooch and then at him. "Not even Lugh or the Morrígan or any of the Tuatha Dé Danaan can say where the spears and arrows may fall. In this hour, I would have you see me as I am."

From the north, a thunderclap sounded, a shuddering peal that shook the ground and rolled across the open country like a shock wave. The blare of horns carried to them on the wind, thousands of horns blown in unison. Beyond the outer wall, the dark sky was taking on an orange-red cast.

Boom boom boom

Even at such a distance, the drums drowned out the sound of wind and horses and soldiers settling into position. At the outer walls, Rowan's horns answered in a blaring call as hundreds of catapults were loosed. The shots rose like meteors, tracing fiery arcs high into the night sky until they disappeared from sight.

The battle had begun.

An hour passed. Then two. Max found their position maddening. He could make out very little of what was happening at the front. The walls were now obscured by a haze of ashy smoke that settled over the land like a pall. Intermittent bursts of light crackled across the sky, illuminating the farms and forests like a flashbulb before the land settled back into shadow. Now and again, the earth shook or there was a cheer as horns rose above the din.

Max was trembling as he walked YaYa back and forth along Trench Nineteen, gazing out at the wall. Already, the Old Magic was stirring within him, its awakening as steady and ominous as the terrible drums from beyond the wall. Even sheathed, the *gae bolga* knew that blood was being spilled. The spear hummed, its shaft glowing a dull red as though it had been pulled from a bed of hot coals.

"I should be out there," he muttered, shifting anxiously in his saddle.

"Your place is with your soldiers," Scathach reminded Max, calming her horse as it snorted and shied away from him.

Scathach's horse was not the only one that sensed a change coming over Max. As the pair rode past the platoons and companies, many of the troops ceased their hushed conversations to watch them. Some were obviously curious about Scathach and the fact that an apparent newcomer was wearing Umbra's armor and carrying her fearsome spear. But most gazed uneasily at Max as though he were the stranger in their midst. When they passed by Tam, the girl who could perceive auras, she abruptly hushed her friend Jack and stood at attention.

"What's the matter, soldier?" asked Scathach.

"His shine, lady," said Tam, staring at Max. "It's *changing*!"

Max said nothing but looked at Jack, who had apparently been crying. There was vomit by his boots. Glancing at her friend, Tam spoke up on his behalf.

"He okay," she explained. "Just getting jitters. I told him to stick by me and he'll be safe. Ain't that right, Jack?"

The boy nodded, blew his nose on his sleeve, and stood at attention.

"Listen to Tam," said Max, gazing down at the boy. "Stick by her and do what she says. Do you understand me?"

Jack nodded, glanced appreciatively at Tam, and sniffled.

"I'll see you after," said Max, riding on.

* * *

The explosion occurred just before dawn, a pluming fireball in the northwest that shone through the haze, rising hundreds of feet into the air. The earth shook once again and there came a distant cry of horns.

"They're breached," said Scathach, standing up in her stirrups.

A foul wind blew in from the north, a brimstone reek that brought clouds of dust rolling down over the hills to settle upon the soldiers in their trenches. Another explosion, this time directly north along the section of wall that Max and Scathach had visited. Black smoke billowed up into the sky, oily and heavy as though from a factory or smokestack. It crested over the wall like a wave, spilling onto the lands beyond.

Huge flares raced overhead from the citadel, screaming past like crimson comets to burst over the outer walls and signal that those forces should pull back. More explosions sent tremors shivering through the ground. The nearby earthworks trembled, spilling dirt and pebbles onto the huddled Trench Rats. The Enemy was already advancing. Gazing out, Max could just make out Stygian crows circling above the walls. At this distance, they looked like thousands of black midges buzzing round a bonfire.

Twenty minutes passed before the first of the retreating forces reached the trenches. They hurried over the open country in glinting streams of armor and weaponry. There was some semblance of order to the retreat, but not much. Many of the troops were clearly exhausted, panting and sweating as they headed for the safety of Northgate. Some were grievously wounded, helped along or even carried by their comrades. Others were anxious to continue the battle and fell in with the trench battalions. Max welcomed them into Trench Nineteen, offering encouragement but also telling Sarah to ride down the line and remind the lieutenants to maintain their existing groups and formations. The reinforcements were most welcome, but they must fit in between the platoons, not among them. Otherwise all the Trench Rats' careful training and practice would be for naught.

The retreating forces thinned. Max heard a gruff voice barking orders, Ajax telling the troops to check their weapons and have a swallow of water. Wheeling YaYa about, Max rode along the trench one last time.

Some of the Trench Rats were praying, alone or in little groups. Others were eating, wolfing down three days' worth of rations as though they were having their last meal. One grizzled veteran was obsessively checking his gear while his neighbor smeared mud across his face like it was war paint. People had their own way of preparing for what was to come, but most simply stared ahead, gazing mutely at the band of flickering orange that was approaching through the miasma of black smoke. The very air seemed to vibrate as the drums grew louder.

Boom boom boom boom . . .

With each drumbeat, YaYa trembled and began to chuff from somewhere deep in her throat. She was trotting more easily, her limp less pronounced as she headed along the broad trench. Heat was rising off her like morning mist off a lake. She walked to the narrow gap between the Trench Rats and the neighboring battalion as Prusias's soldiers came into clearer view.

There were untold thousands of them. They stretched westward from the cliffs in a great curving arc, as though they comprised but one visible portion of a noose that was tightening around all of Rowan. Banners and pennants fluttered high in the morning breeze, the broken and tattered standards of Jakarün and Dùn and a host of lesser duchies and baronies that had fallen to Prusias's forces.

Max gazed out at them. Most were vyes padding about on two legs like men or on all fours like rangy black wolves. But there were ogres, too, hundreds of them in crested war helms along with two-headed ettins, and rotting deathknights holding tall lances decorated with pennons and grisly scalps. Behind them, still tiny in the distance, rolled Prusias's siege engines: great catapults and towers and rams the size of redwoods.

Prusias doesn't want to obliterate Rowan, Max concluded. *Not if he can help it. Otherwise he'd just send the dreadnoughts.*

Even without their secret weapon, this army had broken through the outer walls in a matter of hours. Could vyes and ogres alone do such a thing? Even as he considered this, Max spied lanes forming in the Enemy's densely packed ranks.

The demons that rode to the front were nobility among their kind: proud rakshasas in gilded plate and crowning war helms, fearsome oni wielding sickle swords, and black-masked malakhim. They seemed to care nothing for the dawn or its rising sun, whose rays died and withered in the spreading gloom. As the demons arrived at the front, Max's ring began to sear. The awful drumming ceased and an eerie stillness settled over Prusias's army.

One of the rakshasa urged his mount forward and ventured alone through the gloom toward the trenches, surveying Rowan's battalions like a visiting general. Disdain was stamped upon his tusked, tigerlike features. Turning, he called for one of his attendants—a slender imp on a black donkey. Riding forward, the imp handed the rakshasa an enormous recurve bow and three arrows. As the imp withdrew, Max heard Scathach whispering urgently in his ear.

"Do not take this bait! You have been seen, my love. He means to draw you out."

Indeed, the rakshasa appeared to be looking at Max as he

rode, tall and proud as a samurai, to within a hundred yards of Trench Nineteen. Casually spurring his mount, the rakshasa cantered along its line and raised his bow.

Three shots were fired; three bannermen fell. The arrows struck each in the throat, killing them before they could even flinch or gasp in surprise. They had stood fifty yards apart and yet they fell at the same moment, toppling silently as the standards slipped from their dead hands. Prusias's army roared, raising their weapons high and jeering at Rowan as the rakshasa trotted back and tossed the bow to his attendant. Wheeling back around, the demon drew a long saber and smashed a mailed fist against his chest by way of challenge.

Instantly, Scathach spurred her horse and galloped out to meet him. There was nothing Max could do but watch as she hunched low over the Appaloosa's neck, her hair streaming behind her. With a delighted roar, the rakshasa urged his mount toward the challenger, raising his sword high as though to cleave her in two. The riders raced at one another in a spray of mud and turf as their mounts closed the gap. They passed like jousters at a tourney. As they did so, there was a flash of light and the sharp report of a thunderclap. Continuing at full gallop, Scathach stood tall in the stirrups. But the demon's mount slowed to a trot and then halted altogether.

Sinking low in his saddle, the rakshasa grimaced at Rowan's ranks and clutched at his throat. He appeared as stunned as the thousands massed behind him. Scathach paid him no heed as she circled back around and cantered easily to the demon's speechless attendant. Tearing the banner from the imp's grasp, the maiden raised it high and abruptly shattered it upon her shield.

Rowan's response was deafening.

Every soldier, from the youngest squire to the most seasoned veteran, stood and cried out their defiance. When the rakshasa finally toppled from his saddle, the cheering hit a frenzied pitch. Sarah's horn rose above the din. Other commanders followed suit, and Max turned to see hundreds of bows raised in unison as the pikes were lowered into formations. Scathach galloped back to the ranks, her eyes shining as she circled her horse around Max. Her breathless words sounded like a chant, an incantation wrought with ancient and terrible power.

"You are the child of Lugh Lamfhada. You are the sun and the storm and the master of all the feats I have to teach. You are these things because you must be. . . ."

The *gae bolga* screamed as its blade was freed from its scabbard.

But even its terrible keening was faint in Max's ears. The month was March; the dawn was red and the Old Magic howled in its eagerness to greet it. Scathach drew back as Max wheeled YaYa around and cantered along the trench embankments, staring out at Prusias's army. As the ki-rin's pace increased, all traces of age and weariness fell away. When the archers loosed their arrows, YaYa leaped fifty feet over the trench and charged.

She crashed through the advancing vyes like a tidal wave, leaving broken bodies in her wake as Max pursued the demons and deathknights with frenzied determination. He saw their shine clearly now, flickering, ghostly auras scattered amid a dark sea of vyes and ogres. YaYa tore after them, streaking across the battlefield like a thunderbolt. Even the deathknights could not escape her; she chased them down like Nick used to corner field mice in the Sanctuary. The ki-rin was so swift, so instinctive that Max had only to spy some unholy glimmer amid the throng and seconds later they were crashing down upon it.

Occasionally there was a sharp *crack* as a spear or pike splintered on YaYa's broad chest. Max felt blows upon his shield, twitched at an occasional sting along his neck or arm, but they were no more irksome than insects. Whenever he screamed, the *gae bolga* answered, fanning the flames of the Old Magic until it raged within him.

Layer by layer, Max's mortal identity was peeling, burning away like a skin of tissue paper. He shone so brightly that the Enemy could not look upon him. Whole companies fled from his onslaught, clawing to get past one another, scrabbling madly to get away. Other troops simply fell to the ground, covering their heads or tearing at their eyes as though they burned.

YaYa showed no sign of flagging. They raced deep into the Enemy ranks, scattering the infantry and crashing down upon the advancing siege engines. Rams smashed to the ground as Max slew those carrying them; catapults toppled as YaYa obliterated their heavy beams and supports. Far off, Max glimpsed Prusias's golden palanquin being carried by countless slaves—a moving palace creeping over the murky landscape.

Just then, Max heard the shrill note of Sarah's horn rise above the din. Wheeling YaYa around, he saw that the trenches were besieged. Hundreds of vyes and ogres lay dead from arrows, but more had leaped onto the embankments to engage the Trench Rats at close range. Some pikes held formation, but others were entangled in wild, savage struggles with their opponents using whatever means at their disposal. Another horn sounded and Max saw the Wildwood Knights come charging out of Northgate, their armor gleaming as they drove a wedge through the advancing tide of foes. The collisions were tremendous, bodies flying, horses upended, and vyes trampled. The knights drove the invaders steadily back in a determined offensive of lances and swords. Given some distance, the archers soon loosed another volley but immediately had to take cover as Stygian crows swept down upon them in screeching sorties of razor beaks and talons.

Max glimpsed one archer literally covered by the creatures, which had almost carried the screaming man away before Bob obliterated them with a vicious swing of his cudgel.

To the east, Max spied a troop of deathknights charging along the cliffs. He urged YaYa at them, hurtling over the ground at dizzying speed to intercept the undead cavalry before they utterly overwhelmed that section of the line. The archers had also seen the threat. A hundred Zenuvian arrows were loosed, slamming into the riders leading the formation. Three deathknights burst into green flame, careening off their steeds, which stumbled over the cliffs. But a score of horsemen still remained, bearing down upon the trench. Two more fell as Lucia's firebursts exploded suddenly before them, but the others tightened their formation and galloped at a furious pace to overrun the trench.

With a roar, YaYa broadsided them like a locomotive, shattering bones and crumpling armor as the creatures and their horses were launched over the cliffs. But YaYa went with them, her momentum carrying her far over the edge. Max felt a terrifying weightlessness and hugged her neck, bracing himself for the inevitable, sickening plunge.

But no plunge occurred.

The ki-rin merely galloped over the empty air. Glancing down, Max saw the rocky beach and crashing surf far below. A furious melee was taking place on the beaches below as the Harbor Guard held the Enemy back from the cliff stairs that would bring them up to the main campus.

There was no time to help them. There must have been a hundred such scenes taking place across Greater Rowan. Leaning forward in his saddle, Max held tight as YaYa made a sweeping turn that took them far out over the waves as she circled back and charged toward the battleground at Trench Nineteen.

The scene unfolding before them did not appear real. It was too horrid and beautiful for Max's mind to process. It was a living painting, an explosion of color and light and scale where battalions and mounted companies were no more than toy soldiers scattered across a vast panorama of smoke, sun, and ruin.

Huge storm clouds were circling over Westgate while in the south Max glimpsed a pluming cloud of superheated smoke. There was a flash. From Rowan's casting towers came huge bolts of lightning that lanced across the battlefield, destroying the Enemy's siege towers and catapults in crackling explosions that showered the land with broken timber and debris.

YaYa reached the cliffs, running on solid earth once more. Max struck down an oni as they passed, the *gae bolga* shearing right through its heavy shield. A host of vyes fled before the ki-rin as they crashed back into the fray, scattering like jackals before a lion. Arrows whistled overhead as horns sounded from Northgate. Fresh cavalry came galloping forth, reinforcing the Wildwood Knights in a thunderous offensive.

YaYa fell in with them, charging to the fore as they drove the vyes and ogres back over the scorched earth and ravaged countryside. The Enemy's initial assault was breaking, retreating to protect Prusias's golden palanquin and regroup with the battalions he'd held in reserve.

At a signal flare from Rowan, Max and the knights checked their pursuit. They slowed to a trot and watched the Enemy's withdrawal. Fatigue was overcoming Max. His radiance had dimmed to a flickering halo of light about his brow. Even the *gae bolga* had grown silent, choked and sated from the carnage.

Max was wearier than he had ever been. Dismounting, he saw that his shield was punctured and scored in a dozen places. He tossed it aside, walking around to examine YaYa. The magnificent ki-rin was panting heavily and still growling from deep in her throat. Her black coat was spattered with so much mud and gore, it appeared as though she'd charged through pools of the stuff. Stroking her muzzle, Max rested his head against her chest before stepping back to gaze up at the sky.

The wind had cleared much of the smoke, but not all. Some billows still drifted on the breeze, carrying west across a deepening sky tinged with brilliant streaks of red and pink. Max blinked dully at the fiery orange ball sinking low over the western wood and tried to reconcile how the day could possibly be ending. The attack had begun at dawn. *Could so much time have passed?* It seemed mere minutes since Scathach had ridden out to answer the rakshasa's challenge.

Squinting, Max gazed about, but he could not find her. Not along Trench Nineteen or at the command tent or among any of the mounted cavalry. Terrible thoughts flitted through his mind. His pulse quickened and he stepped around YaYa for a better view of the battlefield. It was hard to pick out details among the devastation, and the sun's rays cast long shadows that obscured much of what he was seeing. Already, the dead and dying were being carried away on stretchers. The Enemy's forces were left to the ravens and gulls, which were settling in alarming numbers.

Max heard cheers from the trenches and from high on the citadel's battlements and the towers of Northgate. In the distance, Old Tom was chiming the hour as though students were being summoned to supper. One of the Wildwood Knights was calling to him. Max glanced at the man who asked again if he would care to ride back with them. Shaking his head, Max anxiously climbed back up onto YaYa's saddle. Taking his spyglass, he surveyed the field again.

As he swept the glass along the cliffs, Max stopped breathing.

An Appaloosa was cantering, tossing its mane and bucking wildly as though it had gone mad. The horse was without a rider.

In his shock, Max barely registered a strange chittering. YaYa gave a sudden start, sidestepping abruptly as something slithered past in a whirl of clicking legs and probing feelers. Glancing down, Max's fears and sorrow were transformed into frantic, disbelieving terror.

The creature was a pinlegs.

And its lights were flashing red.

~ 18 ~

WHEN WATERS RUN RED

Max rode swiftly back toward the citadel, shouting at everyone—every knight and soldier—to flee inside Northgate. Spying Sarah near Trench Nineteen, he yelled for her to blow the signal for a retreat. She hesitated, staring at him like he was crazy until he repeated the order. Taking her horn, she blew the call.

"Pull back!" yelled Max, literally herding people toward the gate and telling other commanders to blow their horns and signal a retreat. Gazing up at the battlements, Max searched anxiously for any familiar faces among the multitude. At last he saw Nigel leaning out from one of Northgate's towers. Max called the man's name over and over until he finally looked down.

"Get a message to Ms. Richter!" Max shouted, cupping his hands. "Sound the retreat!"

"What—why?"

"NOW!"

Nigel disappeared and Max wheeled YaYa away, urging everyone—everyone who could run, walk, or crawl—to get inside the Northgate as fast as they possibly could. Thankfully, people were beginning to respond, to leave their positions and trot uncertainly toward the citadel. But many stopped and looked skeptically over their shoulders, unclear why they were being ordered to abandon the fields where they had just triumphed.

Max could feel the atmosphere changing. The breeze was dying away, but huge clouds were gathering from all directions to obscure the first stars of evening. There was a charged, metallic taste to the air, and even YaYa snorted nervously, swiveling her shaggy head as though searching for an unseen threat.

At last Max heard the great horns sound from within the citadel, a shattering call to retreat as hissing red flares shot out from every casting tower. From inside the walls, even Old Tom's chimes were ringing an alarm as though Armageddon had come.

The peculiar clouds and Rowan's alarm had the desired effect. Whole battalions hurried toward the citadel at full speed. Max looked frantically about for Scathach, scanning the stampede of running figures and mounted knights to no avail. Sarah rode toward him on her charger. Her shield was dented and she was bleeding from a cut upon her forehead, but she did not appear to be seriously injured.

"Everyone's heading in," she assured him. "Are you coming?"

Max shook his head and implored her to go along with the Trench Rats. When it was clear he would not be joining them, she finally left to help evacuate the last of the wounded. Max turned YaYa to gaze out at the emptying battlefield. The ravens and gulls were also departing, hopping off of bodies and taking urgent flight. They wheeled south in dense, screeching flocks as swiftly as their wings would take them.

Twilight was settling upon the battlefield, leaving the grisly shapes in shadow. The wind was picking up once again, blowing in from the north along with a curtain of cold, glittering rain. The drops hissed on hundreds of fires and pinged on thousands of broken shields and bodies scattered across the landscape. Thunder rumbled high above in the swirling clouds, and Prusias's drums began to sound again.

Boom boom boom boom!

Far to the north, Max spied movement. Raising his spyglass, he saw that Prusias's palanquin and troops had regrouped and were moving again, creeping south toward Rowan's citadel. Leaving them, Max swept the glass across the closer terrain and searched frantically for any telltale lights or motion.

At last he found a pinlegs. It was less than a mile from Northgate, scuttling over an ettin's corpse. There was a second one a few hundred yards to the right, descending a shallow hill. Max's heart was racing as he discovered more.

Five . . . six . . .

Hastily wiping rain from the lens, he resumed his count as more tiny red lights blinked in the deepening dusk. He'd tallied nine when the pinlegs seemed to halt their advance. The one Max was watching had climbed atop the empty, smoldering armor of a slain rakshasa and began circling like a dog chasing its tail.

Suddenly, the world went white.

The landscape disappeared in a phosphorescent flash as thirteen bolts of lightning struck the battlefield. With a *whoosh*, the surrounding air rushed toward the strikes as though filling a vacuum. The resulting winds blew with hurricane force, staggering YaYa and bending all the trees inward as though a bomb had imploded. All across the battlefield, bodies and carcasses were rolling and tumbling brokenly toward the strike sites along with acres of dirt and soil to create huge, spiraling vortexes. Thirteen mushroom clouds formed, rising ever higher toward the churning maelstrom above.

At last the swirling plumes crested and began to dissipate. Thousands of broken bodies and horses rained back to earth as the clouds settled. Shapes emerged, dark mountains that seemed to sway and shiver as though stirring from some long slumber.

The earth shook.

Initially, Max thought the dreadnoughts were elephants—colossal war elephants the size of castles. But that impression changed as soon as the creatures awakened.

Many eyes appeared in the gloom, piercing the dusk like monstrous searchlights. They scoured the smoking hills and trampled plains until they fell upon the citadel.

Giant flares shot out from Rowan's towers, arcing through the rain to illuminate the creatures as they began to move. Max watched in mute horror as their particulars began to emerge.

Like the pinlegs, the dreadnoughts appeared to be a hybrid of animal, demon, and machine. Their heads were shaped like that of a pulpy pale octopus, knotted and swollen with muscles and vascular cables that connected them to shiny black bodies that resembled the abdomens of huge, bloated spiders. Enormous black smokestacks jutted from their backs in knuckled ridges, belching fire and smoke into the air as though great engines and furnaces burned at the creatures' cores.

The dreadnoughts had eight long limbs, but they were nothing like a spider's. Four of the limbs were thick, elephantine columns of muscle and flesh that bore the brunt of the creature's

weight and propelled it forward. The others were enormous, bloodred tentacles that sprouted from its sides, swinging grotesquely, digging and dragging through the wet fields as they helped to balance the towering creature.

Max found their uniqueness horrifying. No two monstrosities were exactly the same. The Workshop might have built them, but there was an organic asymmetry even to their creatures' manufactured elements. They looked like they'd been grown and nurtured in colossal vats, a jumble of mutated cells that had been made to grow around a mechanical core until the machinery and engines were subsumed and buried within living tissues.

They had no mouths, not even a truly discernible face. There were only vast, unblinking eyes set atop bodies so colossal that Max could hardly comprehend them. The creatures must have been three hundred feet tall. Just one looked capable of razing Rowan to its foundations and yet thirteen were now advancing upon the citadel fifty yards at a stride.

The *gae bolga* twitched and gave a magnetic pull almost like a divining rod. The weapon tore Max from his spellbound stupor, bringing him back to the rain and wind and YaYa chuffing once again as the ancient ki-rin mustered whatever reserves she had. He gazed up at the attackers, at the smoke billowing from their backs, at the faint red pentacles now glimmering along the creature's underbellies. Max's ring began to burn again.

They're just imps, he told himself. *Imps in huge bodies, but imps all the same.*

He recalled the words and warning of the Fomorian after the giant had reforged the *gae bolga* beneath the waves.

This weapon can never be broken. The wounds it makes will never heal. There is nothing it cannot pierce and nothing it cannot slay, for its essence will destroy both flesh and spirit . . . this blade will slay gods as well as monsters. . . .

That weapon was calling to him now, urging him forward. Max was *not* a mortal being; he was a demigod, a prince of the Sidh who had just driven half of Prusias's army back across the field. The Morrígan could see his greatness; why couldn't he? Max was stronger than they, wilder than the storm, and when his anger was roused, nothing on this earth could stand against him. He was invincible. . . .

Trembling anew, he stared out at the dreadnoughts like a rabid wolf. He spurred YaYa forward and she obeyed, breaking into a trot and then a rolling canter. The *gae bolga* burned, scalding Max's hand as the blade keened and screamed like the Morrígan herself.

Breaking into a gallop, YaYa streaked across the battlefield, as swift as an arrow. She soon left the ground behind, springing into the air and racing over the gales and gusts as though they were a shorter path to her enemy. The dreadnoughts loomed even larger, filling Max's view so that everything else disappeared. It was growing ever hotter, ever louder. Scorched air filled his lungs; all about him was the sound of heavy, churning machinery and the belching fires from the smokestacks. He focused on the nearest one's central eye, so huge and luminescent it might have been the moon. Gripping the *gae bolga*, Max stood tall in the stirrups and reared back to strike as Scathach had taught him.

The impact was like a bomb.

Max and YaYa were thrown back with inconceivable force. They crashed into what remained of Trench Nineteen's embankment, careening over rocks and sharpened stakes until they rolled down into the trench itself. Clawing blindly at the wet earth, Max sensed the *gae bolga*'s searing heat and seized hold of it. Coming to his senses, he glanced about and saw YaYa lying on her side in a small crater. Great waves of steam rose off her, as though the ki-rin were a meteor that had fallen to earth. One of the embankment stakes had impaled her shoulder, while a sickening shard of bone protruded from her foreleg.

Dirt rained down upon them as the creatures continued to advance. Scrambling to his feet, Max saw that the one he'd struck was stumbling. Half its knotted, pulpy head was missing as though it had detonated. Fire and smoke gushed from the gaping wound. Listing sideways, it flailed its tentacles in an attempt to balance, but its momentum was too great. Its legs gave out and the monster toppled like a falling skyscraper.

A savage elation overcame Max. The Morrígan was right; he *was* invincible. He was the son of Lugh Lamfhada, High King and greatest of the Tuatha Dé Danaan. And the weapon Max wielded was no mere sword or spear. The *gae bolga* was a conduit—it was a living tether to the war goddess herself. Together they could destroy the dreadnoughts. Together, they could destroy *everything. . . .*

Twelve creatures remained, advancing steadily in a line like a convoy of battleships. Scrambling out of the trench, Max glared up at them as energy from the *gae bolga* flooded into him, the Morrígan's power mingling, multiplying with his own. He ran at the colossal things with blind, berserk rage. The nearest loomed above him, its bulk blotting out the sky. Raising the *gae bolga* high, Max plunged its point deep into the ground.

The instant it pierced the earth, the spear made a hideous scream and split the battlefield asunder. The shock wave sent Max flying backward, tumbling head over heels until he crashed against an overturned wagon. His leg slammed against its heavy axle, cracking his shinbone down the center. Ignoring the pain, Max focused on the battlefield. The very terrain where the *gae bolga* had struck seemed to be dying, rotting away and collapsing to form a great fissure that spread swiftly beneath the attackers.

With a roar, the fissure became a yawning chasm as the surrounding earth sheared away in a flurry of avalanches and rockslides.

Three of the dreadnoughts vanished from view as they plunged down into the gulf. There was an appalling crash as they struck water far below. Seconds later, jets of steam shot from the fissure like geysers, arcing high into the night and dissipating on the wind.

Gasping for breath, Max watched the geysers plume and drift. He could do little else as the remaining dreadnoughts steadied themselves with their tentacles and continued over the chasm as though nothing had happened. Once across, they began to pick up speed, charging now like Hannibal's war elephants. The entire battlefield was shaking, but there was nothing Max could do. The Morrígan had grown silent and his own powers were spent.

Boom boom boom boom!

Through gaps between the dreadnoughts, Max glimpsed Prusias's palanquin and his remaining troops approaching over the dark fields. Dozens of lightning bolts lanced the dreadnoughts from Rowan's casting towers with no apparent effect. The creatures were running now, their ropy tentacles slapping at the ground while torrents of smoke billowed from their crowning backs.

They strode over Trench Nineteen, stampeding over the remaining terrain. Max was certain one would crush him, grind him into a red smear. He almost wished they would. He had no desire to witness Rowan's destruction, to see its people murdered or enslaved as Prusias's army swept in. Everything around him was blinding light and deafening sound and violent, terrifying tremors.

He gazed up, awestruck, as a dreadnought stepped over him, utterly heedless of his presence. There was a rending crack as the first reached the citadel. Twisting about, Max saw one of the monsters rear up on its hind legs to seize one of the casting towers with its tentacles. With a savage wrench, the creature heaved the entire structure off its foundation, ripping it free as though it were no more than a sapling. Others slammed into the wall, rearing up like great spiders to tear frantically at the battlements and masonry.

An overwhelming sense of anger and shame came over Max. Scathach was likely dead. YaYa too. By dawn, thousands more would join them. All of his efforts had been for naught; he had summoned every ounce of Old Magic in him and still the Enemy was grinding Rowan to rubble. Gazing out, Max saw Prusias's forces halting at the chasm he had made. Already vyes were loping along its ledges, scouting for the narrowest gaps where they might devise a way to cross.

At this range, Max could see Prusias with his naked eye. The demon was standing at the palanquin's threshold like some barbarian chieftain come to view the sack of Rome. Max's anger kindled to blind rage. He had never wanted to destroy another being so badly in his life. If he could just get up, rise once more on this broken leg . . .

And then a dangerous, intoxicating thought occurred to him. *Astaroth!*

Clutching the wagon's wheel, Max twisted farther about so he could see Northgate. It had not yet fallen, but one of the dreadnoughts was lumbering toward it. There might still be a chance to save Rowan if only he spoke those words and called the Demon to him. Astaroth had promised to destroy Prusias's army and protect Rowan if Max summoned him. And Astaroth never lied! He had the power to do so this instant . . . all Max had to do in exchange was slay Elias Bram. At the mere thought of the Archmage, Max gritted his teeth.

Damn Bram to hell!

The Archmage had not lifted a finger to help Rowan. For all his clever arguments, he had abandoned them. What would Bram know about aiding his friends, about helping those he loved? Marley Augur had been Bram's closest companion, and look how he was treated! Bram was a snake; he was a loathsome, self-important snake and deserved to die a thousand times over. Max did not have to do it alone; the Morrígan would help him. Once Bram was gone and Rowan was restored, peace would follow; they would work with Astaroth to create something better, something beautiful and lasting. Wasn't that what the Demon truly wanted? And Astaroth never lied. . . .

Something settled on Max's hand. Glancing down, he saw a brown gypsy moth scuttling over his fingers, twitching its wings and feelers. Was it real? Taking flight again, the moth circled twice about Max's head and then flew toward Northgate. Max followed its progress until his gaze settled on a pale, translucent figure gliding toward him.

It was Astaroth.

The Demon was in his spectral form, no more than a pale apparition walking across the battlefield amid all the destruction. He was smiling, but there was no mockery or amusement in those angelic features. There was only love; there was only compassion and understanding. Cradling the Book of Thoth, the Demon extended a hand and silently urged Max to speak the words that would summon him.

"Noble Astaroth," Max whispered. "Pray favor thy petitioner with wisdom from under hill, beyond the stars. . . ."

As the words tumbled forth, the Demon's smile widened.

He nodded at Max to finish, beckoned eagerly with a terrible gleam in his merry black eyes. But Max trailed off, blinking instead at a tiny figure that came hurtling out from Northgate even as the dreadnought reared up to demolish it.

The figure was David Menlo.

Max glanced back at Astaroth, but the apparition was already fading. Its smile was gone; its features blank and mask-like as it disappeared into the night.

Utterly perplexed, Max pulled himself higher and stared in disbelief at his friend.

David was now directly beneath the dreadnought, screaming in terror and running in staggering zigzags as he sought to avoid the monstrosity's stamping, shuffling feet and keep his balance on the shaking ground. On several occasions he stumbled and fell, but each time he righted himself and hobbled on with crazed determination.

He was making for Max, calling his friend's name as though he could possibly be heard above the din. The sorcerer practically collapsed when he reached the wagon. Yelling for Max to take firm hold of the *gae bolga*, David seized his other hand as he had on Madam Petra's balloon.

Torrents of energy suddenly rippled through Max, screaming through every blood vessel as though David had flipped a circuit breaker. His broken leg kicked and he tried to tear free of David's grasp, but the sorcerer would not let go.

Strange things were happening to Max. He beheld not only David crying out in Latin, but also himself wreathed in a nimbus of golden light and slumped against the wagon. It seemed as though he were also seeing the world from David's perspective, their visions overlapping. As David turned, Max's view shifted. He was now gazing out at the dreadnoughts as they began to clamber and climb over Rowan's broken walls.

Max caught his breath as the dreadnoughts came to a sudden, inexplicable halt. Huge golden pentacles were forming around each, their intricate symbols reflected in the monster's shiny underbellies. The circles trapped the creatures where they stood. Once the pentacles were complete, the abominations could not even twitch without David's permission.

David's voice was growing ever stronger as his mind locked on to each of the spirits that were controlling the gargantuan bodies. Max could sense a mounting desperation as the imps fought against David's will.

They fought in vain.

The sorcerer possessed all nine dreadnoughts, simultaneously shattering all resistance with terrifying strength and dominance. The imps were utterly overwhelmed. Still connected to David, Max became aware of these new presences on the periphery of his consciousness. Whenever he let his mind drift toward one of them, he found himself staring through a dreadnought's many eyes. Through those fragmented, hazy lenses, he glimpsed Old Tom and Maggie within Old College. At first glance, they appeared undamaged, but it was too disorienting and painful to inhabit the dreadnought for long.

David Menlo had no such difficulties.

The boy did not merely command each dreadnought; he *was* each dreadnought. The sorcerer's extraordinary mind controlled the bodies as if they were merely huge extensions of his own intelligence and will. At his silent urging, the creatures now turned slowly about and fixed their attention upon Prusias's army.

The demon's troops were beginning to cross Max's chasm, marching over giant battering rams that had been laid across to form causeways. When the dreadnoughts wheeled upon them, those in front frantically tried to retreat, crashing into those coming up behind them. Many were thrust aside, toppling into the gorge and triggering a general panic as every vye and ogre tried to scramble back.

Sweat was coursing down David's pale face as he followed the dreadnoughts' earthshaking advance. Within seconds, they strode over Trench Nineteen and reached the chasm, obliterating the bridges with their tentacles. Striding over the gorge, the dreadnoughts now loomed directly over thousands of vyes, ogres, deathknights, and demons like smoldering mountains.

The ensuing onslaught was horrific. Whole companies were trampled in seconds; others were destroyed by the sweeping, flailing tentacles that pulverized everything in their path. David showed no mercy as the dreadnoughts began walling the army off and hemming them in against the gorge and the cliffs.

Some escaped, of course. Some vyes managed to flee beneath the dreadnoughts like mice darting beneath a cat. Several rakshasa transformed into spirits of fiery smoke and escaped through the air. But the rest were less fortunate as the dreadnoughts crushed, lashed, and drove them toward the steep cliffs and chasm. Thousands were sent hurtling over the ledges, plunging hundreds of feet to the sharp rocks and wild waves.

Throughout, Max had focused almost all his attention on the golden palanquin. Two dreadnoughts had seized it and were pushing the massive thing toward the cliffs, digging their tentacles beneath and slamming their bodies against it. As the monsters gained leverage, the litter flipped and began to tumble as though the creatures were rolling a gargantuan boulder. With a final frenzied effort, they heaved it and themselves over the edge, clinging to the carriage like hideous octopi as it plunged down to the sea.

The seven remaining dreadnoughts followed their example, charging the cliffs and sweeping along everything in their path as they threw themselves like lemmings over the ledge. More geysers came screaming up once they crashed, their mist floating across the landscape like shimmering veils of silver.

Max heard himself gasp when the dreadnoughts struck the water. A peripheral part of his mind and consciousness had been with them and experienced firsthand the tumbling blur of sky and sea, the awful glimpse of rocks and ocean rushing up to meet them.

Thankfully, David had released the psychic connection right before the monsters had struck. With a groan, Max leaned back against the wagon, feeling as weak and helpless as a newborn. He clutched hopefully at the *gae bolga*, but the spear lay dark and dormant in the mud. Rowan's sorcerer was also apparently spent, for he doubled over coughing and wheezing for breath as steam rose off his body in ghostly wisps.

An eerie quiet settled over the battlefield. There were no more drums, no more horns or the terrible shaking of dreadnoughts. There was only the distant crash of the sea and the sound of their hoarse breathing.

"I'm sorry," David gasped, finding his voice at last. "I didn't have enough power on my own. I had to borrow yours. Can you stand?"

With a grimace, Max took David's hand and pushed himself up on his uninjured leg. Leaning heavily on the spear, he turned to survey the ruin upon the battlefield and the crumbling foundations of Rowan's walls and towers. People were reemerging, streaming out from the remains of the Northgate arch and a hundred other openings to see what had happened. They fanned out to survey the destruction. Some cheered; others fell to their knees in prayer. Most simply stared at the surrounding miles of burning, smoking devastation. Even the earth was trembling and shivering with aftershocks.

It was a minute before Max heard the first scream.

Another followed it and then another. Soon hundreds and thousands of voices cried out as people backed away and then fled from the cliffs.

Prusias was rising from the sea.

The demon had shed his human guise as a serpent sheds its skin. It was no barbarian king that rose above the cliffs, but a great red dragon with seven crowns set atop seven human heads, each slavering with wrath and fury. Max and David were sixty yards from the cliffs, yet the heat that radiated from the demon's red-scaled body scorched their lungs. Prusias had grown since Walpurgisnacht, gorging and glutting himself on the bodies and spirits of his own kind. Each of his crowned, gnashing heads was swaying far above the battlefield, and yet Max could hear his serpentine coils lashing the waves hundreds of feet below.

The heads leered out at all assembled. Blood was coursing from black, festering slashes across several of the faces and throats, grisly legacies of Max's last encounter with the demon. Max had not managed to slay Prusias, but wounds from the *gae bolga* would never heal and so the cuts continued to bleed, dribbling and hissing down braided beards to patter on the scaly necks and the ground below. But despite these injuries and despite the utter ruin of his army, the King of Blys gave a savage smile.

"You think you've defeated Prusias?" he roared, looming monstrously over the battlefield. "Ha! I don't need those insects or machines. I don't need an army to crush this den of fools and tricksters." The demon's eyes settled on Max and David. "I see the faithless Hound and Rowan's cowering sorcerer, but where is Bram? Bring me the Archmage and Richter, too. Pile them all onto a great pyre and beg my forgiveness!"

The heads swayed lower, thrusting forward like great

serpents to loom over the battlefield and its huddling hordes of people. All seven spoke in grinning, leering unison.

"You'll bow down and raise my flag, you groveling little maggots," they growled. "You'll bow down and worship Great Prusias or he'll devour every last one of you!" The central head whipped savagely about to glare in the direction of Old College.

"Where is the Archmage?" it roared. *"BRING ME BRAM!"*

As soon as the demon cried out these last words, there was a blinding flash and the sharp crack of thunder. Something had appeared instantly before Prusias, a radiant white figure amid a cloud of pearly, dissipating mist. But it was not Elias Bram who walked toward the demon.

It was Mina.

Prusias recoiled the instant he saw her, as though she were something grotesque and poisonous. The King of Blys swayed back and forth like an enormous cobra. Each of the demon's seven heads appraised the little girl with a mixture of fear and wonder.

"What are you?" he demanded. "What are you called?"

But Mina did not answer. Spreading her fingers wide, she stretched one little hand toward the demon as though she were grasping at a shiny ornament just out of reach. When she could reach no farther, the girl abruptly closed her fingers and made a fist.

Seven crowns cracked and shattered.

The King of Blys shrieked as they fell from his tangled heads in great shards of hammered gold. Upon each of the demon's foreheads, the Rowan seal appeared, branded into his flesh as though with a hot iron. With a rending scream, Prusias fell back into the sea and fled over the waves like a vast, repulsive sidewinder.

Mina watched him go, then turned and walked to Max and

David. Already, her radiance was dimming and Max realized that the little girl was wearing naught but her nightgown. She padded barefoot through the mud, lifting the gown's hem so as not to get it dirty. Coming to them, she took each of their hands and gazed up at them, utterly oblivious of the gathering crowds.

"I have cast Prusias down," she said.

"I should say so," replied David.

"And I *teleported*," she announced, swelling up as though this was far more noteworthy than banishing a seven-headed demon. "You can't pretend you didn't see! You know what that means."

"Another trinket for your magechain," David sighed. "You shall have it."

She beamed, clutching their hands as though she never wanted to let go, but at last she turned toward the cliffs and watched the white gulls as they circled and soared against the dark sky.

"I have to go down to the beach," she remarked. "My charge is waiting for me."

"How do you know he is there?" asked David.

"Max can say," she replied, gazing absently at the dark ocean.

"*'When the gulls cry out and the waters run red, he'll rise from the sea to find me,'*" said Max softly, recalling the girl's prophecy.

"And he has," she declared excitedly. "Take me down!"

"I'll take you," said David. "I want to see your charge. And there may be something else of interest down there." He turned to Max. "Can you come?"

"No," said Max, glancing back at Trench Nineteen. "I have other things to do."

"But can you even walk?" wondered David, glancing doubtfully at Max's leg.

"I can ride."

And indeed he could. As David and Mina departed, Max called out to a nearby knight and asked to borrow his horse. The man helped Max into the saddle. The climb up was agony, but the pain was manageable once he was settled and so long as he kept his mount to a walk.

Max rode to the embankments along Trench Nineteen, to the section where smoke and steam were still rising in little wisps. Peering down into the trench, Max braced himself for the worst.

But YaYa was nowhere to be seen.

Stunned, Max looked up and down the trench. *Was he in the right place?* Surely he was. There was no mistaking that crater of compacted earth and the smoke still rising from its depths. Prodding with his spear through the wreckage of soil and splintered stakes, Max even saw little pools and droplets of blood. But YaYa herself was missing.

Did ki-rin disappear when they died? Did they simply burn up like rakshasa?

There was no time to solve this mystery. Tugging on the reins, Max rode through the crowds along the ruin of the citadel walls. There was so much commotion, so many cries of jubilation and people streaming past. One group of ecstatic revelers was more than a little stunned when Max snarled at them to move even as they clustered around to thank him.

His eyes were constantly scanning the milling masses for Scathach. He barely noticed Old Tom chiming the Westminster Quarters or the colorful bursts as flares and starbursts exploded overhead. Pushing through, he shouted Scathach's name and gazed about in search for her. Even in this moment of spectacular triumph, Max's heart was breaking.

The dread was numbing. Max had not experienced anything

like it since he'd found his father bleeding to death in an icy stream. He yelled Scathach's name again, gazing wildly, frantically about. So many faces surrounded him and yet none was the one he sought.

He was approaching the citadel's northwest section, riding in the shadow of the ruined walls, when the crowds finally began to thin. There was still an ungodly amount of commotion—ringing chimes and blaring horns and great bursts of fireworks over Old College—but Max could now see each face as people ran past to join the celebration.

As he rounded a tower's remains to head for Westgate, Max reined the horse to a halt as a family passed by. The father was laughing, holding the hand of one child while his wife tried to corral an escaped toddler who was stumbling after some giggling lutins. Max watched them go and was about to urge the horse onward when a rider caught his eye. Gazing up, Max saw Scathach coming toward him.

She was on a different horse and looked wearier than he'd ever seen her, but when their eyes met, the maiden smiled and stood tall in her stirrups. Max's sorrow and dread evaporated. He had never felt such a rush of pure, unmitigated joy. All pain was forgotten as he shook the reins and wheeled his horse toward her. He called her name, grinning wildly and urging his horse into a trot.

As they closed, Max heard someone behind cry out his name. He had no intention of stopping, until the person yelled again with such terrible urgency he could not ignore it. Stopping, he turned around to see someone tearing through the crowds after him. As the person raced past the family, Max finally glimpsed her face.

The person was Scathach.

"Morkün i-tolvatha!"

Even as Max heard those terrible words, he realized his folly. Whipping back around, Max merely glimpsed Scathach's smiling imposter as the mounted assassin swung the blade meant to decapitate him.

With a deafening roar, a huge black blur crashed in from the side.

Max was merely knocked off his startled horse, but the false Scathach was nearly pulverized as YaYa took her to the ground in a furious assault. Arms and legs were pinned instantly. There was a popping of blistering flesh and a piercing, ungodly scream came from the assassin's throat. Max had never seen YaYa so enraged; the ki-rin was shaking violently, her jaws slavering mere inches from Scathach's terrified face.

Already that face was changing. William Cooper's own rough, brutal features were emerging as though YaYa were drawing them forth. The Agent's eyes were black as pitch, his skin cadaverously pale. There were more popping sounds as smoke billowed off of the man's body. Cooper screamed again as though he were being burned at the stake. With furious effort, he tried to writhe free, but the ki-rin was much too strong.

The real Scathach's arms gently closed about Max's shoulders as she crouched behind him.

"YaYa's killing him," Max said, utterly stunned and horrified by the scene.

"No," Scathach whispered, holding him close. "She's saving him."

Max was not so certain. YaYa's teeth were bared, and she was growling with such ferocity that she looked capable of suddenly tearing out Cooper's throat. The man had ceased struggling and now merely offered a bloody smile.

"Go ahead!" he goaded. "There's always another—"

With another roar, YaYa impaled him.

When her horn pierced his shoulder, Cooper's scream was like nothing Max had ever heard before. Nearby spectators covered their ears and drew away. Fiery symbols erupted on Cooper's skin, evil runes and symbols Max had glimpsed in David's grimoires. Cooper was weeping now, pleading with the ki-rin to simply kill him.

But YaYa was unmoved.

At last Cooper's screams and pleas ceased. He simply lay still on the wet grass and took slow, sputtering breaths while smoke hissed and crackled about the ki-rin's broken horn. As the fiery symbols faded, Cooper's eyes returned to their clear, pale blue. His hand twitched, and YaYa raised her bleeding foreleg to release it. Tears ran down the man's scarred, ruined face as he stroked the ki-rin's muzzle. His voice was barely audible.

"Tell them I'm sorry."

When he closed his eyes, YaYa slowly withdrew her horn from his shoulder.

"Is he dead?" Max asked, clutching Scathach's hand.

Dipping her head, YaYa nuzzled Cooper's face. "He is at peace."

~ 19 ~

TÚR AN GHRIAN

Three weeks had passed when Max and Scathach met for a walk one morning beyond Northgate. His broken shin had healed in a matter of days, but Max had not returned to this place since the night of Rowan's victory. He could hardly believe the transformation that was under way. The toppled walls and towers had been cleared away; the blood-churned fields had been tilled and smoothed. Scaffolding surrounded new tower sites and the cool April air was rich with the smell of wet soil, new turf, and budding branches. Max smiled at the sound of saws and hammers, the whinny of horses, and the chirping of innumerable birds as spring chased away the last remnants of winter.

But these were not the most notable changes to the landscape. That distinction belonged to the thousands of small white obelisks spaced in perfect rows. Now and again, he simply stopped to gaze at them, overwhelmed by their simple beauty and the sacrifice that each represented.

"People are calling it Hound's Trench," said Scathach, gesturing at the chasm just beyond them, the very chasm Max had made.

He stared at the great gorge, at its blackened edges and raw, jagged contours. Nothing would ever grow there; that part of the earth was dead forever.

Max shook his head. "I wish they wouldn't do that," he muttered. "It's an ugly name, an ugly thing. I wish the gravestones weren't so close to it. They shouldn't be near anything like that."

"I don't see it that way," replied Scathach, taking his arm. "These people drew a line in the sand, sharpened their swords, and kept a terrible foe at bay. Not one enemy set foot in Old College. Centuries from now, people will visit these graves, see that chasm, and know that heroes are buried here."

Far too many heroes, thought Max. For the rest of the morning, they walked along the rows and looked at the names the Mystics had carved in clean white granite. Most were strangers, but now and again Max came upon a name he recognized. And, of course, there were some that brought him to a solemn halt. These names were not a surprise—he'd already heard of their passing and mourned them—but it was a strange jolt to see them etched with such terrible, beautiful permanence. Whenever Max came upon one, he touched the obelisk and spoke their name aloud: *John Buckley, Rowan Academy, Sixth Year; Jesse Chu, Rowan Academy, Fifth Year; Laurence M. Renard, Senior Instructor; Annika Kraken, Department Chair of Mystics. . . .*

Each sounded a different note in his soul. Max was almost

surprised to find how deeply Ms. Kraken's death had moved him. Apparently, she had cast such a powerful spell beyond Southgate that it destroyed her along with many of the Enemy and their battering ram. Max recalled the huge explosion he had glimpsed in that vicinity while YaYa was galloping over the sea. He wondered if that had been Ms. Kraken's doing. She had always seemed such a cranky old shrew, the kind of teacher students dreaded to encounter in a hallway much less an exam room. But the woman had also been an institution, an academic rite of passage that had challenged and galvanized Rowan students for over sixty years. The school would not be the same without her.

But it was not Ms. Kraken's memorial that brought a tear to Max's eye. It was another set at the far end of a row near the sea and the beginnings of a flowerbed. The earth around the marker was trampled and its obelisk was far dirtier than most. Max smiled to see the varied prints in the grass and the unmistakable mark of a muddy paw above the man's name.

GREGORY WYATT NOLAN
HEAD OF GROUNDS

Max did not know the details of Nolan's death. He didn't want to. It was enough to know that the man had volunteered to serve along the outer walls and that he had died while doing so. Nolan had spent much of his life looking after Rowan's weakest, most vulnerable creatures. Most often these had been charges, but sometimes they were students, too. The man had a talent for putting others at ease and making them feel welcome. There simply weren't enough people like that in the world.

Whenever Max stopped at a grave, Scathach stood aside and let him be. It was a greater gift than she could have known. Max had borne the hopes and expectations of so many people for so long that he had become self-conscious and almost terrified of disappointing anyone. With Scathach, he did not have to mask his feelings or explain them. He could simply experience them and know that she was there.

They were not the only people visiting the gravestones. Hundreds of others were paying their respects. Some were larger groups and families, but often it was a solitary figure walking slowly along a row, consulting their little map and peering at the names.

Walking back toward the remains of Northgate, Max and Scathach passed near one small figure kneeling by a grave and talking quietly to himself. Max's heart sank as the boy glanced up and their eyes met.

"Hello, Jack."

The boy stood abruptly, brushing grass from his knees and removing his woolen cap.

"I didn't steal it," he mumbled. "I was giving it back to her."

Max was at a loss until he glimpsed the pearly disk in the boy's hand. It was the very piece of maridian heartglass Max had given to Tam. Looking past Jack, Max saw the girl's name etched on the gravestone.

TAM
TRENCH RATS BATTALION
2ND COMPANY, 3RD PLATOON

"Did she have a last name?" Max wondered.

"She must have," said Jack, blinking at the inscription. "But I don't know what it was. She never told me."

"Tam was your good friend, wasn't she?"

The boy could not reply. He merely closed his eyes and sobbed.

"I know you want to give that back to her," Scathach said

gently. "But I think you should keep that glass and remember Tam whenever you look at it. What do you think?"

"It was her favorite thing in the world," Jack sniffled.

"Then I'm sure she'd want you to have it."

The boy considered Scathach's words while turning the pearly glass over in his hands. "I won't keep it forever," he concluded. "When I'm old, I'll give it to someone young and tell them all about her."

"I think that's a good idea," said Max. "Do you want to walk back with us or stay out here?"

Jack stayed behind, sitting back down on the damp earth and touching Tam's name with the heartglass. When they had walked out of earshot, Max shook his head.

"Did you see that medal on his chest?" he asked.

"I did," said Scathach, gazing out at the sea.

"A bad bargain," Max remarked. "Swapping a friend for a medal."

"Such things happen in war."

"I told them I'd see them after," he muttered, recalling his words to Tam and Jack as they'd huddled in Trench Nineteen. "What a stupid thing to promise."

Scathach took his hand. "War breaks many things," she sighed. "It can break bodies and hearts. It can break promises, too. But it can't break spirits, Max—not if those who are fighting believe in their cause. Jack may grieve for a long time, but I don't think war has broken his spirit. And I know it never broke Tam's. That girl was very strong and she knew what she was about."

Trench Nineteen had been filled in with earth and smoothed flat. All that remained was a discolored seam along the ground, and even that was disappearing as workers laid out stakes and twine to mark the gardens that would come. Ms. Richter had declared that all the land between the citadel and the outer walls would be transformed into groves and orchards to honor the fallen. Even with the aid of dryads and druids, it would take many years for such an undertaking to reach fruition, but once it was completed, it would be the greatest garden on earth.

Trench Nineteen was gone, but a monument had been erected for its battalion. There were memorials for every Rowan battalion at the places where they had fought. One could see them here and there across the grounds or at the base of walls and towers, larger white obelisks set upon blocks of rose granite. Each memorial flew its battalion's flag and bore the names of the fallen around its base. Max gazed at the Trench Rats' standard flapping in the wind. He counted four hundred and eighty-seven names inscribed beneath it. When he murmured the number aloud, Scathach spoke up.

"I'm no mathematician, but I believe that means there are over seven hundred names *not* inscribed on that stone."

"It's still too many," said Max.

"How many more would there be if you hadn't trained them, or fought with them, or acquired that iron on their behalf? Your losses were half that of the other trench battalions. They were volunteers, Max. Their deaths are sad, but they are not tragic. Look at me."

He did so, studying the sharp planes of her face and the shining gray eyes that studied him in turn.

"You are no stranger to war," she said. "You are grieving, but there is something else bothering you. What is it?"

Max nodded and quietly told Scathach how close he had been to summoning Astaroth.

"I'm glad you did not," she remarked. "A blood debt is ugly business and you must not play the Demon's game. There is a reason he chose you for such a thing, my love. I do not know what it is, but it was no accident. You must be wary of his words."

"I am," said Max, bowing his head. "But there are times, Scathach, when words don't matter to me. There are times when I could turn the entire world into that dead black chasm. It scares me."

"It should," said Scathach sagely. "Some people are born great, but no one is born good. That is a choice they must make for themselves. You were born greater than others. Your choices will be harder and you are not infallible. I know . . . I've read your poems."

Max grinned and pressed his forehead against hers. She kissed him as Old Tom chimed eleven o'clock. When it had finished, she smiled and gazed for a moment at her shadow on the grass.

"Come," she said. "We have honored the dead. It's time to honor the living."

Max would have known the healing ward blindfolded. He knew the number of steps down its hallway and the acoustics of its high ceilings and archways, but most of all he knew the smells. The air in the ward was always warm and faintly scented with the aromas of hearths and oils and innumerable herbs that were laid on tables and patiently mortared into medicines.

The ward was crowded, but it was easy to find the bed they sought. It was in the back, separated from the others and walled off with panels of runeglass whose sigils gave off a soft white glow. Walking quietly to it, Max and Scathach slipped between a slender gap in the panels to gaze at William Cooper.

The man was fast asleep, lying peacefully beneath a white blanket stitched with Rowan's seal. Miss Boon was also there, snoring lightly in a bedside chair and half mumbling some sentence from the tome that was slipping from her fingers. Stepping lightly forward, Max took the book from her hands and laid it on a table. Cracking open her eyes, Miss Boon sat up abruptly.

"I must have dozed off," she said, blinking and looking about. "Forgive the mess."

She gestured absently at several coffee mugs and plates of half-nibbled sandwiches.

"David's had a bad influence on you," Max teased, offering the other chair to Scathach. "How's our guy?"

"Remarkable," she declared, taking Cooper's hand. "He opened his eyes for the first time last night. And whenever I read aloud to him, he groans. It must be therapeutic. It's very nice of you two to visit, but do be careful, Max—you're about to step on Grendel."

Glancing down, Max spied the Cheshirewulf lying at the foot of Cooper's bed. The animal was almost wholly translucent as it dozed, only appearing now and again when it exhaled. There was something standing atop its head, however, perched like an Egyptian plover upon a crocodile. Looking closer, Max saw that it was indeed a bird, a brightly colored kingfisher with mismatched eyes.

"And who is this?" he wondered.

"That's my charge, Aberdeen," explained Miss Boon, laying her wrist on Cooper's forehead. "I was afraid Grendel would eat her, but they get along famously! She chirps; he growls. It's very charming."

Stepping carefully past the two, Max stood over Cooper's bed and looked down at him. The wound from YaYa's horn had closed and the pentacles upon his skin had faded away entirely. His head had been shaved, but already there were scattered patches of short blond stubble. The man's countless scars, box-er's nose, and grisly burns would have appalled many a stranger, but Max merely smiled. William Cooper looked precisely as he should.

Miss Boon reached for the book on the nightstand. "If you two don't mind, I'll continue reading him some *Middlemarch*," she said. "It's just so hefty and satisfying."

Tossing slightly, Cooper groaned as if having a nightmare.

"Quick," said Max. "Start reading!"

Mistaking his urgency for a shared love of George Eliot, Miss Boon quickly found her place. "*Here and there, a cygnet is reared uneasily among the ducklings in the brown pond, and never finds the living stream in fellowship with its own oary-footed kind. . . .*"

Gasping, Cooper suddenly opened his pale blue eyes.

"William!" cried Miss Boon, flinging the book aside and taking his hand.

The man grimaced as he struggled to sit up.

"Prop some pillows behind him and give me a hand," ordered Miss Boon, tossing one to Max and helping Cooper lean back against the headboard.

For a few seconds, Cooper merely looked at them, his eyes going from Miss Boon to Max and then to Scathach, who was sitting quietly by the runeglass.

"I know you," the Agent muttered in his flat Cockney accent.

"We haven't officially met. I'm Scathach."

Cooper nodded slowly, as though emerging from a very long and horrid dream. He glanced up at Max. "I cut you," he muttered, his inflection teetering between question and statement.

"I'm fine," said Max. "Scathach came to my rescue."

"And Grendel . . . ," continued Cooper, horrified.

"Grendel is lying at the foot of the bed," said Miss Boon. "Aberdeen is keeping him company."

Cooper blinked at the ensuing, unseen chirp.

"Xiùměi," he whispered, staring at his hands. "I killed her."

"No, you did not," said Miss Boon firmly. "The *Atropos* killed Xiùměi, not you."

At the mention of the Atropos's name, Cooper sat straight up and stared at Max. "There are clones," he said. "Clones of you. And they're working for the Atropos. The leader gave them my compass . . . the one that points toward you."

"I've met those clones," replied Max grimly. "David buried them under half a palace near Bholevna. They're probably dead."

"Don't you believe it till you've seen the bodies," muttered Cooper darkly.

"That's what I keep telling him," said Scathach pointedly.

"You," said Cooper, turning to her once again. "Who taught you how to fight like that? You fight just like Max."

Scathach shook her head and smiled. "I beg to differ," she replied. "Max fights just like me."

The Agent stared at her, nodding ever so slightly as he came to understand. "You're from the Sidh."

"I was," she replied. "I live at Rowan now. You might even say I report to you."

"What are you talking about?" asked Cooper, frowning.

Pulling back her sleeve, Scathach displayed a small red tattoo on her wrist.

"You're in the Red Branch?" exclaimed its commander.

"The Red Branch needed a replacement for Xiùměi," Max explained. "Ms. Richter was confident that you'd find Scathach qualified and appointed her in your absence."

"Shoot," muttered Cooper, sinking back against his pillow. "From what I've seen, Scathach should be running the damn show."

The man sat quiet for several minutes, periodically gazing at his visitors as though still skeptical that the entire episode was not a dream. At length, he cleared his throat and nodded up at Max. "Gotta question for you," he said.

"What's that?"

"Would you consider being my best man?"

Max was taken aback. He glanced at Miss Boon, whose jaw had come unhinged.

"And what do you need a best man for, William?" she interjected.

"Because I'm getting married," replied Cooper matter-of-factly.

Miss Boon's eyebrows nearly shot off her forehead. "My God, he's still possessed," she said. Leaning forward, she stroked Cooper's hand and spoke to him as though he were a very sweet and dense child. "William, who exactly are you marrying?"

The man's pale, ruined features broke into a grin as he kissed her hand. "I'm marrying you, Hazel."

The teacher flushed fire red. "W-well," she stammered, blinking rapidly. "I'm hardly an expert, but aren't you supposed to *ask* me first?"

"But I have," explained Cooper, placing her hand over his heart. "In here, I've asked you a thousand times. And you almost always said yes."

The woman's glasses promptly fogged. "I shall have to consider it," she replied, primly wiping their lenses. "But it might be prudent for Max to clear his calendar should he be needed to serve in that capacity."

"I'm all for prudence," said Max, smiling. "In any case, we should probably get going."

"Yes," said Miss Boon, rising and smoothing her robes. "Yes, you should. It's going to be an absolutely historic afternoon, and the Director would never forgive me if I kept you. You should both go at once. No need for ceremony."

They had almost escaped when Max heard Cooper call his name. He stopped and turned to see the Agent pointing decisively at *Middlemarch*.

"Take that with you."

At nearly four o'clock that afternoon, Max stood beneath the arched, interlacing canopy of branches that formed the Sanctuary tunnel. He wanted to watch the crowds gathering in the orchard and all along the garden paths to the Manse, but he could not take his eyes off Tweedy. The Highland hare was a nervous wreck, pacing back and forth and addressing his clipboard as though it were his personal assistant. When David sneezed, Tweedy gave a start and snarled his medals on his shawl.

"Look what you made me do!" he grumbled, untangling them.

"Sorry," sighed David.

"Well, come on," said the hare, beckoning impatiently. "Let me have a look at you."

"You have looked me over eight times," growled David. "I look fine."

"A sneeze can wreak havoc on the fringe," said Tweedy knowingly. He stood on tiptoe to examine the silver mantle over David's navy robes.

"This entire outfit is a sham," David declared, flapping his sleeves throughout the hare's careful inspection. "These are instructor's robes. The school expelled me over a year ago. I should just wear my regular clothes."

"You will not," gasped Tweedy, outraged. "I'll not have you looking like some penniless friar for the greatest moment in Rowan's history! Do you have any idea what's about to transpire?"

"I do," said Max drily. "You've made us recite the program twenty times."

"That is because practice makes perfect," retorted the hare, hopping over to reinspect Max's dress. When he could find no fault in the armor's gleam, the tunic's drape, or the boots' polish, he stabbed a paw at Max's spear. "And remember that you are to keep that blade sheathed, McDaniels! We don't want an untimely scream to spoil the ceremony and cause a general panic. It is because I pay attention to these details that the Director—"

"—trusts you with matters of highest importance."

Tweedy's whiskers twitched as the boys finished his sentence.

"You two can stand there grinning like imbeciles, but this is no laughing matter. Oh, why can't you be more like Mina?" he moaned. "She's quiet and well mannered and—dear me—she looks like an absolute angel!"

"Thank you, Tweedy," called Mina, peering down from atop YaYa.

"Don't lean, child," pleaded the hare. "Your robes must remain just so. Now, take a deep breath, all of you, and wait for the signal."

When Old Tom finally began to chime the hour, Tweedy held up a paw and counted the beats.

"And one . . . and two . . . and three . . . and *now*."

Thrusting out his chest, Tweedy led them out of the leafy tunnel and into the sunshine. Max blinked at both the sun and the enormous crowds. He and David were walking on either side of YaYa, each holding one end of a golden sash that was draped over the ki-rin's shoulders. Mina was perched atop the saddle, looking uncharacteristically clean and scrubbed in white silk robes trimmed in silver lace. Tweedy had tried to explain that a magechain was not a proper accessory for an Ascendant's robes, but the girl had refused to part with it. It glittered around her neck, resplendent but for its lumpish centerpiece; a wax-dipped

acorn crudely wrapped with copper wire. Apparently teleportation was such a rare ability that there was no official gemstone
or token to commemorate it. David had improvised. Privately,
Max thought he should have commissioned the dvergar.

But Mina's magechain was not her most interesting accessory. That honor belonged to a thick golden rope that was coiled
around the girl's arm from her shoulder to her wrist. As they
proceeded through Rowan's orchard, Max occasionally gazed
up at it.

And it gazed back at him.

The golden rope was a dragon.

After the battle, Mina had found him amid the carnage on
the beach, resembling a muddy eel, half choked with sand and
seaweed. According to David's account, the girl had identified it
as a dragon right away, but he had been skeptical. No true dragons had existed for a thousand years, and even those compara-
tively meager specimens were more like spiny serpents and scaly
bats than the godlike creatures of antiquity. The ancient dragons had been of the Old Magic, wild spirits of terrible power.

But when Mina washed the creature in the bloody shallows,
David spied a glint of gold and tiny claws folded flat against its
snakelike body. When the creature arched back and revealed
whiskerlike spines along its chin, all doubts evaporated. It was
indeed a dragon. Only time would reveal its kind or purpose.
Mina had not seemed to care. Once it coiled about her arm, she
named him Ember and announced that he was her charge.

As intriguing as Mina's dragon might be, most eyes were
on the girl herself. Thousands of people lined the paths through
Old College and many were straining to get even a glimpse of
the wondrous child who had appeared before Prusias, broken his
seven crowns, and sent him fleeing over the sea.

In truth, the assembly's numbers and proximity made Max

more than a little nervous. He disliked crowds ever since the Atropos had targeted him, but it was not his own safety that concerned him: it was Mina's. A cultlike fervor was starting to gather around the girl. Some had taken to calling her St. Mina and people of various faiths were starting to project their own beliefs and prophecies upon her. Max had experienced some of this himself, but it had never reached such a groundswell of intensity or zeal. Once the Promethean Scholars had declared Mina the first Ascendant since Elias Bram, even some of Rowan's senior faculty seemed to regard the girl as a holy object.

Max could not regard her in this light. For all her astounding and mysterious power, she would always be his little Mina—a girl who liked to play marbles and cook inedible stews and explore tidal pools after a rain. When she grinned down at him, he returned it and dearly hoped that some part of her would remain free from the incredible hopes and expectations settling on her shoulders.

A king's crown is heavy. An Ascendant's robes are heavier still.

Bram never wore those robes and, indeed, never even answered to the title on those rare occasions when an awestruck scholar had the opportunity to address him. David said his grandfather had given up both long ago and had advised Mina to do the same when he'd heard of the pronouncement. But in this, as in many things, Mina was stubborn and took her own counsel.

Max had looked for Bram, but he never saw the Archmage during their slow procession through Old College. He had not even seen him since Prusias's attack. When pressed, David would only say that his grandfather was "gathering himself" and that Max might not see him again for a very long time.

The Archmage might have been absent, but Ms. Richter and just about every other member of Rowan's leadership were gathered at the cliffs nearest the spot where Gràvenmuir had once stood. As they rounded the Manse's pluming fountain and proceeded toward the Director, Max recognized some familiar faces.

Nigel Bristow waved and cheered with his wife and daughter. So did the Tellers and even Thomas Polk and others who had returned to Rowan from the inland settlements. The goose Hannah had to chase down Honk after the willful gosling went tottering after them. Madam Petra was gazing down from a prime perch atop Old Tom's steps, as were many of Max's former classmates. But the greatest joy Max felt was when he saw Bob standing near the front with Sarah, Cynthia, and Lucia. His helmet and cudgel had been put away. Bob wore a cook's apron once again and his favorite blue-striped shirt. When Max passed by, the ogre bowed his head.

The Promethean Scholars stood behind the Director, as did the senior faculty and several leaders from the refugees. The Red Branch flanked the Director and Max's focus quickly zeroed in on Scathach. She returned his smile and quietly urged him to pay attention as YaYa came to a halt before Ms. Richter.

At Tweedy's coughing cue, Max leaned the *gae bolga* against YaYa's saddle and lifted Mina off the ki-rin's back. Setting her carefully on the ground, he took up the spear once again and led YaYa to stand beside Scathach and face the thousands before them.

Just David and Mina stood before the Director now. Each was holding something. Mina's object was clutched and hidden by both hands, but David was leaning upon a very powerful and familiar item.

It was Prusias's cane—the very prop that contained a page from the Book of Thoth. Whenever the demon was in his serpent form, the artifact was embedded in one of the crowns that had shattered. Once Mina discovered her charge, David had gone looking for the cane and found it wedged among the briny rocks along the shore.

When Ms. Richter addressed the crowd, her voice also issued from hovering glowspheres stationed about the Old College and all of Greater Rowan. She spoke of honor and sacrifice, the appalling losses, and the great victory that had been achieved. Max listened dutifully, his gaze straying occasionally to Scathach or the gargantuan war galleons anchored in and about Rowan Harbor. There were twenty of them, twenty crimson galleons that were far larger and more formidable than any ships Rowan possessed. Once Prusias's army had been destroyed, Rowan had captured and claimed the vessels as they tried to escape with mere skeleton crews.

"But that victory is not complete," continued Ms. Richter, reclaiming Max's attention. "We have turned back Prusias, but he is not yet defeated. He sailed to these shores with but a fraction of his forces and he will not underestimate us again. And thus, Rowan must ask more of you. I must ask more of you as we pursue this enemy to his own gates and stamp out this threat once and for all. If we do not, if we succumb to debate and delay, then his armies will surely return with greater wrath and numbers. This is not the end of the war; it is the beginning."

Ms. Richter smiled ruefully and acknowledged the crowd's stunned silence.

"My message today is bittersweet," she confessed. "I know that many of you had hoped to put the sorrows and toil of war behind you. Many of you had looked forward to a quiet life in which you could enjoy our hard-earned freedom and independence. Nobody wants that more for you than I. But we are not there yet. In the coming weeks and months, Rowan may call upon you once again. And I know that you will answer.

"But Rowan will not call upon you alone. We have not merely turned back an enemy; we have gained credibility. Those who could not aid us or feared to do so may now feel otherwise. We will seek their help. We will ask others to strengthen our cause and share our sacrifice. But let me be clear: Rowan is no longer desperate for aid or charity. We are no longer a quaking country hoping to escape the notice of its neighbors. The founders of this school were refugees themselves. They, too, fled an enemy to these shores and sought to rebuild and regain their former strength and dignity. For over four centuries, Rowan has engaged proudly in this struggle. But Rowan has also always dwelled in the shadow of her predecessors; she has been a mere echo of a grander, more storied past. Those days are over.

"Today, Rowan enters a new phase of existence—one that embraces the best of her legacy even as she rises up to break new ground. There have been many schools of magic, but Solas was the finest mankind has ever known and its high tower was a symbol for all that could be achieved. Solas may be gone, but Túr an Ghrian shall rise again."

Following this statement, the Director and scholars and everyone else moved away from David and Mina so that the two were left alone in a broad circle. Max and everyone else watched nervously as Mina approached the cliffs, her Ascendant's robes trailing her upon the grass. Those who were close enough and at a proper vantage might have seen that the girl was holding a small, charred rock. Given a closer look, some Rowan students might have recognized it as the Founder's Stone. Normally, the object was hovering behind glass—one of Rowan's six great treasures. But now it was resting in Mina's cupped hands as she walked toward the cliffs' farthest point opposite the Manse. Kissing the stone, she laid it carefully on the ground and walked back to David.

When Rowan's sorcerer touched his cane to the ground, Max shivered as Old Magic saturated the air and caused it to shimmer. The earth shook and the crowds surged back as a great tower grew around the stone, rising up from the very cliffs where Gràvenmuir had been thrown into the sea. Higher and higher it rose, until the gulls that circled around its gleaming spire were distant white specks. And as the dust settled and the afternoon light turned its pale stone to gold, Ms. Richter announced that Túr an Ghrian—the Tower of the Sun—stood once more.

Back in the Observatory, Max exhaled and sat in his armchair, staring up at the dome's slowly wheeling constellations. He was no longer wearing ceremonial armor but the simple uniform of the Red Branch and some well-worn boots. From the upper level, he heard a sudden rip of fabric followed by a startled oath. The second tear was more pronounced, as was the swearing. The third tear was longest of all, but no cursing accompanied it. Instead, both halves of David's ceremonial robes were tossed over the railing. With a sidelong glance, Max watched them float down like two silken streamers.

"Don't you have to return those?" he called.

"I won't!" yelled his roommate, now flinging down a starchy shirt and a pair of black socks.

Glancing up, Max saw Rowan's sorcerer—the very prodigy who had raised Túr an Ghrian—standing at the railing in his underwear. The boy's face was even paler than usual.

"How much time do we have?"

"They said they'd be here at seven," replied Max.

With a groan, David disappeared. Two minutes later, he stood at the railing wearing leggings and a blue tunic. Max shook his head.

"You look like a page boy. And those leggings keep no secrets."

Mortified, David vanished again. He appeared three more times at the railing, but each outfit was even worse than the last. When there was a knock at the door, David gasped and drew the curtain around his bed.

"Keep them busy!" he yelled. "I just need a few minutes."

Trotting up the stairs, Max opened the door and invited Scathach and Cynthia in. They both looked lovely: Scathach wearing a dark gray dress with a silver belt and Cynthia in her viridian robes with a white daisy in her hair.

"David needs a moment," said Max, giving them a significant look and leading them downstairs.

"Take your time," called Cynthia, scrutinizing the remains of David's robe on the floor. "Are you sure you wouldn't rather go to the celebration dinner?"

"Oh no," wheezed David, evidently straining. "Those formal things are always so stuffy. And you'll love the Hanged Man! Marta's been cooking all day to get things ready. Have you ever had sweetbreads? I haven't, but Marta's a genius at desserts."

Cynthia turned pale.

"Hello, Scathach!" called David pleasantly.

"Hello," she replied, walking around the lower level and gazing about. She stopped at a runeglass case and peered closely at it. "Is this one of those pinlegs Max told me about?"

"Yes," said David. "I spent so much time with it, I thought I'd hold on to it as a keepsake. I call him Chester. He just seems like a Chester."

Scathach raised an eyebrow at Chester's gleaming carapace, lethal pincers, and weakly undulating legs. "And so how did you manage to take control of those dreadnoughts?"

David finally emerged from behind his curtain, having

opted for a wooly brown robe from the hamper. He beamed at Cynthia, who smiled weakly and said something about him looking "very comfortable."

"Oh, Marta doesn't stand on ceremony," he replied, standing on tiptoe to kiss her cheek. "Anyway, Scathach, it was really pretty straightforward once I realized that the dreadnoughts had a fatal flaw. The spirits that controlled them were not only relatively weak, but they were also damaged. I no longer required their truenames to unlock them; I just needed enough power to kick down the doors. And Max helped provide it."

"Fascinating," said Scathach. "So was that Workshop engineer of any use?"

"Not so much. We could never really unravel all of Chester's defenses. But in the end it didn't really matter. Dr. Bechel doesn't even begrudge the fact that we kidnapped him. In fact, he doesn't even want to go back home. . . ."

David trailed off as Max shot him a horrified glance. The boys were silent for several moments before David begged the ladies to make themselves at home. Dinner would have to wait for an hour—maybe two—but he was confident that Marta could adjust. Running up the stairs, David abruptly abandoned their guests and vanished behind his bed curtain.

An hour later, he returned with an outraged smee.

Toby was literally trembling with indignation, twisting about in the sorcerer's hands to lambast him in a thunderous baritone.

"Do you have *any* idea what it's like to be forgotten for over a month!" he roared. "To be left shuffling about a house in Blys, masquerading as some crusty engineer while all of Rowan is celebrating in your absence? Well, I can assure you that you're going to pay for this! The meter's been running, my friend, and when I factor in the overtime . . ."

The apoplectic smee was set upon a pillow by the fire, where he continued to seethe and gasp. But at last Toby sighed and fell still. Uncurling his body, he raised his yamlike head to gaze around at the rest of his audience. Pausing at Scathach, the smee cleared his throat and inched forward.

"Who are you, and why haven't we met before?"

~ 20 ~

UNDER A MACKEREL SKY

A month later, the *Ormenheid* lay rolling on the shallows of
Rowan Harbor. Compared to Prusias's war galleons, the Viking
ship looked no bigger than a dinghy. While she might have been
less imposing, she had her own special gifts. Even as the sun
broke the horizon, her dragon prow faced east, her sail magi-
cally unfurled, and her oars dipped down into the waters.

Max thought she cut a very noble figure under the mackerel
sky, her timbers creaking as the sea lapped his boots with shell
and foam. Sloshing past him through the swells, Cooper climbed
aboard and beckoned for the others to start passing along the
many barrels, sacks, and crates stacked neatly on the beach.

"This is quite the honeymoon," mused Miss Boon, glancing at her wedding band before heaving a sack of flour into Scathach's waiting arms. With an indifferent shrug, Scathach swung the flour along the line to Sarah, who passed it to Lucia, who handed it to Max, who tossed it up to Cooper.

Despite the grunts and occasional griping, the loading of the ship was going smoothly until Lucia dropped one of the crates.

"Eek!" she cried. "There's something moving in there. Lots of things!"

"Sorry!" said Max, stooping quickly to retrieve the crate.

"What is that?" Lucia demanded. "It better not be anything dangerous!" She gestured protectively toward Kettlemouth as the oblivious bullfrog dozed in a converted birdcage.

"No, nothing dangerous," said Max, trotting off with the crate on his shoulder.

Several more boxes went down the line without incident before Lucia dropped another.

"What could be in that one?" she wondered. "It's so heavy!"

"My fault," said Max, promptly scooping it up. "I didn't mean for anyone else to carry it. Sorry—should have marked it."

Lucia seemed content to merely glare and grumble until the smee offered some suggestions.

"You've got to use your legs, young lady!" cried Toby. "My God, you're just flailing about like a broken scarecrow. Bend those knees! How can such a dashing filly be so—"

"Not another word, you!" roared Lucia, wheeling on him. "If you're not going to help, then you just be quiet. I don't have to take orders from some lazy, strutting peacock!"

But indeed, Toby *was* a peacock.

The smee had indulged in many forms since the Director lifted his ban. There had been magnificent tigers, square-jawed knights, and golden stallions, but of late the smee had favored the shape of an iridescent blue peacock that was prone to highly dramatic displays of his tail whenever he believed its sudden appearance might be to his advantage. It rarely had the desired effect, and this occasion proved no exception.

"I was only trying to help," he sulked, having weathered a storm of Italian obscenities.

"Then grab a crate," huffed Lucia.

"But I didn't come down here to *work*," he replied. "I just came to see you off! You know, bon voyage and so forth."

"Are you going to miss us, Toby?" teased Max, lugging a crate to Cooper.

"Let's see," mused the smee. "If 'missing you' means carefree evenings at Cloubert's while Lady Luck whisks me off to fame and fortune, then I suppose I'll miss you a great deal. Ha!"

While the smee reveled in his wit, Max caught sight of a large figure making its way carefully down the many stairs from Rowan's cliffs. Washing his hands in the sea, Max left the others and trotted to where the steps met the rocky beach.

Bob was breathing heavily when he reached the bottom. Setting down his bundle, the ogre reached for a handkerchief and wiped his glistening brow. Catching his breath, he craned his head up at the high cliffs and shook his head. "Too many steps."

"You didn't have to see us off," said Max. "It's so early."

With a shrug, the ogre refolded the handkerchief and gazed out at the *Ormenheid* floating beneath the pale peach sky.

"Pretty ship," he grunted. "Bob wonders if you have room for one more."

"You mean that isn't a care package to see us off?"

Looking down, Bob blinked at the enormous pack that was

overflowing with cooking pans and ogre-sized clothing. Laughter rumbled in his chest.

"No, *malyenki*," he said. "These things are not for you. It is time for Bob to go get his little Mum. Soon he will be too old for such journeys and she has been away long enough. It is time she comes home where she belongs."

"Well, I think we can help you," said Max, grinning. "We're taking Sarah and Lucia to search out Connor Lynch in Blys. Once they're off, we'll be heading north. We'll pass right near Shrope Hovel."

"Where are you going in the north?" asked the ogre.

"The Isle of Man."

"A Fomorian lives there," rumbled Bob. "They are dangerous."

"That's why we're going."

The ogre digested this and gazed back at the *Ormenheid*. "Do you think the others will mind?" he asked tentatively.

"Doesn't matter if they do." Max shrugged, hefting up Bob's pack and trudging toward the water. "She's my ship and I'm captain. If anyone complains, I'll make them cut the jibs and swab the sheets."

"Bob does not think *malyenki* knows how to sail."

Of course, everyone was delighted to welcome Bob aboard. Swinging his leg easily over the gunwale, the ogre settled in to wring out his socks while the others stowed the rest of their gear and prepared to set sail. When Max gave the command, the *Ormenheid*'s oars began to scull gently through the water as the breeze stretched her sail taut. She moved smoothly through the harbor, skimming past Gràvenmuir's dark remains.

Once they were headed for open waters, Max walked back to the stern and gazed up at the cliffs, where he thought David and

Mina might be watching from high atop Túr an Ghrian. The tower dwarfed everything around it, a slender white spire whose summit stood a thousand feet over the sea. Max was enjoying its majesty when a large splash brought him whipping about.

A porpoise had leaped over the gunwale.

"What's an adventure without a smee!" it cried.

Landing heavily, the porpoise slid across the slippery deck until it came to rest against Bob's foot. When no one spoke, Toby changed back into his native form and gazed about dejectedly.

"You just left," he sniffed. "You never even asked me if I wanted to go. And then this big galoot comes along and it's all 'welcome aboard' and 'let me help you with that'!"

Plucking up the smee by one twisty end, Bob began dabbing him gently with a towel.

"What happened to Cloubert's?" asked Max, sitting down by Scathach. "I thought you were on a big lucky streak."

"I lied."

Max opened a nearby crate. "You're more than welcome to stay, Toby, but you might have to catch your own food. We didn't pack for a smee."

"Well, what's in that box?" demanded the smee, pointing with his head. "I'll bet there's plenty of grub in there!"

"There is. But I'm not certain you'd like it."

Reaching inside the crate, Max selected an iron ingot and laid it on the deck. Something in his pocket stirred, and Max brought it forth. He held it on his palm: a glossy black lump that soon stretched and mewled and cracked a coppery eye.

"Is . . . is that what I think it is?" asked the smee.

Max smiled. "Her name is Nox, and she's my charge."

"You never asked *me* to be your charge," the smee observed coldly.

"But you're not a charge, you're a spy," said Max, stroking

the lymrill's quills. "An infiltration specialist, a master of *ruse de guerre...*"

"Quite right," snorted Toby, promptly ordering Bob to set him upon the sunny deck.

Once placed, the smee stretched, flipped onto his tummy, and launched into an unabridged recitation of his many adventures, intrigues, and scandals. After all, the voyage was long, his audience captive, and the smee most forthcoming.

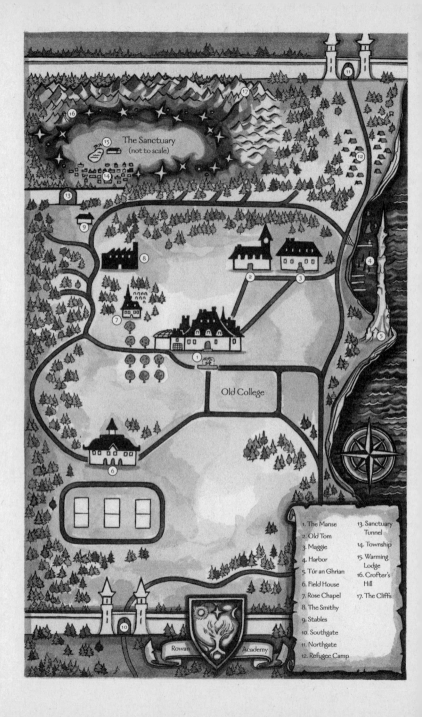

Pronunciation Guide/Glossary

This guide is to help readers pronounce some of the more challenging names and terms found in the Tapestry. Many of the words are of Irish origin, while others are simply the author's own creations. Some nuances have been sacrificed in the name of simplicity, and this should not be interpreted as a scholarly work on Irish pronunciation.

Name/Term (Pronunciation) Definition

Atropos (AH-truh-pos) Among the three Greek Fates, Atropos cut the thread of life; the name was adopted by an assassin guild known for its ruthlessness and fanaticism

Bragha Rùn (BRAH-ga ROON) "The Red Death"; Max McDaniels's alias in Prusias's Arena

Brugh na Boinne (BROO na BOYNE) "On the Boyne"; a river in Ireland

Caillech (KAI-luh) "Crone"; the name Deirdre Fallow gives herself when she meets Max McDaniels and David Menlo in the Sidh

Cúchulain (KOO-hull-in) The Hound of Ulster; an Irish hero who was the son of the deity Lugh and a mortal woman

daemona (DAY-moan-uh) The demons' preferred term for their kind; one that classifies their spiritual essence without automatic association with evil

Emain Macha (EV-in MA-ha) The royal seat of Ulster, northernmost of Ireland's four ancient kingdoms

Emer (AY-ver) The wife of Cúchulain; also the name of Elias Bram's daughter

gae bolga (GAY BULL-gah) Cúchulain's spear, which was forged anew by Max McDaniels and the Fomorian. Its strike is almost always fatal; its wounds never heal.

grylmhoch (GRILLM-hoke) A massive, amorphous creature of unknown origins that Max encounters in Prusias's Arena

koukerros (koo-KERR-os) The transformation that occurs when a demon has consumed enough souls to become a higher order of spirit

Lugh (LOO) A sun deity; High King of the Tuatha Dé Danaan, who slew Balor of the Fomorians. Lugh is the father of both Cúchulain and Max McDaniels.

malakhim (MAL-ah-keem) Fallen spirits that wear obsidian masks and serve the demon Prusias

médim (MAY-deem) Ritualized contests that mark important demonic gatherings; the contests include alennya (arts of beauty), amann (arts of blood), and ahülmm (arts of soul)

mehrùn (meh-ROON) Demonic word used to classify humans who can use magic

Morrígan (MOH-ree-gan) A Celtic war goddess whose willful and terrifying essence comprises the *gae bolga*

Rodrubân (ROD-roo-vaan) Lugh's castle and lands within the Sidh

Scathach (SKAW-thah) A warrior maiden originally from Scotland (Isle of Skye) who has trained many heroes, including Cúchulain and Max McDaniels

Sidh (SHEE) A hidden realm home to the Tuatha Dé Danaan and other magical beings

Solas (SUH-las) Mankind's greatest school of magic; destroyed by Astaroth in 1649

Tuatha Dé Danaan (TOO-ha DAY DAN-ahn) The Children of Danu; a race of divine beings that conquered the Fomorians and ruled Ireland before departing for the Sidh

Túr an Ghrian (THOOR un GREE-un) The highest tower at Solas, where the Gwydion Chair of Mystics resided

ACKNOWLEDGMENTS

Many thanks to Random House and Schuyler Hooke for tightening the manuscript and bringing *The Maelstrom* to fruition. Nicole de las Heras has designed a beautiful book, Cory Godbey has provided another spellbinding cover, and Jocelyn Lange continues to ensure that readers around the world can enjoy Max's adventures. As always, I'm grateful to Josh Adams and Adams Literary for their professional guidance and support.

Every author is indebted to his predecessors and contemporaries. J. R. R. Tolkien showed me the beauty of building a world. Frank Herbert's *Dune* demonstrated the appeal of blending science fiction and fantasy. Ursula K. Le Guin's words fairly crackle with magic, while Patrick O'Brian is unparalleled at using history and humor to explore the human condition. When it comes to concocting primal, nameless horrors, no one tops H. P. Lovecraft. Bill Bryson's excellent *A Short History of Nearly Everything* provided Astaroth's anecdote regarding the dodo's extinction and Sir Isaac Newton's *Principia*. In addition, William Shakespeare's plays *Much Ado About Nothing* and *A Midsummer Night's Dream* provided quotations for Toby and Astaroth, while the smee also recited a stanza from William Cullen Bryant's lovely poem "The Gladness of Nature." James Joyce's brilliant *Finnegans Wake* provided Ghöllah's creative twist on the days of the week. And, of course, there are the overlooked magicians—the creators of the many myths and the folklore that provide the Tapestry's foundation. Without them, we'd have no Sidh, Olympus, or Asgard to populate this tale and countless others.

Ultimately, it is my friends and family who empower me to write and illustrate these books. My mother, Terry Zimmerman, continues to read each chapter as it is completed, while my wife, Danielle, helps me through the creative howls and hiccups with Hannah's love, Bob's patience, and Toby's humor. She even endures well-intended comparisons to geese, ogres, and smees. Every writer should be so lucky.

And finally, I'd like to thank my son, Charlie. I wrote *The Maelstrom* while anticipating his arrival, and the two were delivered within weeks of one another. This book is for Charlie and all the wild, wonderful possibilities his young life represents. A Potential, indeed.

ABOUT THE AUTHOR

HENRY H. NEFF is a former consultant and history teacher from the Chicago area. Today he lives in Montclair, New Jersey, with his wife and young son. You can visit Henry at henryhneff.com.

ROWAN HAS WON A BATTLE, BUT NOT THE WAR.

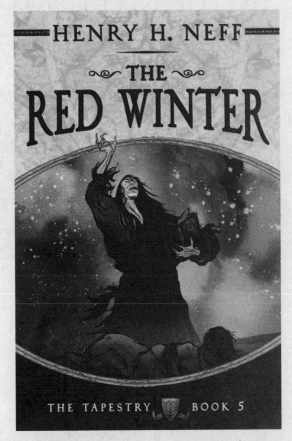

READ ALL FIVE BOOKS
IN THE RIVETING
TAPESTRY SERIES!